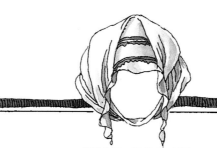

THE GREAT
ENCYCLOPEDIA
OF
FAERIES

TEXT
PIERRE DUBOIS

ILLUSTRATIONS
CLAUDINE & ROLAND SABATIER

SIMON & SCHUSTER

SIMON & SCHUSTER
Rockefeller Center
1230 Avenue of the Americas
New York, NY 10020

The publication of this book is supported by
the Cultural Service of the French Embassy in London

institut français

Designed by Éditions Hoëbeke

Printed in Singapore by Imago

5 7 9 10 8 6 4

Library of Congress Cataloging-in-Publication Data
Dubois, Pierre
[Grande encyclopédie des fées. English]
The great encyclopedia of faeries / text Pierre Dubois,
illustrations Claudine and Roland Sabatier
p.   cm.
1. Fairies   I. Title
GR549.D82819   2000
398.21—dc21

ISBN-13:   978-0-684-86957-5
ISBN-10:   0-684-86957-8

Originally published in French as
La Grande Encyclopédie des Fées

For the little sorceress Capucine,
the faerie Mélanie and Charlotte the imp…
in the heart of the Vendoise.

Contents

Invitation to the Isles of Happiness

My tresses will remain with you; the flowers are "thoughts": the forget-me-not, the buttercup, the little roses are my childhood and they symbolize it: daisies for the purest and most beautiful character.

(Mélanie, *Saskia*)

So here are the Faeries, captured on the page. But "capture" might be misleading to describe this repository of Beautiful Beings. Let us say it is a book in which they will come and wander. An endless path leading from one world to another, with countless alleyways, resting-places and groves where one can learn to get to know each one better. A ritual passage, a spiritual politeness before the engagement. May each page be "climbed" as a stile would be.

This is only a suggestion, because it is always the Wild Ladies who decide and unwind the distaff of our expectations; for our dreams are only a reflection of the sparkling, efflorescent wreath of their own. But these blossoms of star dust lighting up the paths are enough for a nosegay of wonders gathered in these gardens. Of course, this implies a conquest of the heart, an allegiance to faerie enchantment, and the disappearance of any resistance on our part against falling under the spell of their songs.

Having reached the distant shores, we are met with lights and shadows. To walk with the Faeries is to learn to lose oneself. The imps have contributed greatly to this. They tease and play constantly without keeping count, a generous attitude. And yet, nothing can ever be taken for granted. Without warning, the edges of the forests recede into the distance, the bridge crumbles and words remain suspended for an instant before dissolving, or flying away; but this does not displease them, because words are often on the side of the Faeries.

We believe that they are obedient and amenable, that they will repeat and describe the voices and the images of the unlocked kingdom, that linked together they will weave a passage between the banks; but even a spider's web is far stronger, because words may break up and lose the power of their meaning. I have the impression that I spoke of something very similar when I wrote the introduction to *Le Monde des Petites Noblesses*. I shall probably do so again, because magic thoughts ricochet repeatedly, sewing their white pebbles along the meandering curves of their course, and repeating themselves until the meaning is only a rumor, a call picked up while listening for an echo.

It might perhaps be desirable to throw these thoughts into "their" petrifying source, in the secret hope that they might acquire a solid form, thus forever fixing a fluctuating mirage into calcareous concretions; but the Nymphea fountain remains hidden from view and it eludes us. To reach it, the only way is to retrace our first childhood footsteps, towards the edge of the original dawns.

It is always possible to come to an arrangement with an imp—with a fair

exchange, for instance, such as a pinch of snuff in exchange for a confidence, a somersault, a witty remark, or a way of dressing; the deal is done and that's that. Apart from angering them, or happening to come across a particularly unpleasant character, a foul-mouthed little midget, sprites are relatively easy to approach, though minor difficulties may always occur. But different qualities are needed when dealing with Faeries. Faerieland cannot be entered by jumping over the fence. It can only be reached through adventure, trials, enchantment, spells, or love. It is a perilous renunciation, a choice that permits no weakness: the "faerie thought" is a completely "different thought." The soul of the visitor is left behind so as to acquire another, but the soul that has been affected by Faeries no longer belongs in the ordinary mortal world. It has to be said that there is no going back…

With Faeries, it is not a matter of making promises; it is a case of a commitment, demanding the making of a vow…

Faeries have witnessed the past, as they bend over the cradle of our slow, clumsy beginnings, tied to their spindle. They preside over our births, they decide our fate and, when the time has come, they cut the thread of our life. Then, when it all seems to have come to an end, they welcome the defunct souls into a Vendoise and take them to be reborn under the golden apple trees of the rediscovered Eden. They are the goddesses of places, the deities of springs, mountains, meadows and woods, the mistresses of our dreams, the Queens of Avalon, the Serpes of the dark, the Nymphs of the dawn, who make and unmake the seasons. But many of these "All-powerful beings," whose names some dare not speak, have the heart of a woman that can be broken by the slightest failure.

People entering these strange lands must respect the terms of the Faerie Wives without asking about the meaning of the ritual. They must accept the hidden secret of the Lady Serpent, Mélusine, and chastely sit at the bedside of their Sleeping Beauty; without disgust they must kiss the ugly snout of a pure princess who has been locked into a hideous appearance by some spell. Otherwise the perjurer will kill the smile of the Lady, more beautiful than any other, and the land that she had charmed will die at the same time as love escapes through the windows of Lusignan. It is impossible to return, it is irretrievable, and the heart grieves at the sight of the wilting flowers, the crumbling towers and the disappearing hills. The earth vanishes and the fall is fatal. All that is left is the dream of a lost paradise, as sparkling as gossamer but just as fragile.

Those who dream of Faeries must know this before allowing themselves to be taken to the Distant Lands whose elusive access is sometimes discouraging…

But henceforth, Lalie has left the door wide open, by anticipating the Faeries' invitation, by becoming one of them. So, she has left the spirit of her braids among the flowers of childhood, as a lost link between this world and the other…

Now between the Petit and Grand Fayt, the banks, the times, and the edges of forests merge into one another; and gardens burst into bloom again as the May Bride passes by…

She came and landed on these pages to read a few sentences over my shoulder, before carrying me off every evening on her starry wings…

Then at the legendary forester's side road the Sabatiers, husband and wife, arrived, more than ever under the Faeries' spell. They have produced ever more inspired drawings in which they have portrayed the Fayolles, endeavoring to understand the fufolian mechanism of a wing, perfecting the lines of the antennules to reflect their extreme elegance, the volutes of a Pillywiggin's flight, scrupulously reproducing the anatomy of a mirageous Lurcette, emphasizing every time the smallest detail and each embroidery stitch. Claudine has embellished Roland's drawings with faerie rainbows. Whether delicate or bright, these colors enhance the images of enchantment where the dresses are flowers, where butterfly petals stand out against the golden turmoil of a dazzling palette.

I thank them both for their great patience.

Pierre Dubois,
Elficologist

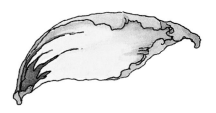

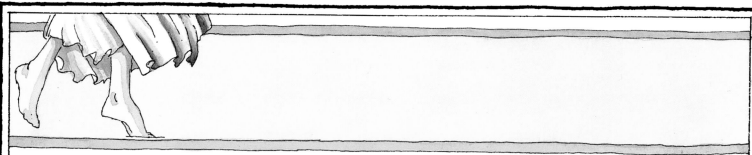

Origins and genesis of Faerieland
Where one learns that one knows nothing about wings…

I do not consider him wise who refuses to believe in the wonders of this world such as faeries…

(Jehan d'Arras)

It would be tedious to repeat in detail here the vertiginous maelstrom of the elfin origins of Nordic mythology. These have already been explained elsewhere, and the serious student could with advantage read, re-read, and meditate on *La Grande Encyclopédie des Lutins*. This tells how the People of the Others were born from the decomposed flesh of the primordial giant, slain by the wild gods. First there was a wriggling of worms to whom Odin gave his face, his magic powers and his habits. The Alfs were born from the somber, icy accumulations of Niflheim, and they then became accustomed to the underground entrails of Svartalfaheimr (a maze of caves, labyrinths and yawning chasms), where they ruled over mines, metals, treasures and obscure sciences. These were the descendants of the black Alfs and Master Blacksmiths—the Svartalfars who were later to become established at earth's level and in the hills, beneath hillocks and cairns, and in the cellars of houses. The gnomic, kobold, korrigan and imp species are a result of their tempestuous crossbreeding.

The white Alfs, those who burst forth from the dazzling brilliance of Muspelheim (the luminescent side of the Ginungagap), are depressed and weakened by life in the bowels of the earth. All they dream of is to return to the surface of the earth and join the birds.

In contrast to their swarthy cousins who are all shriveled up as a result of digging tunnels, the white Alfs are slender and of a delicate opaline hue. Wings unfold from their shoulders, pointing upwards, and in one burst they can escape into the open. They are the Elves, Siths, the lacteipennean vassalage of the Seelies.

Is it possible that the Faeries could be intermediary creatures of a chiaroscuro, a mutant branch of the Great Ash with its antonomic arborescences of terrestrial roots and celestial crown? That would be like a harsh pruning of the subtle luxuriances of the Dreaming Thought; especially because the dark Dwarf sometimes takes on a luminous appearance, and, in contrast, the white Elf may appear very dark.

Our dear "Numineuses" are extremely complex. That is their most important quality, because the most beautiful creations are born from the fluidity of dawns, crepuscular emotions and the promise of roses. Nothing is said. Everything is to be imagined. It is not that their history is incomplete, but it is deliberately veiled with imaginary, butterfly shapes. Later and further distant, other mirage-like realities will appear from secret pollen, distributed randomly in paraphelian clouds, and from threads of lustrous water.

It is true that ingenious scholars have gone back to the singing source of the genealogies of the water. They have deduced the language of the Weeping-of-the-Banks from the consonance of the reeds, while identifying on wild boughs the suckers of the medieval dialects *langue d'oc*, and *langue d'oïl*. They have found Germanic nodules and ancient English nodosities on Latin scions. These findings come from Alfred Maury, Laurence Harf-Lancner and also the spellbinding Claude Lecouteux, master of the archeologies of the marvelous.

First Maury: "Of the various words used by the Gallo-Romans to designate the ancient divinities, only one remained in the memory of the people… this word was *fata*, in the past a synonym for the Parcae, matroe or matrones; the ancient *fata* became the Faeries of the regions of the *langue d'oïl*, the Fadas those of the regions of the *langue d'oc*, and the Hadas those of Gascony. But one should be careful to make the distinction between the noun "Faerie" and an almost identical adjective. The Latin *fatum* became *fatatus* in low Latin, and *Faé*, then *fé* in old French, the adjective meaning "destined" and by extension "enchanted."

Then Lancner attempts to clarify the medley of Parcae and rural divinities. Those places inaccessible to men are inhabited by a host of very ancient creatures who live in the forests, the woods and sylvan sanctuaries, lakes, springs and rivers. They are the Pans, Faunus, Fontes, Satyrs, Sylvans, Nymphs, Fatuiis, Fatuae and Faunae. "The god Faunus, who in the primitive religion of the Latin peoples personified the generating force, was also known as Fatuus; while the goddess Fauna or Bona Dea who, according to legend, was his wife, sister and daughter, had powers of divination, hence the name Fatua. Faunus and Fauna, Fatuus and Fatua, have developed into Fauni and Faunae, Fatui and Fatuae, rural divinities who are often confused with Sylvans and Nymphs."

"By linguistic contamination the Tria Fata, the Fatuae and the Gallic mothers—the matres—benevolent and feared deities, became connected with cults of fertility, birth and destiny." So this is how the seed of the Faerie took root in the forest of gods…

For Lancner the Faerie is a cross between the Parcae and woodland lovers, to which Lecouteux adds his genesis theory, and his wild women, his nightmarish, noctambulant spinners, the Fates…

As he strolled over the heather at Abbotsford, wondering how this extraordinary court acquired its name, Walter Scott said: "The opinion of scholars is that the Persian word *peri*, referring to a non-terrestrial being, is the most likely etymology, if we assume that it was introduced into Europe by the Arabs whose alphabet does not have the letter *P*, so that they pronounced *peri* as *feri*." But in fact he did not favor this theory, preferring to associate the Faeries with the more similar sounding word "Fair."

The genesis of obscure raptures

With this field-dew consecrate,
Every faerie take his gait…
(William Shakespeare,
A Midsummer Night's Dream)

The characters of Great (or classical) Mythology who are too lively to remain immobile as marble statues leave Parnassus for the countryside. As a result of this, the Little Mythology has grown and spread in their wake. Parcae, Hores, Muses, and Nymphs can be seen to mingle at dusk. At dawn, a new maiden will be seen stretching in the crosier of a fern… the start of another story… the rustle of a cult whispered in the ear of a shepherd.

They are also the sacred emanations of the place; they emerge from the filaments of trees and the undulating forms of the flora of rivers and streams; they are born of the earthy pungency of the morning: "The stone, the hill and the mountain are therefore thought of as beings endowed with life, male and female, capable of growing, moving, fighting, copulating, and begetting offspring, and whose substance will be assimilated to a greater or lesser degree into that of a living body. The spirit of the mountain can leave its material body at will, able to take on various shapes and wander along its ridge." So wrote Samivel.

The amazement with which men in that distant past contemplated nature and tried to understand these mysterious transfigurations is merely the embryonic expression of a dormant, intuitive faculty, one that was latent within him: the manifestation of his subconscious. He has a confused glimpse of his surroundings, invisible yet present, active yet concealed, entities whose voices sometimes seem to help him decipher the countless mysteries that surround him. He is aware that the forest is "enchanted" because a tree turns into a beautiful girl who welcomes him and takes him by the hand to the very heart of the Being. "Their world is very different from ours," Yeats said, "and they can only appear as borrowed forms that are within the limits of our awareness. Nevertheless, all the forms take on a particular meaning, as do their actions, and they can be interpreted by an intelligence trained to perceive correspondences between perceptible forms and extra-perceptible meanings." However, the Faerie does not need the clairvoyance of an elect to materialize. While now the soul of a Merlin, poet, fada or elficologist might be needed to perceive them, in those days of the Golden Age when thought was magic, innocent and entranced by the beauty of things, the encounter took place very naturally. So naturally, that the mortal espoused it in spite of damnation by the Church that felt threatened by the sacred shadow of the forest. Until very recently, the "crucifiers" were its executioners. Not so long ago, the fundamentalist knight Gougenot des Mousseaux sent them to stake…

"Exquisite creatures, radiant with youth, endowed with perfect, divine grace. Richly dressed and with an immaterial charm, they resembled ethereal princesses whose feet hardly touched the earth. However, concealed beneath these charms, there lay, more or less hidden, some secret deformity or terrible flaw resulting from their belonging to the Diabolical Beings" (Durville). And yet, it was as a result of the enchantments and noble interventions of these "Beings of passage" that Thomas the Rhymer, the knights of the Middle Ages and the wanderer among the Faeries entered Avalon and the Islands of Wisdom.

At the pale springs of the dawn

I am looking for the key to escape to the lands of our dreams, and perhaps it is death.
(Alain-Fournier)

Between good and evil, the archangel and the devil, legend discovers one being. This being is the Faerie. Between the paradise of Eden and the depths of Hell, legend dreams of a world. This world is inhabited by Faeries.

Between light and darkness, legend creates dusk. This dusk becomes faerieland… With these confused, flashing fragments the Faeries will build a Kingdom of the Dawn…

The Parcae, the Naiads and the wild women have become the queens of orchards planted with the apple trees of eternal youth, of perilous vales, of the "Countries that one never reaches." Time does not exist there. Dead kings have chosen to rest there. Music there is more enchanting than anywhere else. Everything is more beautiful there. But whoever enters this land on a "mad impulse" loses his mortal soul and will not be reborn in celestial havens. That is how it is.

And those who are found wandering on the moors, gray and old with their armor crumbling with rust, they hear only the whispering of the wind. It is said that they know and speak all languages, even the most ancient ones, but the language they are heard to speak is the twittering of birds, the babbling of springs and the sighing of leaves. People who understand this language hear the voice of the gods and of the stars in the sky.

But the kingdom of the gods is very close to the misty regions of death. That is why the monks are constantly clearing groves in their search for the golden doors, destroying in the process the places of "Passage," the intermediary trees, and the large stones on which Faeries gather.

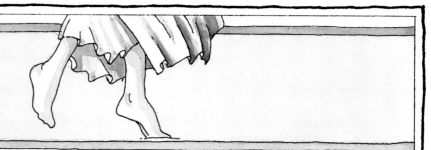

But is their soul as black as the "enchanted one when they kiss him into dark nothingness?" This is what the more moderate scholars wonder as they weigh shadow and light. And popular common sense makes them change their minds, and extrapolate other, less abrupt origins than that of Paradise or Tartarus. If it is recognized that the body and the face are the mirror of the soul, then their very gracious, clear appearance could not—even by trickery—conceal such "evil ugliness of heart." Evening stories and courtly deeds record their "kind gestures" most beautifully. One of the beautiful Ondines saved a child from a neighboring village from drowning. They healed Marianne's broken heart by "giving her a Herb," and they led Huon of Bordeaux and Ogier to victory. But they are also regrettably credited with the death of a few herds and flocks. At the edge of dawn and daybreak, inspired peddlers of gargantuan chronicles will copy out the entire imagery of a blue library. It is said, it has been written, it has been repeated that their soul is neither good nor bad but as innocent as that of birds; that they are the dreams of angels who came to tend the landscape at the dawn of time and who let them slip out of their sleep while burying campion flowers; and that fallen angels found mortal women to their taste and impregnated them with Faerie and Siren children.

It is also said that these "guardian creatures, who during their passage on earth had governed and guided primitive societies with their wise counsel, continued, even after their death, to protect those they had guarded during their lifetime. Before returning to this world to inhabit other bodies, these chosen souls traveled to another kingdom where they lived for thousands of years under the transparent guise of phantoms. Female druids on earth, they were Faeries in heaven."

Or perhaps: "When God made celestial beings choose between good and evil, between His kingdom and Satan's, those who did not come to a decision were separated from the angels and the demons to live in a gray limbo. This is why on the day of the Last Judgment Faeries will not be raised from the dead, but will

gently fade away like a luminous cloud."

They come and go with the weeping shadows and the dead souls, children who have died before being baptized and pale conspirators. They announce deaths and they wash shrouds, leaving behind them

moon trails leading to the banks of the Sidh and the strange bridges to the Other World.

As already mentioned, Faeries undergo a continuous metamorphosis, and they will continue to do so. What seems well-established in one place is crumbling a little further on. A Faerie may seem to be invisible, but she will suddenly appear in the middle of the road. She is thought to be the embodiment of charm and grace, yet she may next appear as a priapic ogre in the whirlwind of a well. She is thought to be material, but as her lover's arms embrace her she becomes a Vendoise fluttering like an elf. Nothing is decided by others. Preceding men at the first light of day, Faeries watch them awaken, embroidering their thoughts and leaving behind those who cling to vain pretensions that do not please them.

They steal little boys—to the extent that, according to Christian Rolland, the Irish of Inisdoon would dress their boys in girls' clothes and give them girls' names to mislead the Faeries. But these abductions were auspicious and gave those mortals ravished by the Faeries an enchanted soul, while musicians and poets became endowed with the gift of seeing the invisible and conversing with the gods.

To mortal women, endowed with spiritual intuition and the gift of hearing the song of the Tribly in the embers of the fire, they bequeathed the knowledge of the Enchantress, thus enabling them to achieve the "Enchanted Status." It is true that during those centuries when kings thought they were stars, people tried to reduce Faeries to the role of ridiculous "précieuses," keepers of white geese and of starchy princes. But the woodland Will o' the Wisps soon regained their great powers, grassing over the alleys of our false virtues and conducting the restoration of the pruned box to its full glory.

Because it is the first spindle of the Parcae, the distaff of the Spinner, the scepter of the White Queen, the prick of the hazel tree of rural Hades, the stick of the catechesis godmother, the magic rod of the blue Pimpernels of cartoons, for all these reasons the Golden Bough of the Faeries is the divining rod of our imagination and of the live springs of our childhood.

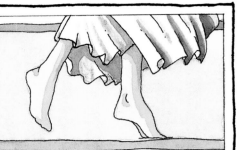

Towards the dazzling glades

All things considered, might not this opening onto the world appropriated by philosophers be a re-opening onto the prestigious world of the earliest contemplations?

(Gaston Bachelard)

To dream of Faeries is to return to the dreams of eternal childhood, to the beauty of the earliest images. That is the key to the enchanted ways. That is when they reveal themselves and when some people have seen them. Some have seen them as a miracle, like an appearance of the Virgin, others have seen them without being moved at all, as if it was a rabbit crossing the road, and others have caught a glimpse of them in a moment of grace.

There are those who see Faeries as a natural phenomenon, and those who have looked for them and are still looking. One might be permitted to doubt the sincerity of these clairvoyances. Even though the photographs of the Cottingley Faeries (which so fired Conan Doyle's imagination) were later discovered to be fakes, what of the Faeries of Marjorie Johnson, president of the "Faerie Investigation Society" (4 Brooklands Road, Nottingham), who followed them for so long and with such love? What were they thinking? We shall never know.

Yet Faeries almost always appear to those who conjure them up through intuitions, apparitions, various signs and psychic communications, such as that received by the medium Lucie Piazzo from Luce, the little Faerie: "We serve humanity... we give fragrance to the flowers... we give dazzling colors to the petals... we cure the sick... we come to the help of humans and we do many other things for them." The Faerie guide cannot ignore the works of theosophists, the philosophers of all things astral, and the inspired visionaries who have described them with the greatest care, approaching them, drawing them and trying to record their transcendental messages.

Yeats wrote as follows about the little Faeries of Ireland: "When one first catches sight of them, they seem small but as soon as one has succumbed to their charm they seem as tall as humans. Sometimes, one has the impression that they can take on any shape they like. They generally travel in groups, and if you are kind to them, they will be nice to you too, but if you are unpleasant and short-tempered with them they will be too. They are like beautiful children, extremely charming but without any coherence."

What was it that Daphne Charters, Sir Quentin Crawford, C. W. Leadbetter, Air Marshal Lord Dowding, and especially Geoffrey Hodson observed: "A wide range of ethereal, astral shapes, large and small, working together in an organized cooperation that might be called the 'life' side of nature. In other words, a completely different evolution, simultaneously parallel with and overlapping ours. Popular tradition has always recognized its existence, and all over the world where hearts are pure and spirits simple, stories of the Little People abound."

Hodson watched in amazement as he saw them at work and play: "The grass and trees shudder under the action of minuscule workers whose magnetic bodies work like the matrix that makes the miracles of growth and color possible.

"The Faeries gather round the flower and give it its coloring by vibration. A tune is produced when the flower is in full bloom; if we could hear it, our gardens would bring us even greater joy." Blessed are those who have come under the spell of the Faeries and who hear the sound of the harpsichord produced by the flowering meadows and the immemorial music of the gods...

Along Faerie paths, the resting place of the soul

What is our country but a dream that we describe to each other leaf by leaf
Golden Bough and golden flower
Fountain, tree, stream,
This invisible Paradise

(Kathleen Raine)

We shall see them blossom and disperse. Fundamental spirits of water and air... mother goddesses and local genies, Parcae, Matrones and Sleeping Beauties of the brambles, Ladies of the snowy mountains and Infusions, Swan Maidens on the ruffled moiré of the Lough, Queen of Avalon, pale Weepers on the lunar shore, White Does of the woods, vengeful Margots, Godmothers, Spinners of destiny, Sirens, shadows of the day and rainbows of the night. Singular and plural, they unknot the tangle of snow clouds and wind manes. They watch over childbirth, rites of passage and passionate love. They lead the re-born child to the gates of the Sidh, towards the fields of reviving corn, or they take refuge in the miniature constellations of elderflower umbels.

They have appeared in so many books: in scholarly and religious works, in books on folklore, in popular stories and edifying tales; in Arthurian and fantasy novels; in counting rhymes and yarns; in the wise words of poets and legendary philosophies; in alchemical explorations of the soul and Jungian dreams; in the dowsing research of Marie-Louise Von Franz... the numinous Faeries of our rediscovered distance, embroiderers of babbling synchronisities inserting the seeds of dreams...

Now, at this moment when forgotten wishes may come to mind and be granted, it is time for the wanderer among the Faeries to set out on the road to faerieland and adventure, and perhaps to become lost in meeting them...

MAIDENS OF CLOUDS AND OF TIME

In the street, women and children
Like beautiful clouds
Were gathering to look for their soul,
Passing from the shade into the sun.
(Jules Supervielle)

To discover what the weather will be like, the faerie vagabond must consult the faerie calendar. The Maidens of the rainbow wrote this almanac of the seasons using the twigs of blackthorn bushes as letters. Everything is in it—the number of days of rain and cold as well as the number of fine days: it is just a matter of consulting it. The birds know this and build their nests accordingly. They are said to see beyond appearances: that the day is within the night and that spring is contained within winter, that April's primrose is really a Christmas rose, and that the future May Queen lies beneath the dead bark.

Behind the white frosted bramble lies Sleeping Beauty, wrapped in an icy shroud… but within her heart a thought throbs as she waits for the arrival of the enchanted visitor.

High above, sitting among the clouds, they arrange snowy festivals, finery of sky blue, love at first sight… and the flowery meadows of summer nuptials.

SIZE:

Gigantic, Titanic, Neptunesque, and also human size.

APPEARANCE:

Those of the first generation bore a striking resemblance to the great meteor gods. As time went by, they took on certain human characteristics; or they could change into a white eagle, a snowman with a cow's tail, a black spotted flying pig, a star-studded wild centaur, a whirlwind, a cloud with a chubby pink face, a cumulus, stratus or nimbus cloud, or a living umbrella. They might also take on the appearance of a witch riding a broom or a country sorcerer.

CLOTHES:

The traveling Tempestaries dress like ships' captains with a sailor's navy blue jacket and cap. The sedentary Tempestaries prefer long capes or dripping raincoats and faded hats. The country Tempestaries, on the other hand, tend to wear wind smocks, faded greatcoats, star-studded floppy hats, and clogs like drain pipes. The Hags love to dress like Faeries with bonnets made of dew, torsades of breeze, little collars of showers, mantles of the changing skies, red moon crowns and trains of the wind.

They brandish swords of flame, spears of lightning, sacks of hail, magic sticks and wands, and branches of wind.

The Spanish Tempestaries Los Estudiantes, El Tempestario, El Escolar, and El Nubero are dressed in black from head to foot, with silver-buckled shoes, vast enveloping capes and cocked hats. They are armed with spoons and forks.

Tempestaries, Tempestarii

Saint Barbara and Saint Flora, who have carried the crown of Our Lord: when lightning strikes, Saint Barbara will protect us.

The Tempestaries have left no written records. Instead they shout out the incantation that arouses and unleashes the wind, and they murmur the prayer that pacifies it and calms it down. No wizard's book of spells, no pentacle, nor any magic amphora has ever been able to contain them for long. The snow melts, the rain evaporates, the rainbow fades away, and the thunderbolt burns its secret in the silence of cinders. But the wind speaks to those who will listen: in spite of the millennia that have passed, its voice is forever young as it recalls distant memories gathered along the road, from the shimmering of green corn to the deepest fossil wells, beneath the damp veil of the woods. The creaking inn sign adds atmosphere to the faerie-tale. When the wind is at its strongest, the rain accompanies it with its choirs, the snow becomes magical and the frost becomes dazzling. The Tempestary climbs down from his cloud, tunes up his street organ and becomes a peddler…

These weather-makers have changed considerably through the ages. Like the happy ending of a faerie-tale, the great meteor gods fell in love, married, had many children and lived happily ever after. But while some marriages were successful, other unions were outlandish or repeatedly in-bred and thus eventually changed the blood. The thunderbolt gods were at the top of the ladder, while at the bottom were the simple old fellows whose only useful divine gift was their ability to forecast the weather from their aching joints or the onset of a bout of lumbago. Other noble families lived in these heavenly abodes, such as the golden haired Dian Rosset family who dispensed good harvests in summer, or the Vendoise Faerie and her spring washing. There were some magnificent giants as well: Roege and Patho, Barabloque, Master Hoar Frost, less impressive than the original Thurses but still capable of flashes of fire and spectacular outbursts.

Then came the Hags, the cavalcade of Faerie witch-goddesses. The Great Berchta was at the head, followed by the Vaudaire, Stabat Mater–Cailleach ny Groamagh, the Old Woman of Gloominers, Cailleach Bheure, Jeanna Paou, and Gryla the Troll. Age will turn every one of these into kindly old Christmas godmothers, but for the time being they are so attractive that they are ceaselessly chased by wild Tempestaries! These are the hunting packs of King Arthur Herod, Hubi, Bassa Jaon of the Pyrenees and Plant Annwn of the King of Elves, Gwyn ap Nudd. They in turn are hotly pursued by cohorts of demons and damned souls, Vassals of the Unseelies and Bogons of black Alfs. Their flying copulation with Succubi, Lamiae, Larvae and Streghes would produce the broom riders and rain slatterns of the Makrâles, Chorchilles, Foxilieros and Brouchos species, which wise men and magicians capture to mate with laboratory homunculi, thus creating apprentice sorcerers.

On the lower rungs, the third generation of the atmospheric gods has become rather bourgeois. This category includes a Bonhomme Hivé, a Mistress of Rain, a Monsieur Durand and a Mister Gray, a Master of the Sluice Gate, Madame de Lausanne, and Father Pépin. They quickly become out of breath, so much so that they no longer pursue the clouds above the towns: they have become choked by urban pollution. Their asthmatic bronchial tubes can now only manage a little fine drizzle or occasional black ice.

Their country cousins, the rural Tempestaries, have become creatures of folklore. The clean air and green spaces of the

countryside have kept them in good health. Until a few years ago people still knew their names and peculiarities and the places where they lived. In Brittany, for instance, people asked old Mother Barnard to make it rain in time of drought. Her boorish, ragged sons were welcomed too: the seven winds were offered soup without frills, and though their table manners left much to be desired, this did not matter. People knew them and respected their little habits, they trusted them. Behind their backs they were given nicknames with a local ring to them, such as D'j'han d'à Vin or Jan d'Auvernha. They tried to please the "Dew Gatherer" who had an abrupt tendency to empty ponds and wells that were badly maintained. In Alsace it was prudent to give a glass of Gewurtz brandy to the "Man without a cow's head or tail" because he could unleash thunderstorms by his yodeling: his downpours would put an end to any banquet and drive all the guests away. On the other hand, Brandhax would be offered a pretty comb to stop him lighting summer fires with his wild, fiery hair. Gods and men breathed the same air, and old people will tell you that the seasons were much more beautiful in the past, "that winter was really winter, and summer was summer"!

Some people believe that gods and humans got on so well that friendly relations continued even beneath the sheets. As a result, many human children had divine characteristics inherited from their godly parent: the last-born of the Martin family was able to drive away thunderbolts and "inflict" burns with just one look of his blazing eyes, inherited from the Tempestary Amigna. In contrast, the youngest daughter of the divine Vendoise sadly inherited the cabbage ears of the human Pochard family. But this only served further to reinforce the links between gods and men.

Sometimes the gods also gave some of their divine powers to holy women, holy men, deserving priests, and wise or innocent people in whom they could detect a "peaceful soul." Thus Saint Barbara, Saint Flora, Saint John and Saint Hubert came to have the gift of driving away lightning, calming storms and ending thunderstorms.

But nothing is ever perfect in this world and there were sorcerers and wicked people who fraternized with black Tempestaries and did evil things to others. They would put a Great Curse on the whole region, bringing drought to their neighbor's fields, destroying his harvest with hail and his vines with frost. Once again the good genies pointed out the best means of defense and counter-attack: "When you see an army of black clouds approaching, led by a raven, you must shoot it right in the middle, with a burst of lead that has been blessed. You will then see the Tempestary fall, with his bag and pockets full of hail."

At certain times the Leaders of the Winds also fight each other. This struggle takes place on January 25 at midnight. The four winds meet at a crossroads where four roads meet. The victor will be the dominant wind for the rest of the year.

HABITAT:
Distant stars and cloud castles: the Emparro, the Tourragat, caverns from which the fountains of the sky gush forth. Snow mills. Somber, atmospheric laboratories of alchemists. Breton sailors often speak of wonderful palaces hanging from the clouds by gold chains, suspended between the sky and the earth.

FOOD:
They are known to love soufflés and vol-au-vents, and they dunk their bread in the soup.

CUSTOMS AND ACTIVITIES:
The good ones do good while the bad ones do evil. A cloud of Estudiantes can easily swallow a man in a single mouthful. Matablat (the dejected) and Galagu (the guzzler) steal harvests. Vudocoryos empties gourds while the "Jardinié" fills them. Baraban protects the dikes against strong tides. The "Agitated One" can make it rain frogs, toads, grasshoppers, asteroids, fire and ashes, and Eltzine can make acid rain.

In addition to their duties as Tempestaries, the celestial Hags also busy themselves with housework.

They are usually giants.

APPEARANCE:

In spite of their differences, whether they are from the north, south, east or west they all have certain characteristics in common, such as iron teeth, claws and wings. They have to be tall and strong, with powerful lungs to stir up storms, to create whirlwinds and typhoons, to erode mountains of ice, or to carve out ice floes. They have to have tanned, tough-skinned hands to strike lightning with their fists, to hammer it into shape, to zigzag it through their fingers and to throw it far, deep down into the earth. They have to have enormous, complicated mechanisms within their stomachs to produce so much mist and to exhale it in drifts of fog and Scotch mist, or to refine it into airy swirls.

CLOTHES:

Tangaroa Ru, bearer of the east wind, and Ruahuttu, bearer of the sea winds, wear Tahitian grass skirts. Hurakan, prince of the wind and thunder who gave the fire to his people by rubbing his sandals against each other, wears the royal robes of the Mayans. Thomagata in Colombia and Pillau in Chili are covered in gold jewelry. Breath-of-the-Wind, daughter of the goddess Ataentsic, and Adekagagwaa of the summer wear a suede tunic embroidered with Amerindian beads.

Genies and gods of thunderstorms, rain, snow and wind

If men on earth knew what thunder was they would turn into ashes and dust.

I n August, the ancient Slavs used to walk in procession to pay homage to Mother Nature.

Turning towards the east they would utter the words: "Mati-Syra-Zemlia, subdue all evil and impure creatures, so that they do not cast a spell over us or harm us," and they poured hemp oil onto the earth.

Then, facing west: "Mati-Syra-Zemlia, engulf all impure force in your seething abysses, in your flaming fire."

Turning to the south: "Mati-Syra-Zemlia, calm the winds from the south and the bad weather! Make the quicksands and whirlpools safe."

Finally, turning to the north, they would say: "Mati-Syra-Zemlia, calm the north winds, clouds and snowstorms." And always, after each invocation, they would drench the furrows with oil. Once the ceremony was completed, they would smash the painted jars on the ground and go home, confident that the goddess of clouds would now intercede in their favor with Striborg, the god of winds, with Warpulis, the master of thunderstorms, and with Erisvorch, the god of sacred storms. She would also calm the three brothers of the winds lying on the island of Bouyan and attract the sweet, caressing breeze of Dogoda to the harvests.

The Lithuanians acted in the same way when they prayed to Perkunas, the king of the gods of the sky, the earth and the elements, asking him to go and throw his thunderbolts further away on wild waste land: "Perkunas, little god, do not beat up the devil on my field, and I will give you a half-side of salted pork"...

There are as many Tempestary genies, gods of the atmosphere, as there are drops of rain, flakes of snow, grains of salt, gusts of wind and blades of grass in nature. Scattered across the celestial seas, these atmospheric gods, crowned with

rainbows, were already making rain and sun long before the most ancient antiquity.

The Nordic Aegir, husband of Ran, the mother tempest of the nine waves, gleams forth with his colorful beer-drinker's face: he is known as the brewer and he makes the sea foam.

Taran, the god of Gallic thunder, resembles a Jupiter with his blond locks; Epona, his fertile companion, has a freckled skin that is as milky as that of her Egyptian sister Bast is bronzed. Hino, the Iroquois archer with thunderbolt arrows, is red-skinned; Fong-po, the count of the winds of China, is yellow-skinned, and Tawhaki, Tempestary of New Zealand, is dark-skinned. The Algonquin Thunderbird has multicolored plumage and his flapping wings announce the lightning unleashed from his eyes. The Ga-oh, the wind bear who knocks the leaves off the trees with his paws in autumn, has brown fur. The Brim-Thursars, Kari and Trosti, the Scandinavian giants of the ice, are blue in color. Kisin, in Southern Mexico, wears armor and he is armed from head to foot. He is a warrior whose battle is never over. Every day and every night he drives back the damned who are trying to escape from the underworld and invade this world. His epic jousts cause mighty earthquakes.

The Scandinavian Jutuls, renowned for their bad beer, make avalanches when they threaten to take their land back from the villagers. But they become reasonable again if offered some food—be it only a weathercock to keep their jaws busy.

In Assyro-Babylonian legends, Adad is the heavenly lock-keeper who fertilizes the soil of the first fertile silt.

Among the Finns, Ukko is the cloud shepherd and his wife Akka causes the mountain ash to bear fruit.

In China, Lei-Kong is the Lord of Thunder; he produces the rumble by beating the drums attached to his blue flanks. Next to him, Tien-Mou makes lightning with the aid of a series of mirrors. Yu-che dips his sword in the jug that he carries round his neck and cuts up drops of rain that he sprinkles over the world. Behind them, Yun-t'-ong, the young man of the clouds, obeys their orders.

In Japan, Take Mikazuchi is one of the gods of thunder and Kami-Nari is his voice. Trees hit by lightning are sacred, and anyone who dares to fell them is immediately struck down.

Shina-Tsu-Hiko the god of winds and the goddess Shina-To-bè who disperses malignant mists were born from the breath of the god Izanangui.

Tatsuta-Huko and Tatsuta-Hime rule over storms at sea. Haya-Ji controls whirlpools and Nai-non-Kami governs earthquakes. Taka-Okami-of-the-mountains and Kura-Okami-of-the-valleys dispense rain and snow.

Bacabs, the four gods of the Mayas winds, support the corners of the world.

Each new season the Aborigines of Australia wake up the gods Wandjma and Bara, who are asleep under the trees, so that they bring back the rain.

Eole, the son of Poseidon, commands Borea, the North wind, Zephyr, the West wind, Euros, the East wind, and Auster, the South wind. It was he who invented sails.

HABITAT:

The "aerial islands" in the celestial seas, some of which are know: Magonia, Bouyan, Eolia, etc. In Brittany, the Palace of the Winds is situated in Bro an Hanter Noz.

On the peaks of mountains, in the depths of caves, inside volcanoes, in cloud castles, in fortresses of ice, in trees, in temples, in blacksmiths' hearths, and in neat little houses. At the center of the earth, inside the halls with the thousand echoes where "They" compose storms on gigantic organs.

FOOD:

They are said to be ogres who devour everything that falls into their hands, with a gourmet's preference for fingers, noses and ears. The ice drunkards swoop down on the vines to suck out all the juices, leaving just a shriveled grape on the vine stock.

CUSTOMS:

Some are cruel while others are good. They are cheerful, playful, magnanimous, peaceful, wise and generous, but they are also vengeful, capricious, mentally unstable, bad-tempered, prone to tantrums, and cataclysmic.

Their insatiable sexual appetites can become a burden to their victims.

Love at first sight is also to be feared.

ACTIVITIES:

In spite of their faults they do much more than just produce rain and fine weather. They keep the planet alive, irrigating it, looking after it, fertilizing it, cultivating it and protecting it from the depredations of mankind; they constantly remind the human race that it is not the master of the universe.

Berchta

The Tempestary Goddesses, the Ladies of Winter and the Christmas Aunties, Advent, Christmas, Epiphany, are all gates to the Great Kingdom…
(Angeles Milhauser, *The Spirit of Feasts*)

SIZE:

She is said to be tall, and mounted on her horse that is the color of foul weather, she seems to be even taller.

APPEARANCE:

She used to be so beautiful that the bravest princes of Elfiria took part in fearless pursuits in order to win her heart. But no one ever succeeded in getting close to her. She has been described as disheveled and hideous, with white eyes and iron teeth, her wrinkled face drained of all color. Or like a queen, haughty and old, whose beauty has become all contorted.

DRESS:

An enormous broadcoat with an interminable train under which the members of her chilly horde take refuge from the elements. It is as black as a storm and the lining is embroidered with stars. She carries a bag full of hail and a lighted Christmas wand. In some places she wraps herself up in a cow's skin and wears a horned hat.

HABITAT:

It is thought to be a star to the north of the North.

FOOD:

There were some rumors, quickly denied, that she was prone to cannibalism. She is quite happy with leftovers which people keep for her at Christmas.

ACTIVITIES:

Being a Tempestary goddess, she influences the weather and brings clouds of snow and hail; but she also brings the lights of the solstice and makes the days longer. As the goddess of fertility she helps women during childbirth and protects large families.

After the lead-up of Advent, Old Christmas starts the cycle of the twelve days or, depending on its Celtic or Germanic origins, the twelve nights. From November 1, the mood of the times changes. The boundaries between the world of the living and the world of the dead, between the world of men and the world of Faeries, becomes blurred because of the arrival of the "Beings of Passage."

From the season of Advent to the feast of Saint Melania, towards Epiphany, the heavens are visited by numerous aerial cohorts. Anticipating the sleigh of Santa Claus, Odin-Wotan, god of storms and of the dead, mounted on his white horse, leads the Lorelei (the Yuletide horde, the furious army or wild hunt), flanked by the blonde cavalcade of the Valkyries, and majestically escorted by the goddess Berchta, Wilda Bertha, Perchta or Eisenberta. Flying over the countryside and the towns of Germany, Bavaria, the Tyrol, and Eastern Switzerland, with their little gabled, half-timbered houses flanked by turrets peeping from the clouds like children's toys, Berchta leads her faerie entourage. A crowd of "misfits" has gathered around her, clinging to her cape of fog, snow and wind, to be comforted by her. A litter of still-born babies twitters inside her hood. Children who have died before being baptized, corpses that have been badly buried, forgotten ones, the souls of murdered people, unfortunate souls who committed suicide because of an excess of love, these all rub shoulders with the shadows of lost sprites, defunct Faeries, abandoned Elves, and wilted ghosts. They are content to roam the countryside together in the company of their benefactress. They visit the houses decorated for Christmas, bringing presents to those who deserve them and punishing those who have been bad. They pick up other unfortunate souls, abandoned by the roadside.

Berchta descends at the crossroads of the four roads where a poor frozen soul is crying, and carries it back to her followers. Keen to comfort it, they cover it with caresses and kisses, thereby restoring it to life and light. And now it has become a firefly, to-ing and fro-ing joyously between the graceful, iridescent shapes, singing with the joyful yelping of a band of tiny, winged dogs.

It is said that the celestial gathering once landed in a field not far from Kufstein

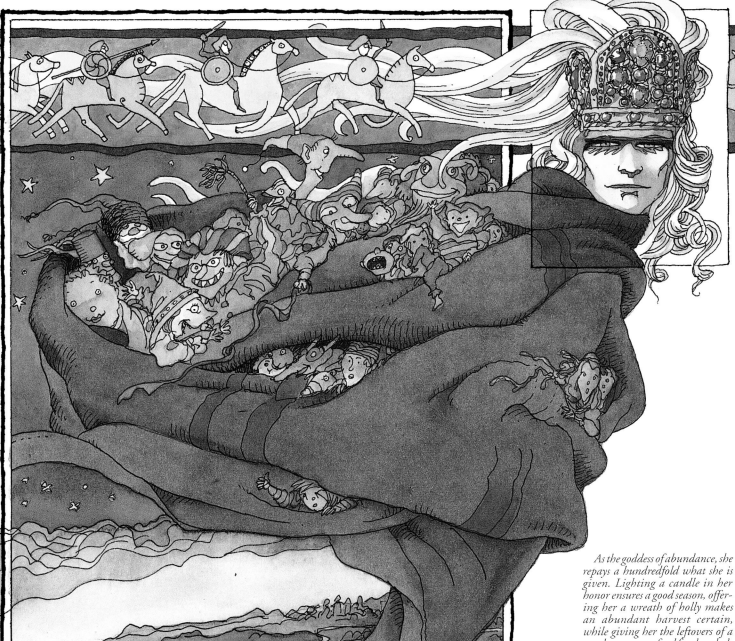

and was playing in the snow while they waited for Mother Berchta, who was busy inspecting the housework of a lazy farmer's wife. The youngest among them, escaping the watchful eye of his elders, got lost in the wood as he ran to catch the snowflakes on the tip of his tongue. His shirt was too long and made him trip at every step. A poor woodcutter who was passing by picked him up, wiped his nose, and removed the hoar frost covering his hair. Noticing that his shirt was too long, he shortened it by putting his own belt round the little mite's waist, and then pointed him in the right direction. Berchta was observing him from behind a bush, and she smiled and walked towards him. She said: "You are a good man. Your children shall be blessed and will never want

for anything." And so it was that, on his way back, the woodcutter found a purse full of gold that he put to good use. As a result, his family lived happily ever after and never forgot to pay homage to Mother Berchta when they were celebrating the feast of Epiphany.

But Berchta can also be terrible in her wrath. It is said that, infuriated by the actions of a bailiff who had made a poor cobbler and his large family homeless in the depth of winter, she seized and threw him into the vengeful claws of the horde surrounding her. At Christmas time, pieces of his torn-up body were placed in the shoes of all the bailiffs of the town as a warning.

That is why people await the arrival of Berchta the Wild with a combination of fear, of joy and of veneration.

SIZE:

Impressive.

ASPECT:

The sizable singers of Wagner's Ring have had a weighty influence on our paradisiacal view of the Faeries of Valhalla. Everyone has laughed—too much perhaps— at the stereotypes of the Bayreuth texts, at the display of overflowing bosoms grotesquely corseted in tawdry, warlike apparel.

Happily, the original Valkyrie has nothing in common with these armor-plated matrons. She is eternally young and beautiful, as naturally graceful as the swan whose appearance she sometimes adopts. She only reveals her colossal size in combat. Her muscles always remain in harmony. She is not a body-building monster; rather her strength is an inner one, contained within the fleshly form of a blonde Venus.

CLOTHES:

She is usually dressed in short, transparent shifts, nipped in by a gold belt that emphasizes the charms of her waist and her delightful buttocks.

The Valkyries (Valkyrja)

Let us conquer here and now
Let us run this race
And this battle with a hundred paths.
(Rig Veda)

Companions of Berchta and daughters of the tempests, the Valkyries follow Odin-Wotan at the center of the wild hunt. But most notably they fly on horseback across the skies of battlefields, selecting the brave heroes who will have to die. Visible only to the heroes whom their spears have targeted, they carry them in glory to Valhalla where a place of honor awaits them at Odin's banqueting table. As the guardians of Valhalla they organize its banquets, serve mead and entertain the assembled warrior guests with their buxom charms.

Superb, muscular, and adorned with breastplates, the Valkyries carry a shield and a spear whose point sparkles like a flame. They take part in every battle and award victory to the army whose leader has succeeded in charming them with his prowess. From the manes of their celestial war horses, dew falls onto the valleys and hail onto the forests.

When they are not taking part in battle, Odin's Amazons enjoy roaming the countryside, taking the form of girl-swans and of particular kinds of Faeries. They land gracefully near lakes and ponds, and in the heart of the lonely forests. People who happen unawares upon these Valkyries may, if they remain invisible and silent, see them remove their finery of white plumes and appear resplendent in their own blond beauty. Anyone smart enough to steal the plumage of one of them can from then on demand total obedience, forcing her to follow him, love him and reveal to him the secrets of his future. But this villainy is accompanied by serious risks, since few men are capable of distinguishing between a Swan Maiden and a Valkyrie who has changed into a swan.

Such a mistake can have fatal results. Indeed, if a Swan Maiden bereft of her plumage is compelled to submit to such an outrage without being able to defend herself, a Valkyrie will use every charm and every enticement known to her to recover the plumage and the power. Woe

betide the loser who dares to defy her.

However, occasionally one of them has been known to succumb to the charms of a beautiful knight and to marry him. In Iceland, the story is told of the passionate, faithful love that united a Valkyrie named Kara and a noble knight called Helgi. They were never separated. She always accompanied him in battle, dressed in her swan plumage. Flying above the mêlée, she would sing to her lover in a melodious, disturbing voice which completely disarmed her lover's adversary, who as a result stopped defending himself against Helgi's blows.

But one day when Helgi was charging and Kara was gliding above him, he accidentally hit her as he was flourishing his sword, preparing to strike the enemy. She was mortally wounded. In despair at the loss of his beloved, Helgi looked forward only to death.

Unlike their cousins the Valkyries who only kidnap warriors, the Kérès (who are often confused with the Parcae, or Fates) strike down everyone whose death has been decided on by the gods. They are sometimes female, sometimes male, and they generate the anxieties and epidemics that shorten the span of human life.

When on the attack she wears a bronze breastplate, a little skirt of steel chain mail, and shoulder and leg guards of finely engraved metal. Her long, flowing hair usually hangs freely down her back, but when fighting it is drawn back and plaited so as not to hamper her in battle. Her helmet is fitted with a nose piece adorned with swan's wings, symbolizing their faerie ancestry.

HABITAT:

Valhalla.

FOOD:

She feasts in heroic company around Odin's cauldron that never empties. She loves venison, ragout of bear, or roast wild boar, washed down with barley beer and the mead of the gods.

CUSTOMS AND ACTIVITIES:

She is sweet, faithful, sensitive, loving, a talented singer and musician, and highly skilled in the art of combat. Somewhat wild, she sometimes takes her revenge when she is captured in her swan appearance and has to submit to the whims of a mortal. Even in the "ecstasy of death" the Valkyrie is never cruel.

This "daughter of Odin" responds above all to her desires and she fights by the side of heroes in the midst of battles.

Mother Holle

Frau Holle! Frau Holle! Another of those witches you must give money to in order to have good weather!

(F. W. Kirchner,
The Antics of the Cupboard)

Another leader of the solar race, Mother Holle is variously known as Faerie Holda, Frau Older, Frau Holle, or Dame Hutt. She leads the march of the Ases, the Spirits of the Cosmos who gather together each year during the twelve nights between Christmas and the feast of the Three Kings to travel through Hesse, Thuringia, and Westphalia. Behind the Faerie marches Old Eckhardt, followed by his horde of horrible phantoms. Fearful noises can be heard, like those of a terrifying chase. At other times the well-armed Spirits go to war, led by an iron-clad chief, and cause chaos everywhere. From her chariot the impressive figure of the Lady Holda can be seen surveying the ghostly procession, according to Henri Durville.

Holle is the German word for "hell", while Hel is the Scandinavian term for it.

Mother Holle, Hel, is the goddess of the damned. She is the daughter of the great, beautiful but cruel Aesir god, Loki, whose name was forged by the flame of his father Farbauti, "he who creates iron by striking," and by the body of his mother Laufey (the wooded island) "who supplies the material needed to light the fire." Mother Holle was born in the land of giants, near the wolf Fenrir and Midgard the great serpent. She lives in the bowels of Niflheim and there she entertains the monster Nidhogg who day and night gnaws patiently at the roots of Yggdrasil, the ash tree of life.

During the day, Mother Holle goes back to the surface of the earth in the form of a White Lady, a woodland goddess and a hunting Diana, to bathe and comb her hair in the sunshine of legends. As Ostera, she can be seen spinning and weaving in the shade of oak trees, cooking, washing clothes near caves in the mountains, protecting new-born babies in their cradles, and picking lilies-of-the-valley in the month of May.

The brothers Grimm also describe her as a gray-haired Faerie-Bogeywoman who lives in a landscape of clouds on the other side of a well. She welcomes and rewards a young girl who helped her with the housework, but punishes a lazy slattern who tried to steal her gold by covering her with pitch.

She is Mary of the Corn in *Contes d'un buveur de bière* ("Tales of a Beer Drinker"). The author, Charles Deulin, places her somewhere above Flanders, in a separate part of Elfland. She gives the same test of cleaning her cottage to children on a quest of initiation. And when her feather-filled eiderdown and pillows are shaken properly and the floor under the Henri II furniture is carefully swept, catkins and down fly from the window, and Mary of the Corn's snow covers the earth to make a beautiful Christmas. Marie Cotron is her cousin.

SIZE:

Tall, haughty, or hunch-backed like a set-square.

APPEARANCE:

Magnificent when she leads the hunt as a goddess. Her profile is straight and crystalline, her eyes are like dark velvet studded with the shadows of the night, her skin glows as if lit by a lunar fire, and her hair is like the tail of a comet. At that moment she is too beautiful to be loved by anyone but a god. But the light of day softens the Untouchable and rounds off the angles. The woodland huntress bares her flesh in the rays of the sun, so she grows languid among the ferns and her movements become those of a Faerie of abundance. This humanization makes her vulnerable in the eyes of men. And once her aura has been destroyed, the country bumpkin turns her into an old bogey-woman, a skittering gray witch, cross-eyed with a long nose… and a hunchback.

CLOTHES:

Her wardrobe becomes drab and turns into rags and tatters as her beauty fades away, crumpling into an old Granny Dust. The precious stones on her dress like moonlight become caught on the bramble hedges. The moiré silk and the sparkling veils begin to shrink, becoming patched with coarse wool. The elegant mare turns into a smelly, slipshod old woman.

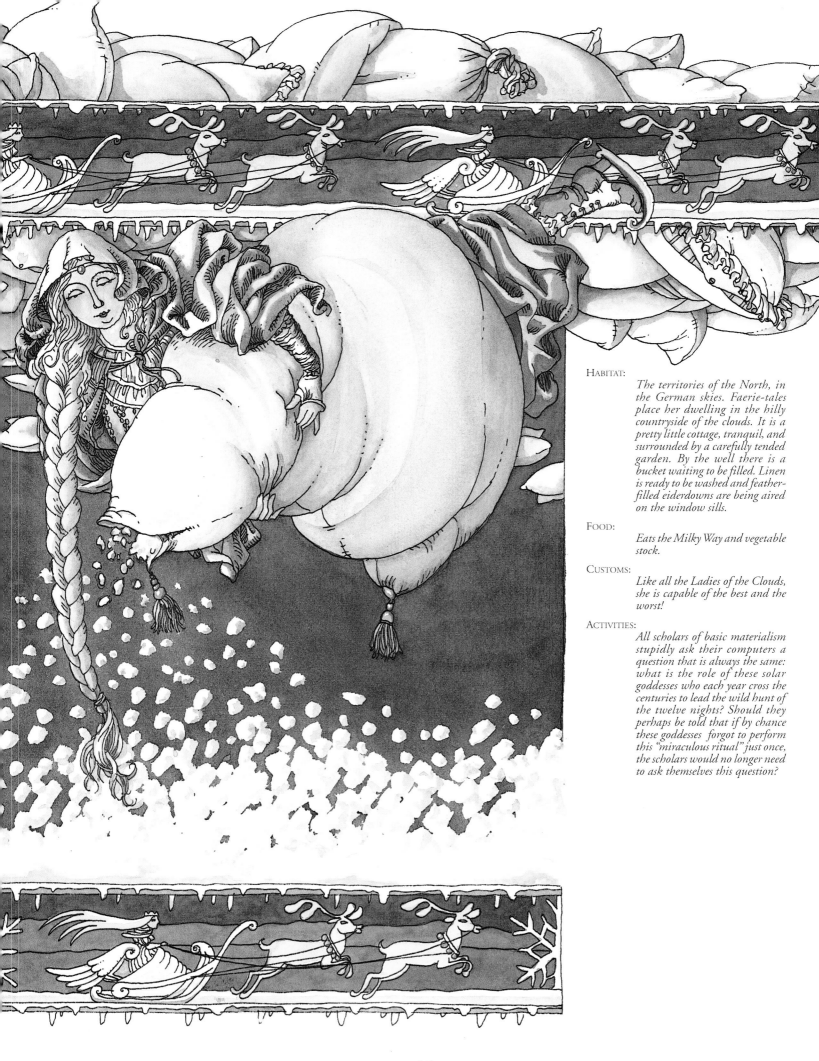

HABITAT:

The territories of the North, in the German skies. Faerie-tales place her dwelling in the hilly countryside of the clouds. It is a pretty little cottage, tranquil, and surrounded by a carefully tended garden. By the well there is a bucket waiting to be filled. Linen is ready to be washed and feather-filled eiderdowns are being aired on the window sills.

FOOD:

Eats the Milky Way and vegetable stock.

CUSTOMS:

Like all the Ladies of the Clouds, she is capable of the best and the worst!

ACTIVITIES:

All scholars of basic materialism stupidly ask their computers a question that is always the same: what is the role of these solar goddesses who each year cross the centuries to lead the wild hunt of the twelve nights? Should they perhaps be told that if by chance these goddesses forgot to perform this "miraculous ritual" just once, the scholars would no longer need to ask themselves this question?

Babouchka

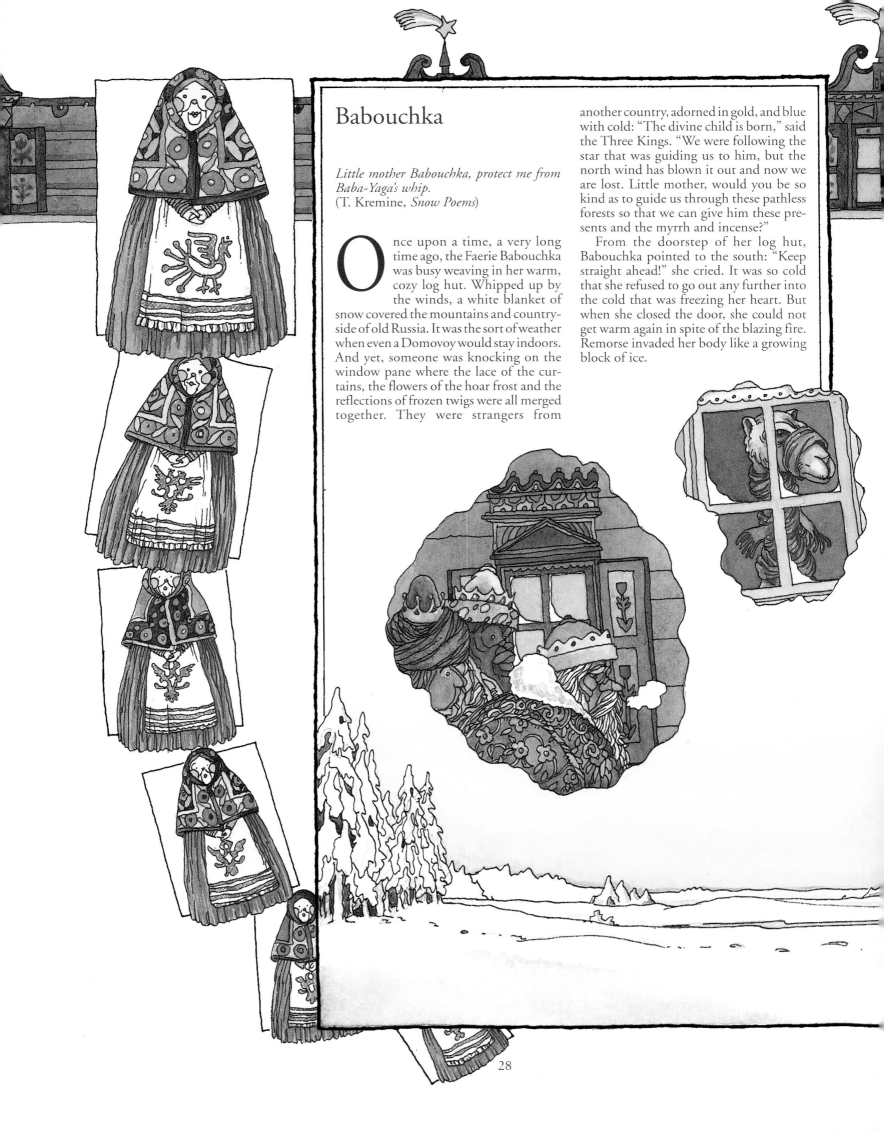

*Little mother Babouchka, protect me from
Baba-Yaga's whip.*
(T. Kremine, *Snow Poems*)

Once upon a time, a very long time ago, the Faerie Babouchka was busy weaving in her warm, cozy log hut. Whipped up by the winds, a white blanket of snow covered the mountains and countryside of old Russia. It was the sort of weather when even a Domovoy would stay indoors. And yet, someone was knocking on the window pane where the lace of the curtains, the flowers of the hoar frost and the reflections of frozen twigs were all merged together. They were strangers from another country, adorned in gold, and blue with cold: "The divine child is born," said the Three Kings. "We were following the star that was guiding us to him, but the north wind has blown it out and now we are lost. Little mother, would you be so kind as to guide us through these pathless forests so that we can give him these presents and the myrrh and incense?"

From the doorstep of her log hut, Babouchka pointed to the south: "Keep straight ahead!" she cried. It was so cold that she refused to go out any further into the cold that was freezing her heart. But when she closed the door, she could not get warm again in spite of the blazing fire. Remorse invaded her body like a growing block of ice.

28

It is true that she was old and tired, but a good Faerie should be good and behave like a Faerie at all times. Since the dawn of time, had she not always brought an enchanted little light to the cradle of every new-born child? Quickly she filled a basket with toys, put on her boots and hood, and started hobbling south. Unfortunately, the wind had obliterated the trail and snow had covered the tracks of the royal caravan.

This is why, every Christmas since she refused to lead the Three Kings to the divine child, she goes from house to house distributing toys to the children, braving the cold, the wind and the snow in order to be forgiven… because she knows that in the eyes of every child shines the joy of the baby Jesus.

SIZE:

Rather short.

APPEARANCE:

She looks just like one of those Russian dolls that fit into one another. In fact, it was she who gave the idea to an old clog-maker who had become too weak to make clogs. Small and rounded like a humming top, her moon-shaped face is lit with a cherry-like smile and two bright red cheeks. Children love her welcoming lap and the comfortable bosom of the eternal wet nurse. She is plump and dimpled, and her podgy fingers are as sweet as corn sugar. She sometimes takes a bear cub with her on her travels.

DRESS:

The traditional costume of the country. Be-ribboned headgear, floral shawl, blouse, embroidered camisole top and bolero. Short poppy skirt, with twenty underskirts, decorated with braid, and an apron embellished with firebirds, its pockets overflowing with sweets. She wears fur-lined boots and a warm coat. On her back is a basket full of toys.

HABITAT:

A log hut ornamented with carvings and painted like a toy, nestling against the background of a Muscovite landscape. A very old and particularly affectionate Domovoy or household spirit keeps her company. Her house can be recognized immediately by its rainbow-shaped weather vane.

FOOD:

Cream soup and cucumber, sweet gherkins, cabbage fritters seasoned with cumin, and Jerusalem artichokes.

CUSTOMS AND ACTIVITIES:

To make up for her past mistake, the good Babouchka distributes toys to the children in her capacity as Mother Christmas, but she also does her utmost every day of the year to protect children, fauna and flora from damage at the hands of nuclear man, who is very aggressive in this part of the world.

SIZE:

Bandy-legged.

APPEARANCE:

Somewhere between witch and scarecrow. For a Mother Christmas she is strikingly ugly: skinny enough to frighten off wolves, and twisted, with corkscrew shaped legs, hands and fingers. She skips or hops rather than walks. The tip of her nose and the tip of her chin meet like a nutcracker. Her long, flaxen hair rests on her hunchback. Her large yellow, teeth gnash together at each step.

CLOTHES:

All black. From head to toe she is covered by an enormous, patched, dirty cape and hood. Only her beaked profile and incredibly long, worn shoes can be seen. She drags behind her a bag of coal and never leaves the broom she rides. Even worse, when Befana feels coquettish, from a pitiable trunk she pulls out a coat of dead rats so hideous that it would terrify the ugly night freaks.

Befana and the Christmas Aunties

One, two, three hundred rats, and here is Befana!
(G. Corvi, *Treasures of Counting-Rhymes*)

"In the past Befana
Befana arrived
Riding her broom
And the wind
The north wind howled
On her back she carried a large sack
A sack filled half with coal
The other half with presents
For rewarding good children."

Befana signifies both the Feast of the Epiphany and its personification, according to G. Rodari (*Grammatica della Fantasia—Introduzione all'arte d'inventare storie*) and N. de Roback (*La Befana, leggenda italiana del Natale*). According to ancient rural tradition, this old hag with crooked teeth is a witch, dressed all in black with shapeless shoes and a bag or basket on her back. On January 5, Twelfth Night, she flies from roof to roof astride her broom to hand out presents. Befana is the Italian Aunt Aria. Having become more kindly with age, this one-time winter ogress puts toys down chimneys to reward children who have been good; but as a punishment she puts coal in the shoes, socks and slippers of those who have been naughty.

The story is that Befana made the same mistake as Babouchka. It is said that one day while she was gathering wood in the forest, the Three Kings asked her to take them to Bethlehem to worship the infant Jesus. But fearing that someone might rob her, she decided to finish what she was doing and put away the bundles of firewood before accompanying them. When she returned the Three Kings had gone, leaving no trace.

Consumed with remorse, Befana distributes toys every year at the feast of the Epiphany to make up for her mistake.

The rowdy noise made in the past to frighten her and ward off her evil spells has been replaced in Tuscany by a new custom known as Bejanata: one of the children dresses up like an old Faerie while the rest of them follow singing in the streets and asking for contributions.

Tchausse-Villha, Chauchevieille or Chauchepaille

She terrifies those who stay at home to feast instead of going to Midnight Mass. She is also much feared in Switzerland; Tsaôthavîde inextricably tangles up all needlework that has not been finished for Christmas.

Snégurochka

Another cousin from Russia, seated in a gondola of light, surrounded by thousands of little snow butterflies that flutter down on hedges and meadows as soon as the handsome Knight of Spring approaches.

Fraü Gaude

A niece of Berchta the Wild, Fraü Gaude roams through the villages on Christmas night, driving before her a pack of cursed dogs with flaming red eyes and fangs.

As soon as she finds a window that is not closed properly or a door left ajar, she sends in one of her boar hounds to sit near the fire. No one can shift it without risking being torn to pieces. If someone succeeds in killing it by shooting it in the head, the dog turns into a rock that comes to life every night at midnight. Each howl is a curse on the inhabitants of the house. Accidents, diseases, and bad fevers will implacably decimate the entire family. No incantation or exorcism can rid the family of Fraü Gaude's curse until she herself comes to remove it the following Christmas.

Trotte-Vieille

A Faerie Harpy of Haute-Saône, she rewards good children and devours the others who are skewered on the long horns growing on top of her completely green head. A cauldron of steaming hot gruel placed on the threshold of the house tends to put her in a better mood. In Lucerne, the witch Straeggel shaves the girls who have not completed their task for the week in good time (by the Wednesday before Christmas).

Kolyada

Another Snow and Christmas Faerie, she also brings toys to the children who sing for her. White-haired with a milky skin and dressed all in white, she appears as white as the horses pulling her white sleigh. It is difficult to distinguish her from the white clouds that surround her. Her arrival is announced by the jingling of bells.

The Guillaneu

The Witch Faerie of Vendée, she haunts the nights between the beginning of Advent and the New Year, mounted on a mad headless horse without a tail.

HABITAT:
Driven out of Bethlehem and northern Europe by Saint Nicholas, who suspected her of being a witch, she fled to Italy where she finds life very pleasant. Giani Corvi (The Befana and the Genies of the Hearth) believes that she lives in a wooden hut in Latium.

FOOD:
She stuffs herself with polenta, panetone, pan d'oro, and pan-forte; she gorges herself on anguilla marinata, zampone with mid-night lentils, and she guzzles pounds of Tortona.

CUSTOMS AND ACTIVITIES:
Like her sisters the Christmas Aunties, she rewards the children who believe in her.

Aunt Arie

SIZE:

Bent in two.

APPEARANCE:

The Lady of Ice and Hoar Frost now suffers from the cold. Her ivory face has turned yellow and her abundant hair has thinned into tow-like clusters. Her iron dentures have rusted to mere stumps. It is said that she has only one tooth left. With the years, her crystal-clear eyes have mellowed with kindness and they sparkle with tenderness behind the bifocal lenses of her glasses. Although she hobbles slowly on her ancient duck feet, she is still bravely able to visit all the chimneys in Franche-Comté every Christmas.

CLOTHES:

She has exchanged her storm wand for a stick and her bag of hailstones and snow for a basket of toys; she seems much happier for it. She now wraps up in warm flannel and woolly clothes, and wears carpet slippers.

HABITAT:

A small chalet on a hillside, nestling in a valley of the Jura. Her house is comfortable, warm and peaceful. You can hear the ticking of a Morez clock. The stove hums and purrs even in summer because her nose and feet are always cold. Still very much present in Montbéliard.

The darkness bore morning in its heart.
(Savitri)

Wrapped in shawls, her duck feet snug in black felt and leather slippers, sitting near the stove, Aunt Arie is dozing to the rhythm of the purring of the cat. Her iron dentures are becoming rusty in a glass filled with water, and many solstices have gone past since her false teeth have bitten winds with their icy pincers. Abandoned to spiders, her bag of hailstones and the lightning wand are gathering dust. As she grows older, the drover of wild clouds, a satellite of Berchta, is no longer interested in the weather or in firing the solar broadside. Through her misted-up glasses her increasingly weak eyes only perceive the behavior of men through the blurred, over-exposed vision of an old Faerie. Her black tantrums are a thing of the past as a result of daily infusions of philosophical decoctions.

The ancients remember her escapades and tantrums; when riding the Hargnes she whipped the countryside with her wand of lightning. If occasionally she spanks some youth with a cane dipped in vinegar, it is because he deserves it. Pleased that she has not lost the knack, she gives them something to comfort them.

Like her companions and for the same reasons, she has became closer to children whose universe resembles hers. They alone are still interested in her, only they read the message of the universe in the swirls of frost on the windows.

Aunt Arie or Faerie Arie now comes out only once a year. At Christmas she emerges from her cottage in the depths of the forests of Franche-Comté, mounts her aerial donkey, and regains the powers of her youth. All night she visits houses, going down chimneys and through keyholes, leaving presents for the good children who have left carrots and turnips for her mount, and scolding those who are good-for-nothing, putting a dunce's cap on them. She checks that the kitchen is clean, inspects the furniture and makes sure there is no dust anywhere.

In the past she used to reward the best spinners with purses full of gold, but now she gives needles and wool to those who knit well. It is said that she can still change into a serpent, she can make it snow by shaking her chemise, and she can find husbands for the young girls who bring her presents. She much appreciates invitations to Christmas Eve celebrations; those who ask with sufficient fervor that their wish should be granted will hear the tinkling of a bell in the distance, the sign that their wish will come true.

When she meets an orphan she picks him up, puts him on her back and lets him suckle on her breasts that she has thrown over her shoulders. Agaberte, the Snow Faerie, also suckles children sometimes.

When she has finished her journey, Aunt Arie travels home via the Jura to visit her friend Bertha the Spinner who no longer sees anyone, and who never leaves her cave since the women have put away their distaffs.

FOOD:

Apparently an ogress in the past, she now loves country cuisine, such as the sausage stew of Morteau, morels served on fried bread, Morbier cheese sandwiches, and grilled Vacherin cheese in season. Her cellar is full of venerable sweet wines: vin jaune de garde and vin de paille that she sips with great delight on Sundays, accompanied by nuts that she crunches with a single bite of her tooth.

CUSTOMS:

Everyone loves Aunt Arie, everyone sings her praises and quietly awaits her arrival.

ACTIVITIES:

The same as Father Christmas.

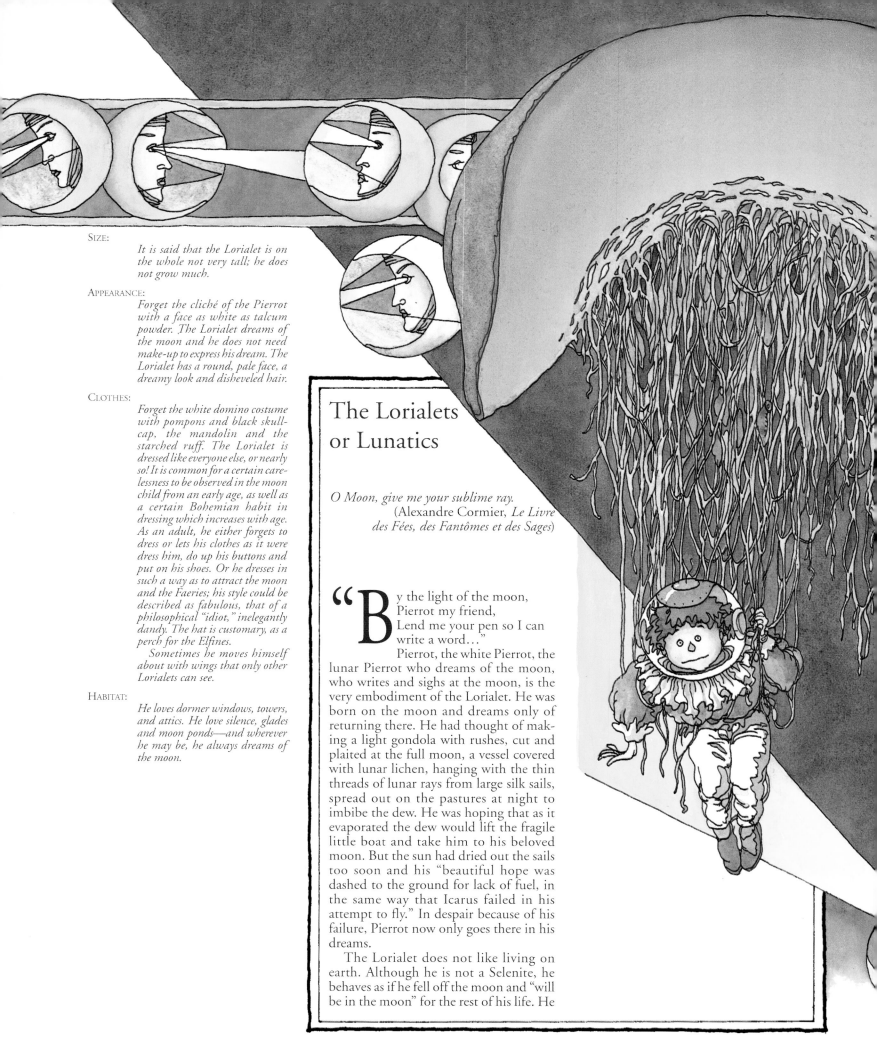

SIZE:

It is said that the Lorialet is on the whole not very tall; he does not grow much.

APPEARANCE:

Forget the cliché of the Pierrot with a face as white as talcum powder. The Lorialet dreams of the moon and he does not need make-up to express his dream. The Lorialet has a round, pale face, a dreamy look and disheveled hair.

CLOTHES:

Forget the white domino costume with pompons and black skull-cap, the mandolin and the starched ruff. The Lorialet is dressed like everyone else, or nearly so! It is common for a certain carelessness to be observed in the moon child from an early age, as well as a certain Bohemian habit in dressing which increases with age. As an adult, he either forgets to dress or lets his clothes as it were dress him, do up his buttons and put on his shoes. Or he dresses in such a way as to attract the moon and the Faeries; his style could be described as fabulous, that of a philosophical "idiot," inelegantly dandy. The hat is customary, as a perch for the Elfines.

Sometimes he moves himself about with wings that only other Lorialets can see.

HABITAT:

He loves dormer windows, towers, and attics. He love silence, glades and moon ponds—and wherever he may be, he always dreams of the moon.

The Lorialets or Lunatics

O Moon, give me your sublime ray.
(Alexandre Cormier, *Le Livre des Fées, des Fantômes et des Sages*)

"**B**y the light of the moon, Pierrot my friend, Lend me your pen so I can write a word…"

Pierrot, the white Pierrot, the lunar Pierrot who dreams of the moon, who writes and sighs at the moon, is the very embodiment of the Lorialet. He was born on the moon and dreams only of returning there. He had thought of making a light gondola with rushes, cut and plaited at the full moon, a vessel covered with lunar lichen, hanging with the thin threads of lunar rays from large silk sails, spread out on the pastures at night to imbibe the dew. He was hoping that as it evaporated the dew would lift the fragile little boat and take him to his beloved moon. But the sun had dried out the sails too soon and his "beautiful hope was dashed to the ground for lack of fuel, in the same way that Icarus failed in his attempt to fly." In despair because of his failure, Pierrot now only goes there in his dreams.

The Lorialet does not like living on earth. Although he is not a Selenite, he behaves as if he fell off the moon and "will be in the moon" for the rest of his life. He

is a bad pupil and a bad employee, and yet he is neither lazy nor badly behaved; his limbate head is just always elsewhere, somewhere among the heavenly infantry.

There are at least two explanations for his origin: the one in the *Légendaire des Astres*, written by Master Herbarius in year II of the elfin era, and the more down to earth one mentioned in the *Chroniques gargantuines*.

The first source claims that he is a child of Selene: Selene, daughter of Theia and Hyperion, personifying the moon. Every evening, illuminating the surrounding darkness with her silvery hair, "having bathed in the ocean, the divine Selene with the Wide Wings and milky skin put on magnificent clothes and flew up into the sky, carried away in her chariot by her magnificent chargers." Sometimes a dragon might try to devour her; she would then hide, thus causing an eclipse, and the magicians who protected her would chase away the Beast. Zeus cast covetous eyes on her and gave her three daughters: Pandia, Neme and Erse (the dew). Pan tried to seduce her by changing into a vigorous ram before enticing her into the bushes of Arcadia… But the beautiful Selene only wanted Endymion (the beautiful sleeping prince) to whom Zeus had granted eternal

beauty and youth on condition that he remained asleep forever. As much in love as a Princess Charming, she lay down next to him and embraced him night after night, and bore him fifty daughters… and one son who was so "enchanted by his surroundings" that he was attracted by the azure color of the blue planet and traveled to earth to marry a Faerie. Since then all his descendants dream of the moon… The Lorialet is said to be the last of them…

The *Chroniques gargantuines* say that the Lorialet or Lunatic is only a mortal conceived by the capricious moon: "When a woman undresses in the light of the rising moon, she exposes herself to the risk of being Lorialated, in other words of being fertilized by the spirit of the moon, and the child will be born under its influence. If a woman accidentally gives birth in a field illuminated by the rays of the moon the child will also be a Lorialet—moonstruck. This Lorialet will become a poet, musician, wanderer or lover of Faeries. He will see the invisible, the past and the future, and his feelings will be expressed through the rain and the sun. Like all enchanted children, he will not find happiness on earth and will forever roam along the moonlit pathways in search of Faerie kingdoms."

And the *Shepherds' Almanac* warns the impudent:

"Those who stare at the full moon for too long risk losing their mind to it" and… "if a man is seen by the moon while he urinates, the moon grimaces in disgust and the children he will father will have the same deformed face."

"… My candle has gone out, I have
    no more fire
For the love of God, open the door."

FOOD:

Squash soup, clover infusions, golden hop medicinal tea, and autumn kippers.

CUSTOMS:

Melancholic, dreamy and gentle, solitary, he is not tempted by human love or by the cooing of Columbine. Cats love him. Glowworms, phalaenas, dragonflies, fireflies, hedgehogs and mushrooms follow him around.

He is sometimes classed among the Tempestaries because he unintentionally brings the rain and makes the sun shine depending on whether he is sad or happy.

ACTIVITIES:

He has the gift of knowing the past and the future but does not use it. He is a poet, musician, and meteorologist, but he only composes or forecasts in the secret of his heart. He is also thought to be an alchemist, but he has never transmuted anything. On the other hand, he has perfected the art of entoptic visions and metaphysical travel. His magical powers and inclinations could have enabled him to become an astronomer or a cosmonaut, but he loathes the idea of expressing the landscapes of the soul as equations and is revolted by the thought of "conquering" and "exploiting" his divine gifts.

Saint Lucia, Cinderella and the Sleeping Beauties

SIZE:

Perfect.

APPEARANCE:

There are several sides to this beautiful Lucia: the primitive witch, the goddess of spring and the saint. She has been seen blue with cold, her mouth studded with shards of crystal.

But "on the feast of Saint Lucia the day progresses like a game of tiddlywinks," and the sparkle of spring troubles the ogress: her marble skin turns pink, her blood begins to circulate and her mouth blossoms. Her frosted hair regains its golden color of the rising sun, decorated with a crown of green leaves, roses and seven candles. The saints are the daughters of the Faeries and, when the first primrose flowers, the Nymph Lucia abandons her pagan tiara for a simple aura. Cinderella leaves her ashy chrysalis for the winged outfit of the Belles of May…

Cook Lucia's cats on the hot plate for about five minutes until golden.
(Mala Powers, *Follow the Year*)

Lying in the shade of a baldaquin of white frost, the beautiful, sleeping creature seems to have abandoned life on earth, and from her dreams the dazzling silhouettes of the Maidens of the Dawn will be born and flower.

Saint Lucia is both a Winter Witch and a Spring Faerie. In Bohemia, with her hair arranged like a shrub caught by the frost, her lips blue with cold, and her petrifying gaze, she haunts the white nights in search of scoundrels. She carries them in her basket to the bowels of the earth where she opens their bellies, stuffs them with straw and adds them to her collection of dolls. In Bavaria and Austria, she disguises herself as a flying goat or as a witch with a bird's mask. In Alsace, she seems more gentle, her face whitened with talcum powder, and on her long, blond, flaxen hair she wears a crown of gold paper, decorated with roses and candles. The silver bell she carries with her wakes the little Spirits of nature: she is the Christmas Maiden. In the northern countries she leaves the forest draped in white, crowned with holly and light, bringing fire and food to each house.

In stories of myth and legend, in folk tales and faerie stories, she appears as the heroine of a rainbow in an episodic tale, as a young princess imprisoned in an underground abyss by one of the ogresses of Winter: Berchta, Befana, or Cailleac Bheur. Sometimes she manages to escape on her own; sometimes she is freed by the son of her wicked jailer who is madly in love with her; but most often it is a valorous Prince Charming who, overcoming many dangers, wakes her with a gentle kiss and takes her to his castle of light. Thereafter, wherever she puts her dainty feet, nature wakes up, the frost-hardened soil becomes green and the dead forest breaks out in buds; when she crosses the frozen river, it comes back to life, singing as it flows between its banks in a countryside bathed in sunlight, studded with a golden sparkle of primroses, and ringing with the call of the cuckoo… Saint Lucia is engaged, Saint Lucia is getting married, here are the bridesmaids of Saint Lucia.

In whatever period or part of the world, everyone knows her names: Persephone, Cinderella, Talia, Snow White, Zelandine, Blanche Épine, Red Riding Hood, Rondallayre, Cucendron, Cernushka, Pepeljuca, La Gatta Cenerentola, Ventafoches, Askepisker, Salie, Aschenputtel, Ashepoester, Florissante, or Lalie. All have the title of Queen of May, of Sleeping Beauty.

In itself, the tale of Sleeping Beauty is capable of opening up the paths of seasonal liturgies, where the cult of the Faeries opens up the original enchantment, where the wings of angels push back the boundaries of the universe to the infinite. Nonetheless, Perrault has diverted and dulled the brilliance of the life-enhancing message with his lusterless, incongruous tale of morality, reducing the seasonal Faeries to edifying bores, with principles and devotions that are quite set in their ways.

"Starting with Perrault, French storytellers take these spirits by the hand, put exquisite shoes on their naked feet, dress them in silk, and take them to elegant salons to curtsey to marchionesses," Lucie Félix-Faure-Goyau enthused, as she buried the goddesses of the Dawn, the genies of creation, with these elegant spadefuls of style: "It is 'exquisitely amusing' to compare our Sleeping Beauty with Talia de Basile, so gauche, so unpolished and close to those primitive roots; Perrault's is finely chiseled, delicate, and elegant. Or to the Snow White of the brothers Grimm. The one has wilder connotations, the other has mythological resonances. Oh yes! Our heroine is unique and incomparable, set in the elegant context of a refined civilization. She does not live with the dwarves of the mountains, she sleeps in the surroundings of a splendid court, still wearing her sumptuous clothes in her sleep, as if Louis XIV's courtiers had fallen asleep at their post while waiting for the King (…) O Basile, go and hide yourself! Would our princess dare to listen to the story of her predecessor? And you, the dwarves of the Snow White, how could you mingle with these courtiers, dressed in such beautifully embroidered and richly spangled garments? (…) It matters not to Cinderella that her ancestor is the beautiful courtesan Rhodopis of ancient Egypt. She has become authentically French [one might say that she has been stuffed, and we can assume that, taught by her godmother, she curtseys with as much grace and happiness as a cadet at Saint-Cyr], sponsored by Madame de Maintenon [she of the Edict of Nantes] and presented to Louis XIV. The Faeries themselves are sincere, very purely so and very pleasantly too. They are Faeries of France, informed, prudent, sociable, not excessively whimsical, moderate, even Cartesian, it has been said"…

In this way the spirit of faerie-tales dies, the Faeries disappear, and the dawn, hearing such arrogant nonsense, fades away. In this way the flowers die, suffocated by the drawing-room frivolities of another Marquise de Sévigné describing the countryside.

In this way the Belle of May lies down under the stone waiting for the arrival of a new spring.

CLOTHES:

The Gnomes of the Peaks carved the wardrobe of the ancient Lucia out of ice, but the spring Fayettes have altered it for the Faeries' balls. They have embroidered it, added veils and pleats, decorated it with lace, shortened it, lowered the neckline, made suggestions… Every year the virgin Lucia, draped in white, with a crown of leaves and light in her hair, opens the gate to the beautiful days. The tinkling of little silver bells attached to her train awakens many thousands of buds.

HABITAT:

Her bedroom is winter; her house is spring; the woods, meadows and gardens summer. She is found in Germany, Bavaria, Austria, Bohemia, Alsace, the north of Italy, and in northern Europe, in the illustrations of Carl Larsson and in faerie-tales.

FOOD:

She used to love fresh food; now she prefers gathering honey from the flowers and fruit without eating them.

CUSTOMS AND ACTIVITIES:

She brings back spring, awakening nature and fertilizing it. According to legend, Saint Lucia saved the people of Sweden during a terrible famine by bringing them food on December 13 one year. That is why on that date each year, every church and every school chooses a young girl to be Lucia for the day. As dawn breaks the Queen of Light puts on a white dress and a poppy belt. On her head she wears a crown of leaves with seven candles. Thus dressed, she goes round serving coffee and brioches known as "Crowns or cats of Lucia."

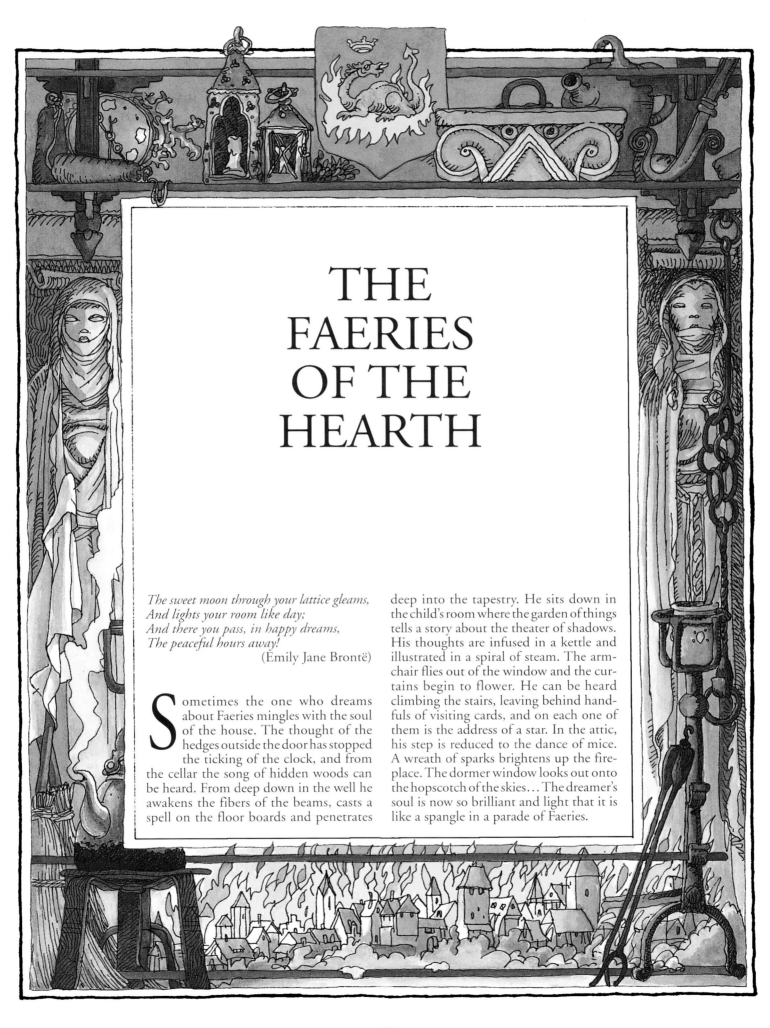

THE FAERIES OF THE HEARTH

The sweet moon through your lattice gleams,
And lights your room like day;
And there you pass, in happy dreams,
The peaceful hours away!

(Émily Jane Brontë)

Sometimes the one who dreams about Faeries mingles with the soul of the house. The thought of the hedges outside the door has stopped the ticking of the clock, and from the cellar the song of hidden woods can be heard. From deep down in the well he awakens the fibers of the beams, casts a spell on the floor boards and penetrates deep into the tapestry. He sits down in the child's room where the garden of things tells a story about the theater of shadows. His thoughts are infused in a kettle and illustrated in a spiral of steam. The arm-chair flies out of the window and the cur-tains begin to flower. He can be heard climbing the stairs, leaving behind hand-fuls of visiting cards, and on each one of them is the address of a star. In the attic, his step is reduced to the dance of mice. A wreath of sparks brightens up the fire-place. The dormer window looks out onto the hopscotch of the skies… The dreamer's soul is now so brilliant and light that it is like a spangle in a parade of Faeries.

SIZE:

Small or large, minute or gigantic.

APPEARANCE:

Beautiful or ugly. They may take on the appearance of Tomte with the wings of a Sylph, of an old Mother of the cherry trees with the legs of Baba-Yaga, of a Faerie or Caraquin. The Bogey Beast loves making himself as ugly as possible: with the hairy body of a Troll, the teeth of the Bogey-man, the claws of a Phooka, the fleece of a werewolf, anything that will frighten children.

CLOTHES:

Magician's cape, knight's armor, Pierrot's domino costume, huntsman's tunic, embroidered garment, fabulous veils, a sprite's hood, the Bogey Beast's wardrobe is as exuberant as the inspiration of the best Faerie couturiers and as inexhaustible as the imagination of the most prolific merchants of nightmares.

HABITAT:

The nursery and bedroom but also the cellar, the attic, garden, stream, or wood—wherever the child thinks he might be.

FOOD:

He pretends to eat.

CUSTOMS AND ACTIVITIES:

The Bogey Beast is as threatening as the Bogeyman and the Alp Luachra, but it only harms the really naughty children or those who do not believe in his existence. His "repelling" presence near dangerous places (slippery steps, wells, caves, forests, torrents, rocks, and ponds) prevents careless children from going near and risking falling, getting lost or drowning. He also takes over from the genies of the orchard and by frightening the children he saves them from many a colic as a result of eating unripe fruit.

The Bogey Beasts

When we are little we are shown so many things that we lose sight of the real meaning of Seeing. Phenomenologically, seeing and showing are in violent contradiction. And anyway, how could adults show a world that they have lost!

(Gaston Bachelard,
La Poétique de la Rêverie)

Are the Bogey Beasts, locked up in broom cupboards and toy chests, the products of the dreams and nightmares of children, or is it they who actually create dreams and nightmares in children? The trick question is interesting only because it appeals to the reason of those who understand nothing, and it enables the reality of the Bogey kingdom to be successfully implanted in them without their knowledge.

The work *Inventaires des Mythologies d'Elfirie* ("Inventories of the Mythologies of Elfiria") gives an official origin for the genies inhabiting children's rooms. They are descended from the French "Portuns,", described by Gervase of Tilbury as tiny, aged creatures, about half-an-inch tall. Having emigrated to England, they became even smaller and were lost sight of, except that children included them in games and faerie-tales under the name Thumblings. According to local folklore, the spirits of the place and the lively imagination of children, they appear in a multitude of forms that change continuously. Borrowing here and there a mossy hunchback from the genies of the willows, a head of seaweed hair from the child-devouring serpent, the jaw of the Bogey-man, the malicious charm of a Puck, and the rustling wings of seraphim, they become protean, both threatening and protective of the nursery legends.

The Etruscan Ferrouer genies were around long before mankind, whom they help throughout their life.

Xin, Gin, Khin are the good genies of the Chinese home. Like Old Shut-Eye, they notice all the actions, good and bad, of the inhabitants of the house. On the last day of the lunar cycle, the genie goes to the Master of the World to give a faithful account of the family's behavior, and they will either be rewarded or punished.

Finno-Ougrians such as the Tonx, who are the guardians of the hunters and fishermen. They often live in the water near the As-iga or Old of the Ob, venerated by the Ostiaks, the riverside inhabitants of the Siberian river. Vu-Muna or Uncle of the Water protects then against Yanki-Must and Vu-Kutis, the "Father Hooks" of the white waters.

Yazatas, the Amchaspends, and the Fravachis open up their wings of guardian angels to protect the Persian soul.

In Japan, living up to the politeness for which they are renowned, everyone keeps the place to which they have been assigned: Jizô Bosatsu manages the household, and Kamado-no-Kami remains near the oven to make cakes. Oku-Tsu-Hiko and Oki-Tsu-Hime are in the kitchen using their swords to ward off the microbe attacks of the cunning demons lurking in the lavatories. Meanwhile Kishimojin, an ogress turned sweet Pie Lady, rocks the children to sleep with sweet dreams.

Among the Assyro-Babylonians, the Outoukkou can be divided into Shedou and Lamasou. They are the luminous shadows of men whom they follow everywhere. They say: "Those who have no gods when they walk in the street shall wear pain like they do clothes."

The evil Outoukkou, the Edimou, persecute them.

Korka-Must protects the home of the

The Innua, the Eskimo Spirits of nature, have set up house in the igloo by taking on the benevolent identity of the Torngak. Makou guards over the hut of the Dahomians while Sseteks-Sskriteks watches over the Moravian hearth… And meanwhile others protect the log hut, shack, cavern, chalet, wigwam, yurt, suburban house, or studio apartment.

SIZE:

He can be as small as a feather in the rays of the sun, or as tall as six feet three inches.

APPEARANCE:

The Old Shut-Eye brothers are twins. Both are good-looking and slim, with a delicate complexion, a little "pale and luminous." The eyes are the mirrors of the soul: sometimes warm, sometimes cold, reflecting beautiful, generous and joyful thoughts, or completely empty, or possessed by demons. One has lunar hair, the other solar hair.

CLOTHES:

The Old Shut-Eye of dreams is well-dressed and wears silk garments "whose color is impossible to tell, because their sparkle is such that they appear red, green or blue depending on how he turns." Sometimes he is only a dazzling light. He wears a top hat decorated with stars, fur-lined socks and no shoes (this absence of shoes clearly indicates his celestial origin). Hans Christian Andersen describes him as carrying an umbrella under each arm: one, covered with pictures, which he opens above good children who then dream all night of beautiful stories, and the other, undecorated, which he opens above naughty children who then sleep so heavily that they wake up in the morning without having had any dreams at all.

Old Shut-Eye

Sleep and become…

Old Shut-Eye comes every night when the curtains are drawn, seated on the last rays of the setting sun. No one hears him jump down, his fur-lined slippers deadening the sound of his steps. No one sees him because his silk clothes shine so brilliantly that the eye perceives only a reflection of sleep. He is very fond of children. He is the sandman without sand. He only needs to pour a few drops of milk on the eyelids and blow a little on the child's neck, or to repeat sleepy incantations in a droning voice for the spirit to leave and rise up in the air.

His skill consists in keeping his little protégé between consciousness and dreaming, on the threshold of deep sleep… The first evening of the week he changes the decor of the bedroom without moving anything: the bed where the bed is, the chest of drawers where the chest of drawers is, not to worry the parents, in case a cry of excitement while tobogganing on the clouds might alert the parents to the dreamer's bedside and propel them into space. He turns the flowers into trees with sufficient subtlety that the branches do not loosen the wallpaper from the wall, that the scent of the cherry trees does not attract all the orioles of the neighborhood, spilling cherry stones all over the stairs.

On Tuesday he tidies up the exercise books, corrects mistakes, removes words that have been crossed out, adds a capital here and there, finishes off the down strokes of letters, and imposes corrective gymnastics on those letters that need it to ensure that they hold themselves as straight as possible and as disciplined as the model drawn in the margin by the teacher. He corrects the sums that are wrong, he turns off dripping taps, he adjusts the points of trains that are late… He revives the colors of picture books.

On Wednesday, he touches all the furniture with his little Troll syringe and they all start to chat, telling the story of when they were still trees, of what they have seen and heard in the deepest forests: tales of robbers, wolves, and white unicorns.

On Thursday he shrinks the sleeping child to the size of a thumb, dresses him in the frogged jacket of a toy soldier and takes him on an expedition to discover the secrets of the house, the universe under the walls, the stairs, the baseboards, in the darkest corners, and in the mice tunnels where dolls are married. Or he opens the window to the swallow who carries the child off to visit the skies.

On Friday everything is possible for Old Shut-Eye. The sea itself follows him to the windows of the nursery where a boat waits for the wind to fill its sails made of curtains before it sets off towards the flowing sands of distant treasure islands.

On Saturday, they go to the land of crêpes, to the painted woodland of the Father Christmas sprites. There they will see stars being polished, mushrooms being painted, snow being made from cotton wool, and sparks and northern lights being created.

On Sunday, Old Shut-Eye opens up the celestial pathway leading to the village

His brother wears a green huntsman's tunic embroidered with silver, a large black cape, thigh boots with star-shaped spurs and a hat shaped like a crescent of moon.

HABITAT:

Unknown. They come from nowhere and return nowhere.

FOOD:

They only eat tea that generous children love to share with them.

CUSTOMS AND ACTIVITIES:

Old Shut-Eye, or Old Luck Oie, is a Bogey Beast different from the others. His powers are greater than those of a simple spirit of childhood. It is true that there is no better storyteller and that no one knows more stories than he does. But his role is not only to help the child go to sleep by rocking him with beautiful dreams; he also wakes the sleeping child by opening the doors of mystery within him and making him aware of transcendency. He takes him beyond the boundaries of life and death, to the revelation of the blessed Spring where people, fauna, flora and objects all understand each other in an eternal and unique harmony.

of reunion. All the people you had thought had gone forever welcome you to the banqueting table. You will find beloved grandfathers and grandmothers and favorite relatives whom you thought you would never see again, all of them singing songs and counting rhymes you thought you would never hear again. And after the banquet, in a room on the first floor, you can play with the toys you thought you would never play with again. Worn teddy bears, broken trains, broken dolls, some of them with missing limbs, torn picture-books—they are all rejoicing and looking forward to the joy of meeting again.

And all the time he tells stories.

Old Shut-Eye's brother is called Old Shut-Eye too. He never visits anyone more than once, and when he comes, he carries the person off on his horse. He also tells stories; but he only knows two. One is so wonderful that no one can possibly imagine it and the other is so terrible that no one dares describe it. He is also called Death. He does not look as scary as he does in picture books where he is represented as a skeleton.

He gallops so fast that he gives the impression of flying. He takes young and old with him on his horse. Sometimes he puts them in front of him, sometimes behind him. But he always asks first: "What is your school report like?" "Good," is the invariable reply. "Give it to me so that I can see for myself," he says. Then each person shows it to him and those who have "very good" or "excellent" sit in front and are told the wonderful story. But those who have "fairly good" or "poor" must sit behind, and they are told the terrifying story. They tremble with fear and

cry. They want to get off but they are held back by chains.

The report which matters is not the school report or the list of social successes. There are some people who are successful in everything, ministers, presidents of the republic, kings, and emperors, who very often have catastrophic marks and big zeros; and there are dunces and truants who are rewarded with first prizes. "The Old Shut-Eye brothers refuse to drive away the nightmares besetting those adults guilty of bad deeds, and condemned to ride behind."

Sometimes he asks his brother to look after special children who have been touched by luminous grace and who ask to be taken to the magical delights of enchanted lands.

"This is the story of Old Shut-Eye. Tonight he will be able to tell you more himself."

The Bogey Nursery

One loves to feel the beneficial influence of a child, to learn from him and, with one's soul appeased, with gratitude to call him one's master…

(S. Kierkegaard)

Awd Goggie: The children of Yorkshire have never agreed on his appearance except to recognize that he runs very fast. He is a malicious spirit of the orchard who, from September onward, comes out of the trunks of fruit trees to catch greedy children who come to steal unripe apples.

Barguest: He is a Bogey Beast with horns. A large hairy creature with prominent teeth and sharp claws. It is said that his burning eyes "bark" and attract wild dogs who then follow him. In his *Folklore of Northern Countries*, William Henderson lists him with the Padfoot and Hedley Kow. He is known to haunt some wasteland between Wreghorn and Headingley, not far from Leeds.

Bulbeggar: His existence is in no doubt since several bodies of his kind have been found while digging in a sandpit on Creech Hill, in Bruton (Somerset). The skeletons had been arranged crossways, and they turned to dust when they were brought back to the surface. In his impressive directory of haunting, Reginald Scott has identified a Bulbeggar's path in Surrey that he followed every night when returning to his barn. In 1906, Ruth Tongue gathered many descriptions of the Bogey Beast's misdeeds: children coming home from school would notice a body lying in the middle of the road that got bigger and bigger the nearer they approached. Unless the child had a piece of burning coal, it would pursue the victim until cock crow.

Billy Blind: Wrongly associated with the Hobgoblins, this graceful Bogey has the appearance of a cloak-and-dagger hero. In children's ballads he travels at the prow of a magic ship breasting the waves. He gives good advice and helps children threatened by robbers or witches. He rescues little girls in distress and takes them to the bridal altar, having found them a Prince Charming. He only leaves when he has heard the word "yes" after a sigh of sacrificed love.

The Bibittes: Strange Bogey Beasts of Brittany. They live like umbrellas, folded in the trees of Ille-et-Vilaine. When a young boy comes and hides near them in order to smoke, they open up, fall on him and gobble him up.

Browney: In Scotland Burnie, Burnie Bee, is the bee. Browney is guardian of bees in Cornwall. It is sufficient to call his name "Browney, Browney" for him to get the swarm together. Even if you cannot see, it is obvious that the queen follows him. He teaches children patience, courage and trust. He teaches the alchemy of feelings into rays of the soul by using the example of work and the transformation of the juices of nature into honey.

Billy Winker: Or Wee Willie Winkie in Scotland. He is the Bogey who is closest to Old Shut-Eye. Being a charmer, he knows how to persuade nannies and mothers to leave the children's bedroom door open. It sometimes even happens that mothers call him when gently rocking their crying baby to sleep.

Clap-Cans: He is a hitting Bogey. He never shows himself but the children can hear him in the middle of the night, scratching and hitting the walls and wainscots in their bedroom in a most terrifying manner.

Tom Dochin: This Bogey with iron teeth devours the children who reject his good advice, starting with the ears.

Tom Poher: Lives in cupboards, wardrobes, wicker chests, under stairs, in the attic, and in all dark places where Bogeys love to live. He makes children shudder by touching the back of their necks with his icy fingers. He loves telling ghost stories. His cousin Mum Poher who haunts the Isle of Wight is much more spiteful.

Wryneck: Like Tod Lowery, Bras Rouge, Tückerle, and Fossegrin, he is a much feared lacustrine genie. In Lancashire, to describe someone with a reputation, they say that he is worse than Wryneck, worse than the devil! In the Lowlands the fox is named after him; in Lincolnshire he is a Goblin. Having left the stream and moved to the house, he has become a Nursery Bogey and an inexhaustible story-teller when he is with children whom he teaches the wonders, the mysteries and the respect of water.

Gralley Beggar: He can be seen sliding happily down the grassy or snowy slopes of Suffolk, crouched on a tray that he uses like a sledge, his head under his arm, laughing heartily. He continues doing this until deep into the night, the slope lit by the luminous halo which surrounds him. The child bold enough to offer to play with him will be king one day, but no one knows of which kingdom.

Bugs, Bug-a-boos, Boggle-boos, Bugbear: "We have always been known to them. Certainly, they had to work very hard to frighten us, growling, trying to make us keep quiet and on the straight and narrow. Mine, the bugbear, had a red beard over his bearskin, trailing down to the floor. But as soon as my wife took over from him he disappeared. Now that I am a widower and retired I miss him terribly; he knew so many good songs" (John Keyne, *Maidstone*). Gillian Edwards in *Hobgoblins and Sweet Puck* believes they are descendants of the Celtic "Bwg."

Bobles or Master Dobbs: Sometimes Elves and Sprites take over from the Bogeys because they love children so much. We have seen Brownies, Hobgoblins, and Puck-Wudjies leave what they were doing to go and look after a nestful of babies and stay with them to their last day on earth. The Dobhs, Dobbies in Yorkshire, Bodachan Sabhaill in Scotland, are the Bogeys of the old people. They bring them comfort and happiness by brightening up their twilight horizon with new dawns.

Urchins-Hurgeons: When Bogeys are not accepted in a house and the children risk being punished if the parents catch them playing and chatting together, the Bogeys hide and turn into small domestic animals or birds. The Urchins take on the appearance of a hedgehog and can thus continue to live their double lives in peace. Barbygère says that the Faeries of early childhood, in similar sad cases, are sometimes also obliged to turn into dolls.

The Dakou Skett': He sows sleep and dreams. Three knocks with his pen-baz on the wood of the bed opens the curtain onto the rich imagery of Breton legends into which the sleeper is drawn. He gets on well with the Korrigans who give him small presents that he gives to children, who love his visits.

Nanny Button Caps: She is the ideal super-nanny, a female Old Shut-Eye. She is said to have been the inspiration for the character of Mary Poppins. Nanny Button Caps is known for making deserving children able to pronounce the longest, most convoluted words, unpronounceable by adults and which, in the mouths of children, acquire the power of a magic formula.

Lalie-Laliocha: Another Faerie-Bogey, elusive and artistic, who has a magician's workshop hidden in the back of attics. In the disenchanted world of the adults she arouses in the child the desire to experience "the Enchantment." She is said to have invented the magic wand and faerie dust. Every year, in May, she gets younger by one year. You can often see her in places whose name includes the word Fayt or Brugh, followed by a string of cats, while the cat in her arms has shiny, solar fur.

Hob: Or Hobthrust. He is from Hartlepool and he keeps sick children com-

pany. He takes them on fantastic adventures, driving away fevers and pain and restoring their health with his magic tricks. There is no whooping cough that can resist him.

The Urluthes: Bogeys of libraries and children's literature. They introduce young minds to the magic of books, revealing to them treasure troves of places, stories and characters that can be brought back to life by activating a simple trigger, as real as the *Hispaniola* knocking against the bedside lamp of the now-grown-up child.

If, in later life, the reader happens to come across one of these works while browsing in a bookshop, he will be overcome with emotion at the mere sight of one of the Bogeys' bookmarks, as strong and pure as it was at the first reading. The Urluthes also prove to be helpful companions to Elficologists whom they guide in their research.

Rawhead and Bloody-Bosses: This is his full name and he does not like it to be shortened. An ancient aquatic monster, he looks like the hideous Breton Spontaïl. But he loves little children who can ask him anything, climbing on his knees, and pulling his dripping wet beard. He teaches them to swim and dive. Little girls even go as far as to call him Tommy Rawhead or Old Bloody Boone. They ask him for jewels and mirrors from the water faeries; he gets these from their glass palace when they are not there.

Freddy: It would be a pity to end this incomplete list of Faerie Bogeys without mentioning the indestructible and very contemporary Freddy. The perfect archetype of the Bogey Beast, born of the obscure, labyrinthine urban legend. The product of the collective unconscious of American teenagers, he has succeeded in reviving with a single blow of his claws the reality of the original viscera beneath the smooth, plasticized surface of an artificial society. Thus he liberates the imagination of the Wild Being atrophied within the cerebral prosthesis of the yuppie clone.

The Larvae

How now, you secret, black and midnight
hags! What is't you do?
(Shakespeare, *Macbeth*)

SIZE:
Changeable.

APPEARANCE:
A kind of flabby, whitish leech at birth. The large, soft sucker that serves as a head already shows the outlines of a hideous face. This primitive digestive tube, loosely wrapped in tissues of fluidic coagulations, will soon go through all the stages of a continuous elastic metamorphosis because of its greedy vitality.

In spite of her many changes, her appearance remains on the whole quite constant. Very small when she is dozing, she looks like a tall, graceful woman without a skeleton when she stands up, her voluptuous body supported by the strength of her muscles. Her gaze is always hypnotic and in some situations it can petrify. When she has not eaten her fill her flesh is a "dirty gray." Her mouth is "deep," her lips fleshy and sensual, her teeth long and sharp, strong, made to tear meat, to crush bones, and to suck the marrow and the blood from all living forces.

CLOTHES:
Naked. She is sometimes represented with membranous wings and shrouds snatched from tombs but her taste for luxurious clothes and expensive jewelry is well-known.

HABITAT:
Everywhere and from time immemorial; all she does is change her name and appearance.

FOOD:
All human fluids, "souls," blood, flesh, even decomposed (especially decomposed, some rival shrews viciously remark).

The cabbala, theurgy, Paracelsism, and the Valentinians call them "Adam's tears," "the children of Adam's solitude." "For three days less than one hundred and thirty years, Adam had no intercourse with his wife," said Elijah. "But he was visited by demons who bore his fruit and who gave birth to demons, spirits, lamiae, specters, lemurs and ghosts."

Larvae are born from nocturnal pollution, the product of onanistic pleasures, and they try to settle in the blood or other living tissue. According to occultists and mediums, these fluidic coagulations, these animated mirages, these outlined emanations of individuals, originate from "ephialte" (the visit of the incubus). An epidemic disease, this spreads infection in a particular well-defined area, where it strikes large numbers of people with the same illness—a thesis that is corroborated in *Loca Infesta* by Father Thyaraeus. Catholic missionaries in China have often mentioned the fluidic ghosts, monsters aborted by the light of life, underlining "the murderous, epidemic nature that overcame entire populations, described by the natives as intercourse with spirits".

"This is not astral coitus during sleep or a somnambulistic crisis, but true carnal relations, usually in the waking state, with objectified specters" (G. Muchery, *Sortilèges et Talismans*).

The threat of memory loss, stammering, deafness, "atrophy," and so on expressed by mothers to the occasional little onanist are quite harmless compared with the risks to which the sinner of the distant past exposed himself.

One thinks with horror of the *negotium perambulans in tenebris* contained in bedside tables, under beds and in dormitory cupboards. However that may be, the monsters have been released… and at the beginning of the chain are the fecund, pregnant mothers: the Larvae. They take shape and reproduce so quickly. The old treatises of magic recommended that women "immediately wash all underwear soiled with menstrual blood, not to dry it within the reach of the Larvae because they made new bodies by coagulating the vapors of the blood."

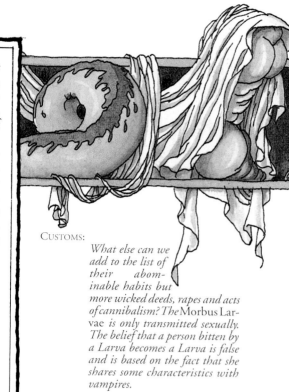

At first just weak, wandering, fluid embryos, they materialize by spontaneously assimilating the corporeal molecules that float in the atmosphere, and by fortifying themselves with the massive absorption of the souls of the damned that are massed around cemeteries and haunted houses, or obtained by devouring corpses. At other times they borrow "a physical existence" from the Lemurs (evil spirits of the dead), compassionate providers of "gloomy flux;" then, strengthened by a constantly renewed organism, the Larvae succeed in confounding the best-informed demonologists by the ever-renewed anarchy of their sinister proliferation: now they have become Mormolyces or Mormolics.

From their encounter with the vengeful Lamia, repudiated by Zeus, they gave birth to the Lamiae who suck the blood of adolescents. As a result of some aberrant intercourse with a group of Djinns, they acquired wings that enabled them to fly above the rooftops, leaving the twin marks of their visit on the throats of their victims: they are the Goules, the Arabian Yfrits, the Druj of Iran, and Draugr in Scandinavia. Associated with the Streghes, they become beautiful and pursue youths from dusk to dawn, using such names as Alouqua, Bu, Bo, or Bhûta. They send three voracious Harpies with clawed feet to the Isles of Strophade, a few Hetaceae here and there… and some Gorgons too.

One of these Gorgons, Medusa, beautifully made up, would become terrifyingly successful: with a head of serpents, a mother-in-law's tongue, wild boar's teeth and retractable claws. Nor can one fail to admire the panoply used by the Empusa, Empouse: one foot in bronze, the other made from donkey's excrement, with the undulations of a serpent, the rear end of a horse and the profile of a sphinx.

And the indefatigable Larvae still continue further and further into abjectness: Bram "Dracula" Stoker encountered one on the edge of Derbyshire, under a lady's hat veil that concealed the rings of white worm. Hogg, a shepherd in the Scottish Highlands, unmasked one under the pink complexion of a fat sow. At night, Beset the Egyptian danced on the ruins of sanctuaries, her hands full of serpents. Nightjars during the day, nestling in the Apache mountains, at night the Gahe or Jajadeh resume their larval activities as cannibal kidnappers of children. With teeth in both their mouth and anus, the Taimu devour the children of the Kagaba people using both orifices. Pricked by *vagina dentata*, the Vulva Ladies of the Apache and Barasana head for the two Americas. The Dzonoqwa of the Kwakiutl sharpens her fangs between two stammerings. Tikokë sucks the blood of the Carib Indians of Guyana with the help of a flute. Phantasmal ogresses of India, the Yoginî and Grakî (grabbers) gnaw babies from inside.

They are very friendly with the witches and Hexen, and they release flights of Makralles and Chorchilles riding Verboucs into the skies of the Sabbath.

Hop! Houp! Riki Rikette!
Over the hedges and bushes
Fly like the devil and even further!

CUSTOMS:

What else can we add to the list of their abominable habits but more wicked deeds, rapes and acts of cannibalism? The Morbus Larvae is only transmitted sexually. The belief that a person bitten by a Larva becomes a Larva is false and is based on the fact that she shares some characteristics with vampires.

ACTIVITIES:

The Larvae, whose name means "mask," took advantage of carnivals to disguise themselves and have intercourse with humans by means of "intrigues" and invitations to farandoles. The children conceived during these festivals were called the "Midgets of Carnival." It was very easy to recognize them because they had the "grotesque" features that their mother had displayed at the time of copulation.

SIZE:
Fat, skinny and tall, like toads and tadpoles.

APPEARANCE:
Repulsive. They are the worst of the Faeries of the dark who in fact refuse to see themselves as Faeries. Even unfortunate exiles from Faerieland describe them as "infamous Bogons." As Harpies, demons and bestial monsters at the same time, they even made the petrifying Medusa look away with disgust.

CLOTHES:
Dirty rags, torn shrouds snatched from tombs and crawling with vermin.

HABITAT:
The Babylonian hell, the ruined underground passages of Burmese temples. Muddy holes, stagnant pools near miry rivers, swamps. At nightfall they come out through drains to roam the deserted streets and alleyways of towns and to slide into houses.

The Chinese Mei live in rocks carved by the wind, ancient trees, certain old objects and domestic animals. They can also make themselves look very beautiful to seduce their victims.

FOOD:
Human flesh, fresh or decomposed.

CUSTOMS AND ACTIVITIES:
Unmentionable.

The Black Sisters

Lamastu

If the baby does not stop crying and screaming: it is Lamastu "the kidnapper," hand of Ishtar, daughter of Anou.
(Labat, *T. D. P. [221, 28]*)

The Babylonian demon Lamastu is a foolish Virgin who attacks pregnant women and steals babies at the breast. Both pure and impure, her father, the god Anou, expelled her from heaven because of her vices. Since then she attacks humans who have no "protecting god." As hideous as the demon Utukku, infertile and jealous of women who are mothers, "she attacks the abdomen of the baby seven times and kills him."

Lamastu is a multiple of seven: seven is the demonic number above all others. There are seven "Bad Demons," there are seven guardians at the gates of Hell: seven demons. There are seven Lamastu. On the other hand, there are also seven "Wise" Apkallu who can ward them off: "Who would I send against Anou's daughter? The seven and seven whose vases are made of gold, whose buckets are made of pure lapis." Seven skirts worn on top of each other protect reapers against snake bites.

The first Lamastu is naked, covered with fish scales: "Her face is like a lion's, her ears like those of a donkey, she suckles pigs and dogs at her breast, her hair is disheveled, her fingers and nails are long, her hands are dirty; her feet are like those of Anzû (the clawed bird), her venom is the venom of scorpions."

The second Lamastu is a sister of the "gods of the streets."

The third one is "a sword that splits skulls."

The fourth one "causes inflammation," brings fever and shivers because her body is filled with a fire which burns.

The fifth one is "a goddess with a pale face."

The sixth one is "entrusted to the care of Irnina."

The seventh one is the "winged demon" who went back to heaven from whence she came through the incantation "In the name of the great gods, fly away with the birds of the sky."

And the sum of this layered charade is Lamastu the Black!…

Ardat-Lilî

Ardat-Lilî is a "beautiful Babylonian Virgin who has not known pleasure, who has not removed her clothes for her husband, who has not known love, and who has no milk in her breasts."

In the form of a she-wolf with a serpent's tail, she steals the light, attacks married men, blows evil into people's homes, and devours children. She is accompanied by the demon Lilû and by the she-demon-succuba Hallulaja "the mole-Cricket."

Madera

Madera or Lady Madela is a Burmese "Nat" she-demon. She kidnaps children, making them feverish and sick. If a baby cries without stopping, it is because the Madera-Madela has taken the child. The incantation to be said is as follows: "You have made my child feverish and sick. You have filled his stomach with air, you have given him stomachache. You make him cry and jump in his sleep. Now may the cries and restlessness, fever and sickness disappear, may my child be healthy and happy: here is a present for you, Dame Madela."

The Songs

The Songs or Belu women are Nat Witches from Burma; they are dangerous and repulsive. The gourds and bladders that they have in their stomachs enable them to float on the surface of the water when anyone tries to drown them. To kill them the gourd in which they hide their soul must be broken.

The Keinnayi haunt ponds, taking the form of wild ducks or cranes with the head and bust of a woman.

Hsing Byu prefers to appear in the form of an impressive white she-elephant.

In Thailand and in Laos the female Nhak or Nhakkhini turn into monstrous animals to satisfy their enormous ogress-like appetites. They can be recognized by the hard, burning, brilliance of their eyes.

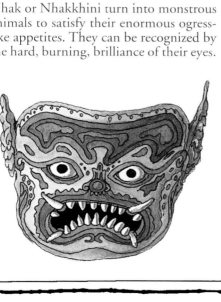

The Mei

The Chinese are the demon Spirits of ancient trees, strange-shaped stones, brooms, old shoes and old animals. They are revived by feeding on their own "essence" before turning into foxes and vixens to attack humans and take their lives. "It is in the form of a beautiful woman that the Mei approaches men and vampires them."

Maja, Mija, Meiga

The essence of Tradition is not a doctrine but a community of spirits that survives throughout the ages.

(*Meditations on the 22 Major Arcana of the Tarot*)

SIZE:

The Maja is small, the size of a ten-year-old child. The Meiga is tall.

APPEARANCE:

Even when she appears like a very old woman with a hunchback, dressed in torn, dirty rags, there is beauty in her wrinkles. Even when she roams the moors and shores as an evil creature, she is still very beautiful with her black hair flowing loosely on her naked shoulders. She has regular, finely chiseled features, a delicate nose, an almost heart-shaped face with strong cheek-bones and a very fine down above her sensual mouth. Her body is supple and graceful, attracting caresses and embraces. Her legs are long with muscly calves. The look in her eyes is unique: violet, green and golden, unfathomable: sometimes the color of dawn, sometimes the color of moonlight.

CLOTHES:

When the good Maja goes out to test souls, to punish the bad and reward the good, she dresses in old, dirty, torn clothes, and a patched cloak; but as soon as she reveals her identity and the mask falls, she suddenly appears seated in the most dazzling coach which would make Perrault's ridiculous précieuses faint with jealousy.

The Meiga favors a wilder look: a plain black dress, short and very tight, belted at the waist, or a straight lamé dress, with slits in the right places. The only aim of her dress is to emphasize the generous beauty of her assets.

"Once upon a time, in a small village in Spain, a very poor boy was setting off to school. His mother Catalina, a widow and sick, could no longer leave her bed because she was so weak. At the corner of the street, Ignacio met an old lady, who was not much taller than himself, dressed in rags and a large black cloak.

'Good morning,' she said. 'You look very sad, child.'

'It is because my mother is so sick and we are so poor that we cannot buy her any medicine to make her better.'

'In spite of everything you are not so poor as I am, because you have a piece of bread in your pocket and I have nothing.'

The old woman seemed so lost and fragile with those beautiful green eyes in her wrinkled face that Ignacio took the bread out of his pocket and shared it with her. The old woman smiled as she put it to her mouth and the child felt the bread become whole again as it had been before he had shared it with her.

'You are a good boy, Ignacio, and that is why I shall give you this.' Digging deep into her rags, she brought out a pot of jam that she gave to him… and then she disappeared.

The boy was so happy that he ran back home to tell his mother about his encounter with the old lady, and he also give her the bread, of which there was a never-ending supply.

'Perhaps she was a Maja? A *Buena Maja*?' she wondered.

Indeed her strength was slowly coming back as she was eating the old woman's food. The food was acting like a medicine. This was without any doubt due to the magical quality of the fruits, picked in a Faerie orchard. Never had Catalina tasted such delicious fare and now she felt so good as a result of eating this magic food that she decided to go and show her embroidery to the shopkeeper. Alas, it had been such a long time since she had touched a needle that there would be little braiding to sell. But maybe there might be enough to buy a few candles to sew at night; indeed, embroidering at night time in the moonlight and by the light of the stars had weakened her eyes. She opened her sewing chest, but instead of a miserable tape-measure she found a large quantity of fine braid delicately embroidered with gold that she guessed was another intervention of the Faeries.

With the money that she made from the wonderful gifts of the Buena Maja, she bought a shop where she sold countless jars of jam from the never-ending pot of jam and endless embroidered braid from the never-exhausted gold-embroidered braid. Because both Catalina and Ignacio knew to whom they owed their good fortune, they never failed to share it with the poor and needy."

So runs the traditional Spanish faerie-tale.

But although the Majas and Mijas are generous and just, there are others who are more elusive, wilder and more dangerous, especially in Galicia: the Meigas. They haunt the moors and river banks. They dance, pursue and bite passers-by, cause storms, and kill the herds of those who do not respect them. They turn into horses and cows with blazing eyes, and they go down chimneys to give nightmares and fevers to those who are asleep. And they are constantly searching for beautiful, male mortals to marry them.

The Maja and the Meiga do not live together and they only meet during the night at particular festivals: in May, at All Saints, Christmas Eve, during Carnival; or when moonlight incites them to debauchery.

HABITAT:

Spain and Portugal, but the Meiga haunts Galicia in particular. They live in the depth of forests, under rocks along the coast, in small palaces consisting mostly of bedrooms.

FOOD:

Raw meat from wild animals and fish. They also appreciate wine, sweetmeats and spiced food.

CUSTOMS:

They are part of the Hadas, the Iberian faeries who were there long before the gods. Passionate in love, they are faithful to their lovers whom they exhaust completely. Capricious and easily offended, it is essential to be on one's guard with them. They love men who resist them, so long as it is not for too long. They are very alert and their anger can cause untold catastrophes.

Their arrival is often announced by flights of ravens and the barking of packs of dogs which follow them everywhere.

ACTIVITIES:

It is said that the Maja does good deeds while the Meiga makes love. But they are capable of many other things, such as attracting or frightening shoals of fish, and influencing the weather. They are obeyed by animals, demons and the Brujas.

SIZE:

Large in their larval stage, they shrink as time goes by until they are only three inches high.

APPEARANCE:

In the past they had a cold, hieratic beauty, but life in the home has softened them. They no longer have iron claws or reptilian hair. Instead they now have long hair decorated with ribbons.

CLOTHES:

They used to wear fur, but later they favored dresses of finely woven cloth embellished with scented plants, and shawls and scarves on their head and shoulders. The males and children wear bright, richly decorated garments: nothing is too beautiful for them. Wives compete to be the one who dresses her husband the best. They then make him stay at home so that he does not crumple, dirty or tear his beautiful clothes.

The Gianes

Are you Larva or Faerie?

(Cirvelo, *Archives of Great Faeries*)

It was with the help of a pentacle that people could distinguish the good Faeries from the Larvae and the Cacodemons from the Agathodemons.

A person approached in a very forward manner by a very attractive person would place the talisman on the heart and say: "If you are who I think you are, go away!" Or if it was carried round one's neck in a scapular, all one needed to ask was: "Shadow or light?" and make all the grains of a stalk of grass fall off by rubbing it once. If the small tuft left at the end was round, it was all right but if the tuft was spiky one was dealing with the Beast.

There is no doubt that this talisman would have burnt the breast of the Giane and driven her out of Sardinia at the time of her detestable youth; but it is centuries since she repented!

The Gianes are the daughters of the Larvae. Like their unworthy mothers, they share a taste for blood, flesh, and the excitement of extreme fornication and bad deeds. Hidden in caves and the mountain forests of the island, they had perfected the art of whistling and singing. They had acquired this skill at the school for Spirits of the Air and from the Sirens whom the Pelasgians tried to befriend; they also learnt from the birds whose appearance they sometimes assumed. A few of them were persuaded by this simple, playful existence between heaven and earth to adopt this way of life permanently: "between the thrush, the cuckoo and the jay," as a species that they always kept secret so as to escape humans and their own kind. They used to build elegant nests of exquisite complexity, true masterpieces of building and fine weaving, concealed in the tops of trees.

With these heavenly songs, the Gianes attracted men who were immediately seduced by their great beauty. For a whole week these unfortunate men became their gourds of blood and sex toys, before dying of exhaustion and anaemia. Each Giane, feeling pleasantly full, would then go to sleep and gave birth three days later to two or three little cannibals. They then turned into she-wolves to hunt and bring back meat for the greedy brood.

Remarkable weavers, the Gianes spun, wove, and embroidered most of the time, when they were not driven by their evil appetites. They were able to make enormous tablecloths of fine white lace that could have covered the entire island with a thin layer of dust-like frost. This lace was so strong, light and invisible that the Gianes

could catch anything they wanted in its mesh: shepherds, dwarves and giants.

By distancing themselves completely from their Larvae family and refusing them access to the island, the tame Gianes who had mated with humans succeeded in creating a new peaceful race of Faeries.

Having become smaller, they ended by marrying dwarves… and this is how the benevolent race of the Gianes was born.

There are two explanations for their change of mood. The most popular says that some very young Gianes, having kept their casual lovers for longer than usual, became accustomed to their tender presence and their kindness; thus they began to experience love, including maternal love. Their pleasant, quiet life, surrounded by the wild beauty of the Sardinian mountains, overcame the cruel side of their nature. Their lewd debauchery was replaced by tender outbursts of affection, their canines lost their sharpness and turned into beautiful teeth, and their enchanting but funereal songs became lullabies…

The other hypothesis is that the Elves were so upset and angry to have lost so many of their brothers and sisters who fell into the traps set by the Gianes that they threatened them with destruction if they did not temper their aggression.

Whatever the reason, the Gianes slowly turned into good Faeries, kind, hard-working wives and excellent mothers.

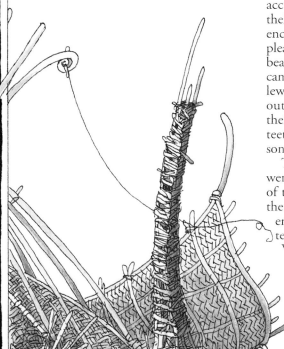

FOOD:
Vegetable and game stews (they still hunt). Salads, goat cheese in oil and honey cakes have replaced their bloody orgies of meat.

HABITAT:
Prettily arranged, well-kept caves in the rocky hillsides of Sardinia. In 1749 a geologist discovered a pile of Giane skeletons, painted light blue, whose skulls were decorated with deep blue solar symbols and spirals.

CUSTOMS AND ACTIVITIES:
The Gianes watch over the natural beauties of the countryside, and the legends and customs of Sardinia. Now old and few in number, they are seldom seen. Women no longer go and consult them to find out about the future, nor do they commission woven and embroidered cloth from them… But although people have forgotten about them, they continue to protect the vineyards, fields and flocks of sheep.

SIZE:

Six feet three inches, but there are also some very small ones.

APPEARANCE:

Very beautiful, with very brown, luminous eyes. Regal and wild at the same time.

CLOTHES:

Traditional Lithuanian costume, enriched with floral motifs, gold embroidery, jewels and ribbons. The brilliance of their impressive hair is further enhanced by crowns of rue flowers.

HABITAT:

Lithuania, Livonia, Latvia, and Estonia. Lithuania had its "Great Sacred One" for a very long time until Christianity destroyed its magic in the mid-13th century. Then the forest of the Laumes used to stretch, alive and enchanted, as far as the eye could see.

FOOD:

They love saltabaciai (cucumbers with cream).

CUSTOMS:

The name of Laumé or Laimé is preserved in the Daïnos, the poems sung on the strings of Kanklés that answered the questions that everyone asks themselves when looking at the stream, the sky and the wind rustling in the leaves. She is a god of happiness and fate.

The Laumes, the daughters of Laumé

Laimé cries, Laimé calls
Running, barefoot, in the mountain.
(Lithuanian song)

L ithuania is beautiful, but Old Statys thought it was even more so in the time of the divine Trinity, when Perkunas, the king of heaven and earth, the master of nature, ruled over all the gods.

At that time the birds were considered superior creatures—subtle creatures of crossroads—capable of knowing and predicting the future.

The Krivé-Krivaïtis, the high priest, the Vaidilutes, the Vestals, the Laoutari, the fiddler and a few others who have the "gift" could interpret the language of the birds and listen to the voice of the souls.

Old Statys had consulted one of them when his wife had gone to the last star of Pauksciu Kélias and he did not know whether to stay in his empty house or become a hired hand at the neighboring farm. After countless visits to the cemetery, he had learned to interpret the messages from his dead wife through the twittering of the small birds nearby and in the tinkling of the little bells attached to the cross above her tomb. His new masters were very appreciative of his affection and showered him with kindnesses. But they were so young, so inexperienced and so lacking in any respect for the old beliefs that they called them pagan nonsense and old-fashioned rubbish. And yet Statys was aware of the bad omens reflected in the worried to-ing and fro-ing of the birds and the frantic tinkling of the bells. Because of this he had clearly expressed his disagreement the night before, when his young master had announced his plan of visiting the market at Sventamiestis. The journey would only take two days. He left his wife, the beautiful Aluité, under the protection of Statys. She was still very weak after giving birth. Her baby was so big and beautiful that he risked attracting the covetousness of the Faeries: the Laumes, the daughters of Laumé!

It was not sensible to leave her so soon after the birth—there would be plenty of other markets. But the farmer laughed at the unfounded fears of Old Statys, and said there was no better guardian than him. "*Melskis uz mus*" ("Pray for us"), Statys muttered worriedly as the farmer's cart left for market.

Night fell. After watching the baby being fed, cuddled and rocked to sleep, Statys placed the child in his cradle next

to his mother's bed. A hundred times he came to ask Aluité if she needed anything, and a hundred times she laughed at the good Statys, telling him to go back to bed, assuring him that everything was well. But he did not feel reassured and a hundred times he checked that the shutters and doors were locked properly. He cursed himself for having listened to his masters when they asked him to throw out the protecting snake, coiled under the bread bin, which was known to drive away the Laumes and the Vokielis with nine tongues from the house; he had done so against his better judgment.

Sitting on the bed in his small room next to the kitchen, he stayed up to watch. When night falls all life in the country stops and the trees are silent; then the mists and the Laumes appear. It is not out of spite that they steal babies, but "to make them happy somewhere else."

He was suddenly woken up by feeling a light touch. How long had he slept? Looking through the keyhole, he could see luminous, faerie-like shapes walking through the walls and materializing. He saw the four Laumes walk quietly into Aluité's bedroom and take the baby very quietly so as not to wake anyone up. They put him on the kitchen table, removed his clothes and wrapped him in golden veils. They then stuffed the baby's old clothes with some straw, made a head, and very quietly went and placed this straw doll in the cradle. Taking advantage of the fact that the baby had been left alone in the kitchen, Statys jumped out, seized the child and hid him in his clothes chest with him. He prayed that the child would not cry. The Faeries were all ready for the baby whom they now realized had disappeared. He could hear their whistling of annoyance and their quarreling, with each accusing the other of not having watched the baby. He heard them search and poke around… getting closer… and then they found his hiding-place. The lid was lifted up and four pairs of flaming eyes stared at him, paralyzing him with fear. But suddenly the cockerel started singing in the courtyard, the light of dawn streamed through the window, and one by one the Laumes faded away.

Old Statys took the baby back to his mother who had woken up crying: she felt an enormous weight on her breast so that she could no longer breathe or move, dreaming that shadowy figures were stealing her baby. He then took the straw doll outside, knowing that he must cut the head off before twenty-four hours were over, otherwise it would come to life. When he cut the straw head, blood spurted out.

No one can go against her will. Some songs describe her as a Banshee, warning men of the disasters awaiting them. She is also revered as a moon goddess. She is often with Praurimé, goddess of the sacred fire, Piluyté, goddess of wealth, and Grubyté, the spring goddess. Laumé is the mother of the Laumes who also protect nature and children.

ACTIVITIES:

The Laumes steal children to shield them from the painful experiences of life and offer them a world that will satisfy their love of enchantment and wonder.

The Laumes visit cradles to endow new-born babies with particular gifts. Those who feared them called them the "devourers." They described abnormal children with large heads as "changed by the Laumes."

SIZE:

Medium height as a woman-Faerie, enormous as a dragon.

APPEARANCE:

She is a winged serpent whose body is covered with fire. On her forehead, she has a single eye, a luminous diamond that sparkles and projects a bright light visible from a great distance.

When she appears as a woman, she is beautiful, tall and slender, well-muscled, her hair either very black or reddish blond.

Marcel Aymé immortalized her in a magnificent book.

CLOTHES:

Her winged serpent skin. Sometimes she wears an aigrette or sparkling crown on her head, and a richly decorated white garment.

HABITAT:

All kinds of clear green waters. There are Faerie-Serpents almost everywhere in the world, but the dominant Vouivre comes from Franche-Comté, more precisely from the Jura and the Doubs. She is so famous there that many rivers and fountains are dedicated to her; she owns castles, and streets in Dôle and Montbéliard.

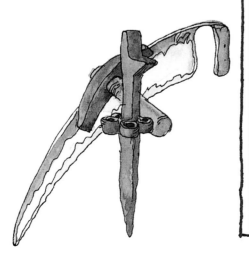

The Vouivre

On the subject of these serpents, vire de vibra, Spanish vibora, Saint Amboise says that they are the cruelest creatures in the world, the most lacking in pity, and the most full of malice.

(Brunetto Latini)

When she shows herself in the shape of a woman she is very beautiful, but she is still as deadly dangerous as when she appears in the guise of a dragon. At night she flies through the air, beating her wings noisily, guided by the luminous carbuncle which serves as an eye. During the day she sleeps until two o'clock in the afternoon, coiled up at the back of a cave. She then goes down to a pond, fountain or river to bathe.

Sometimes she flies there, splashing about in the water and flapping her wings, like the birds do. At other times, she glides through the water with her scaly skin and undulating tail. But usually she prefers to remove her enchanted guise so as to feel the caress of the cool water on her naked skin.

She hides her serpent's skin out of sight in the grass and places her precious eye on top; it is then that she is thought to be vulnerable.

Countless are the curious who came to spy on her there, in the hope of snatching her treasures. It is always the same story. The villain, hidden in the bushes, observes her, a lump in his throat and his eyes fixed upon her, dazed by her beauty when, standing on the river bank, she arches her slender body to dive in. He admires the black brilliance of her hair, the muscled spirals of her arched body, the elegant curve of the small of her back, and her round buttocks.

Were he to speak words of love to her and suggest some frolicking in the ferns, his voice trembling with emotion and his eyes burning with excitement, perhaps the story would have a happy ending. She would listen to him trying to express his love to her and she would smile at his clumsiness as he accidentally brushed against her nipple while offering her a flower. Who knows whether the Vouivre might be charmed by this young man's naive insolence and allow herself a few pleasures of the flesh… But the scoundrel only thinks of the calves, cows, and chickens that Perrine requires before marrying. He has noticed the "exquisite bather" and is fascinated by the sparkle of the diamond that would enable him to buy a tractor, a combine harvester, a hedge-trimmer, an electric milking machine, a chicken factory, and an automated farm. All he has to do is to stretch out his arm while the serpent is swimming, snatch the jewel and flee. It is said that the Vouivre cannot see at all without this carbuncle. But people say so many silly things! He has barely touched the stone when a terrifying whistling makes his blood run cold. The sky has turned black, darkened by an enormous silhouette. All he sees are teeth licked by a forked tongue, and in the middle of the beast's forehead, he can see his own face convulsed with terror, torn into a thousand pieces by the many facets of the diamond.

They are warned that this will happen but it is always the same story. Every time the man's body is discovered torn to pieces, dismembered or burnt, and on being lifted out of the mud, they turn to dust as the Vouivre appears victorious out of the water.

One day, in Peseux, in the Jura, two gentlemen climbed out of a luxurious post-chaise and started looking for a woman who would be willing to look after an eight-day-old baby. The woman first hesitated but made up her mind to accept when she saw forty Napoleons of twenty francs shining on the table. When she undressed the baby she noticed with horror that the lower part of his body was rather elongated, yellowish and covered with scales like the tail of a serpent. Everyone in Peseux and the surrounding villages, and even the local paper dated February 27, 1853, stated that this child was born of the Vouivre.

FOOD:

Calves, cows, sheep, a few pigs that they steal and devour raw at the back of a den.

CUSTOMS:

The mother of the Vouivres is said to be a Philocatrix. The Vouivre is the result of a harmonious fusion of the four elemental spirits: she is linked to air by her wings, to earth by her dwelling, to water by her love of bathing, and to fire by her breath.

ACTIVITIES:

She guards treasures and she fertilizes the earth, the sky and rivers. She brings back spring. She rules over all the different serpents of air, earth, water and fire.

Mélusine

On the cold rampart walks of medieval castles night is developing wings for those who know how to accept them…

(Burneau Perou,
Petites musiques des nuits)

I n the past there was a King of Scotland who was called Elinas. He was a very powerful knight, full of valor. One day, hunting in the forest, he approached a fountain where he saw the most beautiful woman he had ever seen. He greeted her humbly.

"Dear Lady, I beg you to give me your love and affection."

"If you wish me to become your wife, you must swear that you will never try to see me when I am giving birth." Thus spoke the Faerie Persine. They married, were very happy and had three wonderful daughters. The first daughter was given the name Mélusine, the second Melior, and the third Palestine. But Mataquas, son of Elinas from his first marriage, made his father break his promise by pushing him into the room where Persine was bathing her three daughters: "Dishonest king, you have broken your vow, the mother shouted in horror. You will be sorry because now you have lost me forever!"

After Persine left Elinas, she took refuge in Avalon with her three daughters. There Persine and her daughters lived for fifteen years. Every morning she would take them to a high mountain called Eléonos, the flowery mountain from where they could see the distant kingdom of Scotland.

"Daughters, see, that is where you were born and where you should have been living, had it not been for your father's perjury which reduced you to such poverty." She repeated her sad story so often that one day Mélusine said to her sisters: "If you agree, I believe that we should lock up the perjurer in the enchanted mountain of Northumberland, called Brumblerio, where he will be imprisoned forever." And that is what they did. Their mother was very angry: "Mélusine, as the eldest you will be punished first. From now on, every Saturday, you will be a serpent below the navel. But if you find a man who is willing to marry you on condition that he never sees you on Saturdays, you will live the normal life of a woman. In any case, you will be the first of a long line of noble descendants who will accomplish great feats of valor. But if you ever leave your husband, know that you will suffer the same never-ending anguish as before." After that, she punished Melior and Palestine and all four went their separate ways without ever meeting again.

Mélusine went off roaming the deep forests and copses in search of her fate. There she met the beautiful Raymond. They saw each other, looked at each other and fell in love. Sweetly they embraced and kissed, and married in great pomp.

Mélusine bore eight sons, all of them handsome and strong—except for a few details, such as: one had ears that were too big, another had one eye higher than the other, a third one had only one eye, another one had three eyes… But all of them grew up to be extremely powerful. Mélusine had indeed founded a noble line of descendants as predicted by Persine. The rest still remained to be accomplished.

SIZE:

As a Serpent she is prodigiously tall, with a tail fifteen feet long, according to Jehan d'Arras.

APPEARANCE:

"A delightful woman down to the navel, with a serpent's tail whose magnificent blue and silver scales she proudly displays. On her back she has large devil's wings."

CLOTHES:

According to Alexandra de Sancerre at whose bedside she appeared, "she was dressed in a garment made of coarse fabric, gathered by a belt below the breasts, with a white head-dress as was worn in the olden days."

HABITAT:

More or less everywhere in France but especially in Lusignan, Fort-de-Cé, in Poitou and the Vendée, along the Loire and the Gironde. She is also to be found in Belgium, as the guardian of the house of Gavre, at the château of Enghien, and at all the places the Lusignans have passed through. She often appears in buildings that she has built herself: in Mervent, Vouvant, Saint-Maixent, Talmont, and Parthenay.

While Raymond traveled through Brittany, Mélusine started building. She built all kinds of buildings. She erected the castle and town of Parthenay without skimping on stone, she founded the coastal watch towers of La Rochelle, and she built countless churches, chapels and abbeys, so that, on his return, Raymond marveled at the changes she had made to Lusignan. They celebrated their joy at being reunited but their happiness was not to last very much longer.

As he had promised, Raymond never attempted to see her on Saturdays. But his brother, the Count of Forez, was so jealous of their love that he lied to his brother: "Brother, your wife fornicates every Saturday with another." Raymond flew into a rage, grabbed his sword and went to the forbidden door. He pressed the hard, thin point of the sword against the door, twisting it until he had made a hole through which he could see the whole room. He saw Mélusine sitting in a vat some fifteen feet in circumference, with the body of a woman from the navel up, combing her hair. Below the navel, she had a serpent's tail, very long and thick like a cask in which herrings are stored. "Alas my love," wailed Raymond, "I have just betrayed you because of my brother's lies."

Unfortunately, Persine's curse was to separate them forever. "Farewell, my sweet love, my very own, my heart and my joy!" With one leap, Mélusine jumped out of one of the windows of the room, as lightly as if she had wings.

She then let out a long cry of pain and flew off into the air. And then she changed into a large, fat Serpent-Woman, fifteen feet long. She uttered such a strange, heartrending cry that it was obvious that she was leaving this place against her will and with great sadness. And it was not known what had become of her…

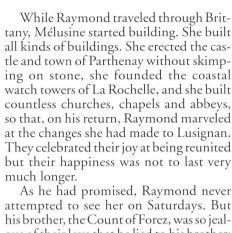

Jehan d'Arras, the novelist-biographer of Mélusine, tells us that she often came back at night to sing lullabies to her children and gently caress them in full view of the nurses who dared not say anything. He also says that she warned them of the death of their father who had become a hermit in Montserrat by showing herself to them three days before his death, flying in circles above the castle towers, uttering wild, piercing cries of pain.

As Persine had prophesied, the Serpent Faerie reveals herself and utters cries of lamentation every time a property in Lusignan changes ownership or an heir of her line is about to die.

FOOD:

Contrary to some rumors, she has never been an ogress.

CUSTOMS:

Mélusine stands for "wonder," "marvel" or "sea-mist."

Mythology experts see in her the Roman Mater Lucina who watched over births or, before that, a Celtic divinity with the shape of a serpent. An old mother of nature and fertility, she is a Vouivre, or serpent, a cousin of mermaids, Meermines, Meeweib-Nixes and the Ladies of the Lake.

ACTIVITIES:

Apart from her Banshee nature, Mélusine is above all a building Faerie; she works by the light of the moon before the cock crows. If she is caught unawares while working she stops immediately without completing the work. That is why one of the windows in Merrigoute is missing, and also why the final stones of the Niort spire and the church of Parthenay are missing.

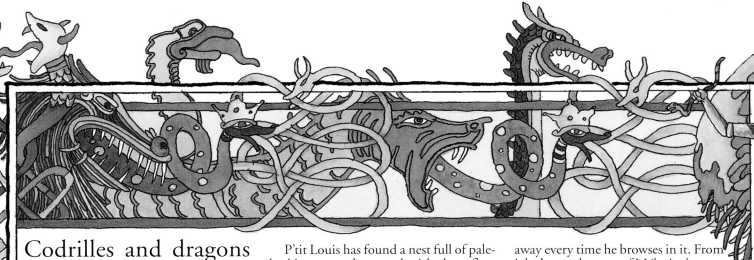

Codrilles and dragons of the countryside

The cockatrice is a feverish beast that is found in the river that is called the Nile.
(Guillaume le Normand)

P'tit Louis is pretty good at ferreting things out. Copses have no secrets for him. Although he is only nine years old, he would still teach the cleverest poacher a trick or two. It is true that the "Woodland Wanderer" has taught him everything from the school of the copse. He reads much better from the grass and leaves than from the blackboard. This little marauder can sniff out nests from afar. It is like a gift from heaven. He is able to recognize a bird in full flight at a glance.

P'tit Louis knows their shape, plumage, song, tricks and habits by heart. The trill, the brief call to the one in the copse, tells him of the amorous or worried mood of the invisible sparrow.

The liquid "stitchitt" and "didelitt" repeated between two twitterings betray the presence of a goldfinch.

P'tit Louis already has a vast collection of goldfinch nests, made of plaited rootlets, grasses, mosses and lichen, lined with wool, horse hair and vegetable down. They are filled with small, mottled, bluish eggs. To gather them, all that is needed is to hang around gardens and orchards when the parents have gone off foraging among the thistles.

He cannot be said to be a friend of the birds, although he does love them in his own way and enjoys their company: the gray wagtails looking like elegant Faerie laundresses and the chaffinch with white stripes, gray-blue head and beautiful wine-colored cheeks protruding from the russet plumage with a green rump. He admires the bird's sinuous neck and his lively song with its distinctive motif: a cascade of twelve notes underlined by a final flourish.

P'tit Louis has found a nest full of pale-looking eggs, decorated with the reflection of flames, concealed among the ivy and climbing plants in a hedgerow. A nest embellished with spiders' webs. The eggs of the hedge sparrow are blue like Easter eggs, those of the fly-catcher are sky blue speckled with rust, the six eggs of the nightingale olive brown. To find these it is necessary to scour moorland and waste land and not be afraid of thistles.

Every day P'tit Louis goes up to the attic to look at his trophies. Each represents a story of watching in the rain, of catching cold, of dizziness while climbing high, of the burning pain of being spanked for tearing one's trousers, but above all, the obscure, breathtaking pleasure of discovering the undiscoverable. A strange feeling comes over him as he bends down to listen to the silence of the fragile shells containing motionless flights and silent cooing. Each nest is a miniaturized field or woodland, each a dream of infinity. On the top shelf of the treasure cupboard are the rarities. Not the most beautiful visually, but in his eyes the most precious. This banal-looking egg is a woodpecker's, one that he had to steal out of an almost inaccessible hole, high up the trunk of a tree, and those very ordinary looking ones are those of a kingfisher that were pulled out of a mudhole in a riverbank. P'tit Louis is also very proud of the four grayish eggs of the wild hoopoe that he found concealed in a nauseous nest, one that sometimes contains grass so sharp it could cut steel.

He does not show them to anyone except his little sister who is the only one who understands; the others have nicknamed him "The Ferret" and often tell him that his pillaging will only bring him bad luck. But he does not worry about the birds' vengeance because he is so excited at the thought of adding the magical egg of the Codrille to his collection. It is the right season to go and search for it, having been newly laid in its circle of stones. P'tit Louis has read about all the "great wonders regarding the eggs of the Serpent Faeries, Vouivres and dragons" in an old almanac whose pages are slowly crumbling

away every time he browses in it. From it he learnt that one of Mélusine's ancestors was a Philocatrix Lady Serpent born of the marriage of the Coquatrice and the Poullatrice. He has learnt so many mysterious things from it: for instance, that if a "mare on heat loses the hairs of her tail in a pond or a pool where they are warmed by the sun, these hairs soon turn into snakes; and that snakes successfully remaining concealed from men for seven years usually grow wings…" And above all, "that the Salamander who has been served by the raven gives birth through her mouth to a Codrille, which she places on a bed of stones, hidden under the yew; and that whoever owns it will be obeyed by all the birds and snakes of the land and of stagnant or salt waters."

That is why P'tit Louis left so very early this morning. "It is necessary to be careful and very quiet when making one's way through the woods to arrive just before the egg hatches; if you are too early the egg will be soft and break in your hand, and if you are late it becomes a very dangerous business. Because if the Codrille sees you before you have seen him he will turn you into stone." But the "ferreter" is not frightened. He knows how to do these things and could probably steal a clutch of eggs from under a woodcock without her noticing.

He has found the yew tree and guesses where the nest will be. He crawls and moves as fast and noiselessly as a lizard under the low branches still glistening with dew. At the slightest movement of the grass he stops, as motionless as a dead trunk. Even the jay, that watchful sentinel of the forest, has not noticed him…

"It" is there, greenish, its shell darkened by a kind of spiral and a crack at the top. P'tit Louis cannot wait any longer and he is about to leap forward when he is stopped in his tracks by a sudden noise nearby. A blackbird with dazzlingly white plumage flies out of the bushes. He has never seen anything like it. But as he turns back to the egg he feels upon him the piercing gaze of the eyes of the creature emerging from the shell. And he feels his heart becoming as hard as stone…

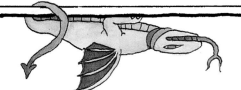

When the Great Serpent Dragon of the distant past, the ancient god of Life and its rebirth, master of wise knowledge, heard the imprecations of the new Church and his condemnation to the eternal fires of hell, he broke his rings and he scattered them among the elements, in the form of thousands of serpents.

The Great Basilisk

A dragon of Gothic times, his glance turns to stone the knights who come to fight him. To defeat him they must send back the mortal ray of his eyes by reflecting it with a mirror. Most Serpent Faeries have this "eye of stone;" even the small Codrille, just out of the egg, is able to turn the first person he sees into stone. Above all the Great Basilisk enjoys the company of "real princesses" whom he keeps prisoner in his cave. He is one of the most beautiful of winged saurians. His crenellated back is covered with enormous emeralds.

The Bouzouc

A gigantic dragon with very short legs and hunched back. He has an enormous head, no neck and an extremely large, hideous mouth: so much so that he is able to swallow a whole ox and two knights in one mouthful. The brave knight Gilles de Chin put an end to his mischiefs by ambushing him and driving him out of the swamps of Berlaimont.

The Karnabo

The Karnabo is known to roam the woodlands on the plateau of Rocroi, in the region of Regniowez. Its face is almost human but with the eyes of a Basilisk and a nose in the shape of an elephant's trunk. Its wickedness is legendary. Its horrible nasal whistling breath paralyzes or asphyxiates those who come too close to the slate quarry that is its lair. It is said that this feared, bloodthirsty monster does not originally come from the Ardennes. Legend has it that it is the product of the union between a migrant Gypsy and a sixty-seven year-old Ghoule.

The Little King Basilisk

So named from the crown of flesh it wears on its head, the woodland Basilisk is the size of a cat, and it is said to have emerged from an egg incubated by a snake or toad. It is a combination of cockerel and snake, a winged lizard with feathers. Every living creature, whether man, animal or plant, perishes before its gaze. The only plant that escapes it is rue (*Ruta graveolens*), the herb of grace. Daylight drives it back into its lair. The Green Wolf is its most effective enemy.

Zaltys

The presence of this Serpent Genie that is neither aggressive nor poisonous is considered very auspicious in the Baltic countries. It can be attracted by offering it cakes and milk, ensuring great happiness, a good harvest, and healthy cattle. But if the farmer does not behave well, it will disappear, and with it all the wealth that the farmer has accumulated. It is very similar to the Russian Tsmok.

The Sangle

A kind of "speckled band" from the Sologne whom Claude Seignolle bravely tackled: "As soon as it sees you it throws itself upon you, winding itself round your body three or four times, holding you so tightly that you cannot breathe any more. It only releases its grip when it has suffocated you."

The Coquecigrue

She is described as a combination of red snake and skinny girl living in wells. She is not bad but very shy and she flees as soon as anyone approaches. Her body is like a little serpent with shoulders as delicate as porcelain and breasts no larger than hazelnuts. Her skin is marble with shades of rust, pink, orange and cherry, covered in places with a lichen-like fleece. She lives mainly in orchards that have turned wild again or near abandoned beehives. She brings luck to those she meets and seems to love the presence of children whom she follows from afar, hiding in the tall grass.

At midnight when Serpent Faeries release their partners from their amorous embrace to reappear whistling at dawn, they carry in them the seed of a new life that will further enrich the great variety of those serpentine creatures that are as much at ease in the water as in the air, in fire or beneath the earth.

They have turned into tadpoles in the course of time but one of them—it was not that long ago—bit Eve in the heel and nothing is finished yet…

Teugghia, Fausseroles and other fallen Faeries

Or voez a je ue meu
Golla en albue ag I reu

(Breton proverb,
Ebria mulier/clavem cunni perdit)

SIZE:

Average.

APPEARANCE:

Her face and body are divided into two distinct parts: the right side is young and pleasant, the left side is decrepit and repulsive. On the one side she has a beautiful, almond-shaped eye, delicate lips, and a velvet cheek, while on the other side she is cross-eyed, her lips twisted and her cheek furrowed with deep lines. Her long hair is black on one side and white on the other. It is the same with her breasts, hips and the rest of her body: firm and smooth on one side, flabby and decrepit on the other. But she is wholly corrupt and evil.

CLOTHES:

Here again, one of the sides is pleasanter and less dirty than the other.

HABITAT:

Fallen Faeries are everywhere; they hide beneath dolmens and menhirs, in abandoned mines, in mountain caves, in ruins, and in derelict houses. They sometimes build flimsy huts that get blown away by the wind. The area surrounding the Teugghia's lair is strewn with bottles.

In the Haute-Vienne, the word Fannette means "bad Faerie." Half women, half Faeries, they hide in the forest during the day and come out at night to follow the local youths on horses stolen from nearby stables.

Only the gods and the Queen of the Faeries have the right to "demote" a Faerie and banish her from the Noble Court. She can only be banished if she has committed a serious offense: either that she has become involved in evil witchcraft, that she is guilty of a serious crime, or that, blinded by the love of a mortal, she has betrayed some precious secrets and thus endangered the Blessed Domains. There have been cruel, unfair banishments that are to be deplored, such as that of the Little Siren. But most of the time, the fallen Faeries have deserved their punishment. But it should not be forgotten that the moral concept of the Ageless Ones is very different from that of mortals. For instance, a barbarous act like pulling the wings off a fly, seen by humans as a minor example of cruelty, would be deemed a very serious, punishable crime in their world. In our world a hedge is cut down; in theirs a hedge is murdered. In faerieland a fault committed by poor, under-privileged people is more easily forgiven than in the society of men where the most powerful person is very often cleared of a crime because of the immunity he has been granted as a result of his position.

Fallen Faeries are banished not just by their own kind but also by humans.

The Teugghia of the Valley of Aosta is one of the most notorious. Crouched in a corner of her cave, she devotes herself to evil, surrounded by her urchins, wicked, hairy children whom she sends out to steal in the neighboring villages.

She was finally defeated by an old woman who advised the villagers to give these begging urchins two loaves of bread stuffed with fennel: "They ate them and when the Faerie saw that they were dead she smelled the fennel and realized that they had been poisoned by this sacred herb." She went to find comfort with the other Teugghia who had all suddenly disappeared—all except Marina, by far the most evil of them all…

Once upon a time, she was seen by a woodcutter chopping wood. Seeing an opportunity here of ridding the country of her evil presence, he said: "This work is much too hard for you, dear lady. Give me your ax, I will help you. But don't you have any wedges to split the wood?"

The Faerie put her hands together so as to form a wedge above the wood and said: "Here is the wedge you are asking for. Don't worry, just hit it with your club." The woodcutter lifted his club and struck the Faerie's hands, which sank into the wood. The woodcutter, seeing her hands caught as if in a vice, lifted the tree-trunk and pushed it down the slope of the mountain to the bottom of the valley, and with it the evil Teugghia.

Since then they have never come back.

The Fausserole, expelled from the Sidh because of her wickedness, is more

FOOD:

They drink more than they eat and live mainly from the looting of their urchins.

HABITS:

The fallen Faeries must not be confused with the black Faeries who are the daughters of the dark Alfs and the mothers of Chaos. Neither are they Larvae, Streghes or Devourers, but fallen Faeries. Some of them may be trying to make amends or free themselves from a magic spell, while others, bitter, evil, and full of malice, are bent on bringing down their victims with them.

They are drunks, evil, vengeful, destructive, and horribly lewd with husky blasphemous voices. The good Faeries have taken all the power away from them but they are still able to curse like a witch and throw a bad spell. They are endowed with a terrifying muscular strength. Their urchins, whose origins are unknown to them and with whom they are very affectionate, will later become ogrelets, then ogres.

ACTIVITIES:

Although some of them try to make amends with good deeds, trials of purification, and mortification in the hope of being pardoned by their sisters, the rest of them drink the gall of their downfall down to the dregs with the greatest delectation…

intelligent than most of her sisters. No nocturnal hunting for her, no howling, no aggressive encounters. She does not threaten, she does not drink and she does not attack. She is very shrewd. With the appearance of a child of Mary, dressed in white organdy, with starched petticoats, her face expressing great piety, she arrives in a village where she rents a little cottage that she makes her home. She helps the old and the poor, and is considered by all to be the most deserving of all women, in spite of the fact that she does not go to church. "The cold of the church is not good for her fragile health, she prays at home."

Such a sweet, hard-working orphan deserves an honest husband. They will find one for her. But the poor dear will not last for very long—because Fausserole kills her husbands. She takes the shape of an enormous weasel, lies on top of him as soon as they are asleep and sucks him dry, down to his bone-marrow. The unhappy widow then leaves the village because she cannot bear to continue living where she has known such unhappiness, and she settles elsewhere.

Once one of them was unmasked. She had designs on a handsome, full-blooded blacksmith, but he was so uneducated that the simpleton could neither read nor write, so he just put a cross on the marriage register instead of signing. When the Fausserole saw this cross, which was reminiscent of the Holy Cross, she shrieked with terror and fled through the window.

Having been turned into moles by Queen Coax as punishment, the Fayettes destroy gardens and fields. This is why moles have such beautiful, elegant hands.

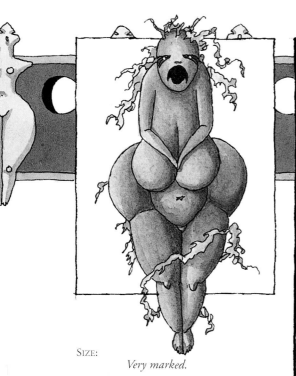

SIZE:

Very marked.

APPEARANCE:

An angular, wild face with her staring eyes surrounded by dark circles, pointed ears, a weak, sensuous mouth and quivering nostrils. The body is emaciated down to the waist from where it widens into monstrous thighs and hips. In the past they were as ravishing as the woodland Nymphs and Faeries. They leave behind a stubborn, musky smell.

CLOTHES:

A few miserable rags.

HABITAT:

Central France. In Berry "where they were seen among the rocks near the torrent of the Porte-Feuille, near Saint-Benoît-du-Sault, and at a very picturesque cascade surrounded by strange looking rocks, known as the Aire-aux-Martes. When the water is low you can see their stone kitchen utensils. It is their men who place the tabletop—that is the stone of the nearby dolmen—on its support while they, fanciful and vain Spirits that they are, try madly to light a fire in the cascade of Montgarnaud to cook the food in their granite casserole. Enraged by their failure they howl and utter wild imprecations" (Georges Sand, Légendes rustiques).

They live in the domain of Montbourneau, near Pierre-à-la-Marte in Saint-Plantaire, in Montchevrier (Indre), in Crossac (Haute-Vienne), and near the Pierre-aux-Martes in Maillac.

Martes, Peïlettes and Trouilles-de-Nouille

The deeds carried out by Incubi or Succubi are so numerous that it would be impudent to deny them.

(Saint Augustine,
De Civitate Dei, XV, 21)

"Ouhououuu ouh ouh laï lél lé… ehéééé leïleïlaléééééé… Tette… Tette!" The love cry of the Marte has just sounded the start of the hunt. Standing on top of a menhir she howls as she expresses her carnal desires. All the people who are still strolling along the country roads, returning from work or drinking at the village inn, must now run as fast as they can to get home as quickly as possible; unless they are too far to reach home, when they must find refuge in a nearby farm, hide in a barn, climb up a tree, hide under a haystack, or disappear to the bottom of a hole, however unpleasant it might be. This is not the time to be difficult. The Marte needs a man!

Even if advanced in years the Marte will give him strength; whether he be a vigorous wood-cutter, a sturdy farmer, a handsome youth, an ugly, fat, hunchbacked gooseherd who has hardly reached puberty: every male is seen as a prey by the Marte!

All those who hear her piercing cry button up their coats, buckle their belts and run away as fast as their legs will allow them. Even the most ardent Casanova and seducer of shepherdesses will not stick around and like the others, he will hide in the bushes, hoping that he will not be discovered, because the hussy has a sharp eye, excellent hearing and a perfect sense of smell…

The slightest rustling of leaves, sound of footsteps or crushing of grass will alert her to the presence of a possible prey. Advancing with care, she searches through the dark bushes and deep ditches. She sniffs and scrutinizes, following the sound of a throbbing heart, the tense swallowing of someone who is panicking. Then she suddenly utters a terrifying howl so as to force her prey to reveal himself with a cry of terror as he tries to escape. But she soon catches up with him, grabs him, forces him down on the ground and rapes him.

Sometimes the tension is too much to bear and some men prefer to give in to her immediately. Docile, beaten, their legs unable to carry them any longer, they fall on their backs and abandon themselves to wild coitus.

Others are braver and put up a fight and, like Monsieur Seguin's goat, resist all night before finally accepting their fate.

Few escape unhurt.

This man started badly. Having left the party rather the worse for wear, he is now walking home in a drunken haze. Surprised in the middle of a field, he cannot find anywhere to hide. All he can do is flee and hope for the best. He soon loses his clogs in the muddy clods of the plowed field. He slips, stumbles and grunts because of the stitch in his side. He ought not to look back all the time to see how close the Marte is. But he cannot help it,

fascinated by the sight of the Marte pursuing him.

Naked, disheveled, with emaciated arms and torso, arched thighs and shamefully disproportioned buttocks and enormous hips quivering at each step, she has slung one of her breasts over her shoulder, and offers him the other with both hands.

He knows he is lost. Already he can feel the Faerie's burning breath at the back of his neck. Without a sound, he slumps down and falls into her lecherous embrace. He falls on his stomach, his arms akimbo, his face resting in a furrow. He hardly feels it when she turns him over, undresses him and then straddles him. A kind angel has come to snuff out his memory and thus spare him the shame of being raped.

But fate was kind to him, the Marte has not carried him off, she does not want him as a partner, disappointed perhaps by the man's few attractive attributes. She has left him dirty, broken, his face streaming with bitter tears, lost in the middle of damp meadows,

He will not dare to say anything when he gets home to his wife. But he will never touch her again. He remains quiet, absent-minded, prostrate and each morning the sounds from the poultry yard break his heart.

FOOD:

They do not live on love alone. Gluttons rather than greedy, these bad housewives and atrocious cooks devour platefuls of cold stew and cabbage, either barely cooked or burnt.

CUSTOMS AND ACTIVITIES:

In the past the Martes or Marses were noble, powerful Faeries before being demoted by their queen. It is because of their dissolute life and vicious turpitudes that besmirched the reputation of the court that Tatiana expelled them from the Blessed Kingdoms. Far from improving, the Martes remained so obnoxious and behaved so atrociously that their woodland sisters and cousins no longer welcomed them in their midst.

They live away from the Elfin worlds, in the company of a few mortals who have gradually become stupid and wild, and their hairy, ignorant, noisy offspring.

In Belgium there are several other kinds of Martes known as Peïlettes and Trouilles-de-Nouille. The latter, the "Truies de nuit" ("sows of the night"), take advantage of carnivals, especially the one at Binche, to pursue their prey, hidden behind masks, and wearing seductive fancy dress and petticoats.

Foireaux Cats, Courtaud Cats, Margotine Cats…

SIZE:

Like an ordinary cat, except that the Courtaud Cats are taller than a very tall man.

APPEARANCE:

There is no physical difference between a Faerie Cat and an ordinary cat except that the Courtaud Cat has no tail. That is why it is possible to have one of them as a pet without realizing it and thus endanger one's entire family. They only way to identify a Faerie Cat is by finding the single white hair concealed in his jet black fur. Furthermore, anyone able to pull it will have all his wishes granted by the black Alfs and demons. It is only when a Faerie Cat attends the Sabbath or goes hunting that his appearance changes: his legs, body and teeth become longer, his fur looks ruffled and his ears stand up, his eyes red and sparkling like glowing embers.

CLOTHES:

Sometimes they wear an old suit of armor that they have stolen from their enemies, the Matagot Cats.

HABITAT:

Everywhere where there are cats. They are very well known in Brittany, Finistère and Ille-et-Vilaine.

They are found in profusion in the Ardennes, Bigorre and Maine. They would have wild parties in the manor of la Gaillardière because it was a "house with many black cats." The wild ones live in forests, cellars, ruins, and sewers; the "tame" ones live in people's houses.

Is that you, cat? How tall and terrifying you are. And no doubt you speak as well.
(Colette, *L'Enfant et les Sortilèges*)

To stop your cat from going to the Sabbath it is recommended to chop off the end of his tail or a bit of his ear, because like that he will not be admitted. Those with burn marks on their fur are also excluded. It is important to know this if you do not want your tom cat to fall under the influence of the Foireaux Cats and be "poisoned" by them.

It is said that you can never be too careful with a cat, even with an ordinary, affectionate cat. When God created the cat, the devil said: "You can create the cat if you want but his head will belong to me." That is why his body is elegant, soft, and pleasant to stroke, but his thoughts drive him to disobey and behave in a wild manner, playing cruel games with harmless creatures and birds. But these little defects in the domestic cat's character are nothing compared to the horrors committed by the Foireaux Cats.

Although a few of the Faerie queens who have fallen in love with various Puss-in-Boots have given birth to pretty white Margotine Cats, the Marcaou of the night are the products of the copulation of fallen Faeries with black Alfs.

They are fearless creatures fond of hunting. They are always on the look-out for young litters and eggs in nests that they can destroy, and they suffocate babies in cradles. They know the paths of the elves, the hillocks where the Elfines dance whom they then attack, tearing them to pieces, leaving behind a terrifying spectacle of mauled flesh and broken wings in this magical place of faerie frolicking. They enter houses through cat-flaps and take the place of the owners' cat, waiting for the right moment to spit in the soup and poison the whole family. If someone is dying they wait near the bed to catch the person's departing soul to take it to hell where they like to laze around in the warmth of the blazing flames.

On the evening of Mardi Gras, in mid-August and during the whole of Advent,

they can be seen coming out of the woods, cellars and drains, responding to the call of the Sabbath. From the tops of chimneys, trees, and gutters, they meow and rally the Foireaux gang and the corrupt grimalkins. They all leave their lairs or borrowed homes to join the Grand Master Marcaou at the great assembly. They regroup and make a circle at crossroads, in deserted places, or near calvaries or large stones. Soon they can be heard shouting as they provoke and attack each other. "And those who hear them are surprised at the shocking blasphemies they utter in the language of the Christians." But you must be in possession of a cat's paw if you want to be able to understand the endless list of misdeeds and crimes the gang members proudly congratulate themselves on as they utter their sinister shrieks. Finally, having sacrificed and eaten one of their own, they start dancing and jumping while they sing the "song of the days of the week."

Once upon a time, a harvester on his way home from the fields late one night, came across a Sabbath in full swing as he walked through the Great Cross heath. All the participants jumped on him to try and tear his eyes out. The poor man escaped by the skin of his teeth thanks to the sharp blade of his brand new scythe. As he twirled his scythe he succeeded in cutting off the head of the largest cat who seemed to be the chief, and thus he put an end to the fight.

It is also rumored that a loyal, affectionate cat, aware that the Sabbath was taking place, went to the fields to try and protect his master by barring his way.

The gracious Margotines with their white, silky fur were not as bad. Some of them accompanied the Faeries on their errands or served charming princesses to whom they reported the secrets and gossip they had picked up here and there by slinking along corridors and ladies' boudoirs in nearby castles and houses. Sometimes they even allowed their mistresses to take on their appearance to wander through the countryside or surprise an unfaithful lover. However, if she was wounded during her "metamorphosis" she was condemned to remain imprisoned in her borrowed form. Other more cheeky Margotines would curl up on the lap of beautiful youths, climb into bed with them and take on the appearance of young girls after the youths had fallen asleep. But some of them were witches who, on horned nights, would join the Foireaux Cats and share in their orgies and dancing.

FOOD:

Delicate meats: mice, rabbits, birds but also little children, imps and sprites, Elfines and little Faeries.

HABITS:

Evil, cruel, hypocritical, destructive, and sadistic. Fortunately their field of action is rather limited. Barbygère puts them in third place among predatory creatures after Man and the Leviathan.

ACTIVITIES:

All kinds of monstrosities. They catch the souls of men and take them to hell. It is said that their blood added to a glass of red wine cures pneumonia. If you exchange eyes with a Foireau Cat you can see what happens behind walls and discover buried treasures.

To make a pact with them, you must sign it with the blood of your left little finger. You can then ask them to steal and murder for you, but you must not forget to feed them on first-class butcher's meat.

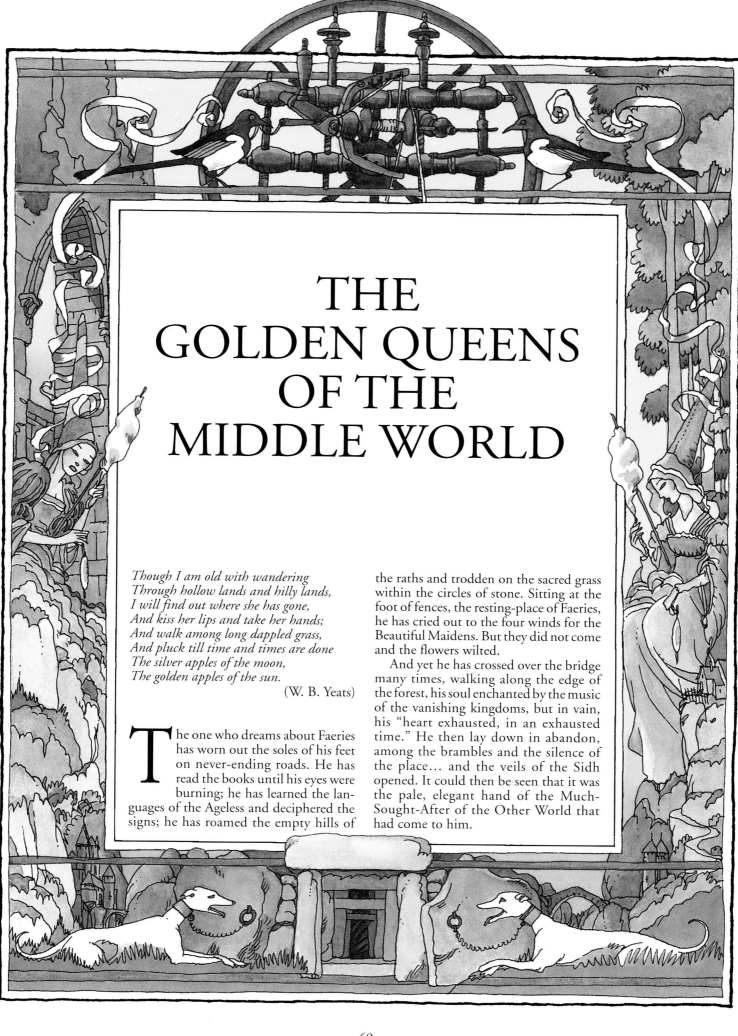

THE GOLDEN QUEENS OF THE MIDDLE WORLD

Though I am old with wandering
Through hollow lands and hilly lands,
I will find out where she has gone,
And kiss her lips and take her hands;
And walk among long dappled grass,
And pluck till time and times are done
The silver apples of the moon,
The golden apples of the sun.

(W. B. Yeats)

The one who dreams about Faeries has worn out the soles of his feet on never-ending roads. He has read the books until his eyes were burning; he has learned the languages of the Ageless and deciphered the signs; he has roamed the empty hills of the raths and trodden on the sacred grass within the circles of stone. Sitting at the foot of fences, the resting-place of Faeries, he has cried out to the four winds for the Beautiful Maidens. But they did not come and the flowers wilted.

And yet he has crossed over the bridge many times, walking along the edge of the forest, his soul enchanted by the music of the vanishing kingdoms, but in vain, his "heart exhausted, in an exhausted time." He then lay down in abandon, among the brambles and the silence of the place… and the veils of the Sidh opened. It could then be seen that it was the pale, elegant hand of the Much-Sought-After of the Other World that had come to him.

SIZE:

Tall.

APPEARANCE:

They were first known as tall and distinguished looking, subsequently becoming old with a hunchback, deformed by years of hard work: one foot flat from working the spinning wheel, the lower lip hanging from constantly moistening the yarn, the thumb flattened by pulling the thread of life.

Today, faerie-tales identify one of them as the Blue Faerie of children's dreams and wishes granted: graceful with a sweet, radiant face, framed by a mass of golden hair, a slender body with wings of blue voile. The second Faerie is Dame Tartine, plump and greedy, voluble and feather-brained, a blundering guardian angel. The third Faerie has the appearance of the inflexible Fate who cuts the thread of life with her scissors: dark and skinny, she has a hooked nose, pointed chin, and crooked fingers: she is the wicked Faerie in all faerie-tales.

CLOTHES:

In the past they favored dark, austere garments. They used to carry a spinning-wheel, distaff and scissors; today they carry a magic wand.

They wear long dresses and their hair is either coiled and held back by an Alice band and a veil; or, parted in the middle, it falls in ringlets on their shoulders.

The Faerie Godmothers

The Moires, the Parcae, the Normes, the Mires, the Matres and the Good Ladies…

She then saw three old women: the first with a flat foot, the second with her lip hanging down her chin, and the third with a thumb like a paddle. The first pulled the yarn and turned the spinning wheel, the second moistened the thread, and the third twisted it and smoothed it down with her thumb.

(Grimm's Faerie-Tales)

On the amphidromic day, the fifth day after birth when the child is named, preparations are made for the visit of the Mires, the Good Ladies who take away milk fever and mysteriously make the eyes of the new-born sparkle. The little house in this Greek landscape has taken on a festive appearance. The grandmother has been busy preparing for this special event. On the white table-cloth reserved for Sundays, she has set out a festive meal of almond bread, honey and spring water, punctuated by silver coins and fresh flowers gathered together by a red thread. Before the open door, after a short rhyming invocation, she makes an appeal under her breath: "Good Moires, Good Mires, Blessed Ladies, pure, luminous, honest ones,

may the gods make your mood today as good as bread, as sweet as honey, as smooth as water, as beautiful as flowers."

She then asks for good luck and wealth for the child she has helped to bring into the world: much property in exchange for a little stone, high earnings for little work and most of all, happiness rather than credit at all times. This is what she asks of the Tria Fata, the Three Fates, mistresses of the individual, inescapable destiny of man, whom the Romans called the Parcae. The first one, Clotho, the spinner, represents the thread of life: she spins the wool into thread. The second one, Lachesis, endows the child with "gifts" and the amount of good luck allotted to each person. The third one, Atropos, represents man's unavoidable destiny against which he can do nothing; it is she who cuts the thread of life.

There are three periods in time: the past, already spun and wound onto the spindle; the present, now passing through the spinner's fingers; and the future, the yarn on the distaff that has yet to pass through the spinner's fingers onto the spindle, in the same way that the present must become the past.

But at the moment the thread has not yet been tied in the neat little white house

near Kastoría, and the soul of the new-born child shines as light and new as the candle lit to welcome the Mires.

Far away, high up in the mountains, near the northern ramparts of the castle, another birth is being celebrated. In the large vaulted hall a crowd has gathered around the cradle. Flaming torches projecting from the mouths of the carved dragons that decorate the beamed ceiling throw light on the horned helmets, the coats of mail, the iron nosepieces of the helmets of the warriors and lords, and the jewelry, toques and finery of the elegant ladies with long plaited hair. The son of a king is born, and next to the child a candle is burning. The sparkle of the sea is already visible in his eyes: he will ride the waves. Birch wine and beer flow in his honor.

Respectful silence greets the arrival of the Normes who go and stand in front of the little prince. The first endows the child with great virtues. The assembled crowd cheers and applauds with joy. The second one says that he will be the best-loved and happiest man among his kind. Once again goblets and horns are filled and emptied, and people jostle to get closer to the child. Suddenly the third Norme falls down, pushed by the jostling warriors. She gets up, livid with rage, her mouth convulsed with anger: "I have decided that the child shall cease to live the moment the candle that is burning next to him goes out."

It seems that nothing or no one can save him now. The assembled guests are horrified. But then the oldest of the three Faeries takes the candle and blows out the flame. Turning to the mother, she says: "The die is cast, but do not worry. Hide this candle in a safe place so that

no one can ever light it again until the day has come for your son to die." This is how Scandinavian legends tell the story of the birth of the hero Normagest, whose name means "protected by the Normes."

Much further away and higher up in the mountains, or possibly much closer and lower down in the valley: in the Faerie Kingdom they are also celebrating the arrival in the "Middle World" of George and Oberon, the twin sons of Julius Caesar and Morgan le Fay. The Elfin crowd has gathered around the double cradle of gold beneath the crystal-domed ceiling of the Dunn: Sidhes, Sylfes, Seelies, Nymphs, Milloraines, White, Green and Blue Ladies, Dracs and Sirens. They are wearing armor made of shells and hennins of dawn light, rustling with gauze, voile and ethereal wings; they chirp, hum, flutter and marvel as they wait the arrival of the three Faerie Godmothers. In their airy carriage drawn by white swans, they descend from the skies. Greeting their vassals with friendly smiles, blooming in their floral finery, they walk to the cradle and bend down over the new-born infants:

– George, the first-born, will rule over the kingdom of men.

– Oberon will be king of the Faerie Kingdom.

And since it is normal, even in Elfyria, to favor those of one's own blood, the third one showers him with gifts. She offers him beauty, the gift of seeing into the hearts of men, and the power of traveling wherever he wishes simply by willing it. She gives him innocence so that he becomes the brother of all animals and able to understand the songs of angels. She also gives him a magnificent horn that cures the sick, feeds the hungry, and fills the hearts of the wretched with happiness; it can be heard from any distance, thereby summoning a vast army of brave knights.

This proves too much for the first Faerie, George's godmother; enraged by the profusion of gifts heaped upon Oberon, she condemns him to remain small forever.

HABITAT:

Moires and Mires live in the skies of Greece. The Fati or Ladies of Rica have been seen in the skies of Albania, the Witte Wjen in the vast infinite spaces of Flanders and Holland, Rojenice in Yugoslavia, the Three Mothers in Switzerland, and the Three Taupes the orchards of Autreppes. They are also known as the Metten, Dame Abonde, Voelur, Vola Spakonur, Femmes Sages, Weisen Fraüen, Bonnes dames, Florissantes, etc.

They can still be seen walking under the beech tree of Pontus in Brocéliande.

FOOD:

Bread, almonds, grapes, and honey. Clear, pure water.

CUSTOMS:

At the beginning were the Fata (from fatum, *whose root contains both the future and fate). It is generally agreed that the Three Fates, the Three Parcae, who are also known as Tria Fata and Fatae, are the divinities who gave medieval Faeries their names and attributes.*

ACTIVITIES:

They preside over births, help mothers in labor and decide the fate of the new-born whom they follow until death.

As soon as a child is born, Verpeja, the Lithuanian Parca, starts spinning in the sky of life. There is a star at the end of this thread. When Fate wants someone to die his or her thread breaks; the star falls down and becomes extinguished in space and the person dies.

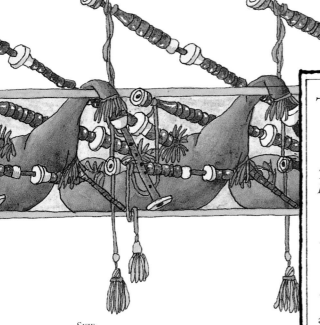

The Banshee

There is a shadow in the wind
I think a tragedy awaits me.
  (Danny Elfman, *The Ballad of Sally*)

SIZE:

> *Tall; although there are now smaller Banshees.*

APPEARANCE:

> *They used to be beautiful and proud, wild and noble of carriage, with a pale, mature forehead, a visionary look in their eyes, sometimes green and ardent, at other times red or milky. Then, with the demise of the clans and the bitterness of men, they became tousled, emaciated and pale, their veins showing their transparent skin, their throats hollow-sounding, their jaws disjointed because of having howled so much, their faces ravaged and their chins trembling. They become very sensual and feline on hunting days.*

CLOTHES:

> *In France they wear the evanescent clothes, characteristic of the White Ladies. In Scotland they wear the colors of the tartan of those who are going to die, or a shroud; in England, a dress with a green underskirt and red slippers; in Ireland, they wrap themselves in a vast, brown shawl.*

HABITAT:

> *Many countries have their own Banshees, but they are particularly abundant in France, England, Ireland, and Scotland—especially in the Highlands. Some live in the ruins of castles, in abandoned towers, on ancient battle-fields, on deserted moorland, and near the sea.*

Four young men had gone hunting red deer in the Scottish highlands. At nightfall they took refuge in a shepherd's hut. Inspired by the heart-warming flames of the pleasant peat fire and the delicious smells of the roast venison, they felt like dancing. One was playing the bagpipes and the others were tapping to the rhythm of a Strathspey reel. They wished they had someone to dance with. Their wish was so heart-felt that the night-wanderer heard it and soon the door opened and four young girls entered, more beautiful than anyone they had ever seen. Three of the girls joined the three youths in the circle, while the fourth one went to sit next to the bagpipe player, clapping her hands and tapping her foot on the ground.

Tune succeeded tune and they were dancing faster and faster, holding the girls in their arms. Then, as they repeated the end of the reel "Mhic Iarla Nam Bratach Bàna," the bagpipe player noticed blood dripping from the green skirts of the girls. He looked closely at their large, green eyes, and their full, red lips and extremely sharp teeth; he felt a cold shiver going down his spine as he recognized the four Banshees. Without interrupting his play he went to the door and fled into the night, quickly pursued by the Banshee who had been sitting next to him and whom he could hear growling behind him. She soon saw him and he tried to hide amidst some horses nearby. The Banshee turned round and round without ever daring to approach because of the iron shoes on the horses' hooves. She continued to circle all night long, now appealing to him gently to lure him to her, now cursing and threatening him with torments so that the hair on his head stood up on end. In the morning she faded away, dissolved by the goodness of the day.

According to an old legend from the Highlands, where the Banshees still abound, he ran back to the hut and found his friends lying in the ashes of the fire, their bodies drained of all blood.

Today, the whole organized structure of pre-Christian tradition has disappeared in Scotland and Ireland. But

although the supernatural atmosphere associated with it has also vanished, the Banshee has remained all-powerful, becoming evil but no longer divine. She is feared but no longer respected. In the past, according to Walter Scott, owning a Banshee was the privilege of families whose origins were pure. They told clan chiefs about forthcoming deaths, disasters, epidemics and defeats. Sometimes they also helped in other ways: they diverted the enemy's blows in battle, watched over and protected the heir to the title during childhood, and even lent a helping hand in chess by indicating the best piece to move, or in card games by pointing out the right card to play.

In contrast to the Scottish Banshee who was a spirit of death, the Faerie Mistress—the Leanan Sidh, or the Lhiannan-Shee of the Isle of Man—was a spirit of life. She inspired the bards and poets allied to the great holy families. She forecast deaths, but also births.

The Fear-Sidh is Ireland's male Banshee; his accomplice is the Far-Gorta, a hungry-looking character, emaciated and as skinny as a rake, who roamed through the rolling Irish countryside during the great famine.

In France, "figures who are not of this world appear to the inhabitants of castles when a disaster is about to happen. They are known as the Banshees," say the old chronicles. They were the souls of Faeries or chatelaines. The most famous of them was the serpent Faerie, Mélusine, who had chosen the family of Lusignan in the 14th century.

The Merluisaine would come out of a chimney of the castle of Piney in Champagne. Her piercing cries would tell the neighboring villages that one of the inhabitants of the castle would die within the year. When misfortune threatened the members of the family of the château of the Mas, near Brood, because a member of the family was going to die, their Banshee would be seen dressed all in white, wandering around the ramparts for several nights and sobbing; she would then go to the great bedroom where she would wake up the sleeping relatives by slapping their faces.

And then times changed and their escutcheons became sullied, probably as a result of some blemish in their character; their divine blood was debased by the white make-up of the courtesans without a past. A handful of noble hearts retained their Banshees, but the others wandered off into the mist to become witches: some are still performing their funereal tasks, while others were abandoned and wander in pursuit of ghostly missions.

In the past, a Banshee took upon her the pain of an entire family, the despair of a clan in mourning. She gathered the suffering and despair and condensed them into a single cry of pain, an ecstatic, never-ending lament, stronger than the storms at sea, that reached such paroxysms that pain faded away in its own death rattle.

Now a solitary creature, she howls to the wind, telling of her anonymous anxiety that the wind returns to her.

Customs and Activities:

The Banshees have lost their reputation as prophetesses and divine guardians to become mere messengers of death, impartial and devoid of any feeling.

Their cry is even more impressive than the lugubrious howl of the black hound of hell on Dartmoor as he rallies his pack to feast on the flesh of stags. One can distinguish three stages in the voice of the Welsh Cyhyraeth. First the distant, plaintive yelping of pain can be heard, getting closer as it is carried by the wind, making the listener's body shiver with horror. The sound then becomes more guttural and wilder as it grows louder, an interminable cry, punctuated by painful inflections without ever weakening; it makes the listener's strength and lust for life drain away. Finally the lament turns into sobs and sighs, fading away, becoming sadder and weaker, and muttering some hoarse, inarticulate regrets before it expires in a death rattle; it is as if the listener's soul has been lost forever.

SIZE:

One or two are gigantic, the others are very small. In spite of their fragile, airy appearance they are amazingly strong.

APPEARANCE:

Beautiful, blond, with a complexion like mother-of-pearl, their limbs as slender and elegant as their spindles, their hair as fine and soft as their yarn. Their great beauty is only visible at night; during the day, one can see that their hair is white, their eyes red and their face wrinkled: that is why they only come out at night and hate the light. They can also be seen as circles of stones when a grumpy saint has cursed them during one of their May dances or Elfin bacchanalia and turned them to stone.

CLOTHES:

White veils, pinafores, aprons, lace and gauze bonnets. Sometimes local costume and head dress, slightly altered by some celestial stylist. They carry menhirs in their aprons or suspended from their distaffs.

Spinners and Ladies of Stone

*If you want to build a lasting monument
That will be beautiful and strong,
A wonderful great monument
Of stones in a circle placed
One on top of the other.*

(Robert Wace)

Once upon a time, the Demoiselles Filandières or Spinning Ladies built an enormous stone spinning-wheel—no one can remember why. The Gargantuan Chronicles and popular tradition have explained their actions in numerous tales, faerie-tales and legends. It is said that they set up these stones:

– to mark their "spinning areas," where they invite young girls to come and be initiated into the art of spinning.

– to mark their "dancing circle," where they invite young people, Elves and Faeries, to come and join the sorority for better and for worse.

– to designate a faerie area where they hold court.

– to erect a tower or a chimney at the top of an enchanted hill, to crown an ancient elfin fort, a rath, or a Faerie's tomb.

– to mark the passage to the "country of lonely women," to conceal the entrance to a treasure, or to forbid access to faerieland.

– as a game or whim: as a picnic area, somewhere where they can have their siesta, or as an umbrella.

The stone spindles unwind their endless reels of "stories."

Some of these monoliths have grown since they were first erected: the menhir of the Lady's Stone was originally a mere pebble the size of a nut, that has grown until it reached the size it is today. The Roches Piquées in the forest of Haute-Sève (in Ille-et-Vilaine) are still growing today, but only very slowly. Some of these monoliths turn like spindles being spun. The great Quintin menhir turns on its own axis, as does that of Saint-Martin-d'Arcé in Maine-et-Loire when twelve o'clock strikes. Others move even during the day. The Stone of the Faeries, also known as the Dancing Stone or the Rocking Stone, dances when the bells of Nailhac ring and it shudders when the thunder rumbles. In the Landes, the Peyre-Lounque jumps twelve times at midday. The Roche-Folle in the Avranchin turns three times when the cuckoo calls for the time in spring. The Stone of the Ladies of Mesnil-Hardray rises every year during midnight mass, and young girls dressed in white, flowing robes appear from beneath it. The sleeping Ladies of Langon rise every May 15 on the arrival of the Faerie Lalie. Some menhirs go and quench their thirst on Christmas Eve, as do the Stone Faeries of Plouhinec who go and drink from the river Intel, leaving their treasures unguarded. But they return so quickly that it is almost impossible to get out of their way. Treasure seekers will almost certainly be crushed to death unless protected by a twig of hawthorn, held in a wreath of five-leafed clover.

The Faerie menhirs have the great privilege of producing sounds. The largest stone of the cromlech of the Forges in

74

Montguillon contains a clock that strikes the hours.

The menhirs of the Spinners are sometimes called the Treasure Stones because of the fabulous treasures buried beneath them. According to an old sailor, the great treasure of the Faeries was buried under one of the many standing stones at Carnac; the Faeries erected these thousands of stones in order to conceal it even better, and nothing but a computation using a formula found only in the Tower of London can indicate its location. But these great riches are well guarded by clawed gnomes, corricks, monsters, ghosts and wolves; only those protected by the Faeries can benefit from this treasure. In fact, it is extremely foolhardy to excavate, move, push over or use these stones in one's work. It is advisable not to plow or cut the hay near them in case the stone is inadvertently wounded. About a hundred years ago, villagers near Vert used to say that if you uprooted the Pierre Piquée, a torrent would spring from the place it had been that would destroy the entire region of Beauce. When people tried to break up the great slab of Peyrolebado in the Aveyron, blood spurted out of the stone at every blow of the hammer and the workmen were mysteriously driven back. Youths who tried to move a rock in the Auvergne were suddenly swallowed in darkness and all died within the year. A house built from the Faerie Stones of the Grande-Roque crushed all the inhabitants to death the day they moved in.

We would do well to leave the stone spindles alone, and not disturb the wise Spinners who are busy spinning the thread of time

HABITAT:

Standing stones, dolmens, cromlechs, and cairns. They have planted them everywhere in the terrestrial world and that of the Good People, in Elfyria, Sylfiria, on the drifting isles and the celestial isles. They have many residences in France and England.

FOOD:

It is said that as well as quince paste the menhir Spinners love vin gris ("gray" wine) because of its bouquet of flint.

CUSTOMS AND ACTIVITIES:

They are as malevolent and as benevolent as the stones they have planted; which is why some elficologists say that they turned themselves into stone while waiting for the return of the Faerie Kingdom. The Ladies of Stone sing, drink, dance, spin, extol, watch, punish, heal...

They are the daughters of the Faerie godmothers and the abdominal Faeries who watch over births; that is why women who cannot conceive come and slide over the stones on their naked behinds or rub themselves against them to become fertile.

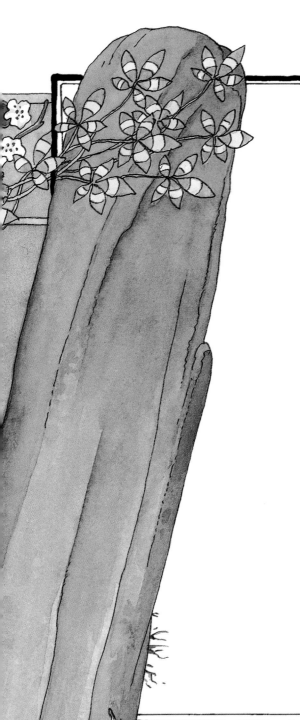

The Filandières and Spinners of the Night

There is no thread more beautiful than that of the moonlight spinners. In the morning the sun gathers it from the dewy meadows to weave his hair.

(A. Marville, *Ariane and the Others*)

SIZE:

Usually average. Sometimes small, very small.

APPEARANCE:

Beautiful, blond, pale, ghost-like or ravishingly beautiful. Sometimes they appear as ordinary peasant women, little old ladies, with wrinkled faces and hunchbacks, or like terrifying witches when they are angry.

CLOTHES:

Long white dresses of fine fabric or regional costume, with pinafores whose pockets are filled with scissors, spindles, yarn, needles… and large stones.

They sometimes use their distaff like a spear or magic wand. According to Claudius Savoye, the Fayettes of the Beaujolais region who used to spin their yarn near a fountain in Pierrefite de Dième wore clothes of different colors, depending on the occasion, white, red or black. Their change of clothes was interpreted as a forecast of the future.

In England the little Spinners sometimes also dress in gray.

Since time immemorial in Epfenbach, near Sinzheim, three beautiful young girls dressed in white came every evening into the room where the villagers met to spin. They always had new songs and new tunes to sing and beautiful faerie-tales to tell, and they knew many amusing games. Their distaffs and spindles were different from everyone else's. No spinner could twist the thread with as much finesse and skill as they could. Every evening on the stroke of eleven they got up, packed their distaffs and left in spite of the pleas of the assembled villagers. No one knew where they came from or where they went. The villagers called them the Maidens or the Sisters of the Lake.

They were very popular with the young men of the village and several fell in love with the Maidens, especially the schoolmaster's son. He never tired of hearing them and talking to them. Nothing saddened him more than to see them leave in the evening. One day he climbed into the clock tower to put the clock back by one hour and, in the evening, everyone was having such fun that no one noticed the time. Then when the clock struck eleven —although it was really midnight—the three young girls got up, gathered their things together and left…

The following day, walking along the lake, people heard some wailing and noticed traces of blood on the surface of the water. The three sisters were never seen again. According to the old German legend the schoolmaster's son became ill as he pined away for his lost love, and he died soon afterwards.

A long time ago the Parcae and the Normes surrendered their power and enchanted distaffs to their daughters, who presided over the destinies of heroes, and later of ordinary mortals. They in turn bequeathed their magic distaffs to their own daughters, the Spinning Faeries, who continued to spin faerie-tales and dreams at the cradle of dreams. The thread has never been broken; if it ever does break the gospel of the distaffs repairs it, like a voice remembered, with the thread of time. At night they roam through the countryside, as white and translucent as the skein they wind off the halo of the moon; during the day they are as dazzling as the golden ball they wind off the sun. They spin between the shadow and the light, good or evil, as mysterious as the thread they draw through their fingers, as strong as steel or as brittle as the gossamer they leave behind in the morning.

Sometimes they are only ghosts. It is said that, in the Semoy valley in the Ardennes, the last chatelaine of Linchamps appeared every night and sat in a recess

among the ruins of the château that formed a natural seat and became known as the "Spinner's chair," because this ghost dressed in white would stay there for hours on end. One could see her spindle going round noiselessly. When she got up she would push a few stones into the river with her foot as if she wanted to remove all trace of her former dwelling. Mothers would say to their children: "Watch out for the Spinner! If you don't behave she will throw a rock at you and crush you."

But they are also generous. In the Hautes-Pyrénées, the daughters of the Lavedan think that if they see a thread lying on the ground near a fountain, they should pick it up at once and wind it: the thread becomes longer and turns into a fabulous ball of yarn from which a Faerie emerges, delighted to have been released from her uncomfortable prison. She gives her rescuer a beautiful present to thank her, lends her magic wand to her, or gives her a spindle of gold thread. But the person who does not bother to pick the thread and thereby fails to rescue the Spinner from her prison can expect to be struck by some terrible disaster.

In Lucs-sur-Boulogne the Faerie who lived in a cave often came uninvited in the evening to the house of the tenant farmers of La Giraudelière. She would sit on a three-legged stool and spin without saying a word. Irritated by this behavior, the people at the farm heated the stool till it was red hot. The Faerie arrived at seven o'clock as usual and sat on the stool as she normally did and was badly burned. She jumped up shouting: "Spin, spin again! Unwind, unwind again!" She came back three nights later in the shape of a "garache" and they all died of fright.

Ever since that regrettable moment, relations between mortals and the Spinners have deteriorated. The forests where they roamed were burnt down, the entrances to their underground dwellings were blocked off, and their dolmens were pulled down; children were kidnapped, cows died, and harvests were ruined by the frost. In the end they disappeared. Some people missed them.

HABITAT:

Prettily arranged caves, coastal swells, under dolmens and in hollow hills, in the former Faerie forts: Dunn and Rath. They are found wherever spinning takes place, and wherever there are megaliths. In Livonia, Pschipolonya is a hideous little old lady with a wrinkled face who terrifies the peasants of Zittau and its surroundings. In Italy, the Nona turns her spindle on the roads of Berbenno. Many traditional faerie-tales mention these mysterious workers, such as the legend of the young girl of Scherven, near Cologne, who can be seen at night spinning a magic yarn.

FOOD:

Anything that is nice.

CUSTOMS AND ACTIVITIES:

They take on the appearance of an old lady, dressed in white, and teach others to spin, encouraging those who work hard and punishing those who are lazy. They preside over births and forecast the future. All these activities clearly show their close association with the Normes, the Great Christmas Tempestaries and the Good Faeries.

Washerwomen and Singers of the Night

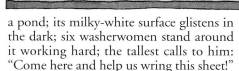

SIZE:

Average. The leaders are taller.

APPEARANCE:

In Provence, the "Masks" who come and wash their linen on the banks of the Var and the Gapeau are very pretty girls, but as the sun starts setting they become wrinkled and disheveled; by midnight they have become witches again. The Kannerez-Noz of Faouët, in Brittany, are terrifyingly skinny. Their white hair is so long that they use it to weave the sheets they wash on the river bank. In the region of the Indre, they are tall women with a reddish complexion. They leap on unsuspecting passers-by without making a sound and wrap them up in bloody sheets. They can make themselves very beautiful to attract people; but they are usually shown with an emaciated body, muscular arms, and long, crooked fingers. A peasant-woman from Sizun-en-Léon who managed to escape from them described them as being "like skeletons, with a skull for a head and puddles instead of eyes."

Sometimes they are only shadows or nothing at all.

CLOTHES:

Occasionally they wear the regional costume but mostly they wear a torn black dress, covered with whitish rags as dubious as the shrouds they wave about. The very beautiful but cruel Toulas and Gallières of Noz-de-Suisse and the valley of the Rhône appear half-naked.

Wring the old rag
Wring
The shroud of the wives of the dead…
(Paul Féval, *The Last Faeries*)

Perronnick walks through the wood on his way home. He has enjoyed the evening and he sings as he staggers along the path, hitting stumps and trees that are like traps set by the night for those who do not treat her with proper respect. He grumbles, swears, and kicks the stones on the ground. Laughing like an ass, he relieves himself against a venerable old oak and battles with the ghostly shadows surrounding him.

Tapping, voices and splashing of water reach him through the fuzziness of his spinning head.

"Fancy doing your washing at this time of the night, in the middle of the forest!"

He suddenly comes upon a clearing with a pond; its milky-white surface glistens in the dark; six washerwomen stand around it working hard; the tallest calls to him: "Come here and help us wring this sheet!"

He has drunk so much that he cannot make out what they really look like. He is rather puzzled because sometimes he sees them as beautiful friendly young women, while at other times he sees them as hideous old women who appear to be threatening him. The fellow would like to turn round and slip away as fast as possible, but it is too late. He is already holding a wet sheet in his hands as an icy shiver invades his body. His limbs are as if paralyzed and he cannot make the sign of the cross that would break the spell. He is almost hypnotized by the song of the washerwomen, "a dull, monotonous, sad song like a *De Profundis*."

Now he knows who they are. He should have suspected it. But he had heard such incredible tales about these Faramic Women and White Ladies that he had never believed any of them. Old people were so afraid of them that they preferred to make a detour of several miles rather than pass by one of those washing places at night time: "Let's go home," they would say, "it is the hour of the washerwoman." And if they heard the sound of sheets being beaten in the far distance, they would run as fast as their legs could carry them. One should never answer their questions or approach

them, still less disturb them. The mere fact of seeing them was already a sign of forthcoming death: "Because the shroud they are preparing is that in which 'he who has been thus warned' will be buried within three days."

"Your shroud is awaiting you, your shroud is awaiting you," they sing.

Their origin is not known for certain. Some say that they were purgatory Faeries who had been punished for the bad spells they had cast; others saw them as night Faeries who were as cruel as day Faeries were good. Or as mothers guilty of infanticide: "If you looked more closely at the sheets they were wringing you would probably discover they contained the corpse of a baby. Indeed, blood would often drip from the sheets. And however much they washed and rubbed and scrubbed the sheet, it would never become white again even on the day of the Last Judgment."

Only a pure or peaceful heart could break the spell and end their punishment. One day, a woman who was returning late from church where she had prayed for her dead was forced to wring sheets with them. After a while, the eldest one said to her: "It is lucky for that you were on your way back from honoring your dead, otherwise I would have wrung you and wrung you again so that no one would have been able to disentangle you after I had finished with you."

Perronnick realizes that being under their spell he could no longer escape from them. The old woman has started to wring the sheet… He also knows that he has offended the night by his loutish behavior. He has cursed himself. He has only one chance of escaping, and that is by always wringing in the opposite direction to that of the old washerwoman. If he forgets, even for a second, the sheet will wind itself round his wrists and tie his arms until they break… his whole body would be crushed and dragged under water. He must not allow himself to be distracted at any time. Men have been discovered near these stagnant waters, unconscious but still alive, their limbs half torn off. Moreover, he must resist till morning when dawn will drive them away with the mist. There are two moons in the old ladies' eyes, two moons dancing, now to the right, now to the left…

Perronnick was beaten and wrung until his remains and shroud merged into one and dissolved among the lost souls at the bottom of the haunted waters where the Singers of the night dwell.

HABITAT:

The Singers of the night only frequent stagnant waters, ponds and disused washing places. During the day they withdraw to a cave, underneath their hunting ground.

Ganipaute haunts the washing places of the Gironde. Jeanne the Washerwoman appears by the pond of Maillebois, near Dreux, while the Teurdons can be seen near Dinan. At midnight on January 13, Beuffenie, the demoniac Washerwoman, attracts and drowns those who walk past her domain in the wash-house of the Source d'Argeot in L'Isle-sur-Serein, in the département of the Yonne. They abound in Brittany, Scotland and other Celtic countries.

FOOD:

They subsist on night and water.

CUSTOMS AND ACTIVITIES:

Spiteful towards "nocturnal offenders" and passers-by who ignore or do not respect the "harmonies of the night," and kind towards innocent souls, dreamers and moon walkers. They spare peaceful souls and reward those whose heart does not need washing.

The Washerwomen redeem bad deeds on the uneven hours of the night and invite mortals in a state of sin to come and cleanse their souls in a terrifying nocturnal ritual.

In Berry they do not wash shrouds or sheets but they work with a kind of vapor of a whitish color and dull transparency that appears to take a human form, and one would swear that it moans and cries under the furious blows of the washerwoman's paddle. They are rumored to be still-born children or the souls of the damned.

The Ielles

The people of Sighisoara and Fagaras, terrified by the haunting Moroï and Ielles, do not leave their houses when night has fallen.
(T. Van Helsing, *Vampirism*)

"However dangerous and malevolent the power of the spirits, the crazy impudence or temerity of man is even worse. (…) He calls for their help because he hopes they will satisfy his curiosity; because he hopes they will be docile instruments of his cowardly or guilty desires." This is the complaint of the fanatical knight Gougenot des Mousseaux in his alarming indictment against Faeries: *Mœurs et pratiques des Démons ou des Esprits visiteurs* ("Customs and Habits of Demons or Visiting Spirits") (H. Vrayet de Surcy, Paris, 1854).

But for once he is right when he warns of the danger of summoning malevolent Faeries and demons and calling them by their real names. People in Romania, Wallachia and Transylvania were so aware of this that they never mentioned their name. "The Ielles are too dangerous to be called by their real name" (T. Van Helsing). "Man is but a toy in their power games" (Marie Holban, *Chants de vie et de mort transposés de roumain*; "Songs of Life and Death translated from Romanian"). The most powerful among these creatures are also the most mysterious because they are the most elusive. Shadows of the Erinnyes, it is not known where they come from or where they are going. Their name is scarcely known, and even that name is now rejected by them. Because the name Iélé or Ielles sounds like the pronoun "Elles," it is prudent to refer to them thus. They are known as the Good Ones, the Courageous Ones, the Brave Ones, the Comely Ones, the Powerful, the Holy Ones. Having no particular shape, they can appear in any form. They are also known as the Pretty Ones, the Radiant Ones, or the Tempestuous Ones. How many are there? Sometimes they are also called the Minuscule and Numerous Ones. Are they really good? They are said to be good, but only in order to make them so. Thus flattered, they may bring happiness and richness, but the worst should always be expected.

It is said that a young mother, who was

both vain and feather-brained, tried to attract the blessings of the Ielles for her baby. One evening she went to an old tree near which the Ielles were known to gather. She placed her baby by the tree, wrapped in lace and in a sumptuous cradle, carved and decorated with gold ribbons. She hung a few necklaces on the branches for the Ielles in the hope of being repaid a hundredfold. Then, summoning Catrina, Marina and Zalina, the most powerful of the Ielles, she told them what she wished for her child: that he should be handsome, rich, and lucky, that he should succeed in everything, that he should always be victorious, that he should later marry a gentle, wealthy princess, and that he should shower gifts on his mother and love her always. When she returned in the morning in the hope of finding all the gifts she had asked for, she was horrified to find serpents slithering over the tree instead of the necklaces, and in a cradle of brambles and nettles, some little white bones, wrapped in swaddling clothes of lichen.

A hunter who had asked the Ielles to help him kill an old stag that he had been pursuing for years was discovered "as if he had been trampled to death by hundreds of hooves and torn to pieces by gigantic antlers."

A rich farmer who had asked them for a bigger harvest than he had actually planted saw all his fields suddenly go up in flames, set on fire by a flash of lightning that had sprung from the earth. Like the Tempestaries, the Ielles are highly skilled in the art of lightning.

They cruelly punish those who have offended them or those whom they do not like. It is known that people have been suddenly turned into dogs, toads or poisonous seven-headed monsters; sumptuous dwellings have been reduced to ruins and dust in a single night, and dreams of power and wealth have vanished in dark smoke.

Habitat:

Romania, Wallachia, Transylvania, at the foot of the Carpathian mountains. No one knows where they live. Shepherds have seen them disappear under sacred tumuli, under old tombs in abandoned cemeteries, said to be haunted by Strigoï and Svircolac… or through holes in hollow trees leading to underground worlds.

Food:

It is best not to dwell on the subject. Some people call them the "Devourers" and peasants believe them to be vampires.

Customs and Activities:

Their power lies in their mysterious nature.

The Ielles, Dînsele (the Elles), Maiestre (the Mistresses) or Puternice (the Strong Ones) are benevolent or malevolent Faeries. They are feared by many, but the wise and the humble, and poets who ask for nothing, are showered with gifts. They influence the weather, the quality of the harvest, the good health or wasting away of the cattle. They protect dreamy girl-Faeries, children who are "different," and those who melancholically and lovingly look after the souls of those who have committed suicide.

81

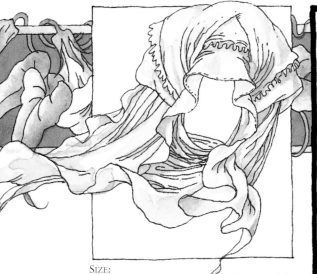

SIZE:

Often tall and slender, graceful. "Li P'tite Blanque Femme" of Liège is minuscule with a hunchback. The White Louisette, the Doucelettes and the Little White Sisters are dwarves.

APPEARANCE:

"She is beautiful and graceful," according to Marnier, "slim and slight like the branch of a birch, her shoulders white like the snow on the mountains and her eyes blue like the springs in the hills." "Her skin is translucent, her body is made up of mercury without blood, organs or other viscera, consisting entirely of soul matter" (Dambruserus).

The White Lady of Montaigu appears without a head.

APPEARANCE:

Whatever she wears, the fabric is always blindingly white "as if made of moonlight." Even her dresses embellished with brocades and richly decorated with sparkling, multicolored jewels, appear dimmed by the whiteness around.

The raincoats, jackets, parkas and other clothes that they wear today are of a similar blinding whiteness.

The White Ladies

In the solitude of the night you keep seeing the same ghosts go past. Night deepens as dreams become engaged.

(Gaston Bachelard)

The friend of the forest returns to the ether. Each blade of grass is a world on its own, each path leads to dream cities. He searches for the herb Paris, the herb of true love, the herb of oblivion, the song of a horn lulling him to the sleep of Elves. Once he has gathered the time and put away his handkerchief, he can sit and wait.

Slowly the blue sky over his head becomes more autumnal. The precision of the leaves recedes into the background as it makes place for the essences, leaving behind only an idea of the forest. The evening sounds have become messages. "He who dreams in the darkness of night discovers the wonderful weave of time in repose." He abandons his book and bares his soul in efflorescent dreams. A star shining at the top of a tree captures his reason, isolating him from the earth. He dematerializes, drawn towards the star by the aerial arms of an ivy. The shining star cries. "We will again hear the music of spheres when imagination is re-established in its active role of guiding human life." The ritual is simple; the growing shade has blurred all points of reference

in order to accustom the Guest to the dimensions of the soul. The aura of a luciola, of a moth or the eye of an animal lights the milky way of the mosses. Movements of air that lived in the past rise above the pond, a shred of mist detaches itself and floats away to cover a soul. A White Lady takes shape as in a suspension, then glides along on a reflection as she multiplies…

They are alchemical creations, the products of imaginary matter and the imagining spirit. In the same way that kingfishers represent the fulgurating fusion of sky, water and sun, they are the subtle alliance of emanations from the forest, the sighing of water and human vapors. Greeted by the song of frogs, they are found draped over the hollow altars of century-old oaks, sacred fountains still echoing with the sound of old prayers. Hanging from the rays of stars, they slide out of a limbo of penitence, a bloody rock, a dream. They borrow veils of sorrow and dancing shoes from the Faeries' wardrobe and, on the stroke of midnight, they relive a secret, long-forgotten story, now only present in the memory of owls.

When the night is dark, the White Beauty of Elven walks on the moors and on the plain near the castle; there are many blood stains on her dress. Often she is met by a ghost, draped in a torn shroud, who walks towards her. They exchange words of love and everyone is careful not to disturb them. They are the souls of the Lady of Elven and a knight who died while defending her; as he lay dying, she kissed him and plunged a dagger into her heart.

The White Shadow of Midon, struck by her father as she intervened between him and her husband, returns every night to pray and cry on the ruins of the château of Montaigle. She wanders silently, desperately searching for him; but every ten years, on the stroke of midnight, she calls out, uttering a single word: "Gilles!"

The inhabitants of Pouencé regularly see a woman dressed in white rising into the air like a column of vapor, a finger to her lips. She sighs as she floats above the ruined ramparts of the castle. She is the ghost of a noble lady, locked up and immured by her jealous husband in one of the underground halls of the fortress. Indeed, a secret room was discovered in the castle containing the dried remains of a woman sitting at a table with a silver plate, fork and spoon. The body was still tied to its chair, and in its wide open mouth was a shiny gold coin.

For seven centuries, the White Lady of Pflixbourg has haunted the fortress overlooking the lower valley of the Flecht. She glides along the ground in her long, snowy dress with veils fluttering in the wind; she cries as she searches for her children, taken from the garden in broad daylight by an eagle that later dropped them onto the rocks on the mountain of the white lake.

Some of these pale creatures guard treasures as a penance.

At night, a white lady looks over the battlements of the castle of Montafilant, near Corseul in Brittany, before disappearing into underground passages from where the clinking of gold coins and sobbing can be heard. This diaphanous ghost is that of a lady of the house of Dinan sold by her equerry for a "large number of coins of the realm." She comes back to claim the money her wicked servant was paid for.

HABITAT:

The White Ladies can be found anywhere in France. The Tall Maidens bathe in the Moselle, the Virgin Sisters of Parameix always follow the same aerial path along the canopy of the forest when they visit each other. The route they have followed along the tree tops can clearly be seen where some of the branches have been bent to the right and others to the left. They are most often observed near fountains, springs, ponds, caves, very old trees, dolmens, ancient places of worship, calvaries, and cemeteries, wandering among the bramble-covered ruins of abandoned châteaux, along a road where there have been accidents.

FOOD:

For a long time the demonizing influence of Christianity has propagated a false image of the White Lady as an ogress, while in reality she only eats honeysuckle perfume and the dew of ivy.

HABITS:

Sometimes Faeries, sometimes ghosts, the White Ladies wander along the narrow shores where the magic clouds meet and merge with the blurred edges of the next world; between shadow and light, in the chiaroscuro of an eternal eclipse. These White Ladies symbolize the world's threatened purity.

ACTIVITIES:

The White Chatelaines wander crying sorrowfully on the site of their death, while endlessly re-enacting the dramatic events which have led to their damnation. Some embittered White Ladies look for a haunting companion along the roads by leading travelers to their death while hunting White Ladies lead ghostly packs of dogs. Others, given to teasing, merely spin and stun their victims. They are harbingers of sorrow and death.

But their activities are not always sad. They also love dancing and frolicking in the countryside, and they have been known to hand out twigs, pebbles and leaves that turn to gold. They feed those who are lost, warn them of possible dangers, and lead them back onto the right path.

A very long time ago, some nuns buried an enormous chest full of gold and precious stones in a cave near the village of Haselbourg. Since then, their souls have been wandering through the countryside at night, and they are condemned to do so until a human discovers the treasure and takes possession of it. From time to time, they appear to solitary walkers. One day, a young man saw a lady dressed in white walking towards him in an orchard. She was holding a bunch of keys in her hand and was trying to give them to him. But the youth fled, terror-stricken, pursued by the desperate cries of the "damned." She then appeared to a young girl who also refused the keys. The nun then burst into tears and disappeared.

The Baselweibchen of Baselwald also offer to guide passers-by to a treasure that it is better not to own. Every hundred years a White Lady appears at the edge of the pond of Offémont. Clenched in her teeth, she holds a key of fire. If anyone agreed to use it she would be freed from her curse.

In the valley of Ogmore in Wales, when the moon is full, plaintive songs can be heard coming from the ruins of the neighboring castle. It is the voice of the White Lady, Y Lady Wen, who guards a "black treasure." People lock their doors, put out the lights and hide for fear that she might come and knock at their door and tell them where it is. Alas, everyone ignores her pleas. People always flee, refusing the

Faeries' gold and rejecting the embrace of the astral body dressed in moonlight— because, when they appear to mortals, all their actions are guided by their wish to free themselves from the curse that condemns them to haunt humans, thus preventing them from resting. As a result the "White Ladies" have become dangerous.

The Demoiselle Blanche de Tonneville has ruled over the moors since the day when she cried out: "If, after my death, I had one foot in heaven and the other in hell, I would put both in hell to have the moors all to myself." A man riding on these moors, now haunted by her, suddenly heard a lady's voice, asking softly: "Where shall I sleep tonight?" Seeing a beautiful young girl dressed all in white, the rider replied: "With me." The young girl immediately climbed on the horse behind him. But when he tried to kiss her, she bared her teeth that were like fangs and vanished. He then realized that she had taken him to the swamps to see him drowned.

In the forest of Serre and the woods of Fau, in the Jura mountains near Dole, the White Ladies attract young men with melodious songs and amorous advances, then turn into Ghouls to devour them. The White Ladies of the knoll of Hogues hurl them into a mud-pit or mire and the Blanquettes of the Dauphiné region throw them over a precipice.

In Strasbourg, the White Lady of the Cathedral takes the careless visitor high up the tower until he is overtaken by vertigo and falls down. The White Maiden with the Mirror makes her victim dizzy and spins him in the air before dropping him again without leaving a trace.

Like the Banshees, the White Ladies are also harbingers of death and catastrophes: a long time ago in Mortagne-sur-Sèvre there was a fountain that inspired great terror among the villagers. If you went round the fountain five times you would see a white shape appear, like a snow statue; it looked agitated and sighed. The apparition would then slowly take shape and a tall woman with fair hair could be seen, dressed in white. Terror-stricken, people would try and flee, but the shadow always caught up and only returned to its watery abode after telling them of their future sorrows and deaths—all of which always came true.

But the White Lady is not just a blood-thirsty Gothic ghost. The Faerie tree of Jeanne la Pucelle also offers her shelter. Dazzled by her appearance in the tree's foliage, people identify her with the apparitions of the white virgin, the Holy Mary of grottos and fountains. Youths say they saw her on Friday September 14, 1984 at 10:30 P.M., in Montpinchon in the *département* of the Manche: "First we saw a cold light appear through the trees, like a piece of bluish ice; this slowly took the form of a tall woman with luminous, fair hair and a long, white veil down to the ground, like a nun's coif. She did not move and her hands were clasped as if in prayer. She had no face, nose, eyes or mouth." "White Lady or Holy Virgin?" the local paper wondered. This confusion has its roots in our collective memory. The White Lady is one of the rare Faeries who has never aged but has always kept up with the times: so much so that her misty veils have even been seen on the screens of audio-visual equipment. The little Blanquette of the fountains regularly makes the headlines in one of the newspapers, and her slender silhouette is very much part of our contemporary mythology. Her "passage" has been filmed at the chateau of Veaucé; car drivers have also given her a lift at night. It is always the same story. It is night time and raining. The driver has just reached a crossroads when the headlights of the car suddenly reveal the slender figure of a young girl, dressed in white. She waves and the driver stops to give her a lift. She seems so frail in her wet dress that the driver offers her his coat from the back seat. After a few miles, she lifts her pale, trembling hand and tells him where to stop; but even before he has had time to slow down or stop, she suddenly disappears without a sound, without opening the car door. Dumb-founded, he gets out of the car and calls her, but the road is deserted. Perhaps she went inside that house across the road without his noticing. He would like to recover his coat that she has taken with her in her haste. He knocks on the door, a lady opens it and invites him inside. She is most upset when she hears his story and starts sobbing when he describes the young girl whose features he recognizes on the photograph she shows him: it is her daughter, killed in a car accident five years ago. She was knocked down by a car at that very crossroads where he picked her up. It is not the first time that she has "come back;" other drivers have had the same experience and told her about it. Each time, the "white passenger" vanishes in front of where she used to live and returns to the cemetery.

When he goes to visit the girl's grave he finds his coat carefully laid out on the tombstone.

SIZE:

Rather tall and straight.

APPEARANCE:

The Black and the Red Ladies are very similar. Although the Black Lady appears sometimes as a "hideous creature with horrible fangs," most of the time she is, like the Red Lady, "of an irresistible beauty," with all the charms and attributes of a "lecherous she-devil and she-wolf." Her sparkling, velvety eyes suddenly disappear under her eyelids at the moment of copulation to reveal a white, milky substance. She then proceeds to bite her victim. "Her skin is so white that the blue of her veins stands out against it," says Dom Anselme (Incubes et Succubes de nos campagnes; "Incubi and Succubi of our Countryside"). She is the equivalent of the Stiga of Hungary.

CLOTHES:

Elegant. Calix-like ruff framing an angular face. They wear long court dresses the color of the night and of blood.

FOOD:

They are insatiable ogresses.

HABITAT:

In order to retain their beauty and the lunar sparkle of their skin, they shelter in the coldest rooms of inaccessible manor houses, huddled against each other.

CUSTOMS AND ACTIVITIES:

Monsters of perversity, they are skilled in the practice of evil. They steal and devour children, forcing their lovers of one night to submit to the most demonic debauchery. They are terrified of mirrors and can only bear the sight of their reflection in corrupt waters.

The Black Ladies and the Red Ladies

I take the place for those who see me naked and without veils,
Of the moon, the sun, the sky and the stars
(Charles Baudelaire)

The Black Ladies are White Ladies who went wrong, who became bad the day they exchanged their beautiful garments made of light for clothes whose colors were those of the night.

In Chateaugay (Puy-de-Dôme), Ladies dressed in black, whose appearances are much feared by the villagers, dance on a knoll in the moonlight. In the Beaujolais, black, hideous Ladies brush against those who walk near ponds on dark nights. The chatelaine of Montanges appears like a Black Lady at the Rieu d'Enfer. She throws her lovers whose charms she has exhausted into the torrent.

The Demoiselle Noire de Gruchy was a magician and she knew how to take on the shape of all kinds of animals. An insatiable lover and mistress, she enticed young men into her tower and, once she had grown tired of them, she changed them into animals or plants. Those who were bold enough to resist her were disemboweled, their intestines laid out to dry on the hawthorn hedges. She was always accompanied by flocks of magpies.

Margot the Black ate children. Mothers were careful to keep them well-hidden because, as soon as she knew of one who was well fattened, she sent her guards for him. One day, her cook, overcome with remorse, cooked a new-born calf in the same way as a little child and served it to his mistress as a veal stew. The glutton had not finished her banquet when dreadful moans were heard in the courtyard of the château. She sent a valet to find out the cause of this commotion. He came back and told her it was a cow searching for its calf that had been taken away. The countess, moved by the story, felt pity for the cow and ordered that her calf should be returned to her. She was told that this was unfortunately impossible because she had eaten the calf in the stew instead of a child. In a blind rage, Margot the ogress summoned the superintendent of the kitchens and reproached him for his treachery and cruelty. "You feel sorry for a poor cow whose calf was taken from her because you have seen her suffering," he said, "but don't you feel anything for those poor mothers whose children you steal?"

When she heard this, the countess died of a broken heart. Since then, dressed in mourning clothes, Margot the Black comes back every night to bewail her crimes near the château that is now engulfed in water. She is accompanied by a funeral procession of repentant ogresses. It is because they walked so often along these liquid shores that the mud in the pond has turned the color of their rotting shadows.

The dress of the Red Ladies is as red as their skin is white. They are like a "pool of blood on the snow," and this contrast perfectly reflects their appetite for lechery and red meat. Their eyes are like glowing embers, and their mouths are like poppies concealing feline teeth. They capture

men by opening their scarlet cloak to reveal "a body whose erotic, magical attraction cannot be equaled by that of other Faeries" (Fleury).

Those who fall into their clutches at night time are found in the morning as empty envelopes of rough skin, drained of all life by these belles of the night, their bones reduced to ashes by the fire of their breath. They collect souls and stick them on hat pins. They have adapted very well to the modern world and many of them have become highly successful actresses in pornographic films.

"When the drowned youths, held prisoner in the Red Lady's magic pond of Tréguier, were freed by a holy beggar who opened the lock gates, he saw them stand up as if resuscitated, and walk towards her on the water."

Gray Ladies
and Ladies of the Well

What a surprising well, she says, I can see myself in the dark.
A Lady of the Well climbs from one beam to the other.

(Jean Paulhan, *Lalie*)

"The name 'Gray Ladies' has often been used as a generic term to designate Faeries, Elves and all kinds of Faerieland's people. Thus, the Ladies of the Well, the Blessed Virgins, Huldres and Vasselage of the hills are all known as Gray Ladies by people who do not hear their song" (Barbygère).

The Gray Ladies live in the vicinity of souls who are missed and ghosts who are awaited. They guard some of the treasures and "resting-places of Faeries."

They haunt old sites, protecting the memory of magical times, as well as visiting secret gardens, children's graves, and winter arbors. Cats often leave whatever they are doing to go and be stroked by them.

According to Jean Paulhan, the Ladies of the Well, the "graceful" ladies, are the play companions of Lalie, whose features

SIZE:
Medium.

APPEARANCE:
They wear dresses the color of lichen, mist and dust. The Ladies of the Well have skinny arms, almost triangular.

HABITAT:
They live in attics, libraries, and hollow roads.

CUSTOMS AND ACTIVITIES:
They play with children behind the parents' back, in abandoned houses, and they protect them from accidents.

    Very little is known about the activities of the Ladies of the Well.

they borrow when they walk hand-in-hand. They appear out of old wells when they are called, when people play at making echoes inside the deep black hole, or dropping in pebbles to make ripples. It is not known how, but they live in waters that are too old to be drawn or drunk; if it is used to water the garden or to clean the house, the result is that forests for Dracs and fish, for Codrilles and for the Groac'h, would sprout up and spread everywhere.

They are simultaneously black, green, red, gray and blue. This is because their shiny, black skin is speckled with red like that of a trout, their tousled hair is colored green with the green talcum powder of beams and stones, their skirt is mousy gray, and their eyes are blue. There are black, green, red and gray sparks dancing in Lalie's eyes when they hold hands as they dance around ponds that are "the color of moonlight and milk," moving "so slowly and silently that they barely touch the shadow of the trees and reeds." Their song is so sweet and blurred that it "seems to emerge from the mist." Afterwards they leap like frogs, still holding hands, and return to their well.

Only Lalie knows what their role is but she has never said anything about it. Perhaps she will later.

SIZE:

Like a wasp.

APPEARANCE:

Resplendent in their beauty. A body of ice and hair sparkling with hoar frost. The daughters of the rays of the Sun, they have pretty shimmering wings.

CLOTHES:

Dressed in the blue shadows of snow.

HABITAT:

The highest mountains in the Alps.

CUSTOMS AND ACTIVITIES:

They cannot stand a human touching their hair and if that happens they are quite capable of abandoning them to the whims of the Faeries of the Echo who will enjoy leading them astray, or to the Faeries of Vertigo who always attract intruders into the abyss.

They plant flowers on the slopes of the mountain, they bring mountain goats back to the safety of vast caverns, they protect chalets from the avalanches unleashed by the spring tantrums of the roaring Wilde Männer and other Trolls of the Alps, they make the grass grow, they sweeten the milk of the flocks, and they teach shepherds the arts of medicinal herbs and of love.

Blue Ladies, Ice Virgins and Mountain Faeries

In spring, when the shepherd dreams of golden flowers in Alpine meadows, the Schneefraülein changes her outfit…
(Eugène Genoux, *Le Chant des clarines*)

It is important not to confuse the "Blue Faerie" of faerie-tales with happy endings, the ones who grant wishes and reward children's good behavior, with the Blue Ladies, the Blessed Virgins or Wild Virgins, the Selingen Fraülein and the Wilden Jungfraüen who rule over the mountains.

"They appear at the entrance of rocky caves and sing songs in a loud, clear voice that echoes far away in the valleys. The shepherd on the high grassy slopes hears this song that reaches him like a sweet echo. He knows what it means: Be careful!" (Karl Grün, *Les Esprits élémentaires*; "The Elemental Spirits"). "They" protect him and follow him step by step, making sure he does not get lost when the clouds are low, shielding him from invisible danger when he pursues his quest to the confines of the earth where knowledge is replaced by the soul.

Faithful spouses of the wild Waldzergen, Nörggen and Lörggenn, the Blue Maidens attach themselves to fragile creatures, children lost in the middle of nature whose "thought" they do not know. When one of them falls, they catch him in their veil that they have placed across the abyss.

Brown-haired Dive is their sister and lives on the Italian side of the mountain, the Fhrön lives on the Swiss side and the Dalien with their goat feet frolic on the Austrian side.

The Ice Maiden, the Snow Queen or Scheefraülein, is all dressed in blue. Andersen describes her as a magnificent creature, her hair as white as snow, all

alone, surrounded by eternal ice, desperate to entice brave visitors to her kingdom of light, that is so cold no man can survive it. In order to keep them under her spell she drives an ice crystal into their heart, opening up the gates of oblivion and irresistible infinities. Unfortunately, the ice crystal always melts and the sleeper always wakes and flees. Being both an aerial and an aquatic creature she takes on all sorts of forms to pursue him: she flies over him in the shape of an eagle, she follows him from cascade to cascade as a salmon, from branch to branch as a stoat, and as a gust of wind she throws him into the abyss. Then the Ice Maiden kneels down and places an icy kiss of

death on his forehead, transforming him into an ice giant.

With delight Grün evokes the Demoiselles Bleutées, Daughters of the Rays of the Sun, frolicking in the sunset of Lucerne: and when they sing together they sound like distant church bells. In the evening they gather in circles at the top of the mountains. They stretch their wings of gold and pink, illuminating the summits of the glaciers with a rich palette of colors and people say that the "Alps are on fire." At night these friendly Elfines sleep in a cradle of snow, waiting for dawn. They are very fond of flowers, butterflies and shepherds.

SIZE:

Very appealing.

APPEARANCE:

Magnificent. The Apsarâ are so seductive that any mortal who catches a glimpse of them is charmed forever. Even the gods cannot resist their charm, with their slender waists, rounded hips and buttocks, muscular thighs, and generous, firm, erect breasts that inspire divine love. They have beautiful oval faces framed by luxurious black, shiny hair, with almond eyes and mouths shaped like lotus petals.

DRESS:

Half-naked, they are adorned with scent and unguents, and with bracelets of gold and rare pearls. They wear tiaras and crowns of flowers, large earrings, and bells on their ankles. Their only piece of clothing is a small loincloth of celestial muslin held in place by richly ornamented belts.

The Apsarâ

Adorned with scent and unguents, perfumed, rich in food and never furrowed, I extol her, she who is the mother of wild beasts, the faerie of the woods.

(Rig Veda)

Purûravas was a prince of great beauty, renowned for his generosity, his piety, his magnificence and his love of the truth. One day when he was hunting in the mountains of the Himalayas, he freed two Apsarâ who had been kidnapped by a pack of demons. One of them was called Urvaçi. He thought her infinitely more beautiful, more graceful and more elegant than any of the women he had known before and he fell immediately in love with her.

"Fair lady, I love you, take pity on me, grant me your affection in return," he begged her.

His prayer touched the beautiful nymph. So, forgetting the delights of paradise, she replied: "I shall answer your prayer, but only if you accept the three conditions I am going to set you. I have two lambs whom I love as if they were my children. At night they always sleep near my bed and no one must take them from me. For your part, you must ensure that I never see you naked. Finally, you may only give me clarified butter to eat."

The prince accepted all the conditions of the beautiful Nymph.

So it was that Purûravas and Urvaçi lived in great happiness in Alaka.

But everyone at Indra's court was missing Urvaçi. The other Apsarâ, the Gandharva and Siddha, were deprived of her beauty and her singing, and they were pining for her.

On her return to the paradise of celestial beings, Urvaçi's companion told the courtiers the details of the pact agreed between Urvaçi and the Prince. The Gandharva decided to ask Viçvavasu, one of their number, to destroy the relationship. One night he made his way to where the two lovers were sleeping and grabbed one of the lambs. Urvaçi, woken by the cries of her beloved animal, cried out: "Woe is me, who has stolen one of my children? If I had had a brave husband, this would not have happened. To whom should I turn for help? Are there no heroes around?"

Cut to the quick and hoping that she would not see that he was naked because the night was dark, Purûravas leapt out of bed, seized his sword and dashed off in pursuit of the thieves. At that moment the Gandharva unleashed a violent thunderstorm. A flash of lightning revealed the prince's nudity. Their agreement having thus been violated, the Faerie was betrayed and disappeared immediately.

For a long time Purûravas traveled throughout the world in search of his beloved. At last, one day he reached Lake Kuruksheta and he caught a glimpse of her swimming amongst a group of Apsarâ, all dressed in swan apparel. He begged her to return and live with him again.

"What can I say to you," she replied, "you have broken the pact between us."

But faced with the depth of his despair, the Faerie felt herself weakening.

"I am pregnant with your child. Go now but come back in one year. Your son will have been born by then and I shall spend an entire night with you."

When one year had passed Urvaçi and Purûravas met once again at Kuruksheta and she gave him Aysus, his first-born son. These annual encounters were repeated until she had given birth to five sons, the fruits of their love.

One morning she gave him the glad tidings: "To please me, the Gandharva have all decided to give you their blessing as my husband!"

This is how Purûravas was granted a place in the kingdom of the Gandharva and was never again separated from the one he loved.

HABITAT:

The golden palaces of the paradise of Indra, the celestial kingdom of Hindu mythology. In the early days of Brahmanism, the Apsarâ lived in banyan trees and fig trees.

FOOD:

Ambrosia and clarified butter.

CUSTOMS:

They were born at the dawn of the world when the gods were stirring the primordial ocean in order to produce ambrosia. They live near their jealous lovers, the Gandharva, but they come down to earth now and again to enjoy the love of mortals who are then raised to the status of heroes.

ACTIVITIES:

The Apsarâ, Nymphs, Naiads and Faeries rule over the kingdoms of fauna, flora and dance.

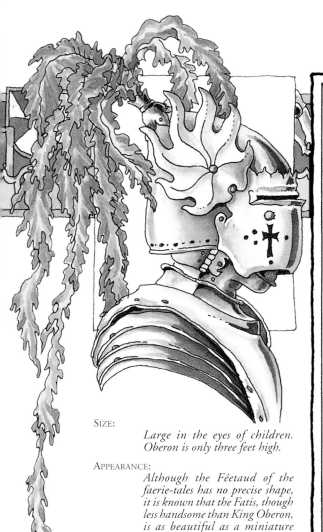

Male Faeries, Fatis and Féetauds

The lay is music to the ear,
The notes easy to retain.

(Marie de France)

SIZE:

Large in the eyes of children. Oberon is only three feet high.

APPEARANCE:

Although the Féetaud of the faerie-tales has no precise shape, it is known that the Fatis, though less handsome than King Oberon, is as beautiful as a miniature Lancelot. In the Golden Age they were tall and as supple as fair poplars. Long hair, a sunny beard, gentle, dreamy eyes, lips that sometimes smiled, a face tanned by long rides in the countryside, with a gait more elegant than warlike.

DRESS:

Gold and azure blue. Plumed helmet, crest decorated with horns, branches, wings, chimeras, and stars. Finely decorated thigh boots, a light coat of mail that no spear could pierce. Wears either hunting or court dress.

HABITAT:

The roads that can only be approached through adventure. Oberon's kingdom, the Fortunate Isles, mirror-châteaux, box tree labyrinths, nurseries. Or caverns and cairns where they are held prisoner by certain Faeries. Some of them can be found in boxes where lead soldiers are stored or in matchboxes. They can also be seen crossing the foliage on tapestries, the clouds and mythologies of certain games such as "Dungeons and dragons."

According to Paul Sébillot in his book *Folklore de France*, the name Féetaud is given to male Faeries near Saint-Malo who have no special name in the classical French language because they do not occur in literary faerie-tales. However deep one delves into popular lore, from the *Chroniques gargantuines* to local mythology, they do not exist. The Male Fairy, the Fé, has no name, no particular appearance, no particular personality. It is as if he only owed his existence to the fact that he is the Faerie's husband, as if her radiating personality has reduced him to the humble role of a helper: fetching the midwife when birth is imminent, hunting, fishing, begetting children. That is the extent of his role in life. But what use would a husband be to her who is able to transport the stones of a dolmen without even stopping to spin, who can make a golden palace rise from the water, a winged horse emerge from a rose-bud; they can grow, disappear, travel through the air, turn into all kinds of animals and flowers, and make it rain or shine. Why be hampered by an ungracious spouse, less powerful than oneself, when one is surrounded by a court of ladies-in-waiting, Elfines, little Imp pages who are all much more gifted than himself?

The Féetauds are said to be clumsy. They are not known for their magical exploits, although it is rumored that one of them turned the fields of a farmer into rough moorland and rocks because he refused to offer him shelter. Another is believed to have owned a boat that grew larger so that it could accommodate more horses, or smaller so that he could carry it under his arm as easily as a basket. Not very impressive really. But this is unfair, because it does not take into account the noble Fatis, the Faerie Knights of the lays and legends, including the beautiful Oberon, the charming Oberon with the golden locks, sovereign of enchanted kingdoms, of Faeries, Elves, Goblins who all lived happily together.

Oberon or Auberon is the perfect image of the Fatis who inspired Shakespeare, Wieland, Weber, and so many magical tales. He is said to be the son of Morgan le Fay and Julius Caesar, or of Flora and Herald-with-the-large-wings. He could build magnificent palaces in a second and set tables laden with exquisite food for his friends. He lavishes kindness on those he loves. And finally, he never ages and can hear the angels in the sky. He owes his small size and special powers to his godmothers. The gold and ivory horn he wears around his neck has magic powers and was made by the Sirens in an island in the middle of the sea. This is how the bards of the Golden Age describe him.

Oberon is the protector of paladins and all those who are on a quest. To Huon of Bordeaux he will lend the oliphant, hanaper and his coat of mail that would make him invulnerable.

Many Fatis are his vassals and celebrated in epic and courtly poems. They have fought dragons, hunted the Bêtes Charmuzelles, thrown the gauntlet at the faces of felons, and driven demons back into hell. They have helped the innocents and seduced many Faeries, mortal beauties, belles-dames-des-margelles. It is true that some dark knights may have slipped in among them, Fatis of the shadows, capable of abduction and worse but never as terrible as the Ganconer Elves and other prowlers with dark hearts.

Time has forgotten about them and only the Faeries are remembered. Like Arthur and the brave knights of Camelot, they did not survive the end of the age of chivalry, preferring to retire to the peaceful haven of the Fortunate Isles, Avalon, Tir Na Nog, near wise Oberon.

There are still a few Féetauds around; the pale husbands of the Faeries, or mortals under the spell of Faeries, slaves of Vily and fallen huntresses. At least that is what is told in faerie-tales… because the *Elfin Chronicles* mention quite a few more. It is often quite difficult for the layman to distinguish them from enchanters, lacustrian genies and wind ringers. Are Lange-Wapper, the Folleti, and the Foireaux Elves, gnomoncules, daymons or faeries? Puck's malice has confused everything, but the elficologist knows which string to pull.

FOOD:

The banquets of Avalon. The Fée-tauds are quite happy to eat the foul soup prepared by the fallen Faeries, and the left-overs they give them.

CUSTOMS:

Irreproachable, although one should not forget the sinister part played by creatures of faerieland in the Protheselaus of Huon de Roptelande.

ACTIVITIES:

They ride the breath of legends.

THE FAERIES
OF RIVERS
AND
THE SEA

I said along the "black" water, but I meant: unknown, there where time flows back, these vessels rejuvenate us.

(Eeva-Liisa Manner)

The devotee of Faeries stops at the water's edge, where the images of the past are condensed. The crossing can only take place through the materialization of the dormant forces of the inner eye projected towards the distant shores. Along the current of the stream or the salt water of the seas, presences become outlined and move between dreaming and reality: the Hydra of the silt is a rose that breathes, and the letter-like form of the heron is a key to the antiphonary of frogs.

A shimmer makes the water imitate a flower… and the scale of a fish fleetingly disturbing the smooth liquid is like a shard of mirror that brings the traveler of deep visions to the Isles of Happiness…

She who now emerges from the clear shadow of the water is like the Ophelian prow of the skiff… The white sails are waiting and the Maidens of the rivers cast off the moorings, while a voice from the depths of the waters invites the guests to attend the nuptials beneath the carpet of water lilies.

Morgans, Mari-Morgans

The wind kisses her breasts and unfolds as a corolla
Her great sails gently rocked by the waters.
(Rimbaud)

The Mari-Morgans are men and women. The men are called Morgans or Morganed, while the women are Morganès, or Morganezed, the plural of Morganès. They bear a great resemblance to Sirens, and towards the end of the 19th century they were often confused with them, although they did not have the tail of a fish and were not aggressive.

At that time, Morganezed could often be seen playing and frolicking, combing their hair, or spinning on the fine sand or on the seaweed along the shore; they would give gold and ivory combs and "distaffs that never become smaller" to young girls who greeted them sweetly. They also used to dry treasures of every kind in the sun, laid out on beautiful white tablecloths. One could admire them for as long as one did not blink, but everything would immediately disappear on the first movement of the eyelids.

The Mari-Morgans have always had a close relationship with humans. They would entice those who reciprocated their love to their glass and coral palaces, as can be seen in this story that contains every

SIZE:
Without actually being dwarves, they are short but graceful.

APPEARANCE:
They are said to have pink cheeks, blond, curly hair, and large sparkling blue eyes. The old Morgans pride themselves on their wonderful long white beards, embellished with gold threads. Morgans become sexually stronger and more seductive the older they get.

CLOTHES:
Morganezed wear long togas of green chiffon, decorated with fine pearls and coral dust. On their forehead they wear heavy tiaras of precious stones. Dressed in short, green tunics, Morganezed protected their chests with breastplates of little silver plates when they went into battle, mounted on their white sea-horses. Their conch-shaped helmets were decorated with long manes of seaweed, falling down to the small of the back.

sign of being true. It was collected by the indefatigable F. M. Luzel on the Isle of Ushant in 1873, a time when there were still many Morgans in the region, although it is said that they are still seen occasionally near Crozon:

"A young girl was sitting on the beach with her companions, and as they talked about their lovers, Mona declared that she was as beautiful as a Morganès, and that she would only marry a lord or a Morgan.

An old Morgan who was hidden among the rocks heard her. He leapt on her and took her to the bottom of the water; he was the king of the Morgans and his palace was more beautiful than any royal residence on earth. His son fell in love with Mona and asked his father whether he could marry her. But the king refused and forced him to marry a Morganès. The betrothed set out for church—these men of the sea also had their underwater churches and rituals, in spite of the fact that they are not Christian; apparently they even have bishops. Mona was ordered to remain at home to prepare for the festivities; but she was only given empty saucepans that were large sea-shells, and she was told that if she did not have a delicious meal ready for the young couple and their guests, she would be put to death. The young man pretended he had forgotten the ring; he ran off and went straight to the kitchens, where by saying a few words and touching various objects in turn he produced a magnificent meal.

The old Morgan told the young girl that she must have been helped and that she was not off the hook yet. When the newly-weds withdrew to the bridal bedroom, he ordered Mona to go in with a lighted candle and to let him know when it had burnt

down to her hand. When the candle was almost out, the young Morgan asked his wife to hold the candle for a while. When the old Morgan was told that the candle had burnt out, he entered the bedroom and without looking, killed the girl holding the candle with a single blow of his sword.

Next morning, the young Morgan went to tell his father that he was a widower now, and he asked his permission to marry the girl from earth. The wedding took place and the young Morgan showered his wife with attentions. Nevertheless Mona still wanted to return to her parents; but her husband did not want to let her go because he was afraid that she would not come back. One day she was looking so sad that he said to her: 'Follow me and I will take you to your father's house.' He said the magic word and a beautiful crystal bridge appeared leading from the bottom of the sea to the earth. The old Morgan wanted to follow the couple; but when they had set foot on the earth, the young Morgan said another magic word and the bridge fell down, dragging the old Morgan down to the bottom of the sea.

Mona's husband advised her to return at sunset, and not to allow any man to kiss her or even to touch her hand. Time went by and she failed to return. She forgot everything that had happened since her departure for the country of the Morgans. Since then she often hears moaning, and one night she distinctly recognized the voice of her husband reproaching her for having left him. She suddenly remembered everything and found her husband wailing behind the door. She threw herself into his arms and she has not been seen since."

FOOD:

The Morgans breed marine cattle: dugong or "sea cows," marine calves and sheep whose meat they eat and whose milk they drink. They do not touch the fish or large mammals who are their allies. They also eat "saffron bread."

HABITAT:

In Brittany, and very occasionally in England. They live in a country under the sea, covered by a transparent vault of solidified water, created by a magic power, through which one can see almost as well as on earth. It contains vast stretches of countryside where strange plants and trees grow, plants that are reminiscent of terrestrial and marine flora. Long avenues lead to beautiful palaces decorated with the richness of the oceans.

CUSTOMS AND ACTIVITIES:

They know and practice the arts of enchantment. They do not sing like the Sirens but they play the marine harp most beautifully. Peace-loving and noble, they always pick up the gauntlet if they have been insulted.

They rescue and look after the victims of shipwrecks.

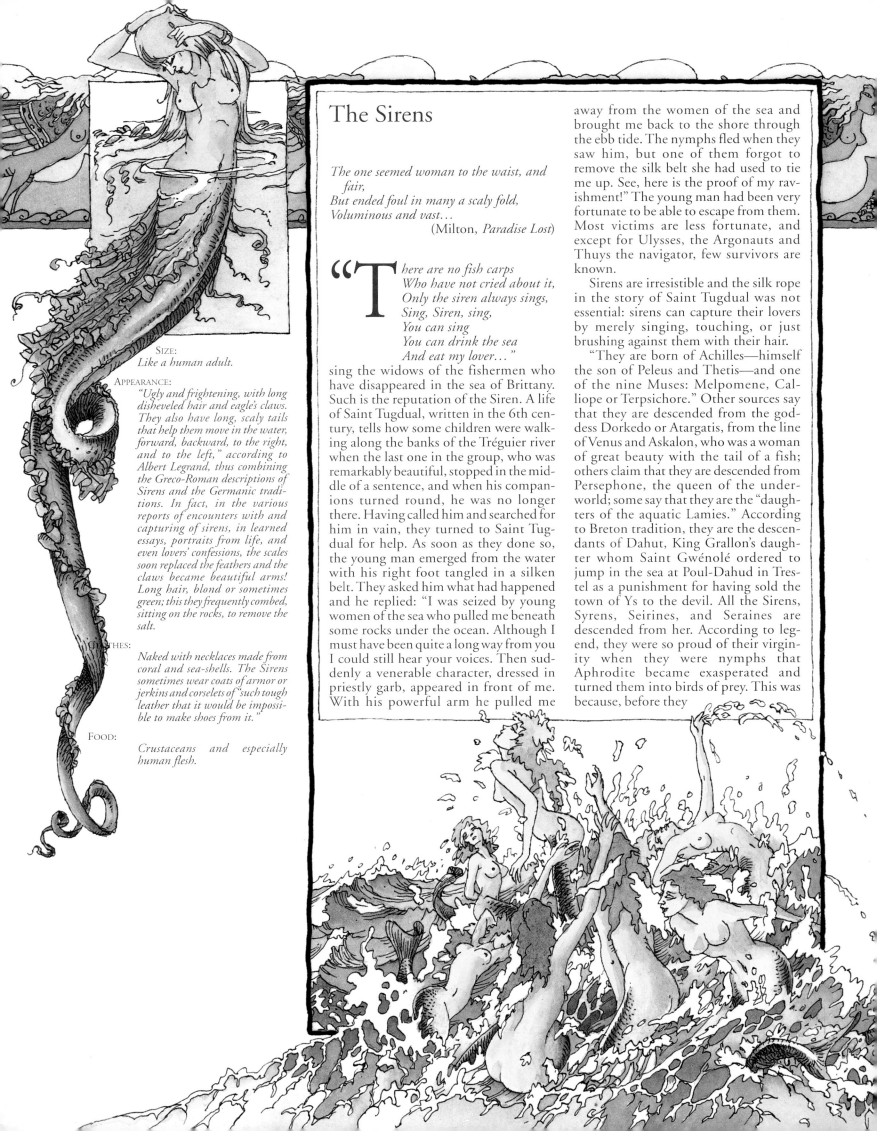

The Sirens

The one seemed woman to the waist, and fair,
But ended foul in many a scaly fold,
Voluminous and vast…

　　　　　　　(Milton, *Paradise Lost*)

"There are no fish carps
Who have not cried about it,
Only the siren always sings,
Sing, Siren, sing,
You can sing
You can drink the sea
And eat my lover…"

sing the widows of the fishermen who have disappeared in the sea of Brittany. Such is the reputation of the Siren. A life of Saint Tugdual, written in the 6th century, tells how some children were walking along the banks of the Tréguier river when the last one in the group, who was remarkably beautiful, stopped in the middle of a sentence, and when his companions turned round, he was no longer there. Having called him and searched for him in vain, they turned to Saint Tugdual for help. As soon as they done so, the young man emerged from the water with his right foot tangled in a silken belt. They asked him what had happened and he replied: "I was seized by young women of the sea who pulled me beneath some rocks under the ocean. Although I must have been quite a long way from you I could still hear your voices. Then suddenly a venerable character, dressed in priestly garb, appeared in front of me. With his powerful arm he pulled me away from the women of the sea and brought me back to the shore through the ebb tide. The nymphs fled when they saw him, but one of them forgot to remove the silk belt she had used to tie me up. See, here is the proof of my ravishment!" The young man had been very fortunate to be able to escape from them. Most victims are less fortunate, and except for Ulysses, the Argonauts and Thuys the navigator, few survivors are known.

Sirens are irresistible and the silk rope in the story of Saint Tugdual was not essential: sirens can capture their lovers by merely singing, touching, or just brushing against them with their hair.

"They are born of Achilles—himself the son of Peleus and Thetis—and one of the nine Muses: Melpomene, Calliope or Terpsichore." Other sources say that they are descended from the goddess Dorkedo or Atargatis, from the line of Venus and Askalon, who was a woman of great beauty with the tail of a fish; others claim that they are descended from Persephone, the queen of the underworld; some say that they are the "daughters of the aquatic Lamies." According to Breton tradition, they are the descendants of Dahut, King Grallon's daughter whom Saint Gwénolé ordered to jump in the sea at Poul-Dahud in Trestel as a punishment for having sold the town of Ys to the devil. All the Sirens, Syrens, Seirines, and Seraines are descended from her. According to legend, they were so proud of their virginity when they were nymphs that Aphrodite became exasperated and turned them into birds of prey. This was because, before they

Size:
Like a human adult.

Appearance:
"Ugly and frightening, with long disheveled hair and eagle's claws. They also have long, scaly tails that help them move in the water, forward, backward, to the right, and to the left," according to Albert Legrand, thus combining the Greco-Roman descriptions of Sirens and the Germanic traditions. In fact, in the various reports of encounters with and capturing of sirens, in learned essays, portraits from life, and even lovers' confessions, the scales soon replaced the feathers and the claws became beautiful arms! Long hair, blond or sometimes green; this they frequently combed, sitting on the rocks, to remove the salt.

Clothes:
Naked with necklaces made from coral and sea-shells. The Sirens sometimes wear coats of armor or jerkins and corselets of "such tough leather that it would be impossible to make shoes from it."

Food:
Crustaceans and especially human flesh.

became the women-fish of Greco-Roman mythology, they were described by Homer, Ovid and the "Palace of Animals" as winged creatures: "The Sirens (in Greek: *seirên*) are deadly monsters who are famous for killing men; they have the appearance of a woman from the head down to the navel, and the body of an eagle; their feet have claws like a bird of prey with which they tear their victims apart." But it is usually in the form of a witch-serpent that sailors all over the world have seen them.

Christopher Columbus is said to have seen three hideous Sirens playing in the water near Santo Domingo. In 1614, the English Captain John Smith saw a woman swimming near the New World. She had beautiful green eyes, a perfectly formed body, and long green hair. The man fell madly in love with her until the instant when she inadvertently revealed her tail.

Sometimes they became stranded on beaches and were captured. But they rarely survived in captivity, or would wreak vengeance on their jailers, or one of their companions would come and free them… according to many witnesses' chronicles.

One of them, dating from 1187, describes the capture of a siren near Oxford. Unfortunately, she managed to escape and return to her natural element.

Thomas de Cantimpré (1201–71), on a voyage to England, was told by a monk that some fishermen had found a monster who looked very much like a woman. She wore a crown shaped like a basket. She ate and drank but did not speak and, when displeased, she would quietly moan. This woman of the sea died three weeks after being caught.

The most fascinating case is that of a Siren caught by some milkmaids in the Purdermeer, in 1403. Guicciardini, Jean de Leyde and Snoyus Meyer all record it. This Siren, hairy all over, was covered in moss and green plants. She did not say a word but now and again she sighed. They washed her and clothed her. She ate and drank like any other human being. She was taken from Edam to Haarlem. She learned to sew but never talked. When

she died she was buried in a churchyard, because she had shown a degree of piety that had been noticed by the widow with whom she lived.

Waling Dijkstra reports the capture in Friesland of "a horseman of the sea" wearing a suit of armour. He was caught in the sea on March 10, 1305. He had a beautiful face and body, and was well-proportioned. He was put on display so that everyone could admire him, but he died three weeks later in Dokkum.

In *Traditions of Holland* by Ter Laan, it is said that there was a sandbank to the north-east of Beverland that had become exposed after the sea withdrew; it was called Minser Olloog, meaning "old village of Minser" in the ancient dialect of Groningen. One day, the fishermen caught a Siren whom they tortured and tied up. They wanted to drag out of her the Sirens' secret remedies for curing diseases and other minor inconveniences. But the Siren remained silent. She even succeeded in eluding the vigilance of her guardians and escaping. As soon as she found herself in the water, she turned round towards the village, and threw salt water onto the dyke protecting it. After this symbolic, premonitory gesture, she dived into the sea and was never seen again. The next morning, the villagers woke up to a terrible storm. The dyke gave way and the village disappeared into the sea.

Jan Van Dorp, the author of the magnificent *Flemish of the Waves*, tells the story of the Siren who implored the fishermen to return his companion caught in their nets. They refused, and he put a terrible curse on them. This took place on the eve of the feast of Saint Vincent. That night a sudden storm broke and completely submerged the town. But the he-Siren arrived too late to free his companion: she had already died. Inconsolable, he comes ashore twice a day with the rising tide, and in stormy weather he can be heard crying and wailing in the sand dunes.

Before the 1914–18 war, the Stracké Museum in Mariakerke, a few miles from Ostend, still had a Siren's skeleton on display.

HABITAT:
Underwater palaces. According to Greek mythology, they live on a rocky island between Capri and the Italian coast. They are often represented on Czech objets d'art. In Russia they are called Moreski Rudi or Melzumini; in Ireland they are known as Merrows or Mara-Warra, and in England as mermaids; in Scotland they go by the names of Ceasg, Daoine Mara, Maighdean mara; in Holland and coastal Flanders they are called Meerminne, Zeemeerminne or Marminne.

CUSTOMS AND ACTIVITIES:
They live in groups or as a couple with their Siren to the age of 29,600 years, not a day more, not a day less… Experience shows that they are not always as bloodthirsty as their reputation says, and sometimes they are even helpful. "When they are left in peace and not interfered with, they sing beautiful songs and warn sailors of bad weather to come, and give them news of their families on land." When whalers, armed with harpoons, sail towards the icy sea, they always bring dainty morsels for the Sirens, who are sworn enemies of whales and show it too!

Sirens are frightened of fire, torches and lanterns. They are also famous for the accuracy of their prophecies.

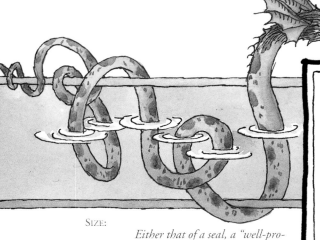

Selkies,
Sea Trows, Sea Lions

Either that of a seal, a "well-pro-portioned" human being, or a giant serpent.

APPEARANCE:

The Selkie or Sea Lion is more or less protean. When they are in their abyssal kingdom they retain their Faerie appearance. It is only when they travel outside their ter-ritories or above the surface that they assume the appearance of seals, turtles or any of the forms mentioned above. One year out of nine, they appear on the eve of the feast of Saint John when the moon rises in the sky; they gather on deserted beaches and reveal their incomparable beauty as they slide on the sand with their silky, smooth skin. They have an exquisite profile and features of "classic beauty." Their eyes are black, large and round like those of seals. Their long, thick hair is greeny blue. Their body is supple, slender, hairless, and their skin is slightly silvery. The Sea Trows wear a wide, natural belt of emer-ald scales round their waist. They have palmate hands and feet.

CLOTHES:

Naked, or sealskin. Maximilian Forestus writes in the fifth volume of his chronicles that a giant sea monster was seen on March 7, 1521, in the Sea of Norway and when caught it vomited forth a Sea Lion wearing a supple bronze armour.

Is it really a seal with a swan's neck?
  (B. Heuvelmans, *The Great Sea-Serpent*)

The origins of the Seal people are very obscure. It is obvious that early elficologists did not go very far under water and merely drew from the sources of the collec-tive elfic memory or from the writings of the last historians of the Golden Age who were themselves quite ignorant regarding their ancestors and brothers of the sea.

Although it seems quite clear that the Sea Trows are an aquatic branch of the legendary family of the Blessed of the Knolls, the ancestry of the Selkies, Silkies or Sea Lions is less clear.

Some experts believe that they are the descendants of the Fins, princely gar-deners of the underwater parks; accord-ing to others they would be the children of traveling Morgans who settled down in the Abysses; or possibly the children of Tritons and Sirens.

Barbygère states (without committing himself too far): "The Sea Lion is the rare and wonderful fruit of the pure love of Ondin and Ondine, born by the Dauphin King and fertilized by the Spir-its of the waters."

According to popular culture, with its more prosaic approach, Selkies (or Otarians) are drowned sailors.

In his meticulous, academic study on the sea-serpent (77 pages in quarto for-mat), Doctor Antoon Cornelis Oude-mans (1893) maintains that the great chimerical sea-serpent is a sort of long, fat seal: "…he is often compared to a snake, but sometimes also to a dog, a wal-rus, a seal or a sea lion. He has a rather elongated snout and sometimes vibris-sae at the end. He has folds under his throat and on the sides of his neck; he has a wide transverse mouth and very large, sparkling black eyes with red reflec-tions. His neck is very long (about one-fifth of his total length), thinner than his head and well defined by a widening at the shoulders where he has flippers like those of turtles or seals. His round body is larger near the top than the bottom, ending in a round, pointed tail of enor-mous size, since it is almost half the total length of the animal (…). His skin is described as smooth and shiny, and only twice have sightings reported the pres-ence of scales; his shiny, smooth appear-ance is due to the fact that his fur is wet and is sticking to his body. Seals look the same when they come out of the water (…). When this animal emerges

from the water he blows noisily, probably through his nose; his breath can be seen coming out from his snout and not from the top of the head, as it does with the Cetaceae. When he comes to the surface, he leaves behind a greasy mirror-like trail and gives off a very bad smell. He often swims with his head above water and he is very mobile in all parts of his body. The sea-serpent moves with vertical undulating movements, but he can also bend his body in the shape of a horseshoe, and when he does so thick folds appear on his body, as is always the case with animals with a thick layer of fat on their body. He swims like a turtle when he moves slowly but when he swims fast, undulating his body vertically, he flattens his flippers against his body. When he moves in the water, only a small part of his body is visible and his tail cannot be seen at all (…)."

The most characteristic feature in the psychology of a sea-serpent is his shyness; this colossal creature has never been known to attack anyone, even if shot at. In fact, he is rather playful, often leaping and frolicking boisterously in the waves.

It is quite obvious that Doctor Oudemans, director of the Zoological and Botanical Society of The Hague, firmly believes that the great serpent is a giant seal, on the basis of some 250 carefully checked observations. It is not the first time that scholars have attributed the origin of fantastic creatures of the sea to seals, lamentins, sea lions and walruses. In 1554, the French naturalist Rondelet

published an illustration of a monk seal "drawn from life" in his Universa Piscium Historia; the creature had been found stranded on a beach on the coast of Norway after a storm. In the same work, Rondelet mentioned another specimen, equally remarkable, whose portrait was sent from Amsterdam to a German doctor. It was said to be a creature dressed in the religious garb of a bishop, that had been discovered in Poland in 1531. "After his death, it was discovered that he was a seal."

"These monks, bishops, and popes of the sea (*Uranoscopus*) who provide the creatures of the sea with a pagan cult often assume the form of dogs, calves, serpents, or unicorns (*Unicornis*) of the sea, as do the Syreines, Selkies, Nyïxes, Colins, Faïes and Fatïaux of the oceans," Doctor Teronimous Leewenhoeck writes in his *New Wonders of Maelduin*.

It is not the first time, and it will not be the last either, that after some lengthy research, scholars have come to the same conclusion as elficologists without realizing it: because if seals sometimes appear as a fish-serpent, sea-monster, devil, woman or man of the sea, it is because some of them belong to the wonderful species of Faerie Seals. These are called Seal People, Sea Trows, Selkies by the sailors in Great Britain, Haaf-Fish in Scotland and Roane in Ireland, and Otarelles or Otarians by those of Little Britain…

FOOD:
Fish.

HABITAT:
The "seal people" live very far away from the coast, deep down under the sea. Not much is known about their dwellings, although legend has it that they live in graceful, light buildings made from phosphorescent pearls. They are said to live near the Shetland Islands, Orkneys, Scandinavia, Ireland, and the Breton coast.

CUSTOMS AND ACTIVITIES:
Intelligent and cheerful but shy. It is not they who attract the humans under water—as the Sirens and other inhabitants of the water usually do—but the men and women who hope to experience love with them. To call them to the coast it was only necessary to shed seven sincere tears in the sea: immediately one of them would appear, emerge from his skin and become lover or mistress. If anyone managed to take away the skin and hide it, the creature would remain with you as the most charming husband or the most adorable wife until they recovered their skin and slipped back into it. They would then return to the water where no one could follow them.

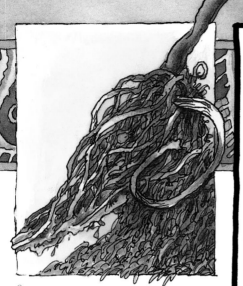

Faerie Horses

While a cloud of smoke with the clear out-line of a giant horse hung heavily over the buildings…

(Edgar Allan Poe, *Metzengerstein*)

SIZE:

That of a horse, a donkey or mule. The Kelpies of the Scottish lakes are very big. The Glashans of the Isle of Man look like pretty little foals or lambs, the Shopiltees of Shetland and the Tangye of the Orkneys are like small, long-haired ponies, covered in seaweed.

APPEARANCE:

The Beast in Cagnes, the Briette, the Beast of La Motte, the "Cheva" of Saint George in Guernsey, and the Malebeste are all terrifying because of their red eyes, their phos-phorescent fur, flaming mane, and nostrils blowing green clouds. But before revealing their infernal nature, they assume a more "pleas-ing shape like that of a Unicorn." Sometimes they also appear as sea-green billy-goats, white or black sheep, a hare, a bull or a barbet spaniel.

L isten, listen to the stories of the Faerie Horses of the rivers, moor-land and countryside. According to a story told in Artois, a magnif-icent white horse used to appear in the Place de Vaudricourt on Christmas eve while young men played there instead of going to midnight mass. The youths approached him because he seemed so gen-tle. He stretched out his neck and withers to be stroked. One of the youths who was bolder than the rest climbed on the horse's back. The animal broke into a gentle gal-lop, traveled round the square, then stopped. The lad's companions then also climbed on the horse's back which became longer and longer until twenty of them were sitting on the horse. When the mass was over, the horse was prancing danger-ously and suddenly jumped into a pond, where all the youths drowned. Since then, the infernal horse appears on the square every Christmas Eve, still carrying on his back his victims whose faces seem tor-tured with suffering. Galloping without a sound, he moves round the village. At mid-night he returns to the square where he started and returns with his victims to the abyss whence he came.

In Brittany they all rule over the waves: especially the magnificent, white Ar Gazek Klanv, the raging mare "who regulates the tides with her kicks or a gentle trot." She is followed by: Ar Gazek Gwen, the white mare; the tumultuous Ar Marc'h Glas, the blue horse who calms the waves; Ar Gazek C'hlaz, the blue mare who leads the fish; Ar Marc'h Hep Kavalier, the riderless horse, and Ar Marc'h Hep Vestr, the horse without a master who whips up the waves into their foamy caval-cades.

In Guernsey, a war-horse grows longer to accommodate a dozen people, then leaps at incredible speed over hedges and ditches and throws them into the mire in the middle of the Grand'Mare.

In the region of Albret, a red horse with a short tail stretches his back to make room for nine riders and then is off like a shot; eight of the riders are thrown onto the rocks while the ninth, who was cling-ing to his mane, disappears with him into a quagmire.

Near Carcassone is a black donkey, cov-ered in rich drapery that turns into a shroud if any one is careless enough to climb on his stretchable back. After a ride through the air and in cemeteries where tombs would rise above the ground to enable the dead to come out and sing funeral songs, the donkey dispatches the riders into the chasm of the Grand Puits…

When the night is black the Beugle emerges from the abyss in the shape of a white donkey. He picks up all the bad people, puts them on his extensible back and hurls them into the Cursed Pond. The horse known as the Gauvin du Jura drowns women on their way to the ball in a mud-pit, just as the horse Malet in the Vendée drowns its riders in a river. In Maisnil, there is the "Ch'blanc qu'vo" whose mane is decorated with bells.

The Bayart horse, a solar war-horse, born of a dragon and a she-serpent, belonged first to the magus Maugis, the Merlin of the Ardennes, before helping the four Aymon sons in their fight against the irascible and versatile Charlemagne.

When the emperor tried to drown him, he broke the stone attached to his neck and, with the heroic foursome on his back, he left the marks of his hooves on the rocks.

Faerie Horses come from very far away and a very long time ago… from the race of Pegasus and Unicorns. According to Barbygère, they have become wild and shy because people did not know how to tame them and win them over. The epic poem of Giolla Deacar extols the exploits of these "Palefrois Side" who came from the sea, of Hy-Breasail and Tirfo Thuinn who could move under water and fly through the air and who was able to carry more than six riders.

Alas, most of them now belong to evil Spirits, to demons who use them to commit evil deeds.

A rider, dressed in red, riding a beautiful black horse with flames sparking from his hooves and nostrils, gallops on the ocean: he comes to buy the souls of those who are going to drown.

Flaming horses push lone walkers towards the cliffs of Henry Chiridillès, a black knight who drowned travelers in swamps. Equally dangerous are the Irish horses of Longfield, and the White Mare of Mélusine, the war-horse of King Grallon who dwells where the town of Ys lies submerged, the Carimaro of Cléry, the "beast with four heads," the decapitated horses of the Moors, and the small gray horse of Jean Gris. In contrast, Roland's horse, often seen on the pont d'Espagne, and the poor old Widecombe nag are quite harmless. The Schimmel of the coast of Ditmarsie in southern Jutland has retained all its magical elegance and mystery.

Listen, listen carefully, the stories are the same everywhere… A white horse suddenly appears in the night, his hooves make no sound: he is so beautiful and looks so docile that riders cannot resist jumping on his back, and go for a ride… If you were ever to encounter such a horse at midnight, be sure to make the sign of the cross and say three paternosters before you get on the horse; you will see him disappear in smoke before your very eyes!

CLOTHES:

The sad Hennequée is dressed in a shroud. Some are covered in such rich drapery and saddles that they attract thieves. The Mare Margot is bridled with her tail.

FOOD:

Almost all are cannibals, especially the Ech-Ushkya of the Scottish lochs. The Elfin Chronicles mention a kind of aquatic red grass on which they graze at particular times of the year.

HABITAT:

Lacustrian and underwater kingdoms. Faerie Horses are also found on moorland, coasts, swamps, and in the cold water of lakes and fast-flowing rivers.

CUSTOMS AND ACTIVITIES:

In the past, they were the warhorses of gods, Faeries and heroes. "There was no war-horse more faithful or high-spirited in the hunt and in tournaments than the White Stallion."

The creatures of Faerieland, Sprites and Farfadets sometimes use them to travel or plow their fields.

The Nekker

When Sir Halewyn sang, all those who heard him wanted to be near him. The daughter of a king, much loved by her parents, heard him sing one day.

She went to see her father and said: "Father, may I go to Sir Halewyn?"

"No, my daughter, don't go. Those who go there never come back."

She went to see her mother and said: "Mother. may I go to Sir Halewyn?"

"No, my daughter, don't go. Those who go there never come back!"

(De Coussemaker, *Flemish Song*s)

Near Parchim, in the region of Mecklenburg, there was a dark lake, surrounded by alders and tall beeches. Deep down, at the bottom of the lake, lay submerged the town of Ninove-la-Noyée. No fisherman had ever dared venture near this ghostly place.

One night around midnight, a few very keen fishermen decided to throw their nets into the black waters of the lake. When they pulled them up they were so heavy that they could hardly carry them. On top of the writhing mass of shiny fish was a giant, one-eyed pike weighing more than a hundred pounds. While the fishermen were preparing to row back to the shore they noticed ripples on the surface of the lake and they heard the voice of a young girl rise above the water. From what she was saying it seemed that she was bringing back a herd of cattle.

"Have you counted them?" a deep man's voice asked.

"There are ninety-nine here," the girl replied. "The one-eyed pig has escaped again!"

And immediately she called him by a curious, barbaric sounding name. And suddenly the giant pike jumped out of the boat shouting: "Here I am!"

A deadly silence now fell over the lake… It was the Nekker, or Nikker, or Necker, and the Nix his companion, gathering their herd. The Nekker—which means black—is an aquatic demon-genie. (The Strömkarl and the Fossegrim live under water-falls.) Sometimes he spends the night hidden in the dunes, lying in wait for those who come to the beach to recover the jetsam left on the sand by the sea. He also hides under the bridges across the Scheldt and in a sumptuous casket placed along the bank of a stream. Those who are inquisitive and open the casket are dragged to the bottom of the stream. He snaps up swimmers and drinks their blood. He imprisons the souls of the drowned in a jug whose opening points down. His prisoners who can be heard crying and wailing on the eve of stormy nights must spin skeins of linen and seaweed until the end of time.

The Nekkers are rich. They own large underwater farms and herds that are minded by Ondine slaves. The Ondines who work in the kitchens and do the washing dry the clothes on the edge of wells when night has fallen. It is very unwise to meet them there because their cries attract the Nekkers who appear from everywhere.

Lange-Wapper

The river and the stream carry out his wishes.
(W. B. Yeats)

Demons of every kind: Ondins, Specters, Kleudes, Bokkenrijders, Berrwtlven and other horrible spirits, driven out of their territories, had in the 17th century taken refuge in a wood south of Antwerp from where they terrorized the neighborhood. They devoured cattle and sheep, ransacked farms, ravished young girls and wrung the neck of any living creature in their reach. The inhabitants were so frightened that they dared not go out any more. They decided to organize a procession to exorcise the infernal spirits. The Dean of the Chapter of Notre Dame, carrying his gold cross as protection, flanked by praying monks and Capucin friars, bravely wielding the censer, chanted pleadings towards the four cardinal points of the cursed copse. From dawn to dusk, he called, pleaded and prayed as he expelled each of the spirits. Each invocation and sprinkling with holy water aroused a cacophony of howling, beating of wings and clicking of enormous jaws.

Gradually, one by one, they all disintegrated, vanishing into smoke and whirlwinds. All of them but one: Lange-Wapper, who resisted the most terrifying attacks, hidden under an enormous stone.

He remained there, unnoticed, until all the exorcists had departed. He then proceeded towards the nearest river and jumped in… and swam upstream towards a safer hiding-place in the canals of Antwerp.

Lange-Wapper lives and sleeps in the water. He prowls along the banks of rivers, streams and canals, he haunts the town's sewers, but he only ventures onto the river banks and quays in the evening when he is driven by hunger. He will then roam the streets, orphanages, and suburbs of Antwerp in search of a victim to devour. He turns into a baby whose cries attract some kind soul who bends over the baby to comfort it… at which point he bites her head off in one giant bite! Then he divides into two and blocks both exits of an alleyway where he drives some poor creature mad before swallowing him. Sometimes he turns into a nun with the head of an octopus and presses his ghastly face against a shop window, literally frightening shopkeepers and customers to death… Because he adores macabre jokes!

SIZE:
Varies a lot: from tweny inches to six feet six inches.

APPEARANCE:
He constantly changes his appearance: from a puppy with big paws, to a baby, a young girl, a confectioner, or a monster. He is very ugly, his body is covered with scales, and his face is like that of a fish with globulous eyes. Long palmate legs enable him to walk on the water.

CLOTHES:
He loves to disguise himself like a girl and decorate his hideous, scaly body with lace and ribbons.

HABITAT:
The canals of Antwerp. Some years ago, he was known to frequent the Wappersrui and the Wapperburg.

FOOD:
Human flesh and eels.

CUSTOMS AND ACTIVITIES:
Apparently immortal. He hates humans apart from children, with whom he often plays by turning into one of them. Not only does he not harm them but he also gives them presents and sweets. He fishes and hunts but avoids churches and chapels which he fears.

SIZE:

That of a cobra or a well-proportioned human being.

APPEARANCE:

The Nâga look like dragons, aquatic hydras, and serpents with a human face. In Sanskrit their name means royal cobra which is sometimes translated as serpent; but the actual word for serpent is sorpa and not nâga.

The original wave is inhabited by a gigantic Nâga on which Vishnu sits. The ruler of the seas, the Indian Poseidon, he is known as the King of the Nâga: Nâga-râja, whom iconography represents on a throne surmounted by a dais of crowns of fantastic cobras with multiple heads.

The Nâga's face is noble and pure. The Nâgi is graceful and an elegant dancer.

The Nâga

There where the serpent goes, a god precedes him.

(K. Wentz)

At that time King Seneka who ruled in Benares entered into an alliance with the King of the Nâga. One day, the latter had left his palace at the bottom of the sea and come to earth to claim what was owed to him. He was seen by some children who started throwing stones at him, saying: "it is a serpent!" The king who was passing by on his way to his gardens asked what was happening. He was told: "Sire, it is children throwing stones at a serpent." The king stopped them and chased the children away.

So, saved from certain death, the King of the Nâga returned to his palace. There he selected a multitude of precious stones and in the night, he quietly slipped into Seneka's bedroom to give him the jewels, with the words: "this is because you saved my life, oh king!"

Having entered into an alliance with the king, he often came to visit him. According to the Khâraputta-Jâtaka, to ensure his new friend's safety he installed a young Nâgi female in the palace and taught him a mantra. The Nâga are the most famous and the most numerous genie-serpents in India. They are generous with those who honor them.

The great Hindu epic poem of the Mahâbhârata tells the story of the legendary struggle between the two clans of the Kaurava and the Pândava in a hundred thousand verses. It says that, like the Gandharva and the Apsarâ, the Nâga and female Nâgi or Nâgîni may marry mortals… One day, Arjun, the great hero, came down to the banks of the Ganges and went into the water to perform his ritual ablutions. Having completed them, he was just about to get out of the water to go and celebrate the morning agnihotra when this powerfully built hero was

suddenly seized and dragged to the bottom of the sea by the beautiful Ulupî, the daughter of the King of the Nâga, who was tormented by the god of love.

And Pându's son who spoke to Krishna was taken to a wonderful palace where Kaurava, the King of the Nâga, dwelt. Smiling at Ulupî, he asked her: "Gentle Lady, what a terrible act you have just committed! Whose is this wonderful palace and whose daughter are you?"

"Prince," she replied, "I am the daughter of the celebrated Kaurava and my name is Ulupî. Tiger among men, when you entered the water, the god of love stole my mind! Hero beyond reproach, know that I am not married; tormented by desire for you, how could I survive? Do me the favor of marrying me this very day!"

"There is one problem. On the orders of King Yudhisthira I made a vow to remain chaste for twelve years! Therefore, O charming lady, I cannot do as I would like. However, I promise to satisfy you and I have never told a lie in my life! So, dearest Nâgîni, tell me how I can be happy with you without being guilty of lying and without breaking my vow, and I will obey you."

Having heard these words, the Nâgî saw to it that Arjun satisfied all her desires, through virtue. All night long he stayed in the palace of the Nâga, only getting up in the morning when the sun began to rise.

Accompanied by Ulupî, he returned to the banks of the Ganges, there where the river leaves the mountains and enters the region of the plains. There the Nâgî left him and returned to the palace of Kaurava, but not without having first granted Arjun a special favor that made him invincible in the water.

The Mahâbhârata does not relate how Arjun satisfied the beautiful Ulupî all night long while remaining chaste. But there is no limit to the powers of the Nâga…!

DRESS:

Silky and gaudy, strewn with precious tones evoking the jewels of fabulous dragons…

FOOD:

Delicious, delicately flavored dishes. Fish, meat, fruit, milk and flowers… and all the other food presented to them, according to the religious ritual of the pûjâ.

HABITAT:

These genies build splendid residences at the bottom of the water from where they observe the world of humans and where they store extraordinary treasures of glittering gold and sparkling stones, guarded by dragons: the name of this fabulous kingdom is Bhogavati.

Their cult is most wide-spread in the Deccan and Dravidian regions. They also live at the bottom of the seas.

HABITS:

The Nâga follow the very strict rules of a king who is himself a vassal of the ruler Nâga-râja. They are faithful to their pretty spouses, but this does not exclude amorous adventures with mortals.

ACTIVITIES:

The Nâga offer magical gifts to those who worship them, answer their prayers, restore them to health and heal their wounds, except for the poisonous bites of their brother snakes.

SIZE:

Varied except for the Vougeote who always remains a little girl.

APPEARANCE:

Take on the most flattering appearances, or turn into a fish, swan, boat, any kind of fishing equipment, brand new, even into a tin of "Dudule bait, the fish pullulate"…

But as soon as they return home, they happily slip into their comfortable scaly dressing-gown and their black felt and leather newt slippers. Terrifyingly ugly: fat myopic larvae, with flaccid, transparent skin revealing a distended and grumbling stomach. Green teeth except for Grandma "with the red teeth."

DRESS:

Scaly mantle, although usually they wear the traditional local costume. The Gorgates and Farates wear large hoods and so does the Havette Beast.

The Groac'h

The ogress of the water, have you met her?
(Bryce)

In the past, to find the body of the handsome young man abducted by the Groac'h or water-witch, the "Macralle d'Aïve," people would plant a wax candle in a loaf of bread and then float it on the pond or river; after a few moments of hesitation, the "hunter of souls" would lead them immediately to the bloodless body of the drowned man. Being more delicate than their male counterparts, the Groac'h only sucked the blood of the adults and only ate the most tender of the children. This funeral ceremony was a frequent occurrence, especially at harvest time when thirsty harvesters would go to springs and fountains to refresh themselves. Shrewder than the Sénandins, they would approach the dewy banks and take on the appearance of graceful nymphs or young girls if their potential victims became suspicious. Fascinated by their physical charms, these innocents were completely fooled, failing to recognize their true identity in the green,
cold sparkle of their eyes! The Groac'h had become experts in the art of seductive deceit.

One of them used to live on the lake of the largest of the islands of Glenans in Brittany. She was said to be as rich as all the kings in the world, so many young men set out to look for her treasures; but not one of them had ever returned. One day, a young man landed on the island and climbed into a swan-shaped rowing boat that was moored on the shore of the lake. This suddenly moved off, taking him far from the shore and diving to the bottom of the lake with him, bringing him to an enchanted palace. There he met the lady who showed him her treasure; she explained that all the chests filled with gold that were lost at sea were carried to her palace by a magic current under her command. The Groac'h asked him to marry her, and he accepted.

One day when she had gone out fishing, the newly-married man started to cut up fish with his knife that he had dipped in the fountain of Saint Corentin, the saint who exorcised bad spells. The fish immediately turned into other young men who told him that the Groac'h had cast a spell on them the day after their marriage. Terrified, the newly-wed man tried to escape, but the ogress, prompted by her "hideous instinct" returned having resumed her real shape.

She caught him in a net and turned him into a carp that she then threw into her fish pond.

Peg Powler was notorious for her pendulous jaw, bloody gums, green teeth and hair. She lived along the Tees in the north of England, attracting little boys and girls by leaving toys, ribbons and lace on the rocks nearby. Having devoured her festive meal, she would place the carefully cleaned bones on the river bank. Jenny Green Teeth found her food in the rivers in Yorkshire. Mother Big Mouth hurls herself on young swimmers splashing about in mill streams; she would shake her prey like a dog to break its back, dive to the bottom of the stream to devour her meal, and then return to the surface for more. Her insatiable appetite won her the nickname of Greedy Granny. In summer children would offer her the contents of the pigs' trough in order to fill her stomach and make her happy in the hope of enjoying a quiet swim.

The Green Ogresses who lived along the shores of the many lakes in the region of Coges (Franche-Comté) fascinated men with their provocative behavior and then threw them to the bottom of the lake.

The Ladies of the Bourbonnais invited young people returning home after the ball to dance with them. Then, having seduced them they would drag them to the bottom… Gwaernardel relied on her beauty, Herodias on her strength, the Vougeote on her youthful grace, the Frisonne on her fair plaits, the Peuffenie on the "puffs," soporific jets of stream that she blew from her wide nostrils protruding from above the water. The Souillarde snatched the ankles of the water lily pickers, who, protected by waterproof leggings, came to harvest the beautiful white chalices to decorate the tables of elegant Parisian restaurants. The Wailing Frisonne imitated the cries of little children drowning and frantically beat the water with her palmed hands in order to hasten the arrival of the rescuers. Marie-Groëtte hid behind the most beautiful flowers. Madeleine with the long hair loved sitting in manure pits and nauseating ponds. The Gofe clambered up whirlpools. The Tiffenotes of Moselle were quite happy to wriggle their pink bottoms and Saurimonde la Fassilière boasted a surprising repertory of salacious propositions to make the most experienced fisherman drop dead with amazement. Marie-Griffon knitted her own nets. The Donseillas played on her exotic appearance. The Echouise turned into an eel, let herself be hooked and fished the wrong way round, and dragged her trophy, still hanging onto his fishing rod, down to the bottom of the water. The Mirtes sang so beautifully in the foaming torrents that adolescents would jump in to follow them. The Seven Ladies asked one of them to chose first and then all of them helped themselves. The Mourning Black Ladies held their head in the palms of their hands and promised the comforter the temperament of a merry widow. The Evil One of the Bas-Poitou tied her hair to the boats so as to drag them down to the bottom: "The floating lake has engulfed them, and they have been swallowed by billowing water."

FOOD:

When they cannot find small children and youths, they feed on the surrounding wild life: rats, waterhens, ducks, small cattle who come to the water's edge to drink. They are not interested in fish, although they will nibble hydras, flatworms, oligochaetas, leeches, decapods, plecoptera, diptera and a few amphibians as snacks, accompanied by groundsel ragwort tea.

HABITAT:

The crystal palace is said to be only a mirage created by magic. The Groach's real dwelling is a large ovoid shell built from solidified sludge and slime.

CUSTOMS:

Infamous; according to ancient texts the "love-sick Meuve spares neither the old man, the deer nor wild boar."

ACTIVITIES:

Lazy. Except for hunting, they do not use their sixteen fingers for anything.

SIZE:

Infinite.

APPEARANCE:

Changing. The Vily take on the appearance of the naiad whom walkers hope to see emerge from the beautiful water and floating islands, Faeries on the surface, Hydras in the aquatic abyss. The vertiginous whirlpools of their flowing hair reflect the luminous passage of drowning.

But the Vily will always remain evil, and even their childish prettiness does not succeed in concealing their sly cruelty or the cadaverous color of their skin.

DRESS:

Naked, with veils of flowers, grass and foliage.

HABITAT:

Eastern Europe. Some have even been spotted further north. "Until the sun shines again on the summer road," they remain asleep in the mud and algae, cold ponds in which the souls of the drowned have taken shelter for the winter. Gradually as it becomes warmer they come up to the surface and take residence under flowers, near whirlpools, mudholes. A few hide under torrents.

The Vila

No supernatural creature, no elf can be fully satisfied.

(Lord Dunsany)

Once upon a time there was a very pretty young girl with long blond hair. According to others she had black hair. When she walked through the village, men and women stopped work, the blacksmith's hammer stopped, leaving its limpid note hanging in the air, the embroiderer's needle missed its point, and everyone looked at her as she passed by. There was no animal in the woods or fields who did not stop running or grazing to look at her and birds forgot their song for that of the most beautiful creature.

Flowers were envious of her perfume. The river blessed her reflection. It was at the water's edge that she was happiest, not to display her charms or to look at her reflection all day long, but she found its company pleasing like that of a sister's.

It was rumored that she was the daughter of a Faerie; but her father remained silent on his death bed. Everyone loved her. The son of the lord of the manor loved her even more. He was a bold knight and so good with words that she believed his stories. He wanted to marry her, he told her, at the end of the summer when he returned from that distant country where his father was sending him. But he did not come back, because he was fickle and he had fallen in love with a wild princess in that distant land.

Every morning the unfortunate fiancée went to the river to wait for her beloved and every evening she came home alone, shedding more tears from the bottom of her heart, heaving more sighs, and losing more of the sparkle of her reflection. She was getting thinner, paler and weaker by the day, her reflection in the water increasingly absorbing her light. It was as if her reflection was more alive than the figure walking away from the river bank.

One night she did not return. People searched for her for many days without finding anything but a white veil floating on the funeral water.

Some said: "She died from grief."

Some said: "It is her mother, the lake Faerie, who took her away to comfort her."

After a while, people forgot about her because the prince had returned home, bringing with him his future wife. The whole country was busy with the preparations for the wedding.

The castle in its finery was buzzing from the kitchens to the turrets. Cook's boys, scullions and valets supervised greasy pans and sauces and set the tables, washerwomen were busy washing, scullery maids were cleaning, laundry women were ironing white tablecloths, and chamberlains were checking the polished furniture with immaculately-gloved hands. Apparently, there was even going to be a tournament.

The betrothed were in a festive mood.

But on the eve of the wedding, the prince who had gone for a walk along the ramparts suddenly heard a voice in the distance. It was a song like a childhood lament from the distant past, like the memory of some forgotten misdeed such as an old toy may suddenly bring to mind. Carried by the effluvium of sludge and damp vegetation, a woman's perfume began to permeate the air, attached to the veils of a floating shape.

Suddenly a face appeared on the surface of the water in the goblet he was lifting to his lips. A face that continued to beg him from the silvering of mirrors and from every glass and flagon laid out on the tables, pursuing him to the very heart of all the flowers strewn along his flight.

A reproachful look and voice called to him…

The arms of the princess could not hold him back, he felt like a wave pushed by the current and taken to distant shores whose flowers meadows kept receding, the ground giving way while drowning him in caresses and hair. People called out to him to come back but in vain. All he could hear was the murmuring of a dream in his ears. All he could see was a face floating on the lake, illuminated by the festive torches, a pale body rising out of the water, standing at the top of the stairs of the castle's reflection in the water, inviting him to exchange their eternal vows.

Her crown was now just a small ring of water on the surface…

So the first Vila was born. She does not swim under the limpid sky of purifying water but in the depths of an aquatic limbo, poisoned by unrequited love and bitterness. Her soul had polluted the water of the lake as it merged with it. Nothing in the transparent clarity of the water and the refreshing coolness of its banks aroused suspicion. Only the star of the epeirid in its hoary rosette does. Everything else is clarity, charm and voluptuousness, but the flower of evil grows in the Baudelairean green, because every man attracted by the sparkling flower of evil carries in him the shadow of the fickle lover. He does not know that the Ophelian sleeping beauty lying on a bed of gladioli is a witch hiding in the sweet water of the lake.

Like a Hydra, the Vila inveigles him with her promises and takes him to her palace where the perfidious nuptials are once again consummated; flesh disintegrates, sparkling ornaments lose their brilliance, substances are digested and the vegetative agglomerate of the larvae resumes its mourning. Autumn leaves cover the river and the river buries its secret in the frozen water. Deep down, the Vila coils its body around organic shadows. She will not move until spring returns; no one will come and drown in her liquid ghost.

The warmth of the sun on the water will begin to awaken her in April when the showers shake their rattle at the frogs' banquet. It will take one month for the old Vila to pass on to the new Vila, the newly born creatures, the inheritance of the Vily, at the same time faerie-like and vampire-like. During the period known as the week of the Vila, the sisters will part ways: some will remain under the water waiting for their prey, while others will roam through the woods where they will hunt.

FOOD:

The cold dish of unsated vengeance.

CUSTOMS:

Although they are sometimes involved in rural activities it is prudent to remember that the Vily are always the executors of an implacable aquatic nemesis whose very existence is a punishment for those who have forgotten it.

The Vily are immortal, they regenerate every year by diving to the bottom of native springs.

ACTIVITIES:

They protect the fish and the entire amnicolic fauna, and frighten the fishermen with their terrifying cries. They tear their waistcoats and destroy their eel pots and bow nets. When they frolic in the mill streams they clamber up the paddle wheels, destroying the paddles and millstones, and breaking down the dykes.

The Vily send torrential rains to ruin the harvest and cast mortal spells on all the pretty girls who come and sit on the river banks to sew and spin. Sometimes they cannot contain their jealousy and drag them to the bottom of the sea.

However they will help the mariners and inhabitants of the river-bank find the bodies of the drowned. They spread malaria, heal ulcers and bring the dead back to life. All Vily retreat if faced with wormwood leaves.

SIZE:

> Very tall and slim.

APPEARANCE:

> Supernatural beauty. Light and supple. Large green eyes. Perfectly oval, opaline face. Exquisitely shaped mouth with pale lips. Very long hair, brown or blond, silvery when the moon is full. Slightly luminescent body with perfect curves. Excessively soft skin.

CLOTHES:

> "White dress of such fine, silky fabric that it appears unreal, woven with the yarn from another world" (Davenson). They never wear jewelry; the jewels humans give them tarnish when they touch them.

FOOD:

> They make an effort to ingest the food of humans. In their own kingdom they feed on dreams of love and fresh water. Yet they are immortal, and give their temporary husbands very beautiful children whom they feed with their own plentiful, delicious milk.

HABITAT:

> Crystal palaces in the deepest lakes, such as Gwagged Annwn in Wales.

Fenettes, Gwagged Annwn and the Undine Lovers

There he found a faerie bathing
Stripped of all clothes
(*Li Romans de Dolopathos*)

"A thunderbolt gives birth to a spring, a broken heart to floods," the saying goes, thus too much love drowns its course…

They are called Gwagged Annwn, Gwragedd Annwfr, Vierges d'eau, Fenettes, Hade, Mümelche, Dames des prés mouillés, Seefraülein, Demoiselles d'eau, Claires Pucelles, Jeannottes, Water Elven, Urgelès… Although they are not malicious, their beauty does not bring luck. Part-Faerie, part-Naiad, part-Nymph, their elfin blood drives them mercilessly towards "passions of the Golden Age" for heroes who no longer exist.

When they throw themselves into the arms of the first-comer it is not—as it is with the Groac'h—to devour him, but in the hope of knowing Love as described in the epic poems of the distant past, guarded by memory and the murmur of ancient springs. Unfortunately, their "difference," their desire for absoluteness, for the faithfulness of Excalibur, and all their interdicts, drive humans away. In spite of the efforts of brave, patient fiancés to become worthy paladins, with a few exceptions they remain cold, sterile virgins, condemned to continue their endless, utopian quest for love forever. It even drives some of them mad…

They then sing and sigh. Their song is sad at first, then turns into a lament that ends in a strange and lugubrious voice: it is the voice of the Fenettes des îles. Sometimes their cries can be heard in the wind blowing through the willows, sometimes they scream in the howling winds of a thunderstorm. When their cries get nearer, fishermen put away their fishing rods, mowers and reapers hurry home, and walkers start running. No one dares look back for fear of seeing one of these "wild Faeries" with their willowy figure, fine features, supple body, green eyes and long hair following them: because anyone who sees the Virgin of the Waves coming towards him will be sure to die within the year.

Once upon a time there was a Faerie who lived in the fountain of Chancela,

in the region of Berry. Sometimes she went for a walk in the Lady's Meadow and the Maiden's Field: "At night the white figure of a woman would be seen to rise above the spring and disappear into time."

This Faerie was incredibly beautiful. The Lord of the manor had fallen madly in love with her and he had kidnapped her several times; but as soon as he put her on his horse she would melt away in his arms, leaving him with such a strong and lasting feeling of cold that it extinguished all amorous sparks in his heart. And it would take him more than a year to get over this feeling and think of kidnapping her again…

Oh, why did this man squeeze so hard! Did he not know that a dream vanishes as soon as it is imprisoned, and that a kind heart and tenderness is needed to warm up the water? Perhaps things would have been different if he had read more faerie-tales! Unfortunate humans who always disappoint and poor Fenettes lost in the incommunicability of enchanted water!

The poor human who had the misfortune of complaining about the excessive coolness of the water of the Chancela fountain and of his embittered lover lost his voice and was condemned to bark for the rest of his life.

In the valley of Azun in the Pyrenees there lived a Hade who had been condemned to live at the bottom of a lake, until a young man who had eaten something yet remained with an empty stomach should come to marry her. One day, a teenage boy went for a walk near the lake. He picked a grain of wheat and cracked it with his teeth to see whether it was ripe. Thus he passed the first test and he married the beautiful creature. They had children together, but because he had called her Hade or Maiden of the Water, she fell under the spell again, because a spirit must never be called by its name…

Oh, why is it that grandmothers and grandfathers no longer pass on this important piece of knowledge to their grandchildren!

Once upon a time there lived a young man who had seduced a Jeannotte of the Loire. She agreed to marry him "on condition that he never worried whether she ate or not, or whether she drank or not, because you must know that I am not like other women." They lived happily together for twenty years and had six children: three girls, two boys and an intermediary. The Lady sat at the table with her family but she did not eat or drink. However, as soon as everyone had finished eating she gathered the remains of the meal and took them to her room. But one day her husband followed her and looked through the keyhole to see what she was doing. He saw that she had removed her clothes and was putting food in an opening in her back without chewing it. She sensed his presence, rushed out and cried: "You miserable wretch, you have just destroyed our life together. Look at this skeleton you can see through the keyhole, well, it is the skeleton of our dead love!"

Certainly, our young men sometimes perjure themselves and they may be a little clumsy, but are not these Maidens of the Water rather contrary?

CUSTOMS:

Passionate, proud and haughty, headstrong when thwarted in love. The particularly difficult conditions stipulated in their marriage contracts make them almost inaccessible. For example: their husbands must never touch them with iron or push them, nor even flick them with their finger; they must not whistle at night in their company, nor embrace them too strongly, they must not smoke, call them by name, swear, expose them to the sun, force them to count beyond five, yawn from boredom, go and visit their parents, nor talk about anything else but love. They are extremely rich and are good matches for penniless farmers.

ACTIVITIES:

They know all the secrets of the water. On the nights when the moon is full, at one minute before midnight, they gather in the meadows, covered with fog and dew, and dance "lightly" until the cock crows. Their lunar hair can be seen flowing in the soft whirls of the silvery mist.

The Irish Leanan-Side resembles them very much although she looks for lovers in the villages.

The Donzelles, Demisellettes of Donzère in Provence petrify those mariners who reject them.

SIZE:

Average and graceful.

APPEARANCE:

That of the haughtiest of the white swans. Those who have seen them in their faerie form describe them as divinely beautiful: their phalaena-like hair steeped in the darkness of night or the dazzle of the sun; their skin is as white and fragrant as lilies, their pubis like the hoary Christmas bloom. Their large eyes reflect the swirls in the sky.

CLOTHES:

Immaculate feathers. Often they wear silver or red gold chains, necklaces or crowns.

HABITAT:

The first swan pair lives in the Mimir fountain, beneath one of the roots of Yggdrasil. Others live in a palace suspended in the clouds by four golden chains, or in the Blessed Isles that are thought to be the location of Sid.

Swan beings have been seen almost everywhere, stretching, flapping their wings in deep fjords, on the Rhine and the Danube, and among the coastal labyrinths of Lettermore, Glashancally, and Cashla Bay, where fresh water mingles with salt water.

The Swan Maidens

Everything takes shape around this water which thinks.

(Paul Claudel)

The oldest evocation of the Swan Maidens in distant memory is by the *filid*, the druids of ancient Ireland, when they sang at wakes in the Green Castle during the reign of the Danann.

The god Lir had had four beautiful children by his first wife Aeb. These were a daughter, Fionguala, and three sons named Aed, Conn and Fiachra. His second wife, Aoife, was very jealous. One day, she took them to Loch Derryvaragh and told them to bathe and swim in the lake. When they were in the water, she waved her wand of druidic magic and turned them into four beautiful white swans. "You will remain like this," she said, "until the union of the woman of the South and the man of the North. No friend, no power that you may have will be able to help you regain your original form, unless you look for it for your entire life, spending three hundred years on Loch Derryvaragh, three hundred years on the Straits of Moyle between Ireland and Scotland, and three hundred years on the isle of Gluaire Breanann. Because this will be your life from now on. However, you will still have your voice. You will sing the most beautiful plaintive songs of the Sidh, songs that will make men go to sleep and live their dreams when they hear your music. It will be more beautiful than any other music in the world. You will also have your mind and dignity and you will never be sad that you are birds."

Thus they lived, outside time, in the kingdom of terrestrial waters. They dazzled princesses and princes, poets and artists, always swimming on the mirage of the lakes, defying the dangers placed by men to entrap these beautiful white swans and the arrows of the hunters.

When they returned to their father's kingdom they found only ruins. The Ireland of Saint Patrick heralded the demise of the gods, and the great race of the Danann disappeared under the ruins of ancient forts, taking refuge in the underground Sidh, their last dazzling cavalcade becoming lost in the movements of the flowers.

They retained their swan shape and took refuge on an island near Saint Mo Caemóc. The monk was kind and noble, and although he preached the new religion he still respected the ancient beliefs of the land. He took them to his house where they followed the hours and went to mass. Then Mo Caemóc fetched a blacksmith and asked him to make sparkling, white silver chains for the swans. He put one chain between Aed and Fionguala and one chain between Conn and Fiachra. No danger or fatigue that the birds had endured could touch them any longer.

But King Lairgrén who ruled over the land of Connaught had heard about these Swan Faeries and tried to capture them in spite of their protector's opposition. As soon as he seized them their feathers fell off. The boys became three skinny, withered old men and the girl a naked old woman without flesh or blood. Startled, Lairgrén ran away. Fionguala then called to Mo Caemóc: "Come and baptize us," she said, "because we shall soon die. And it is certain that it is not worse for you to lose us than it is for us to lose you. Therefore bury us, putting Conn on my right, Fiachra on my left and Aed in front of my face."

After this, the children of Lir were baptized; they soon died and were buried as Fionguala had asked. Steles were erected on their tombs, with their names engraved in Ogam, a magic script from the gaedhilic era. The appropriate funeral rites were performed and their souls immediately went to heaven.

This story comes up again and again like a stone ricocheting over all the lakes throughout the world, from India to Lapland, through time if the weather is

clear and beautiful. The blue sky floats far above the earth, and from a snowy peak, a rustling becomes detached and stretches as it takes shape. Wings of cloud flap in the air, like the sails of a ship lost in the mist. A celestial music, melodious, limpid and yet all-enveloping, accompanies this magnificent parade on the silvery surface of the water. The person watching lies in wait in the rushes and sees the Swan Faeries arrive one by one: slowly, magnificently, they assume the shape of their reflection and abandon their gold chains, crowns and feather dresses decorated with hoary dew, thus revealing their pearly beauty. From there on, the story does not vary greatly, the man behaving either nobly or loutishly. And he is punished or rewarded as the case may be.

These swan creatures are sometimes ordinary princes or poor little princesses whom a wicked magician has transformed into swans for a duration that does not count in faerie life. Another spell will free them from this enchantment in the golden course of ageless time. The human lover, having stolen the habit of the girl or virgin swan, now has her in his power. He can take her home and

make her his bride; it is almost of no consequence to her. One day in spring a flight of swans will fly through the skies singing; she will answer their call, find the key to the closet where her belongings are kept, and fly home with a single beat of her wing. The man will remain inconsolable until his death, an event he is desperately trying to accelerate. But if the white habit that he stole is that of an Elf or Swan Maiden, the thief will repent it bitterly. The operation is extremely dangerous because nothing distinguishes a naked swan girl from a naked Swan Faerie, and this makes it extremely risky. He who behaves like a lout will die like one.

But he who experiences happiness with one of them will never find comparable happiness back on earth. A young man from Galway had this wonderful but fatal experience. Dazzled by the beauty of the Swans, he followed them beyond the seas to an enchanted island where every hour was "like one hundred years of happiness." Having spent seven years on this island, he decided to go and visit his parents. "They sighed sadly when he told them and made him drink from a golden goblet. He woke up on the spot he had left seven years earlier, not far from his father's house.

"For a short time he lived as he had lived before. But in his dreams he kept seeing the beautiful island and the graceful Swan Faeries. He started to waste away, refusing all nourishment, and it was obvious that his mind was elsewhere. He went to sit down on the shore of the lake where he had first seen them, and nothing and no one could get him to move… and that is where he died."

FOOD:

Swimming, they are satisfied with drops of water and ditch grass from water meadows, ponds and rivers. Otherwise, on land they enjoy the saffron gastronomy of elfic cuisine.

CUSTOMS:

The Swan Maidens are gentle, good and patient; they only become dangerous if threatened; their magical powers are without equal. The Elfin Chronicles *tell in detail the story of the wars they fought against the black Alfs and their armies of ravens.*

ACTIVITIES:

According to various legends they invented the Milky Way, the travel dreams of the night watchman, the white butterflies of the marshes, water-lilies, the silver reflection of the white birch, the umbel of the elderflower, white graphite for whitening the veils of the night washerwomen, leucrite, flora petrinsularis, *the snow and clouds; it is also said that they forged the celestial brass and the lily-like bells of the moon. They protect albinos, they lay moon stones, and they make the skylark of the marshes, the tawny reed warbler, sing.*

SIZE:

Tall and slender.

APPEARANCE:

Nixes (Nixes: feminine, Nix: masculine) are very beautiful. They are generally tall and slender, well-developed and graceful. They have delicate features and long blond hair, almost white. Adorable as children frolicking on the rocks along the shores, they are majestic in their old age, as they rest their venerable bodies in the sun.

Later, slanderous rumors described them as scaly monsters, with shark's teeth, hirsute with green hair, with fins from the neck down to the heels…

DRESS:

Red bonnet, blue Renaissance style costume. Nixes wear very full white and gold dresses.

FOOD:

Nixes are neither vampires nor ogres. They eat fish and vegetables, and they cook the black and white goats and poultry people give them in exchange for singing lessons or the repair of musical instruments that are broken or out-of-tune.

Nixes and the Lorelei

This is what the song of the Lorelei, the queen of the water, did.

(Heinrich Heine)

According to the legend, the harmonious song, "the sacred song," has its source in the Altaï mountains where a waterfall sang a most mysterious song.

"Further down," Philippe Barraqué writes in *L'Homme harmonique*, "the Boyen-Gol river attracted many animals with this natural, aquatic chanting. They grazed and bathed in the harmonious musical atmosphere of this haven of peace. The shamans told the people that it was in this sacred place that nature propagated the profound music of the universal soul…" According to the early Alfic chronicles, nature herself learnt to sing and express herself through the voice of the Spirits living in the water, the air and the leaves, and it sang the Spirits' music everywhere in order to transmit it to men and beasts. "Water also has indirect voices," writes Bachelard, "while nature resounds with ontological echoes. Creatures reply to each other by imitating elemental voices." Air and water are the most faithful mirrors of the primordial voices. The Elves and the Faeries were the first to use celestial, aerial voices to convey "harmony" to men, while the magi communicated with men through the intermediary of Aeolian harps. It was through the songs of springs and rivers that Nixes revealed the watery roads that run towards the aquatic golden age…

It has been seen how their words were received and diverted to all these countries… Times have changed and the voices of the gods have become legends, faerietales, superstitions, nursery rhymes, and fables for the "retarded," for "innocents," for children, and for eccentric poets or elficologists.

Now, it is even considered dangerous to listen to the Song of the Sirens.

Do Sirens, Morgans, Nixes, and Faeries of the Water attract young men only for the pleasure of drowning them, or to introduce them to the existence of other pleasures?

According to popular tradition, "He who is strong enough to resist their deadly call becomes endowed with the gift of music."

The village musician who is able to play the King's Melody (Nickus) on his fiddle lures the dancers to the water. He is unable to stop the "flow" unless he plays it backwards, note by note, or cuts the strings of the instrument. And it is well-known that walking, reading, and speaking backwards have always been the means of entering Faerieland, through the back of the mirror. To stop on the way and thereby break the charm would be like abandoning the idea of going further, of crossing the frontier and the bridge. For fear of being unable to resist the call of madness, for fear of entering this other world that is no longer governed by the laws of men. This is where materialistic values crumble down, this where the unknown starts…

The human being demands "butter and the money of butter." He is happy to cheat the Lorelei, the most famous of the Nixes, exploiting her beauty and her musical gifts; he has no qualms about stealing the treasure in her care, as long as she remains on dry land. He will demand that, like Ondine, she gives up her undesirable faerie attributes (these would diminish his prerogatives) and follows him onto dry land where "he feels at home," even if she dies as a result; but he will never condescend to go down to her world. His mother first, then the schoolmaster and village priest warned him against the strange woman! His imagination, entirely created by those around him, is like a nightmare inhabited by dragons, monsters and serpents who have emerged from the abysses of the ocean deeps.

Was he not taught from early childhood not to look at his "reflection," at his "reverse side"? Not to lean over ponds without holding on tight to the edge… not to go near fountains or dream of water… to close his ears to the music of the nymphs, to distrust the beautiful Ladies of the Lake whose beautiful lips conceal bleeding fangs…?

HABITAT:

The Lorelei lives on a rock on the Rhine, 433 feet high and famous for its echo, between "Goar and Oberwesel." There are Nixes in Germany, Iceland, and on the Isle of Man, but the heart of their kingdom is situated to the north of Bergen, between the Norwegian coasts, there where nature becomes legend… there where the fjords lead to the enchanted land of rainbows, sheer cliffs, liquid mists, and cascades illuminated by the sun rays of the gods sleeping in the shadow of the tumuli: Hardangers, Horne, Dalsoald, Laatefors, Sharfors, Espelandsfors, Sognefjord, and Näröfjord, all of which answer the call of golden harp and fiddle of the Nixes!

CUSTOMS AND ACTIVITIES:

They invented the fiddle, a kind of violin whose sound combines metal and gut strings.

It is said that some Nixes are young girls who committed suicide by drowning because of a broken heart. They must live among Nixes for as many years as they would have lived on earth had they not committed suicide. It is also said that the ritual dancing of Nixes above the water at sunset warns of a drowning the following day at that particular place. It is also advisable to carry a branch of oregano or a piece of steel for protection when swimming in their territory.

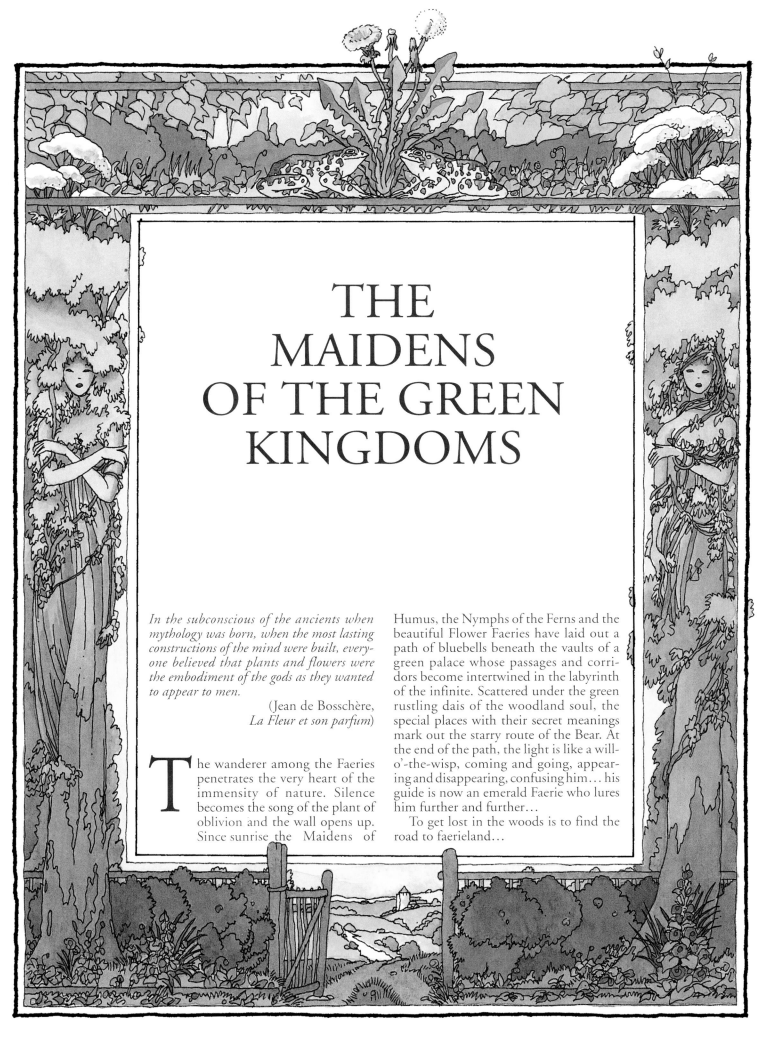

THE MAIDENS OF THE GREEN KINGDOMS

In the subconscious of the ancients when mythology was born, when the most lasting constructions of the mind were built, everyone believed that plants and flowers were the embodiment of the gods as they wanted to appear to men.

(Jean de Bosschère,
La Fleur et son parfum)

The wanderer among the Faeries penetrates the very heart of the immensity of nature. Silence becomes the song of the plant of oblivion and the wall opens up. Since sunrise the Maidens of Humus, the Nymphs of the Ferns and the beautiful Flower Faeries have laid out a path of bluebells beneath the vaults of a green palace whose passages and corridors become intertwined in the labyrinth of the infinite. Scattered under the green rustling dais of the woodland soul, the special places with their secret meanings mark out the starry route of the Bear. At the end of the path, the light is like a will-o'-the-wisp, coming and going, appearing and disappearing, confusing him… his guide is now an emerald Faerie who lures him further and further…

To get lost in the woods is to find the road to faerieland…

121

Faerie Trees

It is thought that great forests attract the inexplicable in the same way as tall peaks attract lightning.
(Félix Bellamy, *La Forêt de Brocéliande*)

"You don't need to be in the forest for very long to have that uneasy feeling that you are being 'swallowed up' by a world that is without end" (G. Bachelard). Once that initial fear is overcome, the wanderer enters the unruly tunnel leading to the high and low places of the Ancient Dwelling. Apart from the woodcutter, the forest ranger, the botanist, and the hunter, who enter the forest without really penetrating into it, it is necessary to be one of the elect, a poet, a wise man, a half-savage, an innocent or a hybrid of man, animal and faerie to be able to cross the terrifying boundary. It is even better to be a child, like Tom Thumb and his white pebbles, who knew that he would overcome the Ogre by just tackling him, or Little Red Riding Hood who was willing to undergo the wild initiation, or Hansel and Gretel who went in search of the forest's double-edged pantry; the list of tales including these little messengers is infinite. Better too to be Robin Hood or Merlin, who deliberately became lost in the forest in order to reach the "supernatural" route to Faerieland as quickly as possible.

Because how many will take fright, get lost, go round in circles, be led astray in the full meaning of the term, and die while penetrating the unfathomable universe of their subconscious? "We are in the forest. The forest is within us." What are the regular visitor and the intruder searching for? Peaceful creatures or dragons? The reality of the bluebells and the "good people," or the projection of their fantasies?

Since the Middle Ages—in the same way as in later years evangelizing blankets soaked in typhoid and alcohol were distributed to savages, and acid rain poured on forests—the church has inoculated its incubi and succubi, against all the homunculi created in laboratories and the infernal menagerie of its vices by means of the atmosphere that is excessively pure, innocent, and favorable to epidemics. There is no need to worry any longer: no one will go and hide in the forest and dream of better worlds any more!

The damage has been done, metamorphosis has begun, degradation is progressing; the most fragile species have already been struck down and are now mutating. Only a few survivors remain and they have taken refuge in the final massif... The fauna, the flora, and the Faerie Trees are all become evil...

The Faerie Trees are supernatural beings whom we must respect. The Amerindians already knew it; they would never have carved their totems in their own woods. Sitting round the last surviving boles in the Indian reserves (another unforgivable example of destruction), people told horrible stories of Faerie Sequoias cut down and sawn up, whose splinters reassembled to turn into little avenging monsters. There are other stories of Faerie Trees transformed into paper pulp that is believed to have perverted writings by infusing them with the miasmas of destructive instincts. These evil books were never those that were

Size, Appearance:
Today we have no idea of how tall these bark-clad colossi were. Dragons would crane their neck looking at their giddy pinnacles. A few ancient Faerie Sequoias in America (where there are trees 4,900 years old) give us a vague idea of what they must have been like. The Baobabs in Africa, the thousand-year old olive trees of the Mediterranean, the great cypresses in Mexico that require at least twenty-five men to surround one of them—these give us an idea of their girth and shape.

But there are also Faerie Shrubs and Faerie Flowers.

condemned to be burnt by rulers and inquisitors.

The cult of trees survived for a long time in Gaul before the arrival of Christianity. The Black Forest was the Dea Abnora, the Ardennes the Dea Ardivina. The inscriptions *Sex Aroribus* and *Fatis Dervonibus* ("to the Genies of the oaks") reflect the adoration of the Sylvans who were still ruled by the Sovereign Faeries. Those who lived on the edge of the forest empire did not much mind the destruction of temples dedicated to Roman divinities or to Romanised Gallic gods, but they were less happy to witness the attacks on the cults and rituals linked to their origins.

For a long time the presence of the Sylvan gods has survived in the memory of men through faerie-tales, legends, and relics of times past, and this attraction still exists…

"Some forests of tall trees are specters planted by Faerie Kings, transformed into trees by time."

On the feast of Saint Peter, people would go and dance round a dozen enormous oak trees in Couze (Doubs). In 1832, these were cut down by the local government. The old women of the village were scandalized by this impious act and complained: "They have cut down our holy oaks, so the harvest will be bad." Indeed since that fateful day crops and grape harvests have never been as abundant or as good as they were.

In Switzerland, each village was dominated by a little forest that protected it from avalanches. An old shepherd had his hand cut off for trying to cut a branch off one of these trees and it was with the utmost difficulty that the flow of blood from the trunk was stemmed. Every year, on the anniversary of this crime, the shepherd hears a terrifying din: it is the Imps of the

Peaks who are avenging the trees of the forest. When he wakes up in the morning, he finds that the goats and sheep are stained with blood; he can only remove this by rubbing it with earth taken at midnight from between the roots of the tree he tried to kill.

In Guernsey, the hawthorn—the king of the woods—must not be used for ordinary purposes. In lower Brittany, the wood of the oak tree is used as a talisman against the Evil Spirits who are powerless against a boat built from this wood. A figurehead made from poplar wood will take a ship to the ends of the earth, protecting it from storms and shipwreck.

The Faerie Trees have always protected enchanted love. Indeed, Faeries are known to have transformed men into trees in order to keep them close to them forever. It is said that one couple loved each other so much and so faithfully till their dying day that the oak under which they declared undying love for each other transformed them into twin trees. In the evening they can be heard talking to each other while embracing tenderly.

But they also punish unfaithful lovers, pursuing liars, crushing them and forcing them to hang themselves…

In order to rid oneself of disease, one would give it to the tree. A piece of string or cloth that had touched the diseased part would be tied to a tree and left to rot; when it started to disintegrate the cure was imminent. Trees were covered with so many bandages and cloths that they looked as if they were covered in cloth foliage. Such miraculous trees still exist, covered with scapulars, ex-votos and candles, but it is the chapels erected above their roots that are now credited with the cures.

CLOTHES:

They do not wear clothes, except for the mountain ash that is sometimes seen wrapped in a gray cape "made of moss and fog." In India, the Spirits of the Tree Faeries sometimes leave their "home trunk" and join the court of Oberon and Titania, dressed in sumptuous clothes.

FOOD:

They eat the same food as the bodies of the trees they inhabit. The bleached, "well-cleaned" skeletons discovered among the roots or in their stomachs have confirmed the existence of anthropophagous Faerie Trees. They eat animals and humans but respect the whole Alfic family, contrary to what many recent "heroic fantasy" novels would have us believe.

The great palm trees with teeth and tentacles, the bloated beetroots, the limpet leeks, and the man-eating baobabs of the Explorer's Magazine, *and all the rest of the pulsating miscellanea of popular travel and adventure, have always been no more than a joke for elficologists. But the bleeding vegetation recorded in* La Montagne morte de la vie *by Michel Bernanos, son of Georges, is genuine.*

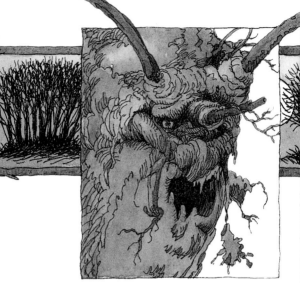

Other creatures of the enchanted boughs

A hedge of trees is looking at me.
(Jean de Borshère, *La Fleur et son parfum*)

For the Faerie people of today, Faerie Trees are the recumbent figures on the tomb of the flamboyant vassalage of their history: an army of immobile silhouettes, conjuring up the armored rides of the heroes of the Ancient Epic. They are vestiges of the great blessed cities of the Golden Age whose pillars, caryatids, and arborescent celestial vaults they were… A single touch of the bark, an ear placed against the trunk, these bring to the Alfic reception the echoes of this rustling that is memorized in the receptacle of the wood.

The Old Heads

Their trunks are usually leaning, and they support a "mass" of gargoyle-like heads: a confusion of hooked noses, eyes rolling in their white orbits, clusters of hirsute brows protruding on monstrous faces that are scowling or jovial, mouths full of stumps and splinters, gums that are rotten and toothless as a result of the boring of the bark-beetle, bumpy foreheads tattooed with wrinkles engraved by a craftsman, and crowned by royal antlers whose number and diameter reflect their power in the hierarchy.

The Sleepers

They originate on slopes to which they cling with the entire might of their rheumatic roots. Some prefer to wrap themselves around enormous stones like tumuli, taking the shape of serpentine, hair twisted like varicose veins. Buried waist-deep in the grassy sludge, the mythical appearance reveals a kind of Hydra hiding under the ground.

The bleached, twisted torso furrowed by the ravages of age displays a mass of holes and galleries creating a passage for the Mustelidae midgets. The hydrocephalic head without shoulders is screwed directly to the trunk, and the melancholic, bearded face carved out of the mass of the wood seems to be frozen in an uninterrupted sleep; but by looking more closely (on stormy evenings) it is possible to catch a glimpse of the thick lower lip, grimacing and twitching.

They are the oldest Faerie Trees. They used to form the Council of the Wise Men but being so old, their memory and powers of reasoning have all but disappeared, and they are only occasionally able to reply to the questions that the elfin woodland people come and ask them.

HABITAT:

Faerie Trees can be found everywhere on the planet and on the Blessed Isles: Avalon, Hy-Breasail, Tir Nan Og, and Tirn Aiel where they do not stop growing. Also to be mentioned are those of Chanctonbury Rings (West Sussex), Mormal (northern France), Coëtquidan: "the wood from below," the underground reverse of Broceliande. Then there are those of the Black Forest, Sherwood Forest, Morrois, Bondy, the Ardennes, the green Scandinavian abodes, the Mangrove Faeries of the Everglades, the Shaggy Faeries of the Caucasus, and the Grows of Yellowstone.

CUSTOMS AND ACTIVITIES:

The Faerie Trees are the guardians, wise warriors, and intermediaries between the visible and the invisible of the forest. It is they who decide whether or not to open the gates of the Sacred Massif to the walker.

He who enters the forest enters his own subconscious. The Faerie Tree is at the same time guardian, judge and… executioner. The main branches of the "Grand Foyaux" resemble—but only in the eyes of the hanged man—the gallows of a welcoming gibbet inviting him to hang himself.

The Limetree Faeries

Very light, aromatic foliage and a smooth trunk. They emit an impression of calm and sweet torpor, and they send to sleep those who lie down in the soporific woolliness of their nets. On waking up "you have the impression of having slept one hundred years in the arms of the most beautiful women in the world, surrounded by landscapes so beautiful that they make you want to cry with emotion" (O'Byrne). Those who have had this exquisite experience will always remember it with the greatest nostalgia. Some of these "charmed men" have been known to put an end to their life in the hope of returning to the Blessed Land of the Faerie Beings.

The Monants

From the outside, they look like ancient, hollow, worm-eaten tree stumps, their face half buried in the mossy layer. On the inside, the trunk extends below the ground, forming a kind of acoustic, spiral tunnel leading to the cavernous Alfic kingdoms. The Monants are thought to be the ears of the Gnomes.

The Leafy Faeries

Only their foliage is Fey. Between April and October the evolving shapes of their "Tenant Spirits" can be seen watching and moving in the foliage: clumps of leaves, soft clouds and moving, whispering figures whose structure changes constantly as they stretch, disperse and regroup, their multiple eyes shining in the light. From November onward, these "Leafy Nymphs" fall with the leaves and turn into invisible, gray birds.

Fire-damaged Woods

These are the famous burnt trees that so terrified the monks reclaiming the land, because they reminded them of the pillars of Hell: "They burnt without ever being destroyed by the flames." Faerie Trees often being the mirrors of the soul, Novalis only saw in them a "flowering flame." He was right: the Fire-damaged Woods, far from being diabolic, guided those Elves who had lost their way during the flight of the Faerie People to sacred woods and welcoming elfic knolls.

The False Faeries of Verzy

Low, extravagant trees. Their branches are as twisted and tortured as any imagined by the German romantic painters. They are only found in the forest of the mountain of Reims, near Verzy, a village renowned for the quality of its champagne. It is rumored that it was the wanton intoxication of a few Nymphs and Dryads that inspired this blossoming of Faerie Groves, claimed by the ancients to be "haunted by the little singing heads of the moss pickers."

The Willow Faeries

At the time of the April moon, the May moons, and the moons of the first seven days of November, these large, shaggy tadpole carcasses resemble giant, disheveled mandrakes. Grouped along hedges or crouched along the banks of ponds, their hollow trunks conceal the aquatic Meuve, Sylvans and other children of the dryad divinities. They are also used as a hiding place by the Lycanthropes who come to remove their wolf-skins and conceal them in it. At night, the Willow Faeries uproot themselves and follow the traveler along empty paths, stopping when he stops to look round and following him again when the unfortunate wanderer resumes his terrifying journey. They show him the whole repertory of their most frightening grimaces, blowing their icy musty breath on his neck.

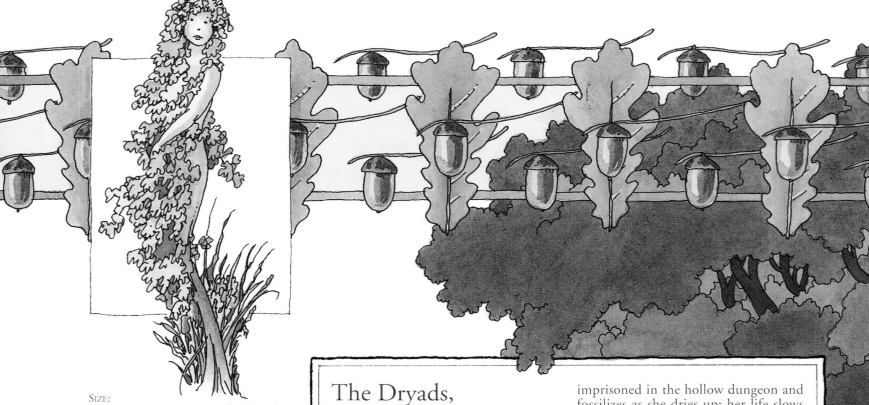

Some are very small while others are two to three feet tall.

APPEARANCE:

The Dryads are Nymphs of the forest, in the same way as the Nappées are the Nymphs of the meadows and copses. They are all very beautiful, tall and slender, slim but vigorous. "The body ends with an arabesque representing the trunk and roots of the parent tree. The skin sparkles like flowers in the light" (Sebaldt Kraft, Causeries autour du Grand Veneur, *1783). Their voice is so clear and musical that it could be mistaken for the bubbling of springs, the rustling of leaves or the song of birds whom it amuses them to challenge, singing endless trills and cooing. Their long floral hair changes color according to the season to match the foliage.*

The Faerie People have dedicated several flowers to the beauty of the Dryads, including a small orchid that has been named the "lady's slipper" because of its arched chalice, and a graceful plantlet of the harvest that they named "Venus's looking glass."

The Dryads leave behind them the persistent fragrance of underbrush on a spring day after an April shower.

The Dryads, the Hamadryads

Listen to the Dryads.

(Norman Gale)

The Hamadryads (*drys, drus*: oak; *hama*: with) are nymphs who live with and inside the Brother Tree without ever leaving it. In the middle of March the Dryad, infatuated by the rising sap, hears the call of the heralds of the Little People blowing their calyx-horns, and breaks loose from the bark to join the first swarm of sylphs. But the Hamadryad does not leave the dense cell of the cambium, or the phloem that houses the sylvan soul, the nerves and the green blood. Driven by a profound impulse, she rests on her roots and breathes in the thousand lives of the renascent humus through her thousand rootlets; she stretches along the trunk as far as the smallest branchlets, sweeping back all her amorous pith whose surplus swells the buds that burst open, and illuminates her still sleepy crown with a tender amorous aura.

It is impossible to describe the Hamadryad, since the only shape she has is that of her original tree whose fate she shares. She suffers, breaks and cries when the tree's flesh is cut—but she lives on even when it dies. If it is uprooted, she flies away and looks for another home in the oak grove. After many centuries when the ancient giant dies, she remains imprisoned in the hollow dungeon and fossilizes as she dries up; her life slows down and becomes like a kind of dream. When the carcass has disintegrated, and turned to dust, she remains on its site like a ghostly Fumarole… unless a generous oak invites her to come and share his fate.

There are ancient giant oaks, with powerful boles and branches as strong as their trunks as a result of having opened their hearts to so many mourning, grieving Hamadryads. (These are found in particular near the château of Comper in Brocéliande.)

Rivulets of dazzling rock crystals with a salty taste have been found under the sprawling canopy of the Nordic forests, concealed among fallen leaves and acorn husks. After careful examination an explanation was found for this strange phenomenon; the salty crystals were certainly tears shed by the Hamadryads over the centuries.

Later and in another region, a botanist traveling through a vast oak grove in the Schwartz Wald or Black Forest, reported that his eye was caught by sparkling crystals on the ground, above which a curious azure blue creature was flying, consisting of elegant spindles of a steamy whiteness and transparent wings; it flew away when he got nearer. There is an inspired painting by Diana Stanley that, apart from a few details, illustrates a similar scene.

The oaks inhabited by the Hamadryads are always visited by the small emerald green foliotocole, the messenger of the Flora and Fauna Faeries.

CLOTHES:

Although always naked, the Dryads, unlike the Nappées, are extremely modest, and they turn immediately into an arbuscle as soon as somebody approaches. They often carry axes or javelins to stop anyone who dares to attack the trees.

FOOD:

Fruit, berries, and flower nectar. Water from the secret fountains of youth. The very small ones who need very little liquid are happy, after playing with the Pilly-wiggins, to drink from the small goblets provided by pitcher plants, nepenthes and sarracenias; they dance around these at night in the light of the tiny lamps of the ragged robin (Lychnis flos-cuculi).

HABITAT:

Driven away by woodcutters and the unfortunate destruction of the universal forest, they doze in the inmost recesses of the "Ancient Massif," inside oak trees that they leave in summertime, sleeping on the moss, in flowers and among roots.

CUSTOMS:

Born of the union of trees and gods, they usually mate with Fée-tauds, Faeries, Spirits and wood-land gods, but some of them like Eurydice may marry mortals on condition that they have been touched by the grace of the muses.

ACTIVITIES:

They protect trees and their mere presence embellishes the woods. Immortal within the protecting bark, they may die if they leave their shelter.

SIZE:

Bent like a little old lady.

APPEARANCE:

Those who have seen her describe her as tiny, shriveled-up and limping. Lively little eyes, sparkling like her fruit. The long hands with hollow fingers, through which she blows to summon the People of the Mosses, clutch the carved handle of a stick "broken" off one of her branches. Her penetrating eyes delve deep down into the visitor's soul. Her smile expresses infinite goodness, but when she is sad or furious, the wrinkles in her face show all the cuts, wounds, notches and burns borne by the trunks of trees.

CLOTHES:

She is dressed very simply in a long green dress, with a black and purple apron, the colors of her berries, and a large fragrant white shawl, like the starry foam umbels of her flowers, knitted into her floor-length hair. She carries a bag full of seeds that she throws out by the handful everywhere she goes.

FOOD:

Rain water and grains brought to her by the birds, who in turn eat her abundant fruit.

The Old Mother

Where are you going, Old Mother of the Woods?
(Peter Woodruff, *The Repentant Woodcutter*)

On the eve of each May 1, a farmer left the farm with a "maypole" in his hand and, instead of taking the road to the village, he climbed a steep grassy path leading to the wood. It was the custom on that night for a man to take a "maypole" to the window of his loved one. The choice of scents in the bouquet, the combination of flowers and the branch used as pole informed the lady as to his amorous

or contemptuous feelings towards her. In this secret language, the heliotrope means "I love you," the ox-eye daisy "do you love me?" the double violet "love is shared," the nettle "love-sickness," and the fir-tree "whore."

It had been a very long time since the farmer had scattered such messages on the shutters of pretty young ladies. He had a wife and three grown-up sons and he never failed to carry out his ritual of placing a twig of eternal ivy on the withered cheek of his sleeping wife: "I am attached, or I die."

While he was slowly climbing the hill shrouded in mist, he was careful to avoid the hidden paths used by the elfin processions on Faerie night when they move from one knoll to another, paths it was

She was born in Scandinavia but the infinite multiplication of flora has taken her everywhere in Europe and the world. She is found mainly in forests but also near houses that accept her presence "to their advantage." She is not rebuffed by old abandoned gardens, factory yards, waste land, or the ruins of unused buildings. Majestically and humbly at the same time, she holds out her hand to everyone, from the smallest to the largest, to distribute her gifts that the stupid despise. She does this in spite of the repulsion and distrust felt towards her by the ignorant recipients—did not Judas hang from her branches? She lets children carve whistles, blowpipes and toys from her branches.

She has many sisters, hidden in ash trees, elm trees, hollies, alders, hazelnut trees and fruit trees: Elda Mother, Fraü Holunder, Plantamyne, Hyldeqvind, Mama Paduri, Grand Chapeau, Fraü Ellhorn, Churn Milk Peg, Marzanna, L'Encoiffée and Blanche Main.

ACTIVITIES:

In spite of everything that has been said or that people have been made to believe about the crimes of the elder tree (that its berries are poisonous, or that its flowers have a horrid smell), the Old Mother is an excellent Faerie. She protects and watches over the happiness of those who come and ask her advice. Those "in the know," the "gatherers of medicinal herbs," those who still have "green fingers" and who listen to the wood, whose spontaneous intelligence is still intact, are well aware of the beneficial properties of her humble treasures: the black elder (Sambucus nigra) is anti-neuralgic, sudorific, emollient, diuretic, resolvent, and purgative.

The Faeries used to produce a cheerful champagne in eight days (the recipe still exists) by mixing 4 ounces of dried flowers, three-quarters of a pint of wine vinegar, 3 pounds of sugar and 10 gallons of water.

advisable to avoid. Showing the greatest respect, he began to walk under the canopy of the dark foliage. Even without a lantern (perhaps habit and the protection of the woodland spirits guided him), he walked straight to a large elder tree dominating a glade at the foot of which he placed his offering of freshly-cut primroses (*Primula veris*). The Old Mother of the Elder Tree gently nodded her wrinkled head and the old man walked down the hill, confident of another year of abundant crops and happiness for his family.

On his deathbed he made his sons promise that they would continue the tradition. But the eldest and second sons were swaggerers and miscreants, and they soon broke their promise in spite of the protests of the youngest brother. In order to get

rid of the whole tedious situation once and for all they climbed the hill, armed with axes, with the intention of doing away with the tree.

When they came back they looked like ghosts, dazed, ashen, covered in splinters and fragrant sap; they went to bed and never got up again.

Next morning, when the youngest brother went to see what had happened, the elder tree looked untouched. The young farmer laid down his primroses and the Old Mother smiled at him.

For years and years, grandchildren and great-grandchildren never forgot to take their maypole offering to the Old Mother, and the cuckoo sings there even more joyfully than it does elsewhere.

The Pillywiggins

Darling, please do not cut the flowers any more.
Janet, why do you cut the rose
That looks so beautiful among its leaves,
Thus killing the pretty child we have together?
(Francis Jammes, *Child*)

SIZE:

Pillywiggins are the final links in the evolution of elves, and with the Tiddy Ones of Lincolnshire they are the smallest: half-an-inch. But all have the power to become even smaller, to grow bigger, or to change both appearance and size.

APPEARANCE:

Faeries, Vairies and Pillywiggins, both male and female, are extraordinarily beautiful. As a result of inter-marrying with dragonflies and butterflies they have developed wings, antennules and various other body parts that they proudly display as an elegant, natural armor.

Eternally young, as time goes by they have a tendency to assume some of the characteristics and colors of the place they live in and of the flowers and plants they eat.

DRESS:

Light muslin, flower petals, tightly-fitting jerkins made of velverette, lizard or snakeskin. They wear acorns, corollas and flower bells as hats.

The Pillywiggins have kept their divine authenticity mainly in Scotland and all over England — except in the Midlands, where they are becoming increasingly rare…

"They have become small and have lost their power, but they are surviving," Lady Trossop wrote in her diary after a long walk "through the topiary garden which hums with their Happy Presence."

It is a fact that English parks and gardens, green relics of the Garden of Eden, are ideal homes for them.

It is in the tranquillity and harmony of the English countryside that the Pillywiggins have chosen to take refuge. There, where the absence of railings and walls allows lawns to merge into the landscape, where branch by branch the rhododendrons naturally become wild again, where the yew tree's broad canopy and sprawling roots reach into the woods… where the ornamental pond leads back to its source, the domesticated duck to the wild teal and the idea of the garden back to its dream…

It is along paths such as these that the "Approaching Being" can catch hold of them… when a walk becomes a timespan with neither beginning nor end.

It is the moment of the "true mirage" when the mist clears before the eyes… allowing the discovery of the realities of the invis-

ible, revealing a luminous path leading to the green, virgin gardens of faerieland tht are sometimes glimpsed through the evanescent layers of the visionary paintings of the Pre-Raphaelites. It is at this moment that Arthur Rackham's delightful creatures and Cecily Mary Broker's flower children come to life, humming and fluttering, and the whole enchanted fauna of a wish finally come true becomes tangible.

It is best not to try to describe the extraordinary beauty of Pillywiggins at play in their paradisiac biotope. The most banal setting becomes transformed when touched by the presence of elves! Flower-like creatures, fluid and luminous, fallen from the whimsical crown of gods, born of celestial efflorescences and the sublimation of the elements: cuspidate Vairies from Suffolk, wondrous lilies and plumules from the marshland of Bodmin Moor, the flabellate beaks of the flower-dwelling Culottins demolishing lupulin, long-eared acorn-eating Patafioles grazing on the green boughs, Farisées with crested craniums nibbling the cerulean carpet of forget-me-nots, Faeries of the flax fields climbing up the tall plants above toothed blades of grass, groups of cheeky Gniafs who, having feasted on clover, now ride on guerliguets in pursuit of the Lawn-Cat beneath the hoops of the nymphs, Feerins from Lancashire, friends of the Sylvanians, tip-toeing on arched feet as a result of trying to reach the bells of hyacinth flowers, minuscule Tiddyfollicoles with small-horned helmets, aristate and downy Processionaries leaving a trail of sparkling arabesques on the green carpet of moss… All these little people, stagnicolous, aerial, small creatures of nettles, of aignail and surcule, of sphagnum moss, musicians of the glassy bells of the dew, young Nymphs of the woodland with sparkling eyes greedily inhaling the scent of wood anemones and primulas, spring flowers whose perfume is so divine that the inebriated senses of the person who sees them are unaware of their intoxication… They vanish as soon as they are glimpsed, leading the observer's spellbound intelligence to doubt this ephemeral yet unforgettable experience…

In an instant the Hotties of Essex turn into green-eyed swallows, the Pillywiggins become toads, pebbles or dragonflies again, the singing of the nymphs sounds merely as the trilling of a finch, and the "Dazzling Vassalerie" becomes a piece of glass shimmering in the evening mist.

"… As the sweetly scented air drifts gently away, only the winding wake of a Pillywiggin's flight remains" (Petrus Barbygère).

HABITAT:

The parks and pleasure gardens of Ireland, Scotland and England. There are some Alvens, cousins of the Faeries, in Holland, and a few families in the north of France on the border of the Belgian Ardennes.

FOOD:

Pollen, sap and the nectar of flowers, shining dew and the beauty of Eden.
The "Greens" are so called because they eat tendrils, buds, shoots and young leaves, and because they blend in with the foliage when they are not moving. The "Grays" prefer lichen and have a green and gray watered-silk appearance... while the Tiddy is green with a velvety sheen like moss.

HABITS:

The "Wild Hunter" is their only enemy. Faeries and Pillywiggins are peaceful creatures, but they hate to see the destruction of plants and they can cause the death of humans who destroy them for dubious reasons or none at all. But to please them a person needs only to plant a flower or a tree.
They hibernate from November to April, when they are woken by the call of the cuckoo.

ACTIVITIES:

They dance, gather honey, make love, flutter, frolic and take care of the smaller fauna and flora that they protect. They leave the task of looking after the taller forests and their inhabitants to the other woodland Spirits.

The Tisanières

See this plant, its shape expresses the living memories of the whole of evolution.
(Rudolf Steiner,
L'homme dans ses rapports avec les animaux et les esprits des éléments [Triade])

Size:

Not very tall.

Appearance:

Tisanière is beautiful; her presence evokes a fragrance, a pleasing freshness and a kindness that emanate from a reassuring shadow. Her figure is not clearly defined, nor very characteristic. She looks like a grandmother, a neighbor, an old aunt whom we loved very much and whose features we recognize in her: a long nose, a wrinkled chin, a prickly kiss, or cheeky eyes full of fun as she bends towards us to listen, comfort and take care of our cuts and bruises.

Others have seen her as a witch, hunch-backed, cross-eyed under wiry eyebrows, a nutcracker chin, her hooked nose bent to mushroom level to sniff out bad herbs, her mouth sneering with malice; with a long tail dragging behind dirty rags. Her legs are as skinny as thorny twigs, her gray hair ruffled with thorns.

She has long been seen as a gatherer of medicinal herbs, bent double with age, eyes like herbal infusion and her hair piled up high like a boletus on a mossy cushion.

Once upon a time there was an old woman who was gravely ill. Doctors said that nothing or no one could save her. The dying woman then whispered to her granddaughter who was sitting next to her: "There is a plant that grows on the highest peak of the highest mountains. It cures the sick and saves their lives. But the journey is so long, so difficult, so full of dangers that I dare not ask you to go and get it."

"How would I recognize it?"

"Someone will point it out to you."

The child left immediately. She wandered along the roads in search of the plant of life. The stones hurt her feet through her shoes, and soon the road became like a river of fire. In the evening she sat down under the only tree she could find. She was hungry and thirsty so she took out the few victuals she had in her bag: a small gourd and three crumbs of stale bread. No sooner had she spread her food out on the white napkin on her lap than a magpie came to sit next to her: "Would you have some bread for my babies? I do not want anything for myself, only for my little ones who are crying in the nest."

And the child shared her crumbs of bread. The next morning, having slept on a bed made of moss and three leaves, she continued her journey. The land around looked like burnt earth without any shade to cool down and rest. She had to keep walking because as soon as she stopped to catch her breath she felt as if the embers under her feet would set her skirt alight, turning her into a torch.

Yet, she never once thought of going back because she knew that on the highest peak of the highest mountains that she was climbing grew the plant of life.

The evening was not like the evenings in the valley where the shadows grow longer to provide a refreshing cool. She stopped in the only small patch of shade she could find around her and sat down on the edge of a dried-up well. As soon as she took out her gourd she heard a little voice rising from the bottom of the well: "You cannot see me because I do not even have enough water to have a reflection. Pour a little water from your gourd into the well because otherwise the only thing I shall have in common with a well will be the name."

So the little girl sacrificed the contents of her gourd, because a well without water can no longer be a well; then, hungry and thirsty, she fell asleep exhausted.

The following morning, she set off once again without ever thinking of turning back, because on the highest peak of the highest mountains grew the plant of life. She walked for a long time along the long road that was becoming steeper and hotter as she went on. Around her the landscape was looking increasingly like a desert, and serpents of fire whistled on the pebbles. When at the end of an evening whose day she no longer knew she finally saw the peak of the highest mountain, the sun had blackened her skin and burnt her eyes. She thought she had become a shadow without shadow.

She could feel the plants under her fingers but she did not know which one to choose. Had she come this far for nothing? Then suddenly in the night of her eyes, a shadow seemed to detach itself and she felt a movement of air against her cheek and guessed the beating of a wing; as her sight was returning she recognized the magpie pecking at a cloud of rain, and it began to sing. Suddenly she felt happy and satiated. It was no longer a magpie nor a well but a Faerie she was looking at. She recognized her grandmother, beautifully healthy, smiling at her as she handed her a plant that seemed to grow between her hands, ever taller and ever greener.

This is how *The Elfin Chronicles* tell the story of the Faerie of plants and medicinal herbs. She is known to mythology as Tisanière. Every flower is the work of a Faerie, and the entire vegetable

kingdom is a book and a garden of Faeries. The whole elfin history is contained in the grass, each blade of which is a reduction of the cosmic Tree linking the terrestrial to the celestial.

The Tisanières live in this meadow. To gather the fragrances, essences and quintessence of elfin thought, to distinguish between the subtle principles—the difference between the dark and the light, the venomous and the elixir—a very wise old Faerie was needed. A Faerie who would have slowly lived through all the phases and stages: from the ether to the grain, from the flower to the star, from ring to ring, slowly climbing up the spiral of a dendrochronology with neither a beginning nor an end. Her art has given Flora, the Nymphs, the Imps, and the People of Faerieland eternal

youth and immortality. By infusing the Spirit of the Golden Flower, the Tisanières have discovered the source of eternal youth. They have taught knowledge to the "listeners" and the wise ones among them have understood. Through legends, popular beliefs, herb soups, old wives' remedies, the witch's gruel, family recipes and the medicine of plants, the Old Art has been transmitted, even among mortals.

Like the Unicorns, the Tisanières have long disappeared from the countryside, but the perfume of their "influences," the memory of their "wish fulfilment," grafted on the wild branches of spells and talismans, old customs and beliefs, continues to decorate the legendary herbarium…

Clothes:
Originally she wore the green dress of the Wise Women with a train of royal foliage, but one more often remembers more sober garments: a white collar decorated with a brooch whose forget-me-not motif was among the first pleasures of childhood flower gathering, a cozy glazed apron, a shawl interwoven with flowers and birds of paradise; the same birds of paradise whose songs are heard before going to sleep. Or strange old rags, black, threadbare and veiled with spider's webs.

Or they may be dressed in gray flannel, carrying bags of coarse cloth filled with fragrant herbs and leaves.

Habitat:
Everywhere in the world, in huts or cottages buried in a sea of ivy, Russian vine, honeysuckle and Polygonaceae. At the heart of an interior overrun with armfuls, bunches, or the strewings of a thousand herbs that are drying in the attic, hanging from the beams, infusing in pots or being distilled at the bottom of large vats. And on the pot-bellied stove and in the pot in the hearth where the vapors of incense and the sighs and whispers of kettles sing and bubble.

Food:
Tisane, infusion, tea, decoction, stock, macaroon and a small drop of eau-de-vie.

Customs and Activities:
Among their secrets they have left the knowledge of healing plants.
They have bequeathed the good use of medicinal plants, the art of preparing plants, of infusion, maceration, decoction, and recipes for angelica wine.

Flower Faeries, Floriales, Floralières

In May the Faeries are busier than ever…
(G. Hervillier,
La Teinture des physiciens et des sophistes)

SIZE:

Average, small, very small, or minuscule.

APPEARANCE:

They are the prettiest of the Nymphs. Giving birth to flowers, living in flowers and for flowers, they share their sparkle, grace and elegance.
In order to pollinate the flora, they adopt the antenullated, winged and colored lures of insects and butterflies. Their essence is the very essence of nature and they have the power to turn into whatever plant, animal or Faerie being may be appropriate at a given moment.

CLOTHES:

Most often naked, they borrow elements of the flora and fauna that surround them, or dress up in the beautiful robes and jewels of Elfirie: spangled robes, decorated with feathers, pearl necklaces, bracelets and anklets, embellished with garden emeralds.

HABITAT:

Underground passages, leaves, riverbanks, roots, flowers. The Noctivagues prefer lorules and overhanging filamentous lichen or the microscosms of the marshes.

The Florales come out first. At dawn, their queen, with three knocks of the yew scepter commanding the "armies of the element," summons her cortège of workers who live below ground, in the oak groves and the deep califlorous mists. One by one, wing by wing, in fragmented flights, the fluidiform subjects of the dragonfly population emerges from the night that is dissipated by the morning; yawning, still sluggish and creased with sleep, they flap their wings and unfold. An apprentice, recognizable by her nigricorn bonnet, is crying because she cannot find her baskets with the phials containing extract from the mountain ash tree. Behind the royal train of the queen's dress, the milky-winged creatures shake their antennules, stretch their leaf-like legs, and produce a melodious musical scale; they chat, jostle, compare the softness of their skins and the elegance of their wings, they adjusts their umbels, quarrel for two pence, and finally respond to the orders as they line up in an erratic row. A planirostral dowager blows her ivory hunting-horn and sounds the start…

The cavalcade deploys into the wood. Viviane leads the march, dressed entirely in green silky velvet. Her complexion is milky and her hair red. Her beauty is enhanced by the color of her coif, that stands out against the woodland background. Nothing more beautiful could be imagined since Merlin's reveries. The squirrel is the living sketch of it. She deliberately walks along ponds and rivers and over the mirrors of puddles to compliment her reflection.

They have stopped in the middle of a building site, a large space, rough and coarse, filled haphazardly with all sorts of vegetation by a primitive god who knew no better. It is beautiful, it is impressive, it is wild: all that remains now is to pollinate the spirit, to sow, to graft the daydreams onto the shrubs, to plant out the herbs of attraction, to lose the paths, to embroider grace and enchantment; they also added mayflowers, September berries and gossamer as they did to the protective hedge of country genies.

When Viviane clicks her fingers everyone unsheaths their dibbles. "Do add armfuls of tall rosebay willowherb and lots of foxgloves to brighten up these thickets: I think there are never enough of them. I would also like the branches of this beech tree to descend lower, like the curtains at an entrance. We could weave a portico of hawthorn to achieve the effect."

As she steps back, she pictures the architecture: an illusory façade with a moon-like rose window at the heart of a tympanum of lime trees; she abolishes the walls, pushes back the vanishing point of the horizon with perspectives of vaults, towers and bartizans; and she gives over the altars of repose to bluebells and lilies.

So the Flower Faeries continue gardening, their wings rustling and humming, catching a beating of light and flying further. The pedestrian workers make their

way along the paths with tiny leaps; they plant, prune, and cut lacy edgings round the leaves.

Perched on a rock, Viviane supervises the work, now encouraging and now chiding.

"Aglaë, I have told you a hundred times not to overdo the red! What brings emphasis to the golden hues of a country landscape does not suit the sylvan atmosphere of woodlands. The coolness of light and dark, the shades of green are the jewel-case for the pearl! The cushion on which the star rests! The receptacle of virginal emanations! Here, the idea of white comes to life, deaf to the suggestion of the mosses, inventing a spontaneous flora made up of oxalis, arums, stellaria, bridal anemones speckled with misty folioles, coifs, calyxes, limbs, and immaculate communicant corollas. I want the walker to get lost here; I want the meadowsweet to hold his memory, to distill it and burst it like a bubble, dispersing its particles in the rays of the umbellules. Thus all that he will remember of the martagon lily, the milky rennet and the angelica will be the beauty of our gossamer veils, fragrant with the perfume of the asperula."

Entering deeper and deeper into the sanctuary of the forest, they stop near a Nemeton, dominated by millenary oak… then after a moment of respectful silence they continue working.

"Stop! don't forget, no flowers near the 'venerable one.' Look at his powerful armor, the beard and wrinkles, the royal head of hair. It would be wrong to surround him with daisies, buttercups, and chattering, turbulent bluebells; but it would be wise and respectful to remove these veils of acacia and replace them with a more austere background of leaves. Let us surround the sacred knoll of his roots with a blanket of lichen and carpet of ferns, crowned by a large ring of *Phallus impudicus*; let us venerate him with the incense of parasol mushrooms, russulas, amanites and lactarius, and let us provide guards of holly."

She has only just finished her speech when a green man descends from the branches, landing in the middle of the crowd of workers: one of those ligniform, hairy elves, with horns on his forehead, and a hirsute body, erect with phallic intentions. "Run for your life!" the cry goes up.

Panicking, as is expected of Nymphs, they scatter and fly away, hotly pursued by the Faun whose hooves echo on the ground. His hairy hand catches and tears the veil of one of them who just has time to turn into a doe and leap over a bramble hedge. The fleeing bodies are all changing shape, turning into hares, weasels, dragonflies, and thrushes; they disappear into the air, into holes and into thickets. But it is the queen whom Sylvanus is after. At the top of a hillock he throws himself on top of her, putting his arms round her, and thus entangled they roll down the slope. Sometimes he is on top, sometimes underneath, and every time his appearance seems to change. Sometimes pieces of his white beard roll off in rings that surround him and reveal a golden body… Finally when they reach the bottom of the slope, Viviane's white body has become free of its robe and she lies among the mayflowers, embracing a beautiful youth whose pointed ears are the only clues to his origin.

"My Puck, Merlin, Robin," she whispers, mixing her red hair with his.

"My Flower, Viviane, Marianne…"

Because he is all of them at once, in the same way that she is each one of them too.

FOOD:
All the pollen, nectar and sap, even if poisonous, on which some of them get drunk. Very fond of fruit: cherries, grapes, berries. Their favorite pear is the Janrinette. They cook sap in winter and distill parigline.

CUSTOMS AND ACTIVITIES:
The same as those of woodland and field gardeners. Under the guidance of their queen they cultivate and organize the flora and look after it. They protect the species, sowing and layering and ensuring their survival. They suggest ideas for the color, fragrance, shape and combination of the plants, and they put forward sweet subterfuges to attract the "visit" of the intermediary fauna needed for reproduction.

They are rumored to practice liabanomancia.

The Flower Faeries have given nicknames to many flowers and plants: bell-flower for bindweed, mariettes for the campanula, scarlet pimpernel, chickweed, or sun spurge for the euphorbia, strangler for the margeline and many others.

They love the flowery, paradisiacal greenery of the English churchyard, but they bemoan the sad sterility of those in many other countries where only abandoned tombs and ones illuminated by the spirit are bedecked with flowers.

The Green Ladies

SIZE:

The Vertes Velles are dwarves, no taller than the stem of a flower or a blade of grass; some are so small that they disappear in the moss; the Green Ladies and Maidens are as tall and supple as a young fir tree.

APPEARANCE:

It is difficult today to describe a Green Lady, daughter of the flora and light. Sometimes she takes on the appearance of the ancient nymph that she once was: the wild virgin with her skin marbled with ivy and the golden coins of the acacia; at other times she appears in the veiled shadow of a jadelaine. The Vougeotes are graceful, the Verdelettes minuscule, the Wild Ladies lanceolate and nectareous, the Green Limbs bewitching. Sometimes their beauty conceals the face of a shrew and the appetite of an ogress.

CLOTHES:

The Green Ladies do not owe their name to the color of their skin but to the color of their clothes: dresses, tunics, veils, coats, hoods, skirts, breeches and slippers. Their dress combines all the shades of green. The most noble among them wear a red hat, the smallest ones a foxglove hat.

Crowds of men of the forest with their friends the Ladies of the Forest, the Green Maidens, and many even more surprising ones.
(Jean Paulhan, *Lalie*)

"Faeries, black, gray, green and white,
You moonshine revelers, and shades of night…"
In the *Merry Wives of Windsor* Shakespeare brings all these Faeries together in a single color, that of the round moon. All the colors merge in the silvery serpentine of the dance, but when the early morning lights silence the notes of the mustanlaria, each one stands out green, white, red or blue.

The Greens were Faeries in the woods before becoming the Beautiful Maidens "in the faerie-tale castle." Then, after many events, they became Faeries again.

In order to make their pyramids grow the Egyptians planted parts of old temples upside down in the earth. Perhaps the gods proceeded in a similar way by building this world on the ruins of ancient ones. As soon as nature was organized, its soul wanted to take shape. It materialized and diversified by borrowing from the fabric of water, the texture of stones, of grasses and of animals. Shaped and molded from the clay of dreams were a butterfly wing, the coat of a deer, the reflection of water in a stream, a flight of birds, the bract of the Arum lily, the view of a burrow or of a fountain covered in ivy.

All the Green Maidens were born at the same time. Before becoming Nymphs, Dialen, Dives, Field Faeries, Junones, Sylviae, Fentha, Wilden Fraülein or Artemis, the woodland Faeries and the Loving Greens were born from the same embryo of vegetable flesh still covered in sap and pollen, brought to life by the breath of dawn…

They emerge from flowers and moss, they slide from leaves, they escape from ferns, and they germinate after the explosion of wild corollas; they gather together from every corner of the forest, touching each other, choosing and knowing one other. Colors, preferences and particular characteristics would be separated later.

The Green Ladies with bodies of leaves and ivy rule over the sylvan luxuriance.

They have names such as: Martagons, Damelis, Vergerettes, Vougeotes, the Fröhn, Sauvagines, Verdelettes, Vertes Velles, Chêneresses, Verteclusses, Vert-Ploumzouc, Vertes Cuisses, Liérandines, Raijonnes, Épervierres, Primulas, Hellebores, Ancolines, Sûrettes, Pervenchèvres, Feuillantines, Aspérules, Belladonnas, Guilledouces, Ladies of the Moss, Green Huntresses, Greenies, Greencoats, Green Hooded Ones, Capucines, and Daisies.

In the elfin era they lived the life of Elemental Beings, of Spirits of the Forest. They worshipped the ancient mothers, and if they were made to cry they hid under the leafy skirts of the White Mothers, the Old Mother of the Elder Tree and Mama Padurii. They became Elves in the time of Merlin, and Faeries in the time of Oberon. They grew taller in the Middle Ages, less wild, and less innocent too. The mortal heroes, paladins, princes, knights and youths who traveled through the forest in search of adventure would often meet them and fall madly in love.

At the start of these legends, they hold the knights in the forest, imprisoning them in chains of oblivion, in an endless sleep, in a bush, in a green wall of a glass, in a bubble of air, or in the clutches of bindweed. And then one day, it is not known why, they follow them. They ride behind them on their palfreys and allow themselves to be locked up in castles of ivy, doubly lost. A sensible hennin holds their leafy hair, a chastity belt closes the bush of perdition; eternity challenges the sand glass. No matter how much one of them might beg for a green room, a window onto freedom, the ultimate secret of Faeries, the husband, still deprived of her charms, would look through the keyhole to catch a glimpse of her lissom waist, her mossy thigh, her leafy arm… and she would escape, diving out of the window and flying away, returning to her wild state; or she would just fade away, leaving a baby in the cradle.

Betrayed and abandoned by others and by their own kind, these unfortunate creatures wander like pale green phantoms in a disinherited limbo between the two closed worlds.

For the people of faerieland, the Green Ladies are still the guardians of the "spirit of the Green Kingdom," and it is in their honor that they wear their color.

If they died there would be no more dreams, no more Faeries, no more dawns; grass would no longer grow, and water would no longer sing; all that would be left would be night and ashes.

HABITAT:

They exist everywhere in the world under different names. It used to be said that there were as many of them in the forests of the North as there were leaves on trees. They still abound in the region of Thiérache and in the hedges of the Avesnois. They live in forests, in the trees and flowers and can sometimes be found at the bottom of wells, rivers and lakes. They can also be found near castles and the peaceful, leafy churchyards of England.

FOOD:

The sap of plants, dew. Some say that they are vampires and ogresses.

CUSTOMS:

In the past they were the goddesses of the forests and woods and were worshipped as such. They protected fauna and flora. They were the companions of the Flower Faeries and Tisanières. Stories in the Middle Ages transformed their image of innocence and kindness and turned them into ghosts, Banshees and Harpies…

ACTIVITIES:

Often the same as those attributed to the White Ladies with whom they exchanged clothes to roam through the forest. The Green Lady of Clairfayts cries near the pond when someone is going to drown in it. In the Meuse region, the Petite Dame Verte au Crochet feeds children to her fish. The Ban-Fionn, the Green Ladies of Ireland, spin near fireplaces at night. They also guard treasures.

The Nymphs

Listen woodcutter, stop your arm!
It is not wood that you are throwing on the
ground;
Don't you see the blood flowing,
Of the nymphs who lived under the hard
bark…

(Ronsard)

They are born on the water, from so very little: a bubble, a drop of water.

The name "Nymph" means fertile woman; a thought is enough to evoke her on the triumphal arch of the rainbow. The ancients were so good at it that they could see her burst forth and spontaneously grow on the leaves of oak trees, and they could hear her laughing in the torrents.

From a drop of water they went upstream towards springs, along brooks and streams until they reached the river… Everywhere there the bubbling of water invited them to rest: in meadows and woods where the ground is moist, on the moss near fountains, on the dew of the flowers, or on steep mountain slopes with lively cascades. By climbing the ether, the evaporated mist, they reached the sky by ladders of rain, or by cloudy shores along bottomless seas.

Each one adopted a site where she lives and which she protects: a delicate periwinkle, a tree, a rock, a lake, a field, or a mountain peak. They have even chosen a name for themselves, and they keep a family record book so that people know who they are and come and visit.

Gods, Titans, heroes, poets and shepherds have fallen madly in love with them.

But the enchanted souls disappeared, the woods suffocated, the watery flowers around them dried out… and the mythologists arrived and pursued them.

Among the celestial Nymphs are the Uranias, sisters of the Muses, and the Hyades of the rain: Ambrosia, Aesylia, Coronis, Phaesylia, Cleia, Phaeo, and Eudora, the seven daughters of Atlas and Aethra. On the death of their brother Hyas, killed during a hunting expedition, their grief was so great that it moved Zeus to turn them into stars, and he carried them up to heaven where they are still crying. That is why the appearance of the Hyades at dawn or dusk always heralds rain.

The Epigae, terrestrial Nymphs scattered in the meadows, woods, and orchards… The Meliades of the apple tree, the Meliae of the ash tree, born from the earth and fertilized by the blood of Ouranos, castrated by Chronos. The seven Heliades, daughters of Helios and Climene: Phoetus, Phoebe, Merope, Helie, Aetheria, Dioxippe, and Lampetie cried so much on the death of their brother Phaethon that their tears became grains of amber and they were turned into poplar trees. Egeria was born from the same tree; she presides at births and gives good advice. Later Diana transformed her into a fountain.

Also living among the trees are the

SIZE:

It varies. The Nereids are tall, the Naiades are tiny, and the Limoniades are as small as the flowers they live in.

APPEARANCE:

A living legend of eternal beauty and grace, they are the image of the ideal woman in the fiery imagination of mortals. They are the luminous, unfurling roundness of the wave, the naive mischievousness of the springs, the juicy maturity of the apple and refreshing acidity of cherries, the velvety softness and promise of mosses, the blowing of leaves, the twining of ivy, the intoxication of honeysuckle, but also the stinging of nettles, the danger of hemlock, the engulfment of algae…

138

Dryads, the Hamadryads, the Syrinx of the reeds, and Daphne, daughter of Peneus, the river god of Thessalia, and of Gaia, whom she asked to turn her into an oleander so as to escape Apollo's amorous attentions.

There are also the Orestiades, the Oreads of the mountains, the mischievous companions of Artemis. They ignore fear and vertigo, leaping over precipices, and climbing up the steepest rock faces. The Napaeae and Auloniads inhabit mountain plateaus and valleys, and the secret Corycides the caves where cryptograms are distilled…

And then there are the freshwater Ephydriads: the Crenises and Pegises of the fountains of whom the most famous, Oenone, was loved by the fickle Apollo; he taught her the art of healing. The Potamides of the rivers, the Limnades of the lakes, the Carmentes, prophetesses of the springs: Pastvorta forecast the future, and Antevorta the past. The Palices, born of Zeus and the Nymph Thalia, ruled over the sulfurous springs of Etna. The Nysiades were wet-nurses to the joyous Bacchus. The Danaides were the fifty crazy daughters of Danaus, grandson of Poseidon. Having ruled over Egypt, he took his fifty daughters to Argolis and offered them in marriage to his fifty nephews with the intention of taking his revenge on his brother. On his command, they cut the throats of their husbands during their wedding night. Punished and thrown into the deepest hell, they tried in vain to fill a perforated barrel with their tears, symbolizing everything that is useless…

The ever-amorous Naiads of the rivers, the mothers of the Silenes and Satyrs…

Finally the leaping, wild Nereides, the fifty daughters of the water god Nereus; riding on the back of sea-horses and tritons, they splash the crests of the waves and accompany the court of Tethys or Amphitrite.

The three thousand wild Oceanides, daughters of the old Oceanus and Thetis, with at the head of the cortege, Admete, Electra, Clymene, Metis, Eurynome, Xantha, Polydora, Astypalaea—whose child walked on water—Adraste, Callirrhoe, and Styx who personified the river surrounding the Tartar with its five loops. By the Titan Pallas, Styx had Zelus, jealousy, Nike, victory, Gratos, strength and Bia, violence. When Prometheus was chained to the rock, the Oceanides rose from the waves and flew to him to comfort him and soothe his pain with their singing.

When Pan died and the cries of mourning dispersed the gods, the Nymphs left their divine dwellings and scattered like autumn leaves in the wind.

Mythologists gathered and labeled them one by one, sticking them between the pages of heavy dictionaries where the faerie-listener hears them rustle and crumple the paper. If a page is left slightly open, even for a moment, then a drop of rain or the reflection from a window will be sufficient for them to escape.

CLOTHES:

Naked or half-naked, veiled with golden or silver hair crowned with reeds, they adorn themselves with garlands of flowers and carry shells, baskets of fruit, sheaves of corn, bowls filled with pearls…

HABITAT:

Each one lives in the place they look after: a flower, tree, thicket, cave, spring, fountain, river, wave, rock, or mountain. The ancients worshipped them in nymphaeums, caves or temples decorated with statues and fountains. The Nymphaeum in Athens was situated on the hill of the Nymphs.

FOOD:

The sap of life.

CUSTOMS:

Benevolent, generous, cheerful, and playful, they behave like children. But they are also capable of feeling anger, great sadness and jealousy; and they can die of a broken heart.

ACTIVITIES:

They protect nature and flora. They are Genies of abundance and fertility; the water of the fountains of nymphaeums has generative, purifying and curative properties. They are prophetesses too and grant the wishes of lovers.

The fifth hour of the day (eleven o'clock in the morning) is dedicated to Nymphs. It is at that time that they return to earth.

SIZE:

Tall and slender.

APPEARANCE:

Their beauty was such that it enchanted the gods of Mount Olympus. Serious, smiling, or thoughtful according to the function of the attributes they each carry.

CLOTHES:

A long white flowing dress, crowned with laurel. In the evening they wrap themselves in a coat of light mist and in the morning they slip on a tunic the colors of the day.

HABITAT:

The lands of light. On earth they live on the balmy slopes of Helicon, near the singing springs. They were worshipped in sanctuaries erected in Delphi, on the banks of the Ilinos, in Sparta, in Trezene, Sicyon, Olympia, Athens, on the mountain of the Muses near the Acropolis, and near Libethrion on the eastern slopes of Mount Olympus.

FOOD:

Crushed wheat grains mixed with honey, milk and water from the springs of Aganippe and Hippocrene, and from the Castalia fountain.

The Muses, Horae, and the Three Graces

*The face of spring is reborn from there
The sun finds even greater brightness there*
(Amadis Jamyn)

The Muses were born at the same time as the Nymphs, from the dreams of a god listening to the music of the waves. First there were three: Melite, Mneme, and Aoede, dedicated to springs, in memory of the water. They listened to the scales of the rain on the slopes of Mount Olympus, to the *a capella* vocalization of fountains, to the choir of rain showers. Rocked by the rhythm of the raindrops drumming on the leaves, they learnt the musical rudiments of conjugation, identifying the clear note of a word from the rainy background, sharing the silence of a breath before being carried away by the harmonious falls of cascades. This is how the Muses became the custodians of the secrets of music, poetry, and inspiration.

According to mythology they were the daughters of Ouranos and Gaia, or of Zeus and Mnemosyne, goddess of memory. After the defeat of the Titans, the mortals asked Zeus to create divinities capable of singing and praising their victory. The king went to the mountain of Pierus disguised as a shepherd to seduce the wise Mnemosyne. He is said to have slept with her nine times, thus producing nine Muses. The first, Calliope, is the Muse of epic poetry and eloquence, she carries the stylus and the tablets.

Clio is the Muse of history and her attributes are the heroic trumpet and the clepsydra that measures time. Euterpe presides over the arts of the flute. Thalia, first a Muse of the countryside, became the Muse of comedy because of her constant tall stories; her attributes are the laughing mask of comedy and the birch for beating. Melpomene, the tragic Muse, has the mask of tragedy and the club of Hercules. Terpsichore, the Muse of lyric poetry and dance, plays the cithara. Erato, the Muse of erotic poetry, holds a lyre in her hand. Polyhymnia was first the Muse of heroic hymns, but came to be that of the art of mime. She is represented in a meditative attitude with a finger on her lips. Urania is the Muse of astronomy and geometry, and she holds a terrestrial globe and a pair of compasses.

Some mythologists add Castalia, the Muse of inspiration, to the cortège.

Permanent guests of the gods of Mount Olympus, they enlivened feasts and ban-

quets. They glorified the assembled guests with stories praising the exploits of mortals, charming them with tender poems and dancing. Their songs would calm Zeus's touchy personality; the Muses could transform a stormy outburst into a summer night's dream with just the opening phrase of a plainsong melody.

Quickly wearying of the pomp of the court and the capricious behavior of the gods, the Muses came to prefer the wooded paths of Helicon, that high mountain in Boeotia where cool fountains echo their laughter, where the monastic vault of the forest reverberates to the song of the blackbird. Here they come and drink the magic essences of inspirational water from the springs of Aganippe and Hippocrene that sprang up under the hooves of Pegasus. Those who come to worship them there return with their soul enchanted.

They often travel to Phocis on Mount Parnassus, near Delphi. There they meet with the beautiful Apollo, god of music, who was the first to undo their chaste tunics.

They discuss the lyre and art in general with him, following him everywhere so that he became known as Musagetes, leader of the Muses. They also accepted his amorous advances. Urania bore him the musician Linos, Thalia the Corybantes; Calliope bore him two sons, Hymenaeus and Ialemus, before marrying Oeagrus and bearing Orpheus... and when they leave him it is to transmit his song to the mouth of the shepherd.

Very close to the Muses—so close in fact that they are often confused—the Horae or Seasons were born from the jostling of rain, hail, sun and wind. Suffering from the general stampede of the elements falling from the sky, sometimes soaked, sometimes cold, sometimes burnt, they patiently organized the succession of the seasons, devising a balanced calendar with equal numbers of rainy and sunny days, with times for waking, times for going to sleep, times for working, and times for enjoyment. They established the length of the months, and the days, hours and minutes, based on the colors and nuances of the rainbow.

It is said that at the beginning of the world there were two of them: Thallo who gave the flowers and Carpo the fruit. But Flora, envious of the splendors of Eden, asked the gods for more Horae to help realize this dream of a magnificent garden. Thus Eunomia, Dice, and Irene appeared, then ten, then twelve: one for each month.

There are Three Graces, Faeries of beauty. They are represented naked, with their arms round each other's shoulder. Aglaia is the dazzling one, Thalia the one who makes plants flower, while Euphrosyne makes hearts rejoice. Daughters of Zeus and of the oceanid Euronymus, followers of Aphrodite, they preside over love, joy and the beauty of things.

CUSTOMS:

Gentle, benevolent, playful, dreamy, the friend and protector of poets and children, they are also very touchy. The Thracian Thamyris challenged the Muses to a trial of skill but lost, so they took away his sight and his voice. The nine Pierides who dared contest a prize of poetry won by the Muses were transformed into magpies on the spot. The presumptuous Sirens, convinced of the superiority of their irresistible songs, were also punished and deprived of their wings forever.

ACTIVITIES:

They preside over the arts and poetic inspiration. They share their gift with those who come to worship and drink from their fountains. It is they who told the Sphinx on Mount Phicion the perfidious riddle that he mercilessly asked every traveler who passed within reach of his claws. The Muses are still invoked today by poets and writers looking for inspiration.

SIZE:

Beautifully proportioned like a doe.

APPEARANCE:

Graceful when she appears as a doe with dazzlingly white fur. Large, gentle dreamy eyes reflecting the face of the soul. The shapely leg with elegant hoof, sometimes made of gold like her antlers. When she takes off her deer skin, the Doe becomes a girl adorned with the most perfect attributes of beauty. Barbygère says that "when naked she still kept one ounce of her white Faerie fleece on her stomach."

CLOTHES:

When she removes her white fleece she slips on an equally white robe. It is said that her silk and satin lingerie owes its virginal sparkle to the moonlight and to being cleansed by the Washerwomen of the night. She adorns herself with pearls and diamonds.

HABITAT:

She loves being near fountains, glades, ruined castles, stone circles and deep forests. But the Faerie kingdom is her real home.

White Does, Faerie Does and Fabulous Ladies

Their music is sweet to listen to.
(Marie de France, *Guigemar*)

"The ones who are going into the woods are mother and daughter. The mother is singing and the daughter sighs.

'Why are you sighing, my daughter Marguerite?'

'I have great anger in me and I hardly dare tell you. I am a girl by day and a white doe by night. The hunters are after me, the barons and the princes, and my brother Renaud, he is even worse. Go, my mother, go and tell him at once that he must restrain his hunting dogs until tomorrow morning.'

'Where are your dogs, Renaud, and the exciting hunt?'

'They are in the woods hunting the white doe.'

'Stop them, Renaud, stop them, I beg of you.'

Three times he sounded his brass horn; on the third time the white doe was caught.

'Let us call the skinner, so that he may skin the doe.'

The man skinning her said: 'I do not know what to say, she has blond hair and the breasts of a young girl.' He drew his knife and quartered her.

Then the hunters, princes and barons were seated at the table in the great hall of the castle, eager to start eating the venison. But Renaud was waiting for his sister to arrive before starting the feast. He wondered about the empty seat:

'Here we all are, except for my sister Marguerite…'

And a voice cried from the roasted meat:

'Why don't you eat, I was the first seated… My head is on the dish and my heart is by my ankles. My blood is spilled everywhere in the kitchen, and my bones are being grilled on the black coals.'"

So ends the sad, sinister lament with twenty-four variants and seven melodies, gleaned on the road from Niort to Saint-Lô.

Poor damsel, what spell turned her into a girl during the day and a White Doe at night, or into a Doe during the day and a sweet girl at night? Is it the same spell as was cast on Mélusine, Ondine, and Charmuzelle, who alternate between being ladies and snakes; or a lady-fish, greyhound, stoat, she-wolf and white mouse at the same time? There are no rules in Faerieland, only exceptions. A young girl may have been transformed thus for her own good, with the help of a Faerie "godmother." She may have wanted to become a doe, a White Beast, to escape certain dangers, to avoid the amorous advances of a loutish lover, or because she wanted to share the natural, simple life of animals. She may hope that one day she would marry a deer-prince, a wild boar, the king of the fish, or even a Selkie, a Drac, or a Morgan; and she hopes that this metamorphosis will enable her to enter the Kingdom of the Others and enjoy its delights for ever. In spite of her fear of the dogs and the arrows of the wicked hunter, she does not regret her fate, she knows that when she lies on the grass, waiting for her throat to be slit, her body trembling under the snow white fur sullied with blood, she will only need to look imploringly, flutter her eye lashes and shed a tear to soften the heart of the intrepid Nimrod. Full of remorse, his heart brimming over with courtly love, he will become again the noble knight of the lullaby, and carry her away safe and sound in his arms…

But as is shown by the lament of the Doe Marguerite, the story does not always end well. The huntsman only spares those who have been helped by a good Faerie godmother; the others who have had a bad spell cast upon them are killed like any other game. The poor girl, metamorphosed as a punishment or simply because of the whim of some wicked witch, is forced to roam the forests for seven or even a hundred years, wearing the white hair shirt of a Fabulous Beast, until the spell is removed.

Tirelessly they haunt the woods and countryside, half mournful and half aggressive, in search of the brave hero who will be bold enough to free them by climbing on their back, kissing their wet nose, and accepting the embrace, and wounding their flesh with a blessed bullet, a virgin blade or with other strange rituals.

A forest near the château of Montfort in the Côte-d'Or is haunted by a White Doe whom the farmers call the Baroness. It is the soul of Amélie de Montfort who lost her mind when she learnt of her father's death and jumped off the top of one of the towers. To save her, she must be scratched between the horns, but no one has ever dared do so yet.

These white creatures have often been associated with the evil creatures of the night: with the Charmuzelles, the haunting she-wolves, the White Ladies and the Banshees.

A child of a magician can also turn into a doe through contact with magic objects or talismans lost in the woods, by drinking the water from faerie fountains, through "scopelism," or through enchantment by magic stones. Then there were seven brothers who turned into deer having eaten a certain "horned grass." Their sister succeeded in freeing them after four years by placing a white handkerchief on their horns.

But according to *The Elfin Chronicles* the girls turned into does by Faerie godmothers or a spell are simply girls who have been bewitched, and they are not authentic White Does, who are Faeries.

Mythologies also tell how at the beginning of time many gods, demi-gods and nymphs chose to be does or deer, wearing woodland crowns on their heads and hooves on their feet, preferring the lively spirit of the animal to the clumsy human body. It was in this form that Merlin meditated in Broceliande, that Gilwaethwy, son of the goddess Dôn, and his beloved Goewin, daughter of Pebin, underwent their initiatory ritual, that God appeared to Saint Hubert…

The White Doe travels between the world and the Other World. She guides Lancelot in his quest and Galahad to the Grail.

But love between a mortal and a Faerie is difficult. Although it may blossom in the heart of Faerie, protected by glass walls, it shatters at the slightest obstacle as soon as it comes to earth; and the ballad of the White Doe ends as sadly as that of her cousins, the Vouivre, the Serpent Woman and the Swan Fairy.

FOOD:

Whether a doe or Faerie, she is vegetarian.

CUSTOMS:

The White Doe is gentle, loving, joyful, and happy: she is not one of those unfortunate "enchanted" heralds of death and misfortune, always in search of a "spell-breaker."

ACTIVITIES:

The White Doe lives among the other animals, she frolics, struts about, attracts the hunter, seduces him or throws him into a precipice, lures him in a swamp where he gets lost… Or through a faerie lover reaches the world of Eden. The White Doe Faeries only appear at dawn or at dusk, in autumn, in spring, at intermediary hours and seasons, on the edge of the wood, along the banks of ponds and rivers, near bridges, stiles, or at the frontiers of one world and another. Half doe, half Faerie, half mortal, half eternal, they have inherited great wisdom and understanding from these paradoxes. They help heroes in their quest and they help the ones who dream of Faeries to find the way to the Isles of Happiness.

THE ETHEREAL ONES OF INFINITE DREAMS

Teach us, Sprite or Bird
What sweet thoughts are thine:
I have never heard
Praise of love or wine
That panted forth a flood of rapture so divine.
(Shelley)

Anyone who dreams about Faeries knows that at night the lake absorbs the light of the moon and swims in its wake, and that, in the morning, it takes on the whiteness of the clouds and reaches up towards the sky.

It is in this fluid nacelle, suspended between the two arcana of heaven and water, that the one who dreams about Faeries hopes to travel to the Enchanted Isles and visit those downy shores that form and unform continuously according to the whims of the Ethereal Ones. Sometimes snowy mountains, sometimes solar castles or griffins' manes, the airy Faeries are forever creating new chimeras, hiding other shores that only chosen souls can reach…

Only by listening for a long time to the chattering of birds will the voice of the Faeries be heard, telling and retelling the secret of wings and the miracle of flight.

SIZE:

Appetizing.

APPEARANCE:

*They emit such a dazzling light
that no human eye can bear such
splendor. The Elfin Chronicles
describe them as rustic and rural
Faeries, similar to pretty, playful
young peasant girls on their way
to the village fête. Beautiful, very
plump, with a florid opulence
that makes for the best dancers
and the most promising lovers.*

CLOTHES:

*Sumptuous garments woven with
gold thread and precious stones.
However, they are most often represented dressed as country
women: a low-cut blouse, a black
top reaching down to mid-thigh,
or a white shirt in serge or cam-
let open at the front and gathered at the waist, a short petti-
coat and skirt decorated with lace
and braid, the number of rows
indicating whether she is a mother
or daughter Margot; a floral dress
with a pleated apron.*

*They wear long knitted stock-
ings and fine, clattering clogs.*

*They wear a coif during the
day and a crown at night.*

The Margot Faeries

*It is on this line that divides the waters,
south of the Armorican Coast, between the
English Channel and the Atlantic Ocean,
in the wild rocky countryside, that the Margots of Croquelien have taken refuge.*
(Jean-Claude, *Contes et légendes de la lande*)

Cousins of the Faerie godmothers, Spinners, Carriers of stone
spindles, the Margots are also
born dancers. Moon dancers at
the feasts of the night, on the
peaks of hills, on Mount Croquelien,
along the peaks of the Mené and on the
moors, in the secret enclave around the
crown of cairns, they dance with little
steps, staccato yet fluid and measured, as
regular as embroidery stitches, they tap
their clogs, and dance an uninterrupted
round. One step forward, one step back,
one step to the side, toe pointed up, toe
pointed down, holding hands, going
clockwise like a lunar spinning-wheel that
the yarn of a gavotte reels off with little
steps, little stitches, little steps… little
stitches…

It is true they are not only dancers; they
are powerful Faeries, "high priestesses of
the moors," as Jean-Claude Carlo records
in his *Légendaire du Pays Gallo*. The Margot looks rather round, rustic and florid,
brimming over with joviality, but her art
is most subtle. But the discreet fragrance
of the humble primrose that heralds the
dawn is even more elaborate. It inspires
those who approach it with endless
dreams.

"The nine Margot Faeries of the moors
are the grand-daughters of Keb, the earth
god, and Nouit, the sky goddess," he
writes. "Their godfather is Poseidon, god
of the seas and oceans. Their parents
Osiris and Isis entrusted them with the
task of educating human beings in every
field. Their power is therefore enormous.
The one called Hertia sits on the chimney seat, invisible, anxious to protect the
peace of the home. She is often accompanied by her sister Cumina who is
responsible for looking after the child in
the cradle. Ceres, another of the Margot
Faeries, watches over the crops in the
fields perched on the back of Horus,
Jupiter's black falcon. If Vulcan is to be
believed, there is always one of the nine
Margot Faeries somewhere on the moors,
night and day, handing out rewards and
punishments to humans, whatever the
time, whatever the season.

They are the forerunners and heralds
of the Divine Judgment, and each one
presides over one moral and material act
of life, with the blessing of Thot, the god
of wisdom, Ouranos, the shepherd of
the stars, and Hera, the goddess and protector of marriage and births. Like their
godmother Venus, they are dazzlingly
beautiful and graceful and owe their eternal youth to the cups of ambrosia that
Jupiter served during the banquets of
the gods, which took place at the dawn
of every season. In exchange for these
favors, they combine their magic powers
with that of Ouranos in order to drive
away the goddess Sahu who had the

appearance of a sow and who ate stars three times a night."

It is easy to imagine the Margot Faeries whispering further embellishments to their mythology in the ear of the inspired poet… They invite the walker among Faeries to dance to the sound of invisible bagpipes, the accents of Kan ha diskan, the song of the wind; encouraged by them he takes part in the dance of the festounoz or feasts of the night. With quick little jumping, sliding, tapping steps they dance endlessly on the endless thread of the endless boundary: one step in, one step out. Like funambulists across a tightrope, they skip once inwards and once outwards, between one world and another, until the intertwining joins up and links together; until the guest dancer, as the druid Gwenc' Hlan Le Scouëzec suggests, reaches another level of Being, another perception of the self and the world, something that goes beyond the customary situations of conscience. He truly reaches another world, or as Plato puts it: he crosses the boundaries of human nature, and becomes an enchanted knight of the eternal Ladies… At dawn he wakes up, dazzled with divine rapture, waiting for the next moon when the circle of the gavotte will engulf him again.

It is said that the first nine Margots had many children as a result of marrying Male Faeries and farmers, whom they seduced with their charms, or lured to their house after having them made giddy with moon dancing. Thus they gave birth to hairy dwarf boys and very pretty girls. During their adolescence, once a year on

a particular day, the girls were forced to take on the shape of a snake from one sunrise to the next. Sometimes a Margot would ask a farmer to go and stand in a particular place, keeping the snake hidden all day under a cloth. In the evening he would lift the veil and instead of the snake he would discover a beautiful young girl. By asking the farmer to look after her daughter she ensured her protection against danger. Indeed, it is true that when Faeries take on the appearance of an animal they run the same dangers as the animal whose shape they have taken on. So it was that one day two farmers were sitting on the grass and eating when a snake came to eat the crumbs. One of them said he would kill it if came within reach of his scythe, while the other thought it would be sad to harm such a graceful little creature. That same evening the second farmer met a Margot Faerie who gave him two belts, one for him and one for his friend, telling him to be very careful not to get the belts mixed up. As he approached the village, he opened his belt and found it was full of gold; he hung the other belt on the branch of a tree because his friend was late and suddenly all the leaves died…

There are so many stories about Margot Faeries that it is impossible to mention them all. Not so very long ago, people in the Mené region used to meet them all the time, always playing tricks, punishing spitefulness and rewarding virtue…

But above all, with quick little rhythmical, skipping, sliding steps, they lead their guest into the gavotte of other worlds.

HABITAT:

There are several places in the villages of Saint-Glen, Gouray and Penguilly where the Margot Faeries have lived in the past. They always live near a pond or a stream. Traces of their presence can be found near these places, such as foot prints or utensils used by them, hollow stones reminiscent of faerie beds or cradles.

FOOD:

Ambrosia, nectar, the finest dishes, but also buckwheat pancakes, curdled milk, smoked chitterlings and kig ha farz.

CUSTOMS:

The Margots are extremely generous, cheerful, and playful, but so enamored of justice that the merest unkind word towards another turns them into the most implacable and cruel avengers.

ACTIVITIES:

A thousand activities. The Margot Faeries are everywhere at the same time, watching over cradles, peace in the home, crops, and the cycle of seasons. They cure the sick, help the needy, reward the deserving and punish the rest. They also like to play "farmer" and watch the flocks, bringing them home in the evening plump with shiny fur.

Above all, they have bequeathed to the Bretons their love of the gavotte, the "enchanting" dance.

SIZE:

Tiny, minuscule, graceful.

APPEARANCE:

The description of the babies in limbo is shamefully terrifying. They can be seen wailing, haggard and desperate, wrapped in sullied winding-sheets, constantly begging for a grace that is being refused. Their appearance is sometimes softened. In Forez, God gives them wings and feathers and they twitter in the elm trees of the churchyard to amuse the dead. Their soul has taken on the appearance of a white flower, ever more beautiful as one approaches, but one that moves away as one tries to grasp it. It sometimes appears as a shooting star.

They appear very pale, evanescent like happy illuminations cut out from the light. With thundering wings, their face and eyes are dazzled by the happiness of enchantment. After a few centuries they take on the appearance of Pillywiggins.

CLOTHES:

Naked, but when the "paranenn" has fallen they look like a chrysalis.

HABITAT:

Though their region is Brittany, their territory is universal.

The Children of Desire
The Reborn of the Faeries

I, the image of light and gladness,
Saw and pitied that mournful boy,
And I vowed, if need were, to share his sadness,
And give to him my sunny joy.

(Emily Jane Brontë,
Child of Joy with Hair as Light as the Sun)

A real midwife knows a little about everything, because she brings little ones into the world and sets them off towards the tomb. Old Fantic was one of these.

Each day to her was like a complete cycle of seasons. She had been called to little Katell's house because Katell was having a difficult labor, and her young husband was rather worried.

To him she said "Quite normal, you always worry with the first one. As long as the baby is in good health, that's what counts." But Fantic had not been wrong and her foreboding was confirmed when she entered the room. The poor girl was writhing with pain, her face as white as the sheets she was wringing in agony.

She wiped and washed the poor girl's cheeks and brushed the hair off her forehead: "Bringing a little beauty to the cheeks honors God and attracts the protection of the angels!"

Already reassured by Fantic's motherly gestures, the girl was breathing more easily and she was taking heart again. The old woman bent down to listen to the beating of the little heart.

There are children you can feel immediately, children with a zest for life who push forward, who are easy to bring into the world; there are playful children who love to tease and escape.

Some children are hesitant, slower to come. Frightened, melancholy ones… who turn back.

She immediately felt the little thing quiver and curl up. She would have wanted to bring him out and reassure him. But her fingers were losing contact. That one would be for the Faeries.

"Let us give him the baptism of desire because I fear he will pass away soon."

Any way, he would not have lasted three days and he would have had to be taken to the chapel of grace, where the rector would have revived the spirit for a blessing in order to spare him the fate of the children of limbo, the still-born, the fireflies. But now she had to hurry and, enunciating each word very carefully, she said the prayer in a sobbing voice: "I desire at this moment that God grant baptism to my child. In the name of the father, son and the Holy Spirit."

And, guiding the clenched hand, she traced the sign of the cross.

Fortunately, although the terrestrial story seems to end in sorrow and pain, it is quite different from the point of view of the souls.

One must be so heavily mortal, so desperately cruel to imagine penitence for children.

Fortunately, angel-children, Elves or

FOOD:

They gather the aura of the plants, of the rising sun and of the rainbow. But the favorite food is the bowl of tenderness and the cake of love placed at the window of the heart by their parents.

CUSTOMS:

Joy, light and jollity.

ACTIVITIES:

The Children of Desire, the Reborn of the Faeries look after lost souls and comfort them, and offer their "damned" brothers the life of celestial Elves. They visit cemeteries and forgotten tombs, looking after plants that are not doing well and flowers that are not blooming, as well as animals who never saw the light. They also go home to reassure their parents while they are sleeping, appearing when their name is called and revealing themselves fleetingly in a reflection or a ray of light. They move the furniture and make it creak, whispering when it is quiet. They lightly brush against a shoulder with their wings, touching a cheek with their breath. The traces of their presence dissipate, they listen, they have talks, and they inspire eternity.

Faeries do not recognize dogma or sin and "naturally" they generously come and get them…

The air becomes musical, and a light rustling of wings beats and flutters around the body abandoned to the high clouds. Alive with the warm breath and voices of children, a fragrant light spreads, descends and rises like the laugh of a skylark.

The child will now be reborn among the Faeries.

Size:
> Minute.

Clothes:
> None.

Habitat:
> Unknown. They disappear at the first light of dawn, and cannot be caught, even by the most determined. It is thought that they rest in deep, narrow hollows in the rocks, wrapped in their wings. They have only been located in Corsica.

Food:
> They drink blood and eat children between birth and puberty.

Customs:
> Distant cousins of the Lemurs, Harpies and Ghouls of the Orient, the Streghes are classed among the fallen Dwarf Faeries, because of their attraction to the creatures of the night.
>
> They live alone, but at dusk they gather together at the Stregoni with the Mother Streghe, the descendant through the generations of Strega: "she who gave the first blood."
>
> There are no male Streghes.

The Streghes

Sophia hears some scratching at the cat flap. Agrementi or Streghes?
(D. Peraldi, *Folklore des montagnes corses*)

A little dog trots through the silent streets of the little Corsican village that nestles on the pillows and quilts of mountains and hills.

A little dog who comes and goes, he lifts its nose in the night breeze and continues on his way, making a gang of pesky, mincing cats take noisy flight—miaaaaow!!!

Suddenly the little dog stops, growls, sniffs, and sits down under an open window with his hair standing on end. He can smell young flesh: the tender, juicy flesh of a sleeping child…

And slowly, just as earlier she had prudently turned into a dog, the Streghe turns into a Streghe again…

She discards her rough fur, revealing a short, curvaceous, naked body. The back legs fill out and turn into muscular thighs, while the front legs spread out and develop into chiropteran wings.

With one push of her talons, the Streghe flies off to the bedside of the little boy.

She bends over the body, sinking two greedy, paralyzing canines up to the gums into his tender neck…

A long time ago, on the evening of the first vendetta, the young Strega was handed the body of her young husband, stabbed ten times. She placed her mouth on his wounds, sucking the blood as a pledge of love and vengeance. Then with her dagger she killed herself.

It is said that the child she carried in her womb was born as she was lying in the tomb; he fed himself as well as he could, and then left his mother's grave and came to earth. Mingling with the small creatures of the night, hunting nocturnal walkers on the moors, and mating with the black goblins, the Streghe gave birth to the race of vampires.

Every night at midnight, the Streghes assemble in desolate places called Stregoni, dancing, sharing some food, plotting, sneering, and barking at their frightful exploits before they disperse to hunt their cursed quest.

It is during the uneven hours between dusk and dawn that they are the most dangerous. It used to be said that if a Streghe was surprised performing her macabre ritual, three blows to her head would be enough to kill her—but the baby died anyway. Otherwise, to destroy one she had to be decapitated, and her

heart pierced with a stake as is done with Oupires, Voudalaks, Goulvas and Vampires.

Their secret abodes are undiscoverable, so a Streghe must be traced through certain hideous clues: bloody ditches, ossuaries with tiny skeletons carefully cleaned, and circles of thicket trampled by wild dancing. Once located, hunters, soldiers, farmers would suddenly appear during their Sabbath; they would surround the place with ramparts of fire, throw nets weighed down with stones to prevent them from flying away… and then the battle would start. The men were armed with shiny swords, stakes and clubs, with which they stabbed, impaled, and pierced. The Streghes, part dwarf, part dog, part bat-like, fought back using their claws, fangs and powerful wings; sometimes they were victorious, and sometimes they were vanquished, depending on the even or uneven hours… until the arrival of the vermilion dawn.

But in spite of regular massacres, there were always a few who succeeded in escaping and, the following night, the sparkle of two sharp canines would be seen shining in the inky darkness of night: the ivory smile of a thirsty Streghe!

151

SIZE:

Approximately five feet seven inches.

APPEARANCE:

Terribly thin with sharp bones, blue with cold, her emaciated face is frozen in a fixed rictus of terror. Her deep-set eyes are like two little pebbles caught in frozen puddles. Her teeth are like stalactites and stalagmites of ice. Her hair is like thatch covered in hoarfrost. Her beard is frozen hard, and she has long, knotty, claw-like hands. She walks with a limp as a result of falling into a crevice on her way back to her secondary lair of Cronk Yn Irree Lhaa. You can still see the print of her heel where she fell. She is often seen on February 1 in the form of a large, black bird with branches in its beak. In Leicestershire she is Cyclops.

CLOTHES:

Long black dress in tatters, a gray shawl on her head. She also wears a torn apron whose pocket is full of hailstones. Her thick studded boots are gaping at the front and reveal her horny toes with excessively long nails.

HABITAT:

The narrow prison of a menhir or a windy cavern. She haunts all the British Isles. She is known as Black Annie of Dane Hills in Leicestershire, Gyre Carline in the Lowlands, Gentle Annie of Cromarty Firth, Caillaghny Groamagh or the Old Woman of Gloominess in the Isle of Man, Cailleach Beara in Ireland, and Cally Berry in Ulster.

Cailleac Bheur

His limpid palm reached the crystal.
(Abou-al-hasin-al-Nouri)

"He who walks from Loch Awe to the summit of Ben Cruachan, following the itinerary of the Sith, will see some wonderful miracles," says Petrus Barbygère. "He must start at dawn, wear strong shoes that have been polished with mosses on which the moon has shone, wear a hat decorated with the plume of a tawny owl, and a sprig of heather, with a shepherd's crook in his hand, not iron-tipped but mounted with a ram's horn whose point is humbly turned outward. After Dunbeg he must leave the road and follow a path leading to Dunstaffnage Castle, the ancient fortress of the Campbell clan that dominates the approach to Loch Etive. Before he goes any further, he must walk through the ruins of the castle gate and stand in silent contemplation before the warriors' tombs shaded by the three round towers and chapel ruins. [...] He will enter the Inverliever Forest, inhabited by birds, deer and Faeries, and climb the mountain slopes, rejecting all thoughts that remind him of the world below. Every time he passes little whirlwinds of dust he must politely raise his hat and say the following words: "God speed ye" to encourage the Beautiful Beings in their removals that take place on that particular spot each quarter. When he reaches the summit he must rub his eyes with a tuft of grass from the highest peak, and he will have the great pleasure of seeing all the ruins of the castles and other buildings built on the top of the Dun-Shi—Faerie hillocks—re-erect their ramparts, dungeons and towers; and he will be able to admire the landscape as it was before Cailleac Bheur's negligence destroyed it."

A very long time ago, Cailleac Bheur was the goddess of spring, fishing and mountains. She protected springs, fountains, and streams, but above all she was in charge of a spring that gushed forth at the summit of Ben Cruachan, cascading down the hillsides with its clear water to irrigate the pastures of the lowlands. Each evening, at sunset, she had to stop its flow by placing a rock in front of the opening and then free it again in the morning. One day, she was particularly tired after taking her flock of deer through the mountains, and she fell asleep near the spring before she had blocked the opening. The fountain started to overflow and rushed down the mountain side like a destructive torrent, destroying everything on its way, people, animals, houses and castles. The thundering roar of the water woke her, but it was too late. In spite of her desperate efforts, Calleac Bheur was unable to stop the flow and soon the whole valley was submerged under Loch Awe.

The sight of the catastrophe caused by her negligence made her blood run so cold that her heart was transformed into a block of crystal and her body into stone. On that sad evening, the goddess of spring turned into the witch of winter.

When the witches of Halloween ring the bells of the churches and chapels submerged in the floods, and dance on the

tombs to wake the dead, Cailleac Bheur emerges from the rock that still bears the imprint of her former beauty and descends into the valley, where her hideously ugly face, still frozen with horror, sends an icy shiver over the land. The earth dies beneath her feet, flowers become crystallized, river banks harden, and streams stop flowing. The icy wand she waves in the air unleashes wild storms.

Leading a band of black Alfs with whom she feasts every night, she drives away the last of the summer Faeries, and howls in the chimneys. Nothing can stop her until the appearance of the first flower of May forces her back to the high snowy peaks. One can then see her become weaker and weaker as she is driven back to the icy summits by the warm breath of spring.

On the Eve of May, she throws away her wand of ice into a holly bush or reed-bed and turns into stone again.

"In the fleeting moment that separates April from May, the observing visitor to Ben Cruachan will be rewarded by a glimpse of her former breath-taking beauty in the reflections on Loch Awe."

A few isolated menhirs have been dedicated to her.

FOOD:

Cannibal; she is often represented sitting on a heap of human bones.

CUSTOMS:

Several times a year old Cailleac Bheur feels in the mood for making love. She then goes to farms that she knows are run by bachelors or widowers who are still young. Those who are not put off by her hideous looks and are willing to lie next to her will have the pleasure of discovering that they are making love to the most beautiful and passionate of young girls.

ACTIVITIES:

There are two suns in the Celtic calendar: the "big sun" that shines from May 1, from Beltane to Halloween, the eve of the feast of All Saints; and the "little sun" that shines from All Hallows to Beltane Eve. Cailleac Bheur is the daughter of Grianan, the little winter sun who sends her every year to kill the crops, petrify nature, and propagate ice, snow and storms in the land. Shepherds watch her so as to discover the weather she is preparing for them.

Cailleac Bheur protects the fauna of the mountain: deer, rams, wild goats, and in the past, wolves. She gathers them together and takes them grazing far from the eyes of the hunters.

Nang-faa and Phi-bird

There is a song dormant in all things that dream constantly, and the world will suddenly start singing, if the you find the key word….

(Eichendorff)

Once upon a time there was a prince who goes for a walk in one of those forests in Thailand that used to be like gardens. He looks at the flowers with such enjoyment that they become alive and tell him to follow a path that strays far from the one usually taken by humans. He breathes the fragrant air with such delight that the air too becomes alive and tells him to follow the stream. He listens so closely to the singing of the birds that a single voice appears to be singing specially for him… and looking up he sees the bird of paradise.

The bird descends, gently brushing the treetops. The prince does not dare to move in case the bird takes fright; its beauty fascinates him, because it would be a most cruel loss for him. He watches as the bird skims the surface of the river and lands on the water's edge, where it discards its feathers one by one in a slow sensual dance. As each feather drops to the ground in graceful swirls, a young girl emerges such as he has never seen before and will never see again. She is like a bird, a flower, water, and perfume, and the most beautiful of women.

He approaches so gently and with such respect that she does not stir when she sees him coming towards her. At this instant he is so close to the joyous soul of things that his human nature fades away in the harmony of flowers, water and air.

They do not need to speak to hear each other. She dances for him and when she has finished, they lie down on the rainbow of feathers and the forest repeats their caresses from branch to branch and the waves engrave their promises of love into the sand.

The prince takes her back to the palace to marry her. They live happily in the magnificent rooms without walls that the prince built in the midst of gardens and fountains. But the king dies and leaves the crown and the burden of war to his son. The crown is like a jail that imprisons the mind and makes it blind. In vain does the beautiful Nang-faa dance for him; he is no longer able to hear the song of the bird-Faerie in the dream of things. He puts on his armor, mounts his horse, and leads his army into war, brandishing his sword.

Three years have passed since the king left and abandoned his wife to the intrigues of the palace. The jealous princes, courtiers, bad counselors and palace treasurers are determined to destroy this fairy who talks to the birds and distributes her wealth to the children and beggars who come to see her dance. This Faerie… this witch!

Already the priests are preparing the stake where she will be burnt. It is so easy to persuade people with promises of gold. The priests claim that she takes the form of a vulture and steals children, devouring them every night at the bottom of a well. She must be burnt at the stake.

She is dragged from the palace onto the market place where the fire is already burning fiercely. Before being thrown onto the fire, she asks that one last wish be granted her, that she may dance a final time in her

SIZE:

>Perfect and tiny.

APPEARANCE:

>Fabulously beautiful, the Nang-faa (Nang: woman, faa: faerie), looks like all the Phi-birds in Asia. Her hair is jet black because it was given to her by the night, her skin golden because it was given by the sun, her lips were given by the fruits of nature, and her eyes by the stars. Her body was molded by the dawn god. With the prince of spring she bathed in the Fountain of youth; perfumed by the most fragrant flowers, she was introduced to love by the god of all things.
>
>Each bird gave her a feather to add to her faerie finery.

CLOTHES:

>Every day she has a new sari cut from one of the hues of the rainbow and the plumage of the bird of paradise.

HABITAT:

>The palace of the Phi and Faa of Asia at the very top of the highest mountains, between the sun and the moon and behind fields of clouds known as "cat's beards."

FOOD:

>The water of the sky, the fruit of the Garden of Eden, the honey of golden fountains.

CUSTOMS:

>She responds to hatred with love. When disappointed by betrayal or the lack of faith in a human, she flees rather than seek revenge, and returns to her bird form. She refrains from any evil thought whose venom might taint the purity of her song and dull the sparkle of her plumage that is the reflection of her soul.

ACTIVITIES:

>All those common to Bird Faeries. Her songs cause flowers to bloom and inspire the sweet melody of the babbling streams.
>
>In China the Phi also turn into flowers.

costume of feathers. Before everyone she then adorns herself with her beautiful feathers: plumes of flowers, the sky, hibiscus, and the sun. She skips and dances on the tips of her toes like birds do. Each of her gestures reflects the movement of the air in the water, the grass and the trees. Sometimes the curve of her hand resembles a hand picking a flower and breathing in the heady perfume of an invisible calyx. At other times her arms open up like wings of light.

But the torturer becomes impatient, and with the point of his scimitar he pushes her towards the flames… She suddenly leaps in the air, and everyone cheers and cries with joy and happiness when they see her fly off above the flames and over the rooftops; she rises into the air and disappears into the skies.

When the king returned to the palace, he was most distressed by her disappearance. Every day dancing girls come to the palace to imitate the never-ending dance of the Nang-faa in the royal gardens. They are the prettiest, most accomplished, most graceful of dancers. They wear golden tiaras pointed like beaks, and dress in tunics as colorful and precious as the plumage of a bird-faerie, but neither their winged costumes nor their songs inspired by celestial melodies can make them fly away.

SIZE:

That of a "sheaf of mist."

APPEARANCE:

Vaporous, graceful, pale shapes, female or male, so ravishingly beautiful that those who have set eyes on them cannot leave. They sometimes also assume the shape of an evanescent doe, of a swan or a faceless cloud whose voice alone is sufficient to lure the listener to his death.

CLOTHES:

Diaphanous dress, tunic and cloak of mist.

The Willies and the Dancers of the Mist

*Through the thin mirror of the water
The spirits of the air and water merge into one another…*

(Jay Lee, *The Hours of Shadow*)

Young men who are lured to the lake by the fragrant night, especially when hearing the sweet melody of the ball still echoing on the sparkling waters and the happy laugh of pretty girls full of promises: turn back! Go no further! And if your soul is yearning for adventure, ignoring the warnings of reason, and guiding you to the fluctuating shores, don't look! Don't listen to the cajoling enticements of the Dancers of the Lake!

They are the expression of the deep sadness burdening the Spirits of the water and air. They need to feed on your love, youth and joy to survive! It is not that they are evil… but they too feel the need to take part in the sweet follies of summer. They are looking for riders… and fiancés.

With long cascading hair and vaporous bridal gowns sparkling in the moonlight, these are the Willies. It is said that they are the spirits of fiancées who died before their nuptials and that their insatiable desire to dance is the result of not having had their fill of dancing. If you join their dance they will leave you for dead at dawn adrift on the billowing water…

The others, slender, fair-haired and pale-skinned, who skim the surface of the water with the tip of their boots like ice-skaters on the ice, are the Bougounskys. The young girl who returns their smile will be lost forever, and as soon as it is dawn, she will vanish with them into the disappearing mists….

Who are these dancers of water and mist? Evil genies? Faeries, or ghosts? They are as elusive, secretive and fascinating as the mysterious universe of funereal pomp that surrounds them. Their enchanted circle goes round and round in the fumaroles without being reflected in the lunar mirror of the lake. Breathtakingly beautiful, they emulate each other in grace and beauty in the hope of achieving a spectral, marvelous communion: they embrace and hold onto each other in a vaporous circle without seeing each other. Invisible in their own eyes, they approach each other and cling to one another, but they can only see those humans who agree to meet their dead eyes, which a mortal pupil will revive at the cost of itself. Anyone who succeeds in escaping their funeral dance will keep the image of their Faerie betrothed forever engraved in their mind and will spend the rest of their life trying to be reunited with them.

The Bogounskys dance on Lake Goplo on the Vistula, the Topielnitsy, the Kerricoff on the lakes of Russia and Poland.

The Altias live and make merry on the plains of Lapland.

The Urlutes, whose bodies reflect the luminosity of summer lightning, flutter along the Meuse on stormy nights.

The White Maidens perform a silent minuet above " bathing ponds."

The Maidens of the Lake have abandoned their Swan Faerie habit on the

shore. Seated in tiny blue boats decorated with golden tears they are taking part in an aquatic ballet… Sometimes they like to "play house" and try and light a fire in the torrent. They can then be heard crying and cursing.

No one should touch the tunics they leave behind in the reeds: anyone doing so will become so numb with cold that they are unable to resist being dragged to their sepulchral abode. Or the ghostly fabric may suddenly come to life and wrap itself around the unfortunate, whom they drag into a frenetic, never-ending pavane… Nor must the Snowy Doe be stroked, and the melancholic Corvie or the Hoar Child must not be followed; anyone doing so will never come back.

The Danis Nokkes punish unfaithful lovers with the utmost severity. "Sometimes they can be seen on a summer's night, skimming the surface of the water, in the form of little fair-haired children, wearing a red hood. Sometimes they run along the riverbanks like centaurs or assume the shape of old men with a long beard dripping with water" (P. L Jacobe, *Curiosités Infernales*).

The White Duiker or Water Jumper can be seen in August in the form of a winged frog with an unyielding look.

In Cheshire and Shropshire a night with a full moon is called an Asrai night, writes the excellent elficologist Nancy Arrowsmith. It is then that once every hundred years the gentle, shy Asrai, or Scarille, comes up to the surface of the water to watch the moon. This fragile little Nymph could be dissolved by the weakest ray of the sun, but she has retained all her youth and beauty in spite of being several hundred years old. Alas, it is this very beauty that has caused her to fall prey to men, because all those who have caught a glimpse of her dream only of capturing her. She lives in the darkest of the iciest lakes and sometimes ventures into the sea. The Asrai never takes part in the rounds of the Water Jumpers, but she sits on a nearby rock until the cock crows, watching the circles of light slowly disintegrate.

The Ferouers, Féeorim, the astral doubles of the humans, the Egregores and the will-o'-the-wisps, sometimes come and join the circles of the Willies.

Young men, when you hear the call of enchanted ponds on a summer's night, lock your door and close your windows: the love of the creatures of the lunar waters is dangerous to mortal hearts!

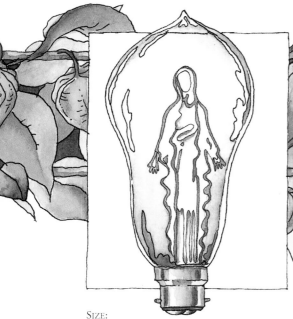

The Encantada and the Luminous Faeries

The vast night lights all the stars.

(Tagore)

When day dies, night lights up. The stars, luciolas, and glow-worms are the mayflowers of the sleeping hedge. The path lost in darkness needs light to wind its way through the gloomy woods and heathland. The large, round eyes of the owl in the hollow tree help the old pollarded head to see. Frogs need the light of the moon to complete their metamorphosis… There are more dreams of light in the secret of the night than in the glaring light of the day. Each light is a spark of thought, a glowing ember of the dawn kept alive by a watchful night watchman whose breath revives it when it dims: a lighter of mushrooms and herder of candles. He walks under the canopy of the miniature flowers, going from one tigelle to another to light the campanulas, ignite a piece of stained glass, and mark out the route of nocturnal processions with beacons using the wick of his faerie light.

It is the hour of haunting and the time of the Faeries of the night, who come and adorn themselves near the silver orbs of fountains.

According to the "dreamers of light," the Encantada is the "most bewildering since time immemorial" of all these apparitions of the "luminous Faeries."

Long, long ago in Spain, children would leave the village at night, and climb a woodland path to the sacred stones in order to admire the apparition of the old Encantada. They would sit down in a circle in front of the entrance to the cave and wait for her to appear. At first the back of the dark cave, covered with ivy and convolvulus, would light up with the "pinkish hues of dawn… and the warm glow of the sky when the sun rises." In the distance a gentle voice singing a song in a mysterious language could be heard. As the glow and light intensified the voice came closer. The walls of the cave turned red, green, blue, indigo, and purple, reflecting the colors of the rainbow, then "a light whiter than white absorbed all the colors and lit the entire cave and its surroundings." The trees, the grass, and the dark branches of the fir trees, turned white and sparkled like snow in the sun… "Everything became transparent, the rocks, the clothes and even the bodies of those who were waiting. All eyes were directed to that light as they tried to locate the precise point where the Encantada would emerge, because it was at the heart of this blinding light that the shape of the Faerie would appear. Everyone held their breath, and as soon as her face began to take shape among the stars, sighs of delight and rapture could be heard all round."

The spectacle did not last long and never changed. The Encantada looked at those gathered round her without seeing them, she smiled at the angels, she sat down, and then she slowly combed her long nebulous hair. No one dared to speak or whisper. As if paralyzed by the magic of this sparkling sight, the children remained there, open-mouthed and wide-eyed, until the light started to fade as she finished brushing her hair. She then gathered her hair and divided it into skeins, while the outline of her shape began to fade imperceptibly. She then put her comb into one of the folds of her dress, got up, smiled again at the angels and, blowing out her own image, she suddenly disappeared.

When the children later returned to the village in the dark, still trembling with excitement, there would always be one missing.

CUSTOMS:

When Good and Evil were still at war, certain Spirits refused to take sides. After his victory, God kept the good angels in heaven with him and threw the devils in hell. To punish those Spirits who had remained neutral, he banished them to earth where they had to cleanse themselves with frequent ablutions. These Faeries who are half angels, half devils are the Incantadès. These genies always do good and never evil. If they are not very often seen today it is because, having been cleansed of all evil, they have been allowed to return to heaven.

ACTIVITIES:

Very mysterious.

159

The Enchantresses

People thought that certain women who had discovered the secret of performing surprising deeds had obtained this gift through communication with imaginary divinities. They were given the honest name of witch or enchantress.

(Furetière)

The knight entered the forest in search of adventure. After wandering for a long time he reached a glade. Several paths led out of it. The trees and undergrowth had become so dense that it had become almost impossible to get through. But gradually the vegetation thinned and the gallant knight entered a circle of verdant meadow. There he saw the most hideous old woman. She was unspeakably ugly and covered in ulcers, with a pig's snout and projecting fangs. Blemished and dwarf-like, she had knobbly arms and legs, a twisted body and an evil nature. She was blind in one eye, and the other rheumy one looked at him through long straggly hair. In honeyed tones she called him "beautiful sire," and he felt faint at the sound of her voice, which sounded like the song of a bird. She said: "Beautiful sire, will you marry me?" He would probably have reacted otherwise had the circumstances been different. He would have laughed or got angry and ignored her as he went on his way. But he stood still, as if rooted to the spot by a magic spell. He even held out his hand to help her climb into the saddle with him. She sat in front of him and huddled against him—so close that he could feel the ridges of her monstrous hunchback.

This time he did not need to force his way through the dense undergrowth, because the trees and bushes made way for them as they approached, and closed up again behind them. They soon came to a magnificent tree-lined avenue at the end of which stood a castle.

Beautiful, richly adorned ladies came to help them and led them through many gardens to a vast hall in which an altar had been prepared for the ceremony. The hideous fiancée walked next to her knight. With great difficulty he slipped the ring on the knobbly, crooked finger of his betrothed. The wedding ceremony was followed by a banquet and ball. At

SIZE:

Very tall; their coif further accentuates their already tall and slender silhouette.

APPEARANCE:

They are usually represented as incredibly beautiful.

They use all kinds of magic—preferably red magic, the magic of love—to get what they want. They love painting their eyelids to enhance the beauty of their eyes but they also paint other parts of their body to emphasize them or make them look thinner. On other occasions they take on the shape of hideous witches and enjoy the surprise they cause when they reveal their incredible beauty.

CLOTHES:

The Enchantresses' wardrobe is unlimited. They wear corsets to emphasize their slender waists, uplifting brassieres to enhance their busts. They wear wasp waisters, stockings, false bottoms, silky garments, but also gold, silver, jewelry and the Faeries' sewing-box: moon yarn, gossamer, mosses, star dust. They love black, red, violet and of course green, the color of Faeries with whom they passionately want to be identified. Their coifs are floral, maritime, vegetable, animal, winged, or astral.

midnight, the newlyweds were invited to go to the bridal chamber.

As the husband hesitated, she said in her sweet voice: "Don't you want to go to bed, beautiful sire?" As if opening his eyes for the first time, he discovered the most beautiful woman he had ever seen. "I am your wife, sweet sire," she said. "By marrying me you have half freed me from the spell cast on me. But every morning I shall turn back into the hideous old woman that you know, and for half the day, unless you can answer one question."

"What is that question?" the knight asked in amazement.

"This is the question: would you prefer me to be beautiful during the day and hideous at night, or beautiful at night and monstrously ugly during the day?"

"Good heavens, what shall I say?" the knight wondered in anguish. This was an impossible choice; but he was so impatient to enjoy the delights of their nuptials that he drew her against him. "Come to me tonight, beautiful as you are now."

"How selfish you are," she said, freeing herself from his embrace. "Why do you condemn me to remain the laughing stock of the world so that I have to live in darkness to hide my shame? I do not expect this from a loving husband. I am bound to suffer from this choice."

"Forgive me," he cried, hearing the fairness of her reproach. "I had only thought of myself. Show your beauty to all in the light of the day and hide your hideous ugliness in the darkness of the night."

He seized her hand but she withdrew it immediately.

"Do you think I am pleased with your reply? Do you love me so little that you do not care how I would feel if I had to share your bed as a hideous, monstrous creature?"

On hearing these words the knight realized there was more to her question than he had first thought.

"My Lady, I am incapable of answering your question. You must decide and choose for yourself."

"That is the right answer to my question," she cried. "Because you have given me what every woman wants: the freedom to choose her own life. Now the spell is broken forever. You will never see the hideous old woman again. And I will be yours forever."

And that is what happened.

HABITAT:

Large mirage-castles, glass towers, pointed dungeons clinging to mountain peaks. In dark forests, deep, dangerous valleys, shimmering ponds. In the forest of Broceliande, the Ardennes, the forests of Briosque and Arnante.

FOOD:

Those who wish to preserve their great powers must follow the strict diet of the "Ladies of the Forest" throughout their life: drinking plain water and herbal teas made from basic herbs. They must never eat the flesh of creatures living in the air, water or on earth.

CUSTOMS:

The Enchantresses are not Faeries, although they themselves claim that they are. They are not supernatural creatures but mortals who through initiation and study have acquired certain skills and magic powers usually associated with Faeries. A very few of them can pride themselves on a distant relationship with the world of Faeries: a great-great-great-grandmother, a godmother, as a result of a mortal and Faerie marrying. At other times they have themselves approached the Faeries to request their protection. Or like Viviane they have been taught the art of magic by a wizard. They in turn can cast magic spells to help those who ask for it.

It is rumored that they are not always kind to others, that they are jealous, and capricious; and that their mortal nature makes them very dangerous.

ACTIVITIES:

Thanks to their special powers they can influence the fate of humans in the same way as Faeries and Parques do. They do this sometimes out of love, or out of perfidiousness, or for profit. The cycle of King Arthur and Merlin and many other knightly romances tell the story of their deeds, good and evil.

It is said that several of them became Faeries after a lifetime of behaving like them.

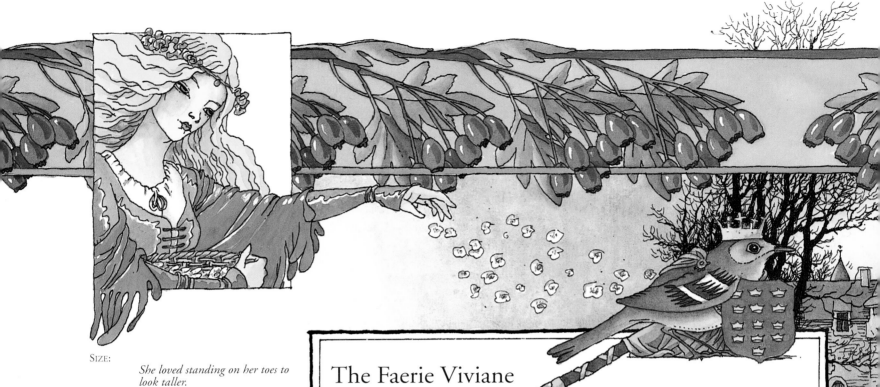

She loved standing on her toes to look taller.

APPEARANCE:

Beautiful like all Faeries, with the disturbing charm that so captivated Merlin. She has something of the nymph, the Enchantress, the Faery, the Fée, of the Arthurian image and faerie-tales. Slender and youthful, with a slightly curved forehead, a pretty upturned nose, a delicate mouth, large eyes with a look of enchantment and pink cheeks. Her long curly fair hair forms an aura around her tiny, delicate body.

CLOTHES:

There is of course the wild, natural dress of the Nymph-Faerie of the fountains, made of veils, water bubbles, aquatic flowers. Also dresses like those worn by the ladies of Camelot, and the coquettish eccentricities of children's books. Hennins with antenulles, starry skirts and long trains carried by processions of little winged pages.

HABITAT:

A crystal castle built in a single night by Merlin at the bottom of the pond in Comper. Some say at the bottom of the lake of Pas-du-Houx. She can be found almost everywhere in the forest of Broceliande, near the fountain of Barenton, near the prison of air where Merlin dreams. And Viviane's house dominates the Valley of No Return.

FOOD:

She is particularly partial to blackberries growing on the brambles surrounding Merlin's tomb.

The Faerie Viviane

I shall walk into oblivion beyond good and evil in order to become reconciled with myself.
(Michel Rio, *Merlin*)

It was a day full of water and foliage that lingered near the fountains. All the roads were enclosed by greenery, their air reminiscent of the smell of wells. Merlin walked behind Viviane. She was hurrying for fear that he might turn round and return to the edge of the forest, drawn by the memory of Arthur. The sooner they reached the heart of the forest the better, because there the roots would hold him back. But close to the edge he could still be lured back by outside influences. She had asked him to wear his woodland habit, which gave him special powers over the trees and mossy rocks of the forest and whose coarse cloth could become speckled like the coat of a doe. She had used every ruse possible and he knew it. He allowed the grass to obliterate all traces of their passage. A kingfisher streaked through the sky and hovered over the river bank. Merlin sighed over everyone he had left behind in their hour of glory: those valorous knights riding through the spring orchards adorned with blossom towards the towers of Camelot decorated for the nuptials of Arthur and Guinevere. He went to them, still young, driving from his thoughts the shadow which followed him. Lancelot took the queen's hand and helped her down. She uttered a word without thinking about it, some of those words

that travel along the mysterious paths of the heart and that Mordred would hear still heavy with sleep in a distant cloud: "What do you see, Merlin?" Morgan had asked, as he leant over the ramparts staring at the plain below covered with corpses, where two armored iron silhouettes could be seen struggling in mortal cut and thrust.

He is not abandoning them, he is leaving a world in which clairvoyance is no longer heard. He has known so many kings—Wortigen, Ambroise-Aurelian, Uter-Pendragon—whose powerful voices have become forever silent while the wren sitting in the hawthorn continues to sing. His memory delves into the distant past when Faeries and oak trees ruled the world. He remembers the forests of Calidon, Arnante and Brequehem, the stone circle where a Duz breathed into his mind when men had barely emerged from the clay and were crawling amongst the saurians. He watched them stand up, stagger on their feet and fight the rival brute for the supremacy of a kingdom. He moved away in search of wild hermitages, looking for the hidden entrances of the Blessed World at the bottom of deep caves. Maybe she would take him back there. He had met her at the height of May, resting on the edge of Barenton, the fountain that smiles when a pin is thrown in it and opens the rivers of the skies if one waters its stone. She was a Welsh Nymph and her name was Vivlain. He had always found her when he gave free way to his mad thoughts…

Viviane could hear all this as they walked

side by side because they had traveled together for a long time. This time, she thought, I shall not let him go again. And she looked lovingly at his body that had become bent, his furrowed face and long white beard. She remembered their first embrace, she the daughter of the moon and water, the Faerie of the Fountains, at first frightened by this woodland god, the god of the oak tree and of stone. He had removed his antlers and wolf's coat to embrace her.

She would spare him the pain of Guinevere and Lancelot's betrayal: Lancelot whom she had taken from her mother Elaine, according to the Faerie custom, and brought up as Faerie Knight. She would conceal Morgan's decline and Arthur's agony from him.

Viviane would keep him far from this world from which one by one the Faeries had fled. She would hide him in this hawthorn bush where their first love was born, and where he would be concealed from everyone behind ramparts of illusions that Merlin had taught her to erect when they were exchanging the secrets of the magic skills.

But he probably already knew about the trap that Viviane was weaving around them. Yesterday he had warned Arthur of his imminent departure without return. What could he have done to change the fate of a decaying kingdom in which his magic spells no longer worked? "I take part of your heart to eternity with me, my king, but I do not belong here any longer, since a cross was made from the wood of Yggdrasil."

Smiling into his leafy beard, Merlin watches Viviane make graceful gestures while reciting the words of oblivion…

CUSTOMS:

Viviane and Morgan are often linked. One of them will always carry the burden of Merlin's prison and the other that of the Valley of No Return. The people judged them both: "Abominably hypocritical towards Merlin," "ambitious, eager for knowledge and power." It was to be quite some time before some Faerie-lover looked into the question of Viviane's behavior towards Merlin and interceded in her favor. "Everyone now recognizes that Viviane's magic spells were cast on a conscious and consenting Merlin who had reached the ultimate boundary."

ACTIVITIES:

Viviane, Nivienne, Vivien or Vivlain is thought by some to be the daughter of Dyonas, goddaughter of a Siren, or of King Cadeu, king of the Redonnes. She is sometimes also depicted as a rather masculine Diana the Huntress. She leads a double life: that of a mortal surrounded by the intrigues of Camelot, and that of a Faerie living in the crystal castle at the bottom of Diana's pond in the forest of Broceliande. She practices high magic, surrounded by her faithful attendants who include the faithful Sayrade. She is the Lady of the Lake in the Book of Legends.

Morgan le Fey

You wonder about the reason that makes me serious and silent…

(Mrs W. C. Elphinstone Hope,
The Star of the Faeries)

SIZE:

Tall.

APPEARANCE:

Her long, shiny black hair is plaited. She sometimes looks cheerful and innocent, at other times dreamy and melancholic or disillusioned and hard. Strange, a little moonstruck like Merlin, her master.

Morgan gradually lost her womanly qualities, taking on the disincarnate appearance of certain Faeries that is illuminated or darkened by a mortal gaze depending on their state of mind.

CLOTHES:

She follows the fashion of the day, preferably in white, black and green.

HABITAT:

Merlin's workshop. She has several homes. The Iron Tower, the steel Chastel, Bellegarde, the Desolate Tower. She has lived in Tintagel and Camelot. But her real kingdoms are those of Avalon and the Valley of No Return. It is known that she still haunts both today.

FOOD:

Apples.

CUSTOMS:

She is at the same time woman and scholar, Water Nymph, witch and Enchantress. She is one of the most fascinating and engaging characters of the Vendoise of Faeries. It is true that she can also be irritating because she reveals to the world the infidelity of all the pure, irreproachable knights of the quest for the Holy Grail.

ACTIVITIES:

Expert in the seven arts, a "high master" of astronomy, a great scholar of all forms of magic and medicine. She has balms for every kind of wounds except for those in her own heart.

O nce upon a time there was a king who ruled in Cornwall. His name was Gorloës, lord of Tintagel. He had had two daughters by his wife Ygerne, one who would become the wife of Loth of Orcania, and Morgan who would become a Faerie.

After her father died, Morgan was brought up by her stepfather Uter-Pendragon. She studied the arts and sciences and become very knowledgeable in many subjects, especially medicine, astronomy, magic and the ingromancy taught by Merlin. This great learning earned her the name of Morgan le Fey. It was probably at this time that she visited the Blessed Isle of Avalon where she soon became the beloved queen, surrounded by her nine sisters who included Moronoe, Mazoe, Gliten, Glitonea, Glito, and Tyronoe. No one in Tintagel knew about her travels, except perhaps Merlin when he saw her coming home from journeys, her hair damp and fragrant.

Time passed and she grew up. Uter was dead by now and Morgan followed her half-brother Arthur and his young wife Guinevere to the fortress of Camelot. All the knights, including Lancelot, were in love with Guinevere. Morgan looked after the pale, wounded knights whom she rescued from lost deserted shores and healed with her knowledge of the sciences.

Finally, Guinevere's cousin visited the castle one day. "Guyomar was a young, handsome knight, well-built with powerful limbs. They spoke to each other at great length and he fell in love with her. The more she looked at him the more he loved her. Their love was so great that they gave themselves to each other."

Poor Morgan, this rare terrestrial happiness would soon be taken from her. Often the lovers would meet in secret. But one morning they were surprised by Queen Guinevere. The latter was furious and forbade the lovers ever to meet again. Betrayed and broken-hearted, Morgan was to hate Guinevere for the rest of her life.

She withdrew from the world to "embalm" her sorrow far from the society of men, but then she suffered another blow to the heart that turned the wise, dreamy Morgan into a vengeful Faerie.

She had recently fallen in love with a knight whom she believed loved her as much as she loved him. But he was unfaithful. The knight and his other lover agreed one day to meet in a secret place, the prettiest, greenest valley that one could imagine. Morgan found out about their secret assignation and surprised them in the act of expressing their tender love to each other. She nearly died from a broken heart at the sight. But she recovered and cast a spell on this beautiful valley, so that any knight guilty of the slightest unfaithfulness, whether in thought or deed, would remain imprisoned in the valley forever. Morgan's knight was the first victim of this spell. When he tried to leave he was stopped by an invisible force. Meanwhile, Morgan's rival found herself imprisoned in ice up the waist, and from the waist to the ends of her hair she was caught in a blazing fire.

Morgan built houses and a chapel for the unfaithful lovers who would become imprisoned in the valley that she ruled from her iron tower.

"The Valley of No Return, the Valley of the Unfaithful Lovers, or the Perilous Valley was vast, surrounded by beautiful green hills. In the middle was a clear fountain. The surrounding enclosure was magnificent: it looked like a thick, high wall but in fact it was only air." When an unfaithful knight ventured into the valley he was immediately caught in a vice of mist that became increasingly tight, imprisoning him forever.

After eighteen years, two hundred knights had been imprisoned in this way when Lancelot, faithful to Guinevere, came to free them… "Then everything in the Valley of No Return disappeared, its castle, gardens, walls, guardians, dragons, and spells, all vanished as a result of the virtue of Lancelot, the knight beyond reproach who was true to his beloved."

Morgan was vanquished once again. Furious, she put a curse on Arthur and his kingdom, but humans do not need a curse to destroy each other: Mordred and his sad intrigues sufficed to bring about the decline of Camelot and to herald the end of chivalrous dreams.

There are two Maeves: the minuscule Mab mentioned by Shakespeare, "no larger than the agate decorating a ring," and the tall, proud Lady of the Raths evoked by William Butler Yeats.

APPEARANCE:

Mab in Romeo and Juliet *symbolizes the graceful procession of winged Faeries, dear to English popular imagery, fluttering among butterflies and wild daffodils. She is the sister of Drayton and Titania's Nymphidia: "The crazy, scintillating little Faerie sovereign who dances on the grass without bending its stems."*

Yeats reports a vision of Queen Maeve as described by an old woman of Mayo: "The most beautiful woman you have ever seen, she had a sword at her side while brandishing a dagger. She was dressed all in white and her arms and legs were bare. She looked very strong and fierce but not evil. She was slender, broad-shouldered and looked about thirty years old."

CLOTHES:

Petticoats made of rose petals, butterfly wings, and a crown of primulas for Mab. A white dress gathered at the waist by an iron belt for Maeve. On her feet she wears some kind of buskins, and on her head a heavy tiara that looks like a helmet.

Maeve, Medb, Mab

… The cairn-heaped grassy hill
Where passionate Maeve is stony still.
(W. B. Yeats, *The Wanderings of Oisin*)

Her story starts when she was a mortal in legendary times. Ireland was a land molded by the gods and the Faeries. The youthfulness of this green isle had been the perfect setting for their spells of enchantment and magic. They erected forts using mountains, they flattened moorland to attack the enemy, and they hurled stones at each other.

Queen Maeve, a warrior queen, was one of the first to enter the pantheon of Celtic Faeries. At the time she ruled over Connaught. She feared nothing and no one, not even the Fey king, the Sidh Ethal Anubal, whom she defied with her arrogance as she led her army of war chariots feared by all. King Ailell lived nearby in his palace of Cruachan. Maeve had chosen him as a husband because he was without "fear, avarice and jealousy." The queen ruled and the king acquiesced. This was Maeve's way, who used her body according to the needs of the realm.

One day when they were making up their accounts and comparing their respective contributions, the queen was pleased at first because she owned as much as her husband, apart from a bull that was the apple of King Ailell's eye. This was a magnificent animal and most virile, known by everyone as the "beautiful horned one." This was an insult that she could not accept, because according to ancient Irish laws sovereignty belongs to the richest. Therefore, if Maeve was to retain her position of sovereign she had to acquire something else of the same value. She knew that in the neighboring kingdom of Ulster, a subject of King Conchobar was raising a legendary bull whose reputation had traveled far beyond the divine Erin; he was the great Brown Bull of Quelgny whom women only looked at with their eyes lowered. She immediately sent Mac Roth to negotiate the purchase of the animal, offering the owner, Dara, fifty heifers, one of best chariots and twenty-one beautiful young slaves.

When Mac Roth came back empty-handed, her warrior's blood boiled in anger. Since she could not buy it, she would have to steal this blessed brown giant of Quelgny; all the more because the goddess Macha was about to put a curse on the inhabitants of the enemy kingdom because they derided her in the past, inflicting a periodic languor on them and making them incapable of moving and even less of defending themselves. She raised her armies and marched triumphantly on Ulster. But she had forgotten that Macha's black magic spared one man, the invincible Cuchulain.

Cuchulain is a legendary hero in Ireland, like a combination of Hercules and Achilles. At the tender age of seven he had slain the mastiff belonging to Culann, Ulster's blacksmith. The god Lugh of the Long Arm had armed him with a magic spear and sword, and when anger filled his heart, he would assume a twisted, hideous appearance while an intense heat would emanate from his body.

And this is how the champion, fulminating with fury, appeared in front of Maeve's soldiers, slaying them one by one. When Cuchulain withdrew at nighttime, Lugh came to his aid by healing his wounds with magic herbs and giving him magic beverages to make him a hundred times more invincible.

The queen wondered how she could destroy this colossus who was turning the rivers red with the blood of her soldiers. She had to find another champion as brave and as strong as this one. Who else but the valiant Ferdia? But was he not a childhood friend of Cuchulain? He would never agree to fight a blood brother. So she makes herself even more beautiful, even more desirable—after all, does not her name mean "intoxication"? She would offer him the most precious presents, her daughter Find'abair, and above all "the friendship of her body," not for pleasure but for the good of the realm. And Ferdia, drugged with wine and caresses, went off to battle

against his will. With a heavy heart Cuchulain struck him down.

Cuchulain was still alive and as a last
resort to beat him Maeve turned to black
magic. She invoked three witches. Three
shrieking Harpies in the shape of ravens
flew to him and lured him on his own to
the plain of Murthemney. They made sure
that his taboos are violated so that he lost
his protection. Without his spear and his
supernatural powers, he was soon surrounded and attacked from all sides.
Bravely he tied himself to a pillar with his
belt in order to die standing up.

Maeve had won. Now the great Brown
Bull of Quelgny belonged to her.

Now, she could climb the mountain of
Knockera, wearing her crown, and lie down
on the stone, dying as a great sovereign.
This is how Maeve, Medb, or Mab became
immortal and the Queen of Faeries.

HABITAT:

*Mab holds court in faerieland.
Queen Maeve's tomb dominates
Sligo. It is an enormous cairn
consisting of forty thousand tons
of rocks placed on the truncated
summit of Mount Knockera. She
lives there with all her court, but
she also haunts other regions of
Ireland such as the Burren.*

FOOD:

Saffron powder.

CUSTOMS:

*Mab is typical of the playful,
cheeky, volatile English Faeries
and Maeve of the seriousness of the
Irish Faeries.*

ACTIVITIES:

*Queen Maeve's activities are
rather mysterious, but Shakespeare gives an idea of a typical
day for little Mab. Seated in a hol-
lowed out hazelnut, carved by
the squirrel carpenter or by the old
mite, coachbuilder to the Faeries
since time immemorial, every
night she travels through the
minds of lovers who then begin to
dream of love.*

*She also loves to play all kinds
of jokes and tricks.*

SIZE:

Rather tall.

APPEARANCE:

They all look alike. Diana is even more beautiful when she sparkles like a sun. Her hair is fair or pure black, her skin soft and fragrant like a peach. The Guaxas have a wild gracefulness, the Janas a more haughty beauty. Sometimes they turn into hideous shrews or serpents to test people whom they ask for a kiss "given without any feeling of disgust."

CLOTHES:

Richly decorated dresses, but also long white veils, or simple dresses in the style of the region. Very modest, they never show themselves naked even when they bathe in flowing water.

HABITAT:

Portugal and Spain. In the Basque country they are called Mari, Maia, Maide, Maindi, Anaia. They live in magnificent gardens at the bottom of caves.

FOOD:

Sophisticated dishes seasoned with saffron.

CUSTOMS:

They are related to witches, the voracious Lamias, but even if they are accused of stealing children to exchange for their "little monster," they always have good reasons to do it. Kind and generous, the Hadas came to earth to redeem man from original sin.

ACTIVITIES:

The same as the Margot Faerie.

The Hadas, the Xanas, the Gojas and Diana

Y no hay hombre que entrase en este lago sin mandano de las Hadas.

(El Baladro de Merlin)

There are very many Hadas or Iberian Faeries; they are often dangerous and linked to the Spirits of the Dead. They are very old and their names have as many roots as the most ancient oak trees of Galicia. It seems that old Jana (Xana), or Spinner of the night, has deliberately tangled all the threads and golden hair of her spindle in order to confuse the curious and prevent them from untying the first knot.

Which Hada is she? This is what the wanderer will wonder when looking at the Faerie that is calling him with her wooden horn. Alike yet at the same time different, they resemble the regions they live in, but the regions are confused because boundaries become blurred beyond the gaze of the millennial Madres. Are not the Hadas the mothers of the earth? Is not every life linked to the shuttle in their hands?

Is she good or bad? This is like passing judgment on the night and the day, the rain, the sun, the wind, the lambs, and the wolves.

Is she a Fada, a Diana, a Bruja, one of those formidable Gojas who is scared of running water? A Xana whose etymological roots (*Xa*: ghost, *Jan*: witch) make

it a kind of hybrid? The apparition of the Faerie is similar to the reflection of a mirror of the soul, and the wandering mortal can but listen and submit to its trials.

"Where do you come from?" the Faerie asks him.

"From Santa Caterina."

"And you are planning to return there?"

"Of course."

"Would you first do me a favor? I am going to give you three oranges that you will take to Cabeço do Castel and place on the Penedo Amarello; you will then go round the Penedo three times, and this will free one Hada from her spell."

"What are those oranges for?"

"They will turn into horses. One will carry the Faerie, another the person who has delivered her, and the last one will carry the treasure that has become his."

So the wanderer puts the three oranges in his pocket and goes to the Cabeço do Castel with the firm intention of accomplishing the mission he has been entrusted with. But he is very hot and it is a long way. He is so thirsty and the oranges look so juicy; surely he could eat one of them? If necessary, he will carry the treasure on his back! And he quenches his thirst with the first orange.

It was delicious, refreshing, and full of flavor, but small, so small that his throat is soon as parched as before. "Well, the Faerie will have to walk," he thinks to himself as he sinks his teeth into the second orange.

Having arrived at the Penedo, he only has one orange to place at its foot. After walking round it three times as agreed,

he hears a voice shouting in anger: "You wretch, not only have you failed to free me but you have brought a curse upon yourself!"

Indeed, from the moment he reached home, he was pursued by bad luck until he died of it.

Thus the trial of the Hadas shows men their weaknesses.

One villager from Asturias was more fortunate when he met a Xana: she offered him a chicken laying golden eggs in exchange for the ribbon of his hat.

Diana, she who scintillates, is the most ancient of the Hadas. She was born with time. This mother Faerie is goddess of both fertility and death; she entrusted the protection of woods, fountains and rivers to the Ninfas, and the protection of fields and herds to the Janas. She is kindly disposed towards humans, and when they die, she places them in a tomb that she guards for three days to keep away the gangs of vulture-like Lamias who have a predilection for dead flesh.

SIZE:

Between four and twelve inches tall.

APPEARANCE:

The Folleti are usually invisible and, when they allow humans to catch a glimpse of them, it is all so quick or amidst such a tangle of graceful little bodies, wings, claws, clouds, hailstones, dust, leaves, and flashes of light, that no one has ever been able to see them properly.

However, it has been observed that the Lazio is pale and grace-ful, and the Colorobetch repul-sive with a red beak. They can also take the form of grasshoppers.

CLOTHES:

The Folleto from the Abruzzo is said to be covered with castanets.

HABITAT:

The wind.

FOOD:

The wind.

CUSTOMS:

At first an unconscious larva, dor-mant in the bowels of the earth, the Folleto divides into one of two species at birth: the terrestrial Fol-leto who is classed as an imp, and the wind Folleto who turns into a Fé when he flies off.

The Folleti del Vento live in a group among the clouds. Their lady companions, the Marzulines, come twice a year to lay thou-sands of minuscule eggs in the cracks of the earth, two thirds of which get devoured by lumbrici, insects and caterpillars. Almost invulnerable, they only obey par-ticular personified winds (Dj'hân d'â Vin, Dj'hân di Bîh, Dzn, the Vaudaire, Père Banard, Dalu, Hardy, A Niss, the Imp of the North and knotter of winds). They fear the sound of bells, the smell of garlic, the power of cer-tain saints and exorcist wizards. The point of a priest's three-cornered hat directed at them drives them away.

ACTIVITIES:

Good or bad, they rule the good or bad winds.

The Folleti del Vento

Little Ludovico, how would you like to climb on my back to join the storm?
(V. Calvini, *The Song of the Wind*)

The wind groans, cries, calls, sings, whirls, tears, howls, sweeps, laughs, lifts, uproots, beats, and plays. As a warm breeze it moves slowly. As a cold breeze it moves fiercely. It can blow in all directions at the same time. The wind is born, it moves, and it takes on the appearance, the mood of the Mad Faeries who animate it.

Caressing breezes for sweet Faeries. Cheerful trade winds for the tropical Farauds Faeries. Bizarre blizzards for the sly. Whirlwind-cotillions for the cheeky. Ghostly squalls for the demons.

These are the Folleti.

Escaping from a crevice in the earth's surface in Italy, the Folleti travel every-where. They take the first passing wind, they gather together and pile up on it, wan-dering round and round and carrying the wind with them. Some of the Folleti like to tease people by rattling shutters, fright-ening children by moaning under doors, lifting skirts up in the street, and making hats blow away. Those who are more rea-sonable bring seasonal breezes with them, they push the sun round and they water the crops with welcome rain. They cool down the sweltering dog days, they cause the sails of ships to fill and the sails of the windmills to go round. The good Folleti brush the Faeries' hair, they rustle the leaves on the trees, they make the butter-flies flutter and the Elves dance, and they caress the petals on the flowering boughs in the orchards in springtime. The evil ones destroy roofs, they take people's breath away, they sting faces, they uproot trees, they topple over pylons carrying electric cables, and they make children fall. The fierce ones unleash storms, tornadoes and cyclones, howling as they destroy, spread-ing death wherever they go. They are responsible for showers, hail, snow and sleet. They create avalanches and make floods, destroying bridges and ruining crops. They flood the valleys and sweep away the houses.

The most dangerous ones come from Sicily.

The Macinghe is a Folleto del Vento who attacks women and young girls. The Mazzamarieddu or Ammazzamareddu only calms down after seeing the blood of a murdered man: he is also responsible for earthquakes. His sworn enemies are Saint Philip and Saint James, who try to exorcise him every spring . In Sardinia a sighting of Sumascazzo heralds bad luck. In Friuli, it is the Grandilini who rules over hailstorms. The Mazzamarelle of the Abruzzo, Calabria and Lazio are other terrible Folleti.

The Basadone of Northern Italy are clouds of male and female Folleti, who climb high in the skies at midday and blow kisses to those who greet them.

While travelling round the world the Folleti mix, merge and mate with other winds, thus creating other Folleti, Elves, Spirits of the Air and other Faerie races: the Tornichauds of dust and sand, Jean du vent of Hainaut, Jean Bijon of Sugny, Trainard, Colorobetch… and the terrible Cornandouets of the tempests.

On the other hand, they hate the Elves of the clouds and the demons of the Hunt-ing Gallery. During carnival they meet the howling packs of Héroguias, the queen of black squalls, in frighteningly bloody battles.

Indefatigable, they continue to fly even when the wind drops, only stopping now and again to sleep under hedges, at the edge of woods, or at the top of trees; or they may let themselves drift with the river current. Every hundred years they may gather together in the cave of the winds, in Bro an Hanter Noz, for great windy ban-quets during which they perform acrobatic tricks, dance minuets, rigaudons, and waltzes, and spin like tops. They also sing ballads, vocal exercises, and lullabies.

These impressive contests, jousts and concerts are followed by magnificent balls that can last all year.

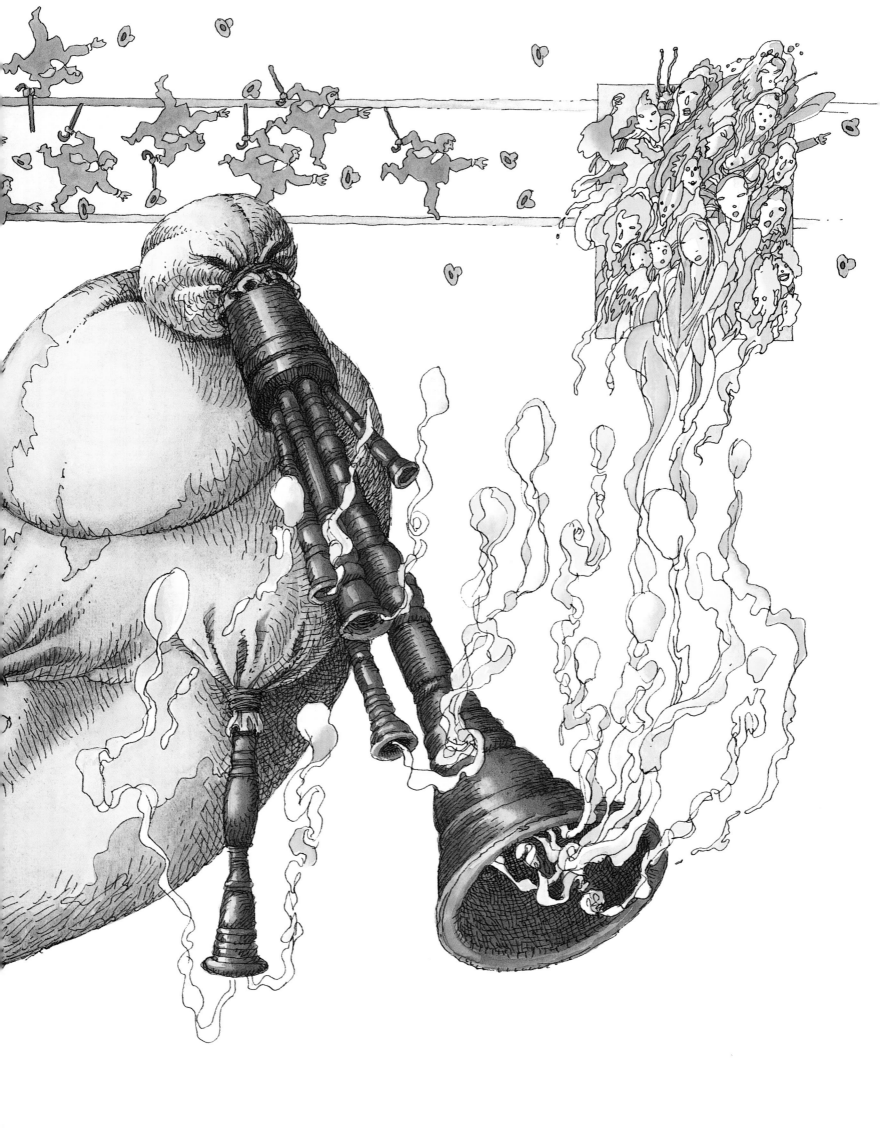

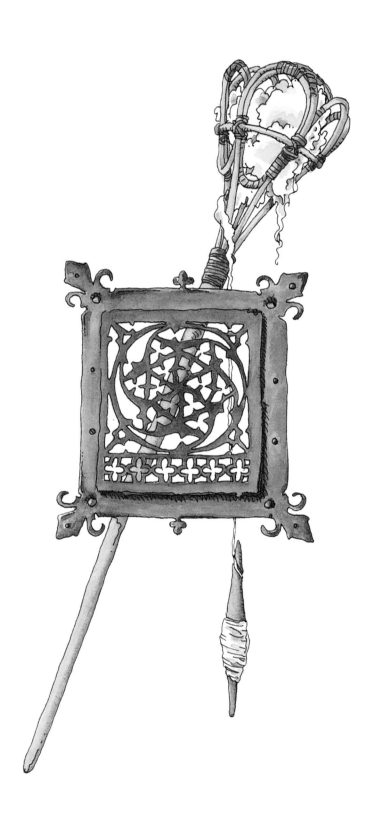

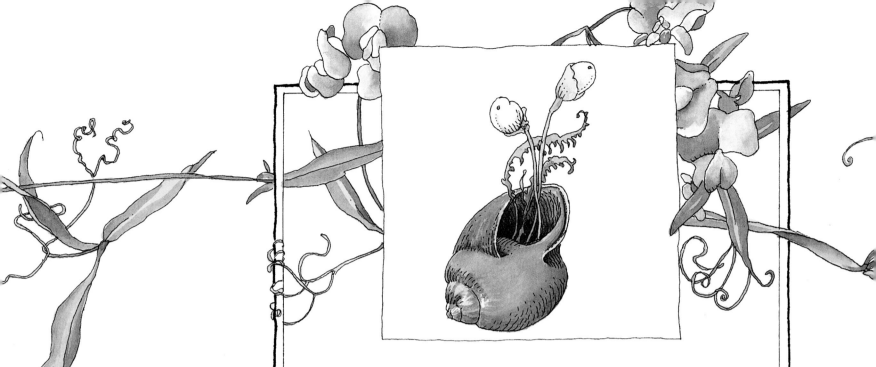

How the White Lady introduced me to Seignolle

Already as a child I dreamt of Faeries. I searched for them at the bottom of the garden, amongst the sweet peas. A damp, mossy hole, inhabited by strange snails, suggested the entrance to the Kingdom that could only be entered through adventure; a Kingdom far away from the vegetable garden and the rows of lettuces. For me it was a world that until then had always been locked in faerie-tale books. I remember reading *Tales of a Beer Drinker* one morning in a wild part of the garden. These told the story of a serpent with a woman's head whose slithering undulations could be seen through flames; they also reported the appearance of a ghost on the road to Culotte Verte, and the red and gold "books of spells," full of mischief. I immediately fell under the spell of the ornamented initial letter of "Once upon a time," and that spell was to last forever, like a secret symbol linking the apprentice wizard to the world of magic. I joined the world of Imps, Gnomes, Elves and Faeries. After "they" had taken me with them I never saw nor heard again of the semblance of a child—the Changeling—abandoned on the little bench beneath the hazelnut trees.

Another day, while on holiday in Morbier, we had to stay indoors because of the bad weather. I settled happily in the library put at my disposal by a lodger with a leafy beard. My parents were worried by my silent ecstasy and anxious for me to join the others in parlor games, but I turned a deaf ear to their calls and slipped through the pages towards the edge of the forest to meet and fraternize with the Man in Gray. A few chapters further on, beneath an oak tree so high that it was larger than the picture, I encountered Merlin who introduced me to my first love, Viviane. She was more beautiful than any woman I had ever set eyes on. This precocious "enchantment" was not entirely innocent.

The fragrance that emanated from these old books was reminiscent of the autumn smells of hedgerows, combining legends with the reality of the woods. I blew into a pine cone because the curve of its scales was similar to Oberon's ivory hunting-horn that summoned the vassalage of the Beautiful Helmeted Ones to the glade. We would then ride the ferns to the deepest recesses of the hollow trees.

Later I would take my friends along to discover the Delectable Valleys ruled by the ancient divinities.

It was rumored that a White Lady of the Fountains sometimes appeared almost naked near Caillou-qui-bique, a place believed to have been the haunt of a highwayman called Moneuse and his gang of hell raisers. The pagan trail was still fresh there. So was the water of the Honnelle, a stream that one normally walked across barefoot. Then suddenly torrential rain began to fall from the blue sky, determined to obstruct our Way. It was a pouring, pelting downpour, whipping our bodies and slowing us down. Slopes collapsed under our feet, brambles became entangled and formed impassable barriers. The whole forest responded to the cries of the angry Lady. In the end, the force of a final spell sent me back to bed, shaking with fever, and with my throat painfully swollen by tonsillitis.

I had failed miserably in my first elfilogical quest and I was devastated: not only had the Faerie of the Pointed Rock slammed the door in my face but, scornful of my fervent homage, she had taken revenge for my audacity. What must I do to establish a dialogue and get closer to her? In what rare and valuable palimpsests would I learn the formulas of the Abraxas?

My mother, worried by my state of mind, and unconsciously inspired by some good Graces, found the magic solution to my torment as she went shopping for food. Still stuck in the mesh of the shopping bag, emerging from a Broceliande forest of vegetable, was a copy of *La Malvenue* by Claude Seignolle, fresh from the local bookshop.

I can still feel the thickness of the book between my hands like the offering of a talisman. Thus the budding knight meets the Scholar on the moving course of his quest. I had also met the Enchanter—he who had come to outline my fate.

"The hidden, fleeing beings forget to flee when they are called by their real name," wrote Bachelard. This is also what Seignolle taught me by suggesting that I should listen to their furtive passage, when Merlin had pointed me in the right direction and disappeared, leaving me on the road. But I was only on the edge of this forest of words and the author remained an inaccessible legend. So, with my pockets filled with words and pebbles, I penetrated deeper into the forest in search of the Strange Isles…

A few years later, a stray postman arrived and brought me my "military call-up papers and marching orders."

The barracks nestled against a hillside, in Epernay, in the quartier Marguerite, and they were famous for their peacefulness. Discouraged by my inability to mark time and present arms, the noncommissioned officer very kindly forgot about me, allowing me to take refuge in the retreat under the roof where I spent my time writing and drawing. Perched on the tubular framework of a bunk-bed, I spent every evening staring through the window at the gothic outline of the ruins of a building lost in the misty distance. Its tower was highlighted in the evening twilight, and it dominated a scene that seemed to be about to burst into life. But no road appeared to lead to it. How could I reach it? Should I cross the fields and the vineyards and walk straight towards it? I did not even know how far it was. Would it be possible to go and come back without any one noticing? To try and locate it on a map and calculate the distance would be scorning the rules of the Approach that I had long ago learnt to respect. I therefore approached it in my dreams before venturing there on one of my free days. Dawn still enveloped the distant hill in a dazzling, powdery light, and each grape was a jewel in the vine's crown. The well-defined chalky ribbon disappeared, quickly drowned like a river under the influence of the Frenzied Ones of the waves, a blur of water bubbles, and I recognized under my feet the fleeting texture of an enchanted path. The "ruins" I had seen were in fact a church, the church of Chavot. The shimmering light of the setting sun on the crenellated architecture had made it look like a romantic ruin.

However, the church I entered was a most inspiring place. Surrounded by a churchyard with wordy tombs, the square tower, swarming with darting lizards, stood against the green, leafy background of rustling trees. An invisible torrent seemed to have turned this haven of silence into an organ giving forth music. As I crossed the worn steps of the entrance, I thought of those who cut a starling in two in order to find the gold promised by the gold dust on feathers. I only saw white walls. Climbing the stairs I disturbed crowds of squawking crows who flew away noisily as they rejoined the tumultuous celestial cascade. I was breathing the salt of the stones, the flour of the old wood, and I remained hanging from the clock tower above a motionless landscape. Oblivious of the passing of time, I flew towards the rolling hills and green groves and peered through the discreet curtains of little cottages. I learnt later that in one of them Cazotte had dreamt of the "Devil in love." Beyond a pretty curve a hamlet had gathered near a gushing spring, and in the distance I could imagine the reverse side of the barracks and my face glued to the pane…

Finally, tearing myself away from the sweet influence of the lullaby, I returned to the road, moved by the painful realization that each step on the asphalt took me ever further from the loving embrace of the subtle soul of the place.

In those days, soldiers still looked dowdy, each badly dressed in an ill-fitting khaki uniform with a navy blue beret screwed onto a shaven head. And without even trying one could be certain that some

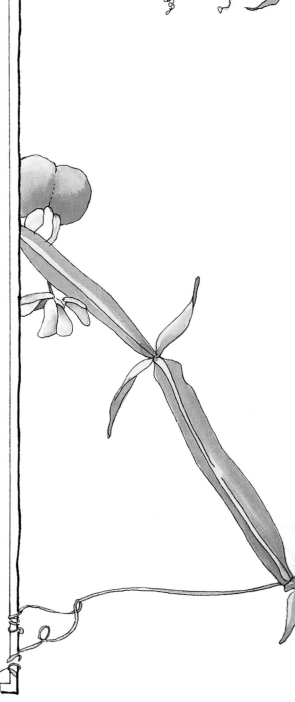

Good Samaritan, full of memories of the old days, would be more than happy to help the soldier of the French Republican Army.

"How long till you are demobilized, young fellow?" In the kind of voice that goes with a mustache, he would tell me barrack room stories, stories of fatigue parties, of drunken demobilizations, or of sergeant majors keeping a lookout to catch marauding privates. And then he would express his delight in the sweetness of the Champagne region. "We love it here." (Anyway, was I not here because I loved it too?) "Isn't our church, the church of Chavot, picturesque? By the way, this is where the White Lady appears!"

I was speechless when I heard this and asked him to repeat it. What White Lady? A rural goddess, a Faerie of the harvests… Had I been close to my beautiful secret love without realizing it? He knew no more, except that she was often seen surveying her domain, but he said that "I would find lots more on the subject" in the library.

Indeed I found a lot more than I had expected. I remember the rooms inhabited by the silence of the pages being turned, and the murmur of the words escaping from the shelves brimming over with knowledge. There was woodwork decorated with elaborate carvings of branches and foliage on which sumptuous bindings in shiny leather seemed to multiply. In a glass globe, goldfinches sitting on a branch sang an imaginary song to the sleeping reader… and to a lady with pale hair sitting behind a desk.

She was the daughter of Arnold Van Gennep, the founding gardener of folklore and the orchards of legends, and she told me stories of a White Faerie, of Banshees, and of wild women. She then opened an exercise book with beautiful calligraphy, and filing cabinets full of notes, while with her fingers she shuffled skeins of golden leaves. Now and then she would pick up a leaf and read it, then little by little she wove another tale. I listened to her for hours. Then in conclusion she said: "One day, a young man full of passion, like you, came to ask father's advice. He was dreaming of finding out more about devilry. He has published many books since then: *Le Diable en sabots, Marie la louve*… He would probably see you if you told him I sent you!" As well as books by Sebillot, Frazer, Le Braz, Pourrat, Souvestre and many others, she also showed me a row of books, the top one of which fell into my hands: *La Malvenue* by Claude Seignolle. So it was that a White Lady who had finally forgiven me gave me this book me as a symbol of a secret alliance.

Three weeks later, I took advantage of special leave to cross the bridge to the Seignollian domains. That day my khaki uniform radiated a distinctive elfin green. It was somewhere along these rough banks, frequented by Vouivres and wolves, that Leather-Foot, as I used to call him, made me a present of these indefatigable boots to walk along the eternal paths, the paths that constantly flower again…

Although this *Great Encyclopedia of Faeries* finishes here, that of the Elves will start further along, there where the Trolls crown the pine forests, and where the Huldres prepare for the May processions, in the moonlight at Puck's Fair…

A short inventory of the elficological library

Shelves of the enchanted paneling of Ferral

Les Fées, Henri Durville, Bib. Eudiaque, 1950.

Les Fées du Moyen Age, Alfred Maury, Lib. philosophique de Ladrange, 1843.

Les Fées au Moyen Age, L. Harf-Lancner, Lib. Honoré Champion.

Le Folklore dans les deux mondes, H. de Clarencey, Paris, 1894.

Superstitions et survivances, Béranger-Feraud, Leroux, Paris, 1896, 5 vols.

Le Paradis de la reine Sibylle, Antoine de la Sale, ed. Fernand Desonay, 1930.

Mitologiae, Fulgence, Rudolfus Helm, Leipzig, 1898.

Confessio amantis (*Tales of the Seven Deadly Sins*), John Gower, ed. H. Morley, London, 1889.

Li Roman de Dolopathos, Herbert de Paris, Bib. Elzévirienne, 1856.

Etymologiae, Isidore of Seville, ed. W. M. Lindsay, Oxford, 1911.

Lais, anonymous from the 12th and 13th centuries, ed. Prudence Mary O'Hara Tobin, Geneva, 1976.

De nuptis Philologiae et Mercurii, Martianus Capella, Leipzig, 1866.

De correctione rusticorum, Martin de Braga, ed. C. P. Caspari, Christiana, 1883.

De pythonicis mulieribus et Lamüs, Ulric Molitor, 1926.

Le Merveilleux dans l'Antiquité, Apollonios de Tyane, Philostrate, Paris, 1862.

Japanese Mythology, Masaharu Anesahy, Cooper Square, New York, 1973.

Les Mythes de l'outre-tombe, Fernand Benoit, coll. Latomus, Brussels, 1950.

Dissertations sur la mythologie française, J. B. Bullet, Moutard, Paris, 1771.

The English and Scottish Popular Ballads, F. J. Child, Boston, 1882.

Storia del folklore in Europa, Giuseppe Cocchiaria, Turin, 1952.

Demonology and Devil Lore, Moncure, Daniel Conway, New York, 1886.

Fairy Legends and Traditions of the South of Ireland, C. T. Croker, London, 1834.

The Folklore of China, N. Belfield Dennys, Trübner, London, 1876.

Les Plus Anciens Contes de l'humanité, H. Théodore Gaster, Payot, Paris, 1953.

Sicilianische Märchen, Laura Gonzenbach, Engelmann, Leipzig, 1870.

La Vie et la Mort des Fées, Lucie Felix Faure Goyau, Perrin, Paris, 1910.

Songs and Stories of the Ch'van Miao, David Crockett Graham, Washington, 1954.

The Fairy Mythology, Thomas Keightley, London, 1850.

Legendary Fictions of the Irish Celts, P. Kennedy, Macmillan, London, 1866.

La Mythologie primitive, Lucien Levy Bruhl, F. Alcan, Paris, 1935.

Das Eurapäische Volksmärchen, Max Lüthi, A. Franke, Berne, 1947.

Fiabe, novell e racconti popolari siciliani, G. Pitre, Pedrone Lauriel, Palermo, 1875.

Cultes, mythes et religions, Salomon Reinach, E. Leroux, Paris, 1908, 1923.

Celtic Folklore Welsh and Manx, John Rhys, Clarendon Press, Oxford, 1901.

Les Portes du rêve, Oeza Roheim, Payot, Paris, 1973.

Contes russes, Léon Sichler, Leroux, Paris, 1881.

At the frosty window where Father Christmas appears

Du Groenland au Pacifique, Knud Rasmussen, Plon, Paris, 1929.

Popular Tales from the Norse, (translated from *Asbjørnsen*), Sir George Webb Dasent, Edinburgh, 1888.

Norske Folkeventyr, selected by Helga Krog, introduction by Frederick Pasche, Stockholm, 1942.

Barnets Legender, Leif Werenskjold, Riksmalsforlaget, Oslo, 1966.

The Norse Myths, rewritten by K. Crossley-Holland, F. T. Folklore Library, Pantheon.

Norske Folkeviser, Gerhard Munthe, Dreyers Forlag, Oslo, 1943.

Det mørke Landet, Edward Ruud, Fonna Forlag, Oslo, 1980.

Gamle Norske Folkeviser, collected by Sophus Bugge, Universitets Forlaget, Oslo, 1971.

Great Swedish Fairy Tales, John Bauer (illust.), Delaporte Press/Seymour Lawrence, 1971.

D'Aulaire's Trolls, Inger and Edgar Parin d'Aulaire, Garden City, Doubleday & Company, New York, 1971.

Norwegian Trolls and Other Tales, Theodore Kittelsen, ed. Florence Ekstrand, Washington.

Halnarfiördur, Huidsheimahort, Erla Stefánsdóllir, Sjaandi.

Fairy Tales, Hans Christian Andersen, edition consulted: *Contes*, Mercure de France, 1953–54, 4 vols.

Under the roof of Sylphyria, at the perch of the White Lady…

Le Conte de Gabalis ou entretien sur les sciences secrètes, Montfaucon de Villars, A. G. Nizet, Paris, 1963.

Grimoires de Paracelse: Des Nymphes, Sylphes, Pygmées, Salamandres et autres Êtres…, translated, introduction and notes by René Schwaeble.

Démonologie et Sorcellerie, Sir Walter Scott, Payot, Paris, 1973.

Découverte de la sorcellerie, Reginald Scott.

Sadducismus Triumphatus, Joseph Glanville, Edinburgh, 1700.

Le Livre des merveilles, Gervais de Tilbury, Les Belles Lettres, Paris, 1992.

Anecdotes historiques, légendes et apologues, selected from the unpublished collection of Etienne de Bourbon, 13th-century Dominican monk, ed. Lecoy de la Marche, Paris, 1877.

The Archaeology of the Cambridge Region, G. Fox, Cambridge, 1923.

Lalie, Jean Paulhan, Gallimard, L'Imaginaire, 1982.

La Bière du démon and *L'Enclos des chats*, Saskia Barbygère, Le Chemin Herbu, 1947.

Le Merveilleux dans l'Occident médiéval, J. Le Goff, L'Imaginaire médiéval, Paris, 1985.

The Idylls of the King, Alfred Tennyson, London, 1859–85.

Le Cabinet des Fées, Cuchet, Paris, 1785–89, 41 vols.

Le Monde enchanté, M. de Lescure, Lib. Firmin-Didot & Cie, 1883.

Contes de fées, Ducray-Duminil, Bernardin-Béchet, 1860.

Les Fées de la famille, S. Lockroy, Hetzel, 1880.

Les Farfadets, A. Mélandri, Quantin, 1886.

Les Divines Fées de l'Orient et du Nord, Sébastien Rhéal, Fournier, 1843.

Contes de fées, Comtesse de Ségur, Hachette, 1860 .

Le Roman d'une fée, H. Belliot, Trene et Stock, 1895.

L'Etoile d'une fée, Elphinstone Hope, translated by Stéphane Mallarmé, La Pléiade, Gallimard.

Contes de fées, Charles Perrault, Garnier, 1850.

Quand les Fées vivaient en France, Y. Ostroga, illust. Félix Lorioux, Hachette, 1923.

Contes de fées, Gabrielle de Burlet, Bruxelles, 1910.

Le Château des fées, J. Dervallière, Ed. de Flore, 1946.

Bonnes Fées d'antan, E. Pilon, E. Sansot et Cie, 1900.

Les Esprits élémentaires, Karl Grün, Verviers, 1891.

Contes et légendes d'Irlande, Georges Dottin, Ed. Terre de Brume.

Brocéliande, Charles Le Goffic, A. Dupouy, Ed. Terre de Brume.

On the lunar lectern and the shelves of Petit Fay

La République mystérieuse des Elfes, Faunes, Fées et autres semblables, Robert Kirk, Bib. de la Haute Science, 1896.

Les Origines, la vie et l'évolution des Fées, Daphné Charters, La Diffusion spirituelle, 1953.

Les Fées au travail et au jeu, M. Geoffrey Hodson, Ed. Adyar, 1995.

Le Côté caché des choses — L'occultisme dans la nature, C. W. Leadbeater.

Voyage dans le monde astral, Mme Anne Osmont.

The Night Bell, G. S. Arundale.

Fairies, Edward L. Gardner, Theosophical Publishing House.

Occult Book — The Fairy Tradition, Frank Lind, Rider.

The Kingdom of the Gods, M. Geoffrey Hodson, Ed. Adyar.

The Coming of the Fairies, Sir Arthur Conan Doyle, Theosophical Publishing House.

Les Perversions du Merveilleux, Jean de Palacio, Séguier, 1993.

Le Livre des Fées, des Fantômes et des Sages, Alexandre Cormier, Sansot et Cie, 1906.

L'Homme dans ses rapports avec les animaux et les Esprits des éléments, Rudolf Steiner, Ed. Triades.

Le Calendrier de l'âme, Rudolf Steiner, E.A.R., 1912.

L'Esprit de Goethe, Rudolf Steiner, E.A.R., 1918.

Les Carnets de Lalie and *L'Epousée de Mai*, Ed. Le Clos des Huldres, 1993.

Per amica silentia lunae, W. Butler Yeats, edition consulted: Presses universitaires de Lille, 1979.

The Celtic Twilight, W. Butler Yeats, edition consulted: *Le Crépuscule celtique*, Presses universitaires de Lille, 1982.

The Secret Rose, W. Butler Yeats, edition consulted: *La Rose secrète*, Presses universitaires de Lille, 1984.

Essais et introductions, W. Butler Yeats, Presses universitaires de Lille, 1985.

Mythe, folklore, religion, occultisme, unpublished prose: "Come, Faeries, take me far from this gloomy world,/ I would like to ride the wind with you/ And dance on the hills like a flame", W. Butler Yeats, Université de Caen, 1989.

Occultisme pratique, H. P. Blavatsky, Ed. Adyar, 1973.

Mythologie des arbres, Jacques Brosse, Plon, 1989.

L'Homme dans les bois, Stock, 1976.

The White Goddess, Robert Graves.

The Greek Myths, Robert Graves, edition consulted: *Les Mythes grecs*, Paris, 1967.

La Peur de la nature, François Terrasson, Le Sang de la terre.

Isis errante, Kathleen Raine, Granit.

Le Premier Jour, Kathleen Raine, Granit.

Le Roi du monde, René Guénon, Gallimard, 1958.

Symboles de la science sacrée, René Guénon, Gallimard, 1962.

Faune et Flore sacrées dans les sociétés altaïques, Paris, 1966.

Le Veda, translated by J. Varenne, Paris, 1967.

Mystères celtes, John Sharkey, Paris, 1985.

Les Dits et Récits de mythologie française, Henri Dontenville, Paris, 1950.

La Mythologie slave, L. Léger, Paris, 1901.

Le Paganisme et la Russie ancienne, E. Anilkov, Saint Petersburg, 1914.

Le Polythéisme hindou, Rabain Daniélou, Paris, 1960.

Le Latin mystique, Rémy de Gourmont, Paris, 1913.

Forêts — Essai sur l'imaginaire occidental, Robert Harrison, Flammarion, 1992.

Ancient Mystery Cults, Walter Burkert, Harvard, 1987.

The Golden Bough, Sir James Frazer, edition consulted: *Le Rameau d'or*, Robert Laffont, Bouquins, 1983.

Le Symbolisme des contes de fées, Leïa, Ed. du Mont-Blanc, 1942.

Les Contes de fées — Lecture initiatique, François Roussel, Amrita, 1993.

Elfes, Fées, et Gnomes, Ellen Lórien, Johfra et Carjan, Amrita.

Les Lis des champs et les oiseaux du ciel, Sören Kierkegaard, Ed. de l'Orante, 1966.

L'Interprétation des contes de fées, Marie-Louise Von Franz, Albin Michel, 1995.

L'Ombre et le Mal dans les contes de fées, Marie-Louise Von Franz, Albin Michel, 1995.

La Femme dans les contes de fées, Marie-Louise Von Franz, Albin Michel, 1995.

La Synchronicité, l'âme et la science, Marie-Louise Von Franz, Albin Michel, 1995.

La Légende du Graal, Marie-Louise Von Franz, Albin Michel, 1995.

La Voie de l'individuation dans les contes de

fées, Marie-Louise Von Franz, La Fontaine de pierre, 1978.

L'Ane d'or, interprétation d'un conte, Marie-Louise Von Franz, La Fontaine de pierre, 1981.

Symbolik des Märchens, Hedwig von Beit, Berne, 1952.

Gegensatz und Erneuerung im Märchens, Hedwig von Beit, Berne, 1956.

Märchen und Traüme als Helfer des Menschen, Hans Dieckmann, Stuttgart, 1966.

Märchen und symbol, Hans Dieckmann, Stuttgart, 1977.

Die Mutter in Märchen, Sibyl Brikhaüsen, Stuttgart, 1977 (see also *C. G. Jung et la voie des profondeurs,* Etienne Perrot et Francine Saint-René, Tallandier/La Fontaine de pierre, 1980).

Synchronicité et Paracelsica, C. G. Jung, Albin Michel, 1988.

Mysterium conjunctionis, C. G. Jung, Albin Michel, 1982.

De Dieu aux dieux — Un chemin de l'accomplissement, Etienne Perrot, La Fontaine de pierre.

Rencontres avec l'âme, Barbara Hannah, Ed. Jacqueline Renard, 1990.

La Montagne et sa symbolique, Marie-Madeleine Davy, Albin Michel, 1996.

L'Homme intérieur et sa métamorphose, Marie-Madeleine Davy, Ed. de l'Epi, 1974.

Homme, cimes et dieux, Samivel, Arthaud, 1973.

Le Rêve du papillon, Tchouang-Tseu, Albin Michel, 1994.

Curious Myths of the Middle Age, Sabine Baring-Gould, London, 1867–68.

At the beam of the Pixies, at Milk Tooth's cat door

The Fairy Tradition in Britain, Lewis Spence, Rider & Company, 1948.

The Fairy Mythology, T. Keightley.

Folklore of the Northern Countries of England, W. Henderson.

The Fairy Faith in Celtic Countries, W. Y. E. Wentz.

The Fairy Mythology of Shakespeare, A. Nutt.

Popular Romance of the West of England, W. Henderson (in Devon at Easter).

Traditions, Superstitions and Folklore, W. Henderson.

Popular Rhythms of Scotland, R. Chambers.

Popular Superstitions of the Highlands of Scotland, W. Grant Stewart.

Superstitions of the Highlands and Islands of Scotland, J. G. Campbell.

The Savages of Gaelic Tradition, D. MacRitchie.

Folk Tales and Fairy Lore, J. MacDouglas & G. Calder.

Folklore of the British Isles.

Myth, Tradition and Story in Western Argyll, K. W. Grant.

Scandinavian Folklore, W. A. Craigie.

Old Lore Miscellany of Orkney, A.W. & A. Johnstone, Shetland, Caithness, Sutherland.

Shetland Traditional Lore, J. M. E. Saxby.

Celtic Folklore, J. Rhys, Welsh and Manx.

Bristish Goblins, Wirt Sikes.

Fairy Legends and Traditions of the South of Ireland, Crofton Croker.

Ulster Folklore, E. Andrews.

Minstrelsy of the Scottish Border, Walter Scott.

Ancient Legends of Ireland, Lady Wilde.

Visions and Beliefs in the West of Ireland, Lady Gregory.

The Wee Folk of Menteith, H. Terrell.

Goblin Tales of Lancashire, J. Bowker.

More West Highland Tales, J. G. McKay.

The Darker Superstition of Scotland, J. G. Dalyell.

The Book of Elves and Fairies, F. J. Olcott.

English Fairy and other Folk Tales, E.S. Hartland.

The Science of Fairy Tales, E. S. Hartland.

Folklore of Scottish Locks and Springs, J. M. Mackinlay.

British Fairy Origins, L. Spence.

Strange Stories from Devon, Rosemary Anne Lauder & Michael Williams.

Supernatural in Cornwall, Michael Williams.

My Dartmoor, Clive Gunnel.

Devon Mysteries, Judy Cord.

Legends of Devon, Sally Jones.

Ghosts and Witches of the Cotswolds, J. A. Brooks.

Demons, Ghosts and Spectres in Cornish Folklore, Robert Hunt.

Folklore of Somerset, Alan Holt.

After Dark on Dartmoor, John Pegg & David Edgley.

A Book of Dartmoor, S. Baring Gould.

Traditions, Legends, Superstitions and Sketches of Devonshire of the Borders of the Tamar and Tavy, Mrs A. E. Bray.

The Haunted Cotswolds, Bob Meredith.

Minster Lovell, Barrie Rodgers.

The Middle Kingdom, Dermot MacManus.

Celtic Fairy Tales, Joseph Jacobs.

Atlas of Magical Britain, Janet & Colin Bord.

A Field Guide to the Little People, Nancy Arrowsmith & George Moore.

A Dictionary of Fairies, Katharine Briggs.

The Fairies in Tradition and Literature, Katharine Briggs.

The Folklore of the Cotswolds, Katharine Briggs.

The Personnel of Fairyland, Katharine Briggs.

Rhythms for the Young Folk, William Allingham.

Fairyland : A Series of Pictures from the Elf-World, Richard Doyle, poem by William Allingham.

The Poetical Works, Christina Rossetti.

Fairy Tales from the Isle of Man, Dora Broome.

The Enchanted Land, Lovey Chisholm.

Mopsa the Fairy, Jean Ingelow.

Dealing with the Fairies, George MacDonald.

Fairies and Enchanters, A. William-Ellis.

The Types of the Folktale.

A Bibliography of Folklore, W. Bonser.

The Lost Gods of England, Brian Branston.

Fairies and Pubs, Lord Brett, Maam Cross, 1932.

Under the ridge of the five stars

Au-delà du Merveilleux, Claude Lecouteux, Presses universitaires de Paris, 1995.

Fées, Sorcières et Loups-Garous, Claude Lecouteux, Imago, 1995.

Mythologie du vampire en Roumanie, Adrien Cremene, Ed. du Rocher, 1981.

Dictionnaire de mythologie et de symbolique celtes, Robert-Jacques Thibaud, Dervy, 1995.

Méditations sur les 22 arcanes majeurs du tarot, anonymous, Aubier, 1984.

Mythe et épopée, Dumézil, Gallimard, Quarto, 1995.

Mythes et dieux des Germains, Dumézil, PUF.

Les Contes de Perrault, Pierre Saintyves, Robert Laffont, Bouquins.

En marge de la légende dorée, Pierre Saintyves, Robert Laffont, Bouquins.

Les Reliques et les images légendaires, Pierre Saintyves, Robert Laffont, Bouquins.

Les Fées, Brian Froud & Alan Lee, Albin Michel.

Le Monde des Esprits, Alain Kauss, B. F. Ed., 1993.

Les Elfes et les Fées, Ed. Time Life.

Contes de l'Ille-et-Vilaine, Adolphe Orain, Maisonneuve et Larose, 1968.

La Magie des mégalithes, Anne-Marie Le Masson, Ed. A.M.

Contes et légendes de haute Bretagne, Albert Poulain, Ed. Ouest-France, 1995.

Traditions, histoires, légendes du pays Gallo, Jean-Claude Carlo, Yves Castel, Eric Rondel.

Iseult et les Sœurs celtiques, Bernard Felix, Coop Breizh, 1995.

Les Contes de Luzel, Presses universitaires de Rennes/Terre de brume.

Merlin l'enchanteur, M. P. Page, Ed. Corentin.

Ondine, F. H. Karl de la Motte Fouqué, Ed. Corentin.

Enchantress, Benwell, Gwen & Arthur Waugh, London, 1961.

Mermaids and Mastodons, Richard Carrington, London-New York, 1957.

Mermaids, Beatrice Phillpotts, London, 1980.

Franche-Comté, pays des légendes, Gabriel Gravier, Ed. Marque-Maillard, 1980, 2 vols.

Contes et légendes de Bretagne, Mikaël Lascaux, Ed. France-Empire.

Des Fées du P'tit Louis, Serge Aillery, Beaupréau, 1990.

Contes et légendes de Bretagne, Elvire de Cerny, La Tourniole Ed., 1995.

Légendes et récits vendéens, Jean Robuchon, La Découvrance, 1995.

Le Légendaire de la Rance, Jules Haize, Rue des Scribes Ed., 1993.

La Forêt de Brocéliande, Félix Bellamy, Lib. Guénégaud, 1979, 2 vols.

Les Prophéties de Merlin, Jean Macé, 1498.

Les Veillées de l'Armor, E. du Laurens de la Barre.

Barzaz-Breiz, de la Villemarqué.

Voyage au pays de Joyeuse-Garde, Miorcec de Kerdanet, Brest, 1823.

La Légende de la mort, Anatole le Braz, Robert Laffont, Bouquins.

Vita Merlini, Geoffrey of Monmouth.

Légendes rustiques, George Sand, Marabout.

Promenades autour d'un village, George Sand, Calmann-Lévy, 1888.

Le vieux bocage qui s'en va, Jehan de la Chesnaye, Notes du folklore vendéen, 1911.

Mystérieux haut Anjou, Patrick Planchenault, Château-Goutier, 1984.

L'Insolite dans le Maine, le Perche et leurs confins, Robert Guy, Ed. Siloë, 1984.

L'Ile d'Yeu, terre de légendes, Yves Logé, L'Etrave, 1995.

Faërie, Tolkien, 10/18.

Contes et légendes des pays celtes, Jean Markale, Ed. Ouest-France, 1995.

Guide de la France mystérieuse, Tchou, 1964.

Guide de la Bretagne mystérieuse, Gwenc'Hlan Le Souëzec, 1966.

Bretagne terre sacrée, Gwenc'Hlan Le Souëzec, Beltan.

Légendes et récits populaires du pays Basque, J. F. Cerquand, Aubéron, 1992.

La Sorcellerie en Vendée, Joël Perocheau, Le Cercle d'or/Rivages, 1979.

La Mer magique, Albert Van Hageland, Marabout, 1973.

Les Cavaliers du Gâvre, Claude Pédron, Reflets du passé, Nantes, 1992.

Les Contes populaires du Poitou, Léon Pineau, Ernest Leroux Ed., Paris, 1891.

La Vieille Lituanie, P. Klimas, Wilna, 1921.

Les Druides, Françoise Le Roux/ Christian J. Guyyonvarc'h, Ouest-France université, 1986.

Les Fêtes celtiques, Françoise Le Roux/ Christian J. Guyyonvarc'h, Ouest-France université, 1995.

Textes mythologiques irlandais, Christian J. Guyyonvarc'h, Rennes, 1975.

Enquête sur l'existence des Fées et des Esprits de la nature, Edouard Brassey, Ed. Filipacchi.

Near the greenery

Lo Cunto de li Cunti ouvero lo trattenemiento de li peccerille, Giambattista Basile.

Lo Cunto degli Cunti, Giambattista Basile, translated by Michelle Rak, Garzanti Ed., 1986.

Le Conte des contes, Giambattista Basile, translated by Myriam Tarrant, Ed. l'Alphée, Paris, 1986.

Folleti, Farfarelli, Giani & Cinzia Corvi, Bergame, 1904.

I Demoni nella tradizione popolare, Lodovico Giovanni Corvi, Castel l'Arqueto.

Hadas, Princesas, Brujas, Curiosas y otras heroínas de Calleja, introduction and selection by Carmen Bravo-Villasante, Biblioteca de Cuentos Maravillosos, 1994.

Cuentos de Hadas celticos, introduction and selection by Carmen Bravo-Villasante, Biblioteca de Cuentos Maravillosos, 1994.

Almacén de cuentos — Cuentos de Calleja, introduction and selection by Carmen Bravo-Villasante, Biblioteca de Cuentos Maravillosos, 1994.

Cuentos del abuelo, S. Calleja, Biblioteca de Cuentos Maravillosos, 1994.

La Fe, Armando Palacio Valdès.

Las Tradiciones popolares asturianas, Constantino Cabal.

Mytología ibérica, supersticiones, cuentos y leyendas de la vieja España, Constantino Cabal, ed. J. M. Gomez-Tabanera.

Description philosophale de la nature des Fées, J. P. Croquet, Lille, 1888.

Les Métamorphoses, Ovid.

Disputatio de Lamiis sen Strigibus, Thomas Erastus, Basel, 1572.

Les Lieux fées, Gonzague de Lapidaire, Grand Fayt, 1793.

Discours sur les passages de la Vendoise, Eisengott, Gand, 1448.

Le Folklore flamand, Is Teirlinck.

Les Reposoirs des Fées, Bucane Noctiflore, Le Chemin herbu, 1923.

La Légende de Petit Fayt, Bucane Noctiflore, Le Chemin herbu, 1947.

Traditions et légendes de Belgique, Baron de Reinsberg, Düringsfeld, 1870.

Esprits et Génies du terroir, Albert Doppagne, Ed. Duculot, 1977.

Légendes, curiosités de la Champagne et de la Brie, A. Assier, 1860.

Le Folklore de la Flandre et du Hainaut français, Arnold Van Gennep, 1935.

Le Folklore de l'Auvergne et du Velay, Arnold Van Gennep, 1942.

Contes des landes et des grèves, Paul Sebillot, 1898.

L'Epopée celtique en Irlande, Henry d'Arbois de Jubainville, Ed. E. Thorni, 1892.

Traditions, légendes et contes des Ardennes, Albert Neyrac, Charleville.

Les Evangiles du diable, Claude Seignolle, Maisonneuve.

Invitation au château de l'étrange, Claude Seignolle, Maisonneuve.

La France mythologique, Henri Dontenville, Ed. Tchou.

De spectris, lemuribus et magis, L. Lavater, 1886.

Magia naturalis et immaturalis oder dreifacher Höllenzwag, Dr Johannes Faust.

Kinder und Hausmaerchen, Jacobs Ludwig, Carl Grimm, Göttingen.

Teutonic mythology, Lib. of Education, London, 1900.

Poèmes héroïques, ballades et contes du vieux danois, W. C. Grimm.

Les Eaux Etroites, Julien Gracq, José Corti, 1976.

Around the pond of the golden salamanders

Mélusine, Jean d'Arras, Ed. Robert Morel, 1961.

Mélusine ou la robe de saphir, Franz Hellens, Gallimard, 1952.

Génies, anges et démons, Sources orientales, Ed. du Seuil, 1971.

Le Folklore des sources et des fontaines, H. de Bonneville, Rouen, 1902.

Biographie du Père Noël, Catherine Lepagnol, Ed. Hachette, 1979.

Hauts Lieux de Brocéliande, Claudine Glot, Ed. Ouest-France.

L'Irlande et les musiques de l'âme, Artus/Ouest-France.

Innisdoon, Christian Rolland, Denoël, 1996.

Ys dans la rumeur des vagues, Michel Lebris, Artus, 1985.

On the road of the Sìd across the bridge of Petit Fayt

Les Chroniques elfiques, Petrus Barbygère.

La Poétique de l'espace, Gaston Bachelard, PUF, 1957.

La Poétique de la rêverie, Gaston Bachelard, PUF, 1960.

Le Droit de rêver, Gaston Bachelard, PUF, 1970.

L'Intuition de l'instant, Gaston Bachelard, Denoël, 1971.

L'Eau et les rêves, Gaston Bachelard, José Corti, 1989.

Campagne anglaise — Une symphonie pastorale, Autrement, 1990.

La Mystique sauvage, Michel Hulin, PUF, 1993.

Poèmes, Emily Jane Brontë, Gallimard, 1963.

Sous le pommier en fleur, John Galsworthy, Heinemann & Zsolnay.

Le Sentier de l'Elpe, Saskia Dampierre, Valenciennes, 1994.